Troubles in Bellmount

by

Nicki Pascarella

A Miranda Albright, Ph.D. Mystery
Book 1

Troubles in Bellmount

Cover Art by *Diana Carlile*

The Wild Rose Press, Inc.
PO Box 708
Adams Basin, NY 14410-0708
Visit us at www.thewildrosepress.com

Publishing History
First Edition, 2022
Trade Paperback ISBN 978-1-5092-4204-7
Digital ISBN 978-1-5092-4205-4

A Miranda Albright, Ph.D. Mystery Book 1

Published in the United States of America

"I know. Do the best you can," I said. "We need to move this along. We might be running out of time."

Neither of them commented on my plea for urgency. Keisha sat in quiet reflection, and Winona flipped through her notebook.

"Miranda, I've been thinking, what if it was Shultz? He's a pervert and likes younger women. What if he purposely messed up the investigation to cover up his crime?" Winona asked.

As I have previously indicated, I had concluded that Shultz had thrown a wrench into the investigation for three reasons. First of all, he was a klutzy cretin. Second, he was trying to keep Mayor Reynolds happy, and the mayor wanted the crime solved and closed so that nothing reflected poorly on his perfect little town. Third, and the most disturbing realization to me, was that he had tried to erase me from the scene because he was terrified someone would discover he had stopped a woman on her way into town and behaved like an atrocious debauchee.

"Hey, Winona, you're a moron. She would never have slept with that piece of shit cop, meaning it wasn't his baby, meaning it wasn't him. It was those damn frat boys. I could see it in their lecherous little eyes."

The Albright Detective Agency was working like clockwork.

Kind of.

Dedication

To my Guardian Angel, Julie Lokun.
Thank you for helping me find my voice.

Prologue
Bellmount, Pennsylvania, 1989

Small town rumors are a lot like snowballs careening downhill. They begin their descent, take on speed and fresh flakes, and grow in size until they crash into a brick wall.

Eventually, they melt, leave a pile of mud, and disappear. Life goes on, and everyone waits in anxious anticipation for the next chilly gossip-ball to fly. Much to my chagrin, my recent arrival had kept the town of eight thousand inhabitants entertained with an incessant bombardment of the icy orbs.

As I stood behind my podium studying lecture notes that I had penned three days prior, someone pushed a paper cup under my nose.

"Coffee?" a young man asked.

Steam wafted from a vent in the lid, warming my cold cheeks. I breathed in fragrant vanilla and moaned. "Thanks."

"In case you stumbled over another dead body last night. I thought caffeine would help," Mason Bitz explained.

"No corpses last night," I assured him.

Mason grinned and sauntered to his seat.

"I'm the one that deserves a drink," chirped the wispy figure standing beside me as he reached for the cup.

Since explaining a levitating hot beverage to a room full of first-year college students wasn't something I felt up to tackling, I swatted at the translucent hand.

A coed wearing a denim skirt and lavender jelly shoes approached my podium. She ignored my waving hand and seemed unfazed by the scowl I bestowed on my perverted poltergeist as he scrutinized her legs.

"Dr. Albright, I love the book. I think I have a crush on Gatsby," the enthusiastic girl said.

"Don't we all, Shelly?" I sipped, then smiled.

Shelly Byers beamed back at me before settling into her seat in the front row and looking at the clock above the door.

I followed her gaze to see that the little hand was on the X, and the big hand was on the XII. I lapped at the brew before clearing my throat. "Listen up, people. Do I have everyone's attention?" Once all gazes were fixed on me, I began my lecture. "What was the inciting incident in yesterday's reading assignment?"

"Dr. Albright, what was the exciting event in your story?" called class clown John Gibbons.

Missy Henderson turned from her seat in the second row to face the back of the classroom. "Enticing, not exciting. John, you're a moron."

My drink-free palm met my forehead. "Inciting, people. Remember that means the event that hooks the reader into the story."

Luckily my students couldn't hear the ghost's insulting proclamation. *"Elite private school, my ass!"*

"Dr. Albright, I was hooked the time you wore the itsy bitsy teeny weenie purple polka dot bikini and went swimming in a kiddie pool full of beer." Gibbons bobbled his head about and added, "And then you ate live goldfish. I heard it was super cool!"

I sighed and rubbed my forehead. Although Mr. Gibbons's ribbing was good-natured, and most of the time, I found him quite humorous, we had a lot to cover. As usual, I had the delicate task of squelching rumors while keeping my class on task. A welcome quaff surging into my body took the edge off my walking scandal of a life and allowed me to keep a light tone in my voice.

"Where did you get your information, John? I did not eat goldfish."

"You did swim in beer in a tiny bikini, though, right?"

I twisted my lips as I studied the smart-alec gleam in the jokester's eyes. "I wasn't wearing a bikini."

He chuckled. "So, you were naked?"

Gibbons' classmates gasped.

I rolled my eyes at the lewd suggestion. Then, since the incorrigible ghost who had recently become my shadow was distracting me with his guffaws, I shot him my best hairy eyeball. Keeping one phantom and thirty nineteen-year-olds on task felt a lot like trying to stop three dozen loose marbles from rolling down a steep decline.

I deepened my voice and squinted my eyes in an attempt to seem intimidating. "People, back to the saga of our protagonist, Jay Gatsby."

"I bet it was the time you became a harvest princess, and then the pastor called you a witch and threw holy water on you and the bartender when you were doing the, um—"

I considered pitching a chalk-filled eraser at Gibbons's grinning visage. Since I had the aim of a wingless albatross with vertigo, I refrained and chose to refocus my class. I tapped my fingers below the lecture notes on the chalkboard. "Back to our novel."

"You did shoot someone with a fourteen-karat-diamond-encrusted gun that once belonged to a sheik, though, right? It would break my heart to find out you never actually shot someone in the ass." Gibbons dramatically clutched at his sternum.

I muttered, "Oh, fudge," and my unwelcome specter mumbled, "Fucking hysterical," as he plopped himself into my chair and doubled over in laughter.

"Come on, pony up, Dr. Albright. Give us a real-life example of an 'inciting incident' so we can learn better." Gibbons used quotation fingers around our current vocabulary word and puffed up his chest.

I assumed he was proud because he had finally pronounced the term correctly.

"Besides, your life is way more interesting than this Gatsby dude."

I never did "pony up," although I did recall my inciting incident. I mumbled "Shultz" between clenched teeth as I pictured my nemesis, a lemon of a cop who was a master at creating chaos. Then, for a second, remembered a young girl's insect-covered corpse. Finally, the most horrible image of all settled in my mind—my handsome specter's disfigured face covered in blood. Nightmarish doesn't begin to describe the last two months.

"Cut Dr. Albright a break," Shelly admonished Gibbons. "I heard the most recent crime scene was super bloody."

"*Yeah, because she shot me.*" My ghost propped his legs onto my desk, crossed one foot over the other, placed his hands behind his head, and pushed his filmy torso into

4

the back of the chair.

For the record, I have only shot one person, and it wasn't my delusional specter.

I glared at my ghost before cutting my gaze to Gibbons and slicing my index finger under my neck.

Gibbons cringed. "I'm sorry I got us off track, Dr. Albright. I was just joking around. I think the inciting incident was when the narrator met Gatsby."

I shook the unwanted memories and Gibbons' annoying taunts off at the exact moment that the clock hand clicked onto the V. At least there was a silver lining to my five minutes of lecture gone wrong. My students finally understood the meaning of the word *inciting*. Despite the rough start, I decided it was the perfect day to make a dozen literary breakthroughs.

I projected my voice. "Thanks, John. Can someone explain why this incident might hook the reader?"

I attempted to wink at my ghost; however, it came out as an awkward two-eyed blink. Then I tilted my head back, drained my cup, wiped the rogue dribbles from my chin, and smiled as two dozen hands rose into the air.

Chapter 1
Ten weeks ago

Years of hard work had paid off. I drove across the state of Pennsylvania, my hair blowing in the breeze as I daydreamed about the splash I would soon make.

Bye-bye to the socially awkward little Randa, who had no life outside of school books. Hello to the sophisticated Dr. Miranda Albright, who would fit in and be the best professor Bellmount College had ever seen.

I had just checked my speedometer, popped out the *Moby Dick* cassette I was halfway through, and turned on the radio which played a tune I suspected might be popular when a police siren blared.

Even though he aggressively demanded I leave my car to wait on the steamy macadam shoulder, I refused to cower. I kept my stance wide, my gaze lifted, and my arms at my side as I did my best to put up a spirited defense.

"Do you know how fast you were driving, young lady?" Sheriff Edgar Shultz twisted his lips into a distorted grin.

"Sixty miles per hour," I said.

"The speed limit is fifty." He pulled on one of my long red corkscrews, and his rat-like eyes watched as it sprung into place.

Once it dawned on me that I was dealing with a libertine with the intellectual quotient of a sea cucumber, my heart thudded. I rubbed at my chest and considered how I might get myself out of the dilemma. I cringed, then went for it.

"There was recent legislation to change the speed limit to sixty. There's even a sign about a mile back indicating this." I placed a hand on my hip and lifted my chin into the air. "And, I will not ask you again. Please remove your hand from my hair."

As his hand retreated, his palm landed on one of my breasts. His lip quivered, and the right side of his mouth lifted to form a misshapen sneer.

"Perhaps we can work out a way to pay off this ticket."

I narrowed my eyes and called forth a venomous voice. "If you like having your cloven hoof attached to your limb, you better get it off me."

He lingered three seconds longer as he studied my expression. Then his arm dropped to his side. The pistol hanging inches from his limp fingers caught my eye, and I forced my shoulders back.

It wasn't that I was courageous or spent my days looking for ways to anger authority figures. I was terrified, but if I hadn't manufactured a facade of bravery, the cop would have continued groping me. The truth was, I found the false legal accusation as disturbing as the disgusting proposition. I had no desire to break any law and had been obsessively watching my speed.

I drove a 1971 monstrosity that my father had given me as a present following the defense of my doctoral dissertation, "Pamela or Virtue Rewarded: The Implications of Richardson's Epistolary Writings on the Contemporary Feminist Heroine."

Although I knew a lot about literature, I knew very

little about cars. I did know if I drove my gas hog under sixty miles an hour, it shook like the engine might fall out. Besides checking my speedometer, additional proof of my adherence to the speed limit was that for the past four hours, my brain, teeth, thighs, and D cups had been shimmying like I was hooked to an old-fashioned vibrate-the-fat-away belt.

The Tank needed to have the idle fixed. Russ, my aunt's live-in special friend, was a fabulous mechanic. I explained all of this—minus my penchant for books and my bouncing bosom—to Officer Odious.

"Edith and Russ. You mean Edith Marshall, who owns The Bellmount Inn, and Russ Jenkins, the caretaker?" Shultz asked.

"Yes, that's my aunt, and Russ is going to fix my car." I shot the cop what I hoped was an intimidating glower. "I tried to tell you this already. I'm the new English professor at Bellmount College, and I'm staying with Edith."

Raising his hands in the air as if to say he was throwing in the towel, Shultz backed away. "Since Edith's your aunt, I think we can forget about this. I'll let you off with a warning this time. If I were you, I'd keep this incident to yourself. You wouldn't want to upset her with your irresponsible driving. Be more careful. Follow the speed limit."

The second he finished blabbing, he hopped into his cruiser and left a puff of dust in his wake.

"Fudge."

I slid into my absurdly large eighteen-year-old car and locked the doors to check my road atlas without further incident. It was impossible to concentrate. My body vibrated with equal parts of anger and fear from an adrenaline rush. I put the map down and rested my head on the steering wheel. After a deep inhale and a twice-as-long exhale, I lifted my head, willed my body to stop shaking, and focused my eyes out the windshield.

A ray of sunlight reflected off something that sat a few feet in front of my car. I'm not sure why I put on my gloves and got out to pick up the object. With a deviant cop running amuck, why would any sane female ignore the safety the locked door afforded? Was it curiosity? That I couldn't resist shiny things? Or one of my other bizarre issues?

I turned the nickel-plated ring every which way to study it. The metal wove around in a circle until it formed a black cross with an oval-shaped top. It was too large to belong to a female and was slightly spooky looking. Heebie-jeebies crawled up my spine. The unattractive item wasn't as distasteful as the sweaty sheriff, but it came in a close second.

I'm also not sure why I decided to wander into the tree line alongside the road. I was aware that my normally acute common sense had failed me, but I couldn't stop myself. Something magnetic pulled me into those woods. I picked up a stick and swung it in the air in front of me. At a young age, I had found this to be an effective way to protect myself from trudging headfirst into spider webs.

I trampled over twigs and branches for about twenty-five yards before the sickly sweet smell of rotten eggs overtook me. I covered my nose with a gloved hand. Unfortunately, the rank funk crept right through the yarn, overpowering Mother Nature's pine and honeysuckle perfume.

More than anything, I wanted to retrace my path to The Tank. Instead, my legs carried me toward a pile I prayed was deer guts.

The most terrified I have ever been was when the Triple Looper at the Chocolate Empire Park broke down. My cousin, Liam, seemed to enjoy being stuck mid-fall on the coaster. Nope! Not me. At twelve years old, my heart had raced at triple speed, and I was afraid it might explode out of my chest. My belly had tingled like poisonous butterflies were banging at my core. I thought my stomach was about to fall into my feet, through the floor of the Looper's cart, and splatter onto the spectators below. I experienced that same exploding heart and crashing stomach sensation as I traipsed in a trancelike state toward the unknown source of the stench.

"Six times six is thirty-six. Six times seven is forty-two," I recited, trying to steady my nerves.

I never got close enough to the corpse to look directly at it. However, I had seen more than enough of the carrion in my intuitive visions—or my overactive imagination—or my hallucinations. At that moment, I wasn't sure what they were. Finally, I broke free and sprinted toward the road, where I vomited up my lunch on the door of my ginormous brown automobile.

Since it was the fourth day of a late August heat wave, the sun blasted the left side of the mountain. Heat radiated from the asphalt, creating shin-high steam. The air hung heavy, and the oppressive temperature took its toll. The only thing that moved was my stomach as it dry-heaved.

I ran my forearm across my mouth to wipe away the repulsive remnants of my spill. Then placed my glove-protected hands on the scorching metal hood, leaned forward, and breathed.

"Miss, I'm a doctor. Can I help you?" someone

behind me said.

When I didn't answer, he repeated himself.

"Miss, I'm a doctor. You seem to be ill. Please let me help you."

Composing myself, I turned to face the stranger. He appeared to be in his thirties, and his blue eyes were a bright sapphire.

"I'm a doctor, too."

It was such a stupid thing to say. It wasn't a response made in the spirit of one-upmanship. I said it out of confusion because the chunks of fast food cheeseburger and fries decorating my car door was a bit distracting. The smell of my digestive mishap had mingled with the decaying body in the woods, then morphed into a live malodor that clung to my ringlets.

"My name is Brad," the man said. "Do you think you're motion sick?"

It took me a moment to process what he said.

"No. I found this over there." I handed him the ring and pointed.

He held it close to his eyes and squinted. "It's an Egyptian symbol called an ankh. It's also sometimes a symbol used by other pagan religions."

I nodded then scooted us away from my lunch to finish our conversation in a less offensive location.

"Did finding this upset you? Is that why you were sick?" he asked.

I scrunched up my nose and gave my head a frantic shake. "No. It's the smell and the bugs. They're disgusting."

"Bugs?" the doctor asked.

"All over the girl's corpse." I shivered. "Can't you smell it?"

His eyes went wide, and he sniffed. "I think so. Can you show me where the body is?"

I mustered courage and walked back into those woods with Dr. Brad. Since he was massive and muscular, he could probably fight off perverted police, hungry maggots, ancient Egyptian gods, and small-town murderers.

I stopped about fifteen feet from the pitiful blob. He lifted the collar of his polo shirt over his nose and continued to walk toward it. I turned my back to the scene and concentrated on reciting the poem "Jabberwocky." Reciting usually calmed my nerves, and multiplication tables weren't going to do it this time.

When the doctor returned, he placed his hand on the small of my back and escorted me to the main road, where he encouraged me to sit in his car. He leaned across me, reached under the dashboard, pulled out a contraption that looked like half a telephone, closed the car door, and walked away.

I sighed in relief. I had always been an excellent judge of character, and I knew that, unlike the sheriff, the doctor didn't pose a threat to my safety.

He paced in front of his car as he talked into the walkie-talkie/phone thing and gesticulated toward the woods. After he finished speaking, he bent over the scorching metal trunk of The Tank. He stayed like that for a couple of minutes. Finally, he straightened, shook his body, and frowning, joined me in the front seat of his car.

"I called 9-1-1. The dispatcher said the state police and forest ranger are on the way." He slid the talking device into a box labeled *Radio World. TC-1 Mobile Cellular Telephone*. "We're to wait until they get here." Then he asked, "What's your name?"

"Miranda Albright. Dr. Miranda Albright."

He smiled. "Oh, you really are a doctor." His lips only turned up for a moment; then, his expression twisted into one of concern.

Was it my casual attire, my young age, or my upchucked meal that caused his original skepticism? He rummaged in his back seat, grabbed a bottle of water, and handed it to me.

I was a headache-kind of thirsty but declined his offer, afraid that I might vomit all over his super cool Radio World cellular phone. Besides, taking in fluids would cause me to need a ladies' room, and there wasn't one for miles.

"You need to rehydrate," he advised me.

I refused again. He gulped half the bottle. He wiped a hand across his sweat-covered brow. Even though I only had on short-shorts and a thin T-shirt, at least five layers of sticky perspiration coated my skin and soaked my gloves.

"I'm assuming you're a medical doctor? I have a Ph.D. in Literature," I said.

"Are you Edith's niece?"

"Yes. How did you know?"

"I'm psychic," he said.

A wave of goose-pimples shot down my neck, landing in my center. "What? You are?"

"No." He laughed. "I'm friends with your aunt. She's excited about your new job and hasn't talked about anything except 'how brilliant and beautiful Miranda is' for the last month."

"Oh." Although I was glad that my aunt was proud of me, I was disappointed that he wasn't psychic.

He looked at his watch, then tapped the steering

wheel. "You have on gloves. It's over ninety degrees today."

It was unclear if he meant this as an observation or a question.

"Raynaud's syndrome," I lied. I had learned that once I explained the benign circulatory disorder, people usually stopped asking questions. Since he was a physician, I shouldn't need to explain myself further.

"Ah," he said. "I have a blanket in the trunk."

The liquid soaking my hairline, sliding down my neck into my cleavage, and drenching my thighs forced me to pass on his offer.

"How long do you think the body's been there?" I asked.

He took a minute to think it over. "Well, my specialty is the living, but I'm going to guess a couple of weeks from the amount of decomposition."

"That's horrible. She was so young and pretty."

He peeked at me from the corner of his eye. I knew he probably discredited my response because there was no way I could have known this from viewing the indistinguishable mess in the woods.

Finally, he faced me. "Do you know who she was?"

I bit my lip. "No, I'm just guessing." Then I let out a long sigh. I didn't want to come off as a crazy witchy woman who believed she had psychic abilities. I sounded insane when I mentioned my intuition, so I no longer discussed it with anyone, not even my dad. However, my vision indicated that the rotting corpse had been a pretty girl before being covered in insects.

"Someone cut out her heart," he announced.

My strange vision depicted a damaged bra and a ripped open chest cavity.

He swallowed. "The wildlife got to her."

Buzzards had picked at her eyes and face, and maggots, flies, and a hideous variety of crawling things left me with a nausea that would haunt me for the rest of my days.

"Her body was inside a red spray-painted pentagram." He shivered and looked straight ahead.

Was he picturing her empty eye sockets and the large nails driven into her palms and feet?

"It's a disturbing scene. I doubt they'll be able to identify the body without an autopsy. How much of it did you see?" he asked.

I was reasonably sure I had envisioned the girl before the elements and critters had done their damage. "Enough."

He tapped his steering wheel again. "Cool car." He lifted his chin toward The Tank.

"That's what my dad said when he presented it to me. I had been hoping for a smaller, newer, less brown car." I wrinkled my nose. "Not a spot of rust," I added with a touch of flippancy.

He mulled my comment over and chuckled. "What were you doing in the woods?"

Thank goodness I didn't have to answer because a white truck with a Park Service logo pulled in behind us.

The doctor opened his door and called over his shoulder, "It's the park ranger."

I did a double-take because I recognized Tommy Little, my childhood friend, instantly. Tommy's face still hadn't grown into his ears, and as usual, his hair was too short.

"Tommy," I called, exiting the car and running toward him.

"Randa, little Randa Albright."

The park ranger's grin consumed his face. He picked me up and swung me around.

"Well, what a fine welcome back this is."

We exchanged a few niceties before he said, "You want to take me to the body? I need to secure the scene until the state police arrive. It might take them a while to get here."

Brad offered to escort him to the corpse when a municipal police car, siren blaring, passed us and parked in front of The Tank.

"Oh, shit! What's he doing here?" Tommy frowned and kicked at an invisible clump of dirt.

Boom! Boom! Boom! The earth violently rumbled as a burbling Jabberwock galumphed toward us.

"Oh God, it's Officer Bandersnatch." My voice echoed to Saturn's fifty-ninth moon.

"You again?" The slimy cop glared at me.

"I guess you've met Sheriff Shultz, Bellmount's finest?" Dr. Brad whispered as he rolled his eyes.

Chapter 2

It was dusk when I parked The Tank in front of my aunt's three-story Victorian. At least a dozen baskets overflowing with purple geraniums and cascading ivy hung from the rafters of the olive green wraparound porch. Intricate gingerbread lattice in shades of burgundy and cream adorned every corner and edge of the inn.

Even in the fading light, I could tell the gardens that graced its walkways were well cared for and lush. Nothing had changed since my visit seven years prior.

The inn had once upon a time belonged to my Grandma Zoey Wilson. Aunt Edith had taken control of the business when she was seventeen years old. My mother had been fifteen at the time and didn't understand how mentally ill her mother was or why her older sister had become so "pissy and bossy." Rumors circulated declaring Grandma Zoey thought she was a witch with special powers. Consequently, my grandmother often found herself sequestered at Bear County Hospital.

Aunt Edith worked tirelessly to keep their home from falling into a state of disrepair, and she had fought tooth and nail to keep the county social services from stepping in and taking my mother away.

My aunt had continued to work her fingers to the bone through my cousin's birth, her husband's death, and my grandmother's chronic hospitalizations and eventual death.

Including my infancy, I spent eighteen summers playing in the inn's gardens with my older cousin, Liam. They had been the best times of my life: long, lazy days that consisted of mornings reading on the wraparound porch, afternoons swinging on the rope vine at the river with Liam and his gang, and evenings catching fireflies and eating s'mores around the backyard bonfire.

Dr. Brad broke my reverie when he knocked on my car window to see if I was okay. He had proven himself quite helpful in more ways than one. Shultz was on his best behavior around the doctor. Although, perhaps, the sleazy sheriff's perversions halted because of the presence of Tommy, Miller, the state police detective, and the coroner.

Or perhaps it was that I had called the sheriff *diseased vermin dung*.

Meanwhile, the brave physician, with his stomach of iron, had cleaned my car. Once the ancient Detective Miller finished his inquisition, Brad insisted on following me to the inn to touch base with my aunt. His final Good Samaritan act of the day was unloading possessions from my car.

"Oh, Miranda, thank God you're okay. I expected you hours ago." Aunt Edith descended the front porch and wrapped me in an embrace.

When her cheek brushed mine, I understood how worried she had been. Then she did a double-take and addressed the volunteer packhorse behind me.

"Bradley?"

"Hi, Edith. I wanted to make sure Miranda arrived safely."

I supposed he paused to give me a chance to fill in the details.

I wiped a bead of sweat from my eyes, tried to lubricate my mouth with saliva, then gave a feeble explanation. "I found a corpse about ten miles from town. We waited for the state police and coroner to show up; it took them forever, and then there were so many questions."

"Oh, my!" Aunt Edith declared. "Come on inside." She used a curling hand to usher us into the foyer, where we continued our conversation.

Brad stood beside me as he related a few details. "Edith, I happened to be driving past, and it was horrible. The cops believe it was some sort of Satanic ritual."

I didn't correct him. It wasn't his fault that the police were clueless. Maybe I was wrong. I secretly hoped I was. Knowing all sorts of odd things was exhausting, and I had no desire to be locked away like my grandma. But this didn't feel like a cult murder.

"Aunt Edith, would it be okay if I got a shower right away? I'm filthy, I threw up, and I've been sweating for hours. I'm also thirsty," I said.

It took a moment for the shocking declaration to sink in.

My aunt cut her gaze from me to the doctor. "A Satanic murder?"

When neither of us responded, she said, "Of course, the blue room is ready for you." She pressed a key into my hand.

I grabbed the suitcase containing my overnight clothes and toiletries and passed the once gas, now electrified pole lamp. The four-ball shades of opaline glass illuminated my climb in an otherwise dark stairwell. I was in a hurry to rid myself of all the foul things that clung to me and knew my aunt would forgive my haste.

I was halfway up the first flight of stairs when I turned to thank my caregivers. The doctor's muscular frame juxtaposed next to my aunt made her seem more petite than I remembered. He towered over her by almost a foot. His thick black hair contrasted with her short graying curls. I supposed the horrors of the day had kept me from realizing how incredibly handsome Brad was, and his dimpled smile stole my breath.

Although she was only forty-seven, Aunt Edith's pale blue eyes sat below a forehead lined with deep crevices. Something besides my late arrival was worrying her.

"Thank you, Brad. I don't know what I would have done if you hadn't been there," I said.

He acknowledged my gratitude with the shifting of his weight and a nod.

Aunt Edith scooted me along. "Honey, there are clean towels in your bathroom. We'll finish unloading your things. Russ will bring up your luggage when he returns from walking the dog, and I'll bring water up right away."

"Hey Edith, do you think I could have some whiskey before I finish unloading the car?" the doctor asked.

Unless my knight in shining armor was a heavy drinker, and I was reasonably sure he wasn't, he had been more shaken up than he would have me believe.

The oak staircase was wide on the first floor, but the higher I climbed, the more it narrowed and curved, causing me to struggle with my suitcase. By the time I took the last step to my new abode, I was both tingling with excitement and panting from exertion.

The blue room had been mine every summer. Built into a turret, it contained a semi-circular cushioned window seat that allowed me to pretend I was a princess looking out my castle window to view my kingdom. It looked as lovely as I remembered.

Aunt Edith had added a new floral wallpaper, reupholstered the window seat in a contrasting blue and white fabric, and accessorized with half a dozen frilly throw pillows. The headboard, dresser, nightstand, and small table in front of the bay window remained the same as they had been during my childhood. A Moroccan swan neck lamp still sat on the nightstand beside the bed. Its Tiffany-style glass, in multiple shades of blue, had been casting a magical glow for as long as I could remember.

"Oh, my lovely castle, I have missed you." I tossed my room key onto the dresser.

I lifted an armpit and gagged. I stripped, then piled my germ-ridden clothes beside the door. I hoped Russ still built bonfires so everything could be discarded in flames. I retrieved my toiletries and stepped into the clawfoot tub that had been converted into a shower.

I had scrubbed my body raw, rinsed my hair of the rancid odors it had absorbed, chugged the glass of water my aunt had placed on my nightstand, and finished unpacking my bags when there was a woof at my door.

A tiny golden-haired collie nudged the door open and pranced in to greet me.

"Oh, my." I squatted to pat him on his regal head. "You must be Spot."

Because I hadn't been to the inn since I was a college freshman, this was my first time meeting the Shetland sheepdog. Spot was a ridiculous name for such a beautiful dog. He should have been named Lassie or Prince. I was certain Russ had chosen the most unlikely name for their pet as a way to tease my perfectionist aunt. I ran my finger along the white stripe through the center of his nose, and the Sheltie smiled at me.

Aunt Edith entered and placed a tray on the round table in front of my princess-throne window seat.

"Bradley suggested you may only be in the mood for tea and toast tonight." My aunt studied the plate and frowned.

If my aunt wasn't serving a gourmet four-course meal fit for a queen, she felt her hostess duties were subpar.

"I made the jam with the wild elderberries growing in the woods out back."

She sat beside me, Spot at my feet, while I spread the jam on thick slices of homemade bread.

"It's perfect."

Aunt Edith's concoction was loaded with cinnamon and cloves and tasted like my childhood.

She fidgeted with one of the lacy window coverings. "Bradley's worried. He said Shultz trampled all over the crime scene before the state police arrived."

"Men like Shultz need to be castrated," I muttered before taking a huge bite. I was hungry, although, after my day, anything more than bread would have caused me to balk.

Her eyes widened. "What did he do?"

"Nothing. I can just tell he's a creep."

"Bradley also told me that the homicide detective the state police assigned to the case wasn't receptive to you."

"I overheard Shultz tell him I was a troublemaker. I can't imagine how they would have treated me if Tommy and Brad hadn't been there. Are the state cops and local cops in bed together?"

My aunt thought this over as I prepared my cup of tea. "Probably, but why would Shultz call you a troublemaker?"

Probably because I called him diseased vermin dung. I shrugged.

"I noticed you are wearing gloves," she said.

"I have Raynaud's syndrome. It's this circulatory condition in which my hands become cold."

I recognized the look she gave me. It was the same crooked-eyebrow gape she had bestowed on Liam and me fifteen years ago when we knocked over her antique vase and blamed it on Russ's innocent dog.

She stood. "Honey, if you need to talk about anything—what happened to you today, your mother's passing, your circulatory disorder—I'm here for you. The inn is your new home. I know I'm not your mother, but I plan to do my best to look out for you." She withdrew a pill container from the pocket of her robe. "Bradley left this for you. He said it should help you sleep. He also said to make sure you rehydrate, and he will swing around to check on you later this week."

I wasn't plagued with a terminal illness. I simply had a long drive and vomited up an unhealthy lunch. The doctor seemed to be overly concerned. Although, since I had just witnessed my first heartless, decomposing maggot picnic, I wouldn't take it for granted a movie-star handsome man was worried about me. It comforted me to know that my aunt intended to look out for me. But I wasn't an orphaned child; I was an adult with a career. "Thank you, Aunt Edith."

"Liam will be here for breakfast," she announced.

I clapped. "Awesome!"

Two years my senior, Liam was like my super cool big brother, and I was like his pesky little sister.

"Remember, breakfast at nine on the weekends. Greet

the guests, grab your coffee from the sideboard, then come to the kitchen for your meal."

She didn't need to remind me. I remembered her rules by heart.

"Get a good night's rest, honey. You have a busy week ahead of you." She picked up her tray.

Spot jumped to his feet, and I bent forward to scratch his ears. He licked my cheek, then, wagging his tail, followed my aunt to the door. Before leaving my room, she picked up my damp laundry.

She laughed and called over her shoulder, "I'll run this through the washer—twice." Then she closed the door.

I crawled into my bed and pulled a fluffy powder blue blanket to my chin. Smiling, I closed my eyes and inhaled my new life.

Chapter 3

Even though I had swallowed a sedative large enough to knock out livestock, I awoke excited to begin my day. An afternoon of vomiting in front of a handsome stranger and conversing in the front seat of a fancy car while waiting for the coroner was the closest thing to a date that I had experienced since 1982 when Tommy Little had taken me turtle hunting.

The only difference between the date in 1982 and the dozens of previous excursions Tommy and I had gone on was that he had said, "Randa, we should go on a date. Wanna go look for turtles?" So I'm not sure it counted as an actual date.

If I faced reality, the gorgeous doctor probably didn't consider cleaning vomit off my car to be romantic. Maybe I had never been on an official date. No matter; I was happy! Nothing compared to the excitement I felt starting my new life as an adult.

The window beside my bed was propped open, and a late summer breeze blew across the room, adding to my elation. The smell of my aunt's Oriental lilies wafted up three stories to my little blue turret, and a cheerful cardinal chirped away, foreshadowing that the day would be incredible.

It didn't take me long to dress. I applied mascara to my light lashes and neatened my out-of-control hair. Then I dressed in red pants, a white blouse, large red hoop earrings, and red jelly shoes.

Since I was ready early, I sat at my plush window seat and peered out over my kingdom. From my one-hundred-twenty-degree bay window, I could see across the southwest end of town, all the way to the west branch of the Susquehanna River. The Methodist church steeple, an old-fashioned five-story department store, a 1920s movie theater, the gables of Konicki's Funeral Home, and the clock above the town hall stood out.

It was a beautiful view, as long as I didn't look too closely at the square architecture and neon sign of Grainey's Gun Shop. Aunt Edith had a long-standing feud with her fellow council member, Greg Grainey, the materialistic womanizer who owned the family's eyesore of a store.

At the very edge of town, down a steep hill, stood The Bear Claw Pub. Two of the seven Westinghouse siblings owned the restaurant bar. Weston the Second—fondly referred to as Pop because he looked out for his regulars—and his younger brother Will purchased the pub in 1959. Pop had named his only child Weston the Third. Will was married to a woman named Polly, and they had two daughters, Winona and Willa.

I found the most fascinating of the Westinghouse clan to be Weston Westinghouse the Third. West was both my childhood friend and my teenage crush. The Bellmount consensus was that it wasn't Pop's fault his son was incorrigible.

According to over two decades of rumors, the woman who had birthed and abandoned the rambunctious toddler was one hundred percent to blame. The last time I had seen West, he rode a red motorcycle and carried a black comb in his back pocket. He was constantly removing his feathered locks from his hazel-colored, amber-speckled eyes so he could "wink at pretty girls."

West, Tommy Little, and Liam spent my eighth summer chasing me around town, throwing bugs into my hair. My fourteenth summer, they delighted in pulling my red ringlets, insisting I looked like some popular chubby cartoon character. By my thinned-out sixteenth summer, West had become obsessed with touching my breasts— not that I had ever let him.

By my eighteenth summer, he ignored me since he was twenty and had focused his attention on older girls. West had seen it imperative to inform me that those women *put out*. That same summer, Tommy Little lavished me with invitations to search for amphibians. Although Liam found having a younger cousin an annoying responsibility, he also protected me with a loyal fierceness.

As we got older, Liam didn't allow Tommy, and especially West, to get too close to me. I guess he felt it his responsibility as my stand-in-brother to keep his hormonal friends at bay.

Five minutes before the hour, I put on my red gloves and raced down the stairs, excited to see my bug-taunting, overly protective, favorite cousin.

Aunt Edith's insistent etiquette had been fun as a child and torture as a teenager. Now that I was an adult, it was merely a way to repay my doting aunt. My first stop was the parlor, where I introduced myself to the guests and performed my duties as the innkeeper's niece. I politely greeted two couples dropping their children off at the college, and then a man with roving eyes, who was in town to study the local river trout.

Next, I prepared my coffee and grabbed a raspberry

muffin at the sideboard. Finally, I headed to the family common area in the kitchen.

Aunt Edith and Winona Westinghouse were preparing eggs Benedict and fresh fruit. Winona was my aunt's other pretend daughter. West's older cousin worked at the inn a few mornings each week and the pub most afternoons and evenings. Winona had her cousin's pretty coloring and gorgeous eyes, but the resemblance stopped there. She was curvy and round and as tall as a redwood.

"Good morning, honey. How'd you sleep?" My aunt balled a piece of cantaloupe.

"Gwait," I replied, my mouth full of muffin.

"Hi, Miranda. Wow, you got pretty. Edith was telling me you found a Satanic murder victim on your way into town. Who was it? Do they know? Was it bloody? Were you freaked out? Isn't Bradley gorgeous?"

Winona came up for air and adorned the egg entree with fresh melon balls before handing it to me. I plopped my half-eaten baked good on my plate and cleared my pre-coffee fog with a quick back and forth head shaking. Seven years had done nothing to change Winona's game of let-me-see-how-many-questions-I-can-ask-at-once.

I took three quick sips of coffee. "Hi, Winona. It's good to see you. Sorry, I don't know anything." It wasn't a lie since nothing I knew was official. I chose not to address the comment about the handsome doctor.

"Aunt Edith, where's Liam?" I carried my plate to the family dining table.

"Right here, little cuz," Liam said, the kitchen door swinging behind him. "Was saying hi to Mom's company."

"Liam," I squealed, leaping to embrace my cousin.

Although my mother and aunt were blue-eyed like my Grandpa Lucas, Liam and I had inherited Grandma Zoey's emerald eyes. His long lashes matched his copper brown hair. He lifted me off of my feet, swung me around, and kissed my cheek.

"It's been a long time. I haven't seen you since the funeral." His body tensed, and he let out a sigh.

I dismissed the comment and focused on my cousin's kiss because he still had the remnants of a pretty brunette with big brown eyes on his lips. I supposed I knew this because brunettes had a distinct smell, or so I told myself. It surely wasn't because I could see his girl smiling at him as they said goodbye—because reading minds was crazy!

"Look at you! You've turned into quite the heartbreaker," Liam declared.

The truth was I had a tough time getting physically close to people. I chose not to mention that earning my bachelor's degree and Ph.D. in seven years left no time for dating, men, or being a heartbreaker. My goal had been to be prepared for Professor Lingle's job at Bellmount College when he retired. That meant seven years without semester breaks, or summers in Bellmount, and no romance. Besides, Liam was the "heartbreaker," evidenced by his handsome face, lean physique, and early morning sport of passionately kissing some pretty girl.

"No men for me. Do you have a girlfriend?" I intently studied his body language.

"Nope. No serious girlfriend." He gave me one of his charming smiles.

Liam and I spent the rest of the day swaying on the front porch swing, munching on a picnic lunch, and visiting our old swimming hole. He told me about his new apartment across town and explained the day-to-day grind of being an accountant for the Lancaster Firm. When I explained I was wearing gloves because I had a syndrome that made my hands cold, his lips formed a straight line before telling me that Grandma Zoey had the same affliction but refused to wear her gloves—so not a comforting thought!

While sitting on the bank of the river, he coaxed my second biggest secret out of me by holding a spider that resembled a tarantula and was the size of The Tank, inches from my nose.

"Yes, I'm a virgin! Liam, get it away from me. Now!" I swatted at his hand, punched him in the shoulder, then stomped away from the river and toward the inn.

Chapter 4

The Bear Claw Pub was the town's equivalent of a time capsule. Locals, visiting sportsmen, and college students packed the room. Liam informed me the music that blared from the brightly lit vintage jukebox was southern rock.

Old copper camp lanterns hung over the long bar and above each of the round dining tables. Nineteen-fifty-style photos of the local wildlife—bear, deer, fish, and fox—adorned the paneled walls. A "Go Bellmount Grizzlies" sign sporting the high school mascot was the most prominent banner in the establishment. Under it hung a smaller sign celebrating the local college. I smiled as I read "The Bellmount Bears." The realization that this was now my place of employment made me swell with pride.

I glimpsed back the long hallway that started at the left end of the bar and led to the small game room and restrooms. A comforting warmth washed over me because the pub hadn't changed.

Tommy Little was waiting for us at the bar. "Randa!" He hugged me. "It's been so long. An entire twenty-four hours."

"Under better circumstances this time." I took a whiff.

Tommy had traded in his childhood odor of dirt and dead fish for the more appealing *eau de parfum* of

Stallion Cologne.

Liam perched on the other side of me. Tommy and I had a few minutes to catch up before Pop, Will, Polly, and Winona accosted me with greetings.

"Where's Willa?" I finally asked.

"Moved to Pittsburgh with her boyfriend," Polly said.

I ran my hand over the varnished maple bar. "Where's West?"

Pop patted me on the shoulder. "He's in the storeroom, should be back any minute. I gotta head back to the kitchen. Glad you're back in town, kiddo."

He waved then retreated into the kitchen.

It took all my effort to concentrate on the conversation because I searched the room, anxiously anticipating West's entrance.

"Liam says you're teaching at the college. So cool," Tommy said.

"Always knew you were a smart one," Will declared.

Polly kissed me on the cheek. "We've missed you these last few summers, so you better visit us a lot now that we're neighbors. I'll make sure you get tons of mozzarella sticks. I know how you love them." With the promise of mountains of fried cheese, Winona's parents went back to their barkeep duties.

Tommy and I resumed our conversation

"It's my dream job. I'm teaching three English classes and one journalism class. I'm also the advisor for the campus newspaper."

"Smart and beautiful." Tommy's ears turned scarlet.

"Back off, buddy," Liam actually growled. "She's way out of your league."

Tommy shifted on his stool as I tried to ignore Liam's absurd comment. I wasn't out of Tommy's league in the least. I figured chit-chat would alleviate the embarrassment we both felt, so I searched for a new topic.

"So, you're happy at the Park Service?"

"Yep." Tommy took a swig of beer. "It's a good livin'."

Tommy had wanted to be a forest ranger since he was five years old. He had always been obsessed with turtles, amphibians, and all manner of four-legged creatures. He had gone to college to study environmental science and had attended the local police academy for a year. It seemed that both Tommy and I were currently pursuing our dream careers.

Winona plopped beers in front of us, singing out, "On the house."

I eyeballed mine suspiciously, decided to be appreciative, took a sip, then cringed.

Winona propped her elbows on the bar and bent forward so that she was at eye level with us. "Tom, I heard you got called in on that Satanic murder investigation. I wonder if it was connected to those murders a few years ago. Was the body in a pentagram? You know, devil worshippers do that; they put sacrifices inside pentagrams." She tapped her forehead. "Anyone else wonder if she was a virgin? I bet she was—you know—a virgin."

Winona Westinghouse needed a new hobby that didn't involve a fascination with my crime scene. I prayed nobody was sacrificing virgins or I was in terrible trouble.

Tommy swirled the contents of his mug before taking a sip. "Shultz heard the call over the dispatch and showed up before the state police. He made a mess and then wrote up a shit incident report that contradicted what I said."

"What do you mean?" I asked.

Liam added his two cents. "Damn local cops."

"To top it off, I think the murder interrupted the homicide detective's nap," Tommy said.

I laughed.

Tommy's brow furrowed. "Shit, I shouldn't have said that. Forget I said anything."

"Why? I thought Detective Miller seemed a bit narcoleptic." I chuckled for an eternity at what I thought was a humorous observation.

"Seriously, Randa, let it go. I was wrong to bad-mouth Miller," Tommy said.

I didn't have a chance to ask him to elaborate because Weston Westinghouse the Third put down the crate he was carrying and headed straight toward me. I popped off the barstool and met him halfway.

"Wowee! Ya still look like a yummy strawberry shortcake," he called out in his country boy drawl.

He looked me over from head to toe. "Ya turned out really hot!" He grinned, lifted me into the air, and squeezed me.

"Hi, West," I said, a little breathier than was seemly. "It's so good to see you!" I felt West's appropriate embrace in very inappropriate places.

It had been years, and West still made me realize I had girl parts that did tingly things. His five-foot, eleven-inch frame was leanly muscled. His biceps and chest belonged to a man who lifted heavy items and had a love of outdoor sports.

I ached to run my fingers through his dirty-blond hair, which was more golden than brown. It waved about uncontrollably—a lot like the man whose head it adorned. I wanted to touch the flaxen scruff that indicated he had missed a day or two of shaving. He wasn't as pretty as the twenty-year-old West, but the sweaty working man look suited him.

He came around behind the bar so he could wait on customers while we talked. Tommy was filling him in on my new job when two heavily made-up women from the other end of the bar called for him.

"West, oh Weston," the more attractive of the two practically purred. "Where have you been? I'm so thirsty."

He winked. "Be back in a minute."

West's mischievous look was the same one that made me accept his lamebrain dares when I was a child and had my heart doing flip-flops when I was a teenager. A blush scorched my cheeks.

Liam cleared his throat. "Forget about him, little cuz." He pointed to West's back since two half-naked barflies were currently entertaining his front. "He may be my best friend, but he isn't the boyfriend type."

Tommy uttered an "Amen."

I wanted to throttle my squad of protectors. The boyfriend type? I had my career; men didn't find me attractive, and I was a freaky nerd who had weird visions. Besides, West probably told everything with breasts they were hot.

Additionally, it was unfair to say such things about him since he was across the bar flirting with the bimbo twins and couldn't defend himself. I decided if Liam had stepped up his protection service because of the arachnid-coerced confession, he was no longer my favorite cousin. Besides, he was the one who had appeared at the inn with some girl's kisses still lingering on his lips.

I huffed out, "Well, isn't that the pot calling the kettle black?"

Had I been a child, I would have stuck my tongue out at my cousin. Okay. I confess, it made a brief appearance, but Liam had a way of bringing out the five-year-old in me. Tommy chortled, his drink exploded from his mouth, and the returning West ended up wearing a mouthful of beer.

"What the hell, Little?" West wiped the beer spittle from his eyes.

My chuckles turned into obnoxiously unattractive snorts.

West looked me in the eyes, my heart fluttered about, and he grinned.

I didn't want the evening to end. Since I hadn't had friends at home, hanging out with Liam, Tommy, and West when I visited Bellmount had always made me feel special. I gave myself a mini pep talk. You live here now; you can see them every day if you want.

Unfortunately, Liam gave me an earful on our short walk up the hill. "You need to be careful. You're fresh meat in this town."

I grunted. "Are you seriously projecting your philandering onto me?"

Liam grunted back. "If you're interested in a boyfriend, stick with someone in your league, like Doc Gordon. He's available since his divorce."

I silently agreed. Brad Gordon was a spectacular specimen, but he was so far out of my league we didn't exist in the same plane.

"And, if you decide you want to slum it, Tom is a good guy."

Tom Little was a great guy, although I couldn't help but still see him as my friend, Little Tommy, the freckled-faced boy always covered in mud and smelling like decaying wildlife. Of course, no man, not even the kind-hearted Tommy, would be into a weird woman who wore gloves to run her hands over his chest and couldn't touch his cheek without thinking she knew every one of his secrets.

"But stay away from West. He's a scoundrel!"

I poked Liam in the chest. "Scoundrel? When did you turn into a middle-aged woman with a penchant for romance novels?"

Liam snorted, then hugged me. "Have a great first week at work, and see you next weekend, little cuz."

My frustration with my cousin instantly faded. "Thanks, Liam. I missed you and Bellmount so much."

I ran up the porch steps, popped onto my toes to wave, then dreamily strolled into the inn.

Chapter 5

In 1985 Forbes published a list titled "The 100 Most Beautiful Small Town Colleges in the US". The article included a short description accompanied by a photo of the Bellmount College entrance. *Number twenty-six: Set in the Appalachian Mountains, the mature trees, majestic stone architecture, and manicured lawns give Bellmount College a bucolic old-school charm.*

In 1989, that same stone archway boasted a banner that read, "Bellmount: Celebrating 150 Years of Excellence".

After passing under the entranceway, I navigated strategically placed buildings, each an architectural masterpiece in its own right. Eventually, the evergreen and oak-lined pathway led to the largest of the Georgian Colonials. Resplendent with four mammoth Grecian columns, Sutton Hall was the center of the private liberal arts college and housed Admissions, Student Services, and my new office. Since classes were to start in two days, cars lined the roads to the right and left of the main quad. The steady stream of parents dropping off students and students carrying boxes into the dormitories created an ongoing wave of activity.

My office was on the third floor of Sutton Hall. I'm almost positive no one witnessed me hop about when I read the brass nameplate beside my door, *Miranda Albright, Ph.D. English Studies.* Even though my personal space was small and only consisted of a desk, two chairs, and an old wooden file cabinet, opening that door was one of the most rewarding moments of my life.

My joy met with a warm breeze that entered through the narrow lattice window. Although it was only nine a.m., my powder blue gloves, floral sundress, and blue linen jacket had me perspiring profusely. I plopped down, retrieved a folder from my backpack, and studied my meticulous lecture notes. Eventually, needing a break, I spun around in my swivel chair and took in my surroundings. Every once in a while, a gust of wind threatened to scatter the papers on my desk.

"Hasn't air conditioning been invented in Bellmount yet?" I asked the hot air.

Puff, it answered, blowing a paper onto the floor.

I reached down to retrieve the rogue note, and a man's voice called out, "Knock, knock!"

When I sat up, a distinguished-looking gentleman with a full head of white hair and a matching beard filled my doorway. Dr. Lincoln Harrison, the psychology professor assigned to be my mentor, pulled up a chair and filled me in on everything from job responsibilities to faculty gossip.

By the end of his visit, I knew Ms. Brown ran the campus and was the only person who could control Dean Johnson—and at all costs, I should avoid Johnson on Mondays. Lincoln also warned me not to fraternize with crazy Professor Michelson and advised that Margie in the cafeteria dished out giant portions.

"Are you cold?" he asked, looking at my hands.

"I have Raynaud's syndrome. My hands are numb, but the rest of me is burning up." I pointed to a bead of sweat at my hairline.

"Late August is a bitch." He lifted an arm to acknowledge his damp pits.

Lincoln was charming and talkative. An old friend of my aunt's, he had been instrumental in keeping her apprised of my predecessor's retirement. We made a Thursday lunch date so that he could introduce me to my new colleagues.

I also met Keisha Brown, the delightfully outspoken assistant to the dean. She entertained me with stories of Dean Johnson's temper and toupee gone wrong. Then she wowed me with tales of the barefoot Dr. Michaelson's "hairy-ass toes." She made me laugh until I snorted.

My morning was a dream come true until I met Liza Smith. Her sweet voice interrupted the reading of my *English Curriculum Guide*.

"Hello. Dr. Albright, I'm Liza Smith. I'm in your journalism class and editor-in-chief of the campus newspaper."

"Oh, fudge!" I said as the girl in front of me combined with my memory of the girl in the woods. Then I blurted out, "Fudge!" as I knocked a glass of iced tea onto the binder I was reading.

For the record, I believe an ambitious college professor should have a more sophisticated way of expressing herself.

The coed ran from my office.

Still, at a loss for my more refined thesaurus, I blurted out another "Fudge" as I helplessly watched the dark liquid permeate the pages.

My attempts to shake off my disquiet failed as my heart seemed to drift two inches above my chest cavity.

Liza returned a couple of moments later, carrying a handful of paper towels.

My taut shoulders relaxed. "You didn't run off?"

"Run off?" she repeated, handing me the towels.

After I wiped the spill from my desk and blotted tea from the pages, I extended my mucky palm, indicating Liza should take the seat in front of my desk. "Thank you, and please sit."

She stared at my stained glove and sat. Winter couldn't come soon enough. People rarely took notice of my hands once temperatures dipped below the freezing mark.

"I have some ideas for the newspaper. Could I run them past you?"

"Of course," I answered.

She took a folder out of her backpack. I shuffled through her papers as she filled me in on the details. Liza appeared to be organized, bright, and creative. Her paper towel rescue proved that she was also helpful.

I reorganized her folder and handed it back to her. "Beautiful work. Are you a senior?"

"No, a junior." Then she offered unsolicited information. "I'm from Bellmount. I know most people don't want to go to college in their hometown, but I love it here, and I've never wanted to go anywhere else."

"I understand. My aunt owns The Bellmount Inn. I spent my childhood summers here, and my dream has always been to call this my home. I love it here, too."

"My sister couldn't get away from here fast enough." She rolled her eyes. "She's a handful and fights with my dad non-stop. He's kind of strict, being a pastor and all."

"Your sister?" An ominous dread poked at my chest.

"Yes, I have a twin sister. She went away to State College."

"A twin? What do you mean?" I asked. "Is she at

school now?"

Liza tilted her head to the side and took a moment to form her response. "Yes. She was fighting with our dad, so she left for her campus about two weeks early. Why are you asking?"

"Your ideas are great. Let's talk Thursday before class. Sorry, I have to go now," I called over my shoulder as I sprinted out the door, leaving my editor-in-chief gawking after me.

****

The Tank had a bad habit of getting hungry at the most inopportune moments. Unfortunately, the insatiable beast was hungry almost every minute of every day. I simply wasn't in the mood for his appetite when I was in a hurry. After my conversation with Liza Smith, I needed to get to the crime scene immediately. Regrettably, nothing went my way. In my haste, I passed by the gas station and had to double back. Then the officer guarding the area turned me away.

I was in a snit by the time I harassed Tommy Little at the Forest Visitor Center. I'm not sure I even greeted him.

I plopped myself down at the seat in front of his desk and blurted out, "Why is there a cop standing there? Why is there yellow tape everywhere?"

Tommy looked up from a pamphlet he was reading. "Hiya, Randa. What are you doing here? If you are talking about where we found the body, it's because it's a crime scene. Haven't you ever watched a detective show?" He chuckled.

My studies had left me in a decade-long culture vacuum, and I found no humor in my situation at that particular moment. I grunted. "Can you get me inside the tape?"

"No. It's a crime scene. The armed cop and tape are there for a reason. The state police have kept the scene locked down a bit longer than expected because of some…" He chose his words carefully. "Well, some things went wrong with the investigation, and there were inconsistencies in the incident reports."

"But the state forest is your jurisdiction, right?" I asked.

Tommy put the pamphlet down and rubbed his eyes. "You know something. When you're obsessed, you're relentless." He sighed. "Randa, I'd do anything for you, but no, I can't get you near it until they clear the scene. Detective Miller with the Homicide Division is still in charge of the investigation."

I sat forward. "Fine, we won't get too close. Have the police identified the body yet?"

Step number one was getting Tommy to go with me. Step number two would be convincing him to let me inside the tape.

Tommy leaned back in his chair. "Look, you need to stay away from this. It's a hell of a mess right now, and no, they haven't identified the body."

"So, Shultz screwed up the investigation?" Shultz had become my sworn enemy. I was sure he was responsible for the AIDS plague, the Chernobyl disaster, and the recent Valdez oil spill.

I hoped Tommy didn't play cards because his poker face needed work. He ratted out the cop with an eye roll. Fortunately, I knew Tommy's weakness. It happened to be a little red-haired girl with green eyes and a smattering of freckles across her nose. Good thing I knew her personally. I swallowed my grumpies, flicked my hair over my shoulder, and gazed up at him through fluttering eyelashes.

"You wouldn't want me to go back there by myself, would you?" I was the pits at flirting, but Tommy was easy prey.

"Come on." He groaned as he grabbed the keys to his truck and slid into his official work jacket.

****

Tommy and I greeted the officer who guarded the scene.

"Kline, this is Dr. Albright. She's been helping with the investigation and thinks she may have lost an earring the other day. She's going to look around for it." Tommy turned to me and pointed. "Over there."

I sulked to my relegated spot. I hunched in the grass but stayed close enough to eavesdrop on their conversation.

"I'm waiting for a radio call from Miller. I think they have everything they need, and we should be opening the scene soon. Ridiculous, we have had to post someone here this long," Kline said.

"I know. Shultz stomped all over the place. He even tripped and fell on his ass," Tommy said.

I giggled at this precious tidbit.

"If that wasn't bad enough, when he tried to stand up, his foot got stuck in the mud. Get this. He rolled right onto the corpse and freaked out." Tommy imitated the sheriff by throwing his hands into the air, frantically wiggling his fingers beside his face, and raising his voice a few octaves. "Jesus Christ, get it off me.' He was covered in, well, disgusting shit."

I was no longer chuckling. I crunched myself into a ball and held onto my stomach.

"I know I shouldn't be laughing out of respect for the

dead, but his stubby limbs were flailing all over the place," Tommy added.

Kline snorted. I whimpered. While Shultz's lack of coordination and slapstick antics were comical, defiling the young girl's corpse was inexcusable. Shultz was an inept nincompoop.

"Then the stupid bastard butchered the incident report. He said Doc Gordon was the one who discovered the body. I'm not sure why he left the professor out of the report," Tommy said.

The distance between us muffled Kline's response. I inclined my ear toward them but only made out the words "Miller," "Reynolds," and "fast."

"Dr. Albright claims she found the ring by the road. Shultz says Doc Gordon found it beside the body. I hate to say it, but I trust her over Shultz any day of the week," Tommy said.

Kline waved to me. "I hope you find your earring Dr. Albright, but we have scoured these woods. We would have found it if it was about."

I conjured a big smile and stuck my hand in the air. "Thank you," I called back. "It was my grandmother's. I would hate to lose it."

Wow. Who knew? I was a good liar. I congratulated myself.

Tommy left Kline's side to stand with me. He nervously shuffled his feet as I caressed the vegetation and ran my hands over the ground. I wasn't able to pick up any helpful information.

Thank goodness I was a college professor because I made a terrible Sherlock Holmes. What good was my freakish intuition if I couldn't help solve a crime?

My body worked in overdrive whenever I tried to live

a normal life. The times I needed it most, it failed miserably.

"Randa, what are you doing?" Tommy asked.

"Looking for my earring." I tried to wink, but I think it came out as some sort of weird grimace. "And clues."

"On the leaves?" Tommy watched me concentrate and rub my fingers on a leaf.

He was correct. I wasn't getting anything useful from the foliage. I focused my eyes on the statue-like man in the blue-gray uniform, guarding the neon tape.

"No way!" Tommy said, his understanding dawning.

"Come on, Tommy. Isn't investigating this part of your job?"

"Look, park rangers just help out in state lands when law enforcement asks. I haven't ever had to investigate a murder. Usually, I chase poachers and teach kids how to avoid poison ivy."

I sighed and dramatically grasped at my heart.

Tommy crinkled his nose and thought for a moment. "Once I had to put out a cabin fire for some irresponsible Nature Scouts, and I administered first aid to a hiker who broke his leg."

I feigned disappointment with the overdone theatrics of a silent film actress. "Didn't you go to the police academy?"

"Yes, and occasionally I have to put a hand on my gun and follow Greg Grainey around to make sure he isn't hunting out of season."

I smiled as I pictured Tommy putting a bullet in my aunt's enemy.

"Randa, come on. Don't do this to me. I can't get you in. It's a murder scene." He frowned and studied his shoe before looking at me. "I'll bring you back tomorrow.

Kline said he thinks the scene will open soon."

"I guess I'll have to come back tonight without you and hope that Shultz isn't lurking about." I wasn't above using puppy dog eyes on my animal-loving friend.

"What's the hurry?" Tommy asked.

I didn't have time to answer because Kline interrupted.

"Hey, Little, I gotta take a piss. Can you keep an eye on things?"

"Sure thing, Kline," Tommy called before addressing me. "You have about three minutes—if you're lucky."

I clapped and hopped over the tape.

The body was gone, but the smell lingered. I paced around the spray-painted pentagram and thought. Tommy split his attention between watching me and keeping an eye on the path.

"Doesn't it all seem a bit overdone and dramatic to you?" I asked.

"It's a murder. They all seem overdone and dramatic."

I knelt, traced the pentagram, closed my eyes, and concentrated.

"Randa, what are you doing?"

"Shh!" I said.

A warm feeling traveled from the ground up my body, then caught fire. A fuzzy vision faded in and out. The intensity grew until it felt like a hot poker was stabbing at my chest. I held my breath and tried not to panic.

I could see the pentagram and hear men talking.

One of the men said, "Did you even read the article? The paint is still wet, so be careful. Don't be a klutzy fuck."

Another said, "The guy who killed her is so fucked up. I think she was pretty."

They talked about what seemed to be useless nonsense, including something about bonds, a run, and pirates. Although "I'm gettin' out of town. Lowalski won't see a dime of what I owe him" seemed to be pretty significant.

"Come on. Hurry up," Tommy said, breaking up the disjointed impressions I had conjured.

I shot him a squished-eye frowny-face. Since I usually did my best to avoid seeing, hearing, and feeling anything that didn't have to do with an immersion into Steinbeck or Dickens, I wasn't very good at my task. His nervous energy made it difficult to concentrate. I placed my fingers in the location I thought Suzy's hand had been and closed my eyes again.

Tommy's frantic voice continued to break through. "Randa, hurry. I hear someone coming!"

I ignored him and focused. This time the image that flickered was horrible. I watched as a hand drove a nail into Suzy Smith's palm. She didn't flinch because she was dead.

Tommy's voice had become ten shades of alarm. "Randa, out now! I'm serious."

"Oh my God," I cried, falling backward onto the torso of the drawing. I watched as a blurry knife sliced into Suzy's chest. "Oh my God," I cried again.

Tommy grunted as he picked me up and tried to lift me over the yellow tape. "We need to go!"

I panicked, fought his embrace, and tripped, landing on my knees. A victim of poor planning, I hadn't considered how I would react if I gleaned information about the murder. I also hadn't considered how odd I would appear to Tommy or his questions that might follow.

"Oh my God," I repeated for the umpteenth time as I got back onto my feet.

It was Tommy's turn to silence me. "Shh! We need to get out of here."

Tommy dragged me to the other side of the tape a moment too late because not only was Officer Kline returning, but Shultz, and two men I didn't recognize, were headed toward us from the opposite direction.

"You again." Shultz's gaze traveled the length of my body. "Little, what's she doing here?"

My beating heart drowned out my jittery voice. "I lost an earring the day I found the body." I pointed at the dangling blue hoop in my ear. "Tommy helped me find it." I tried to appear innocent, although I'm pretty sure I resembled a bad puppy who had just eaten trash.

"Yep, we found it, and we're leaving," Tommy said.

I pulled my shoulders back and focused my gaze straight ahead as we strolled past the three men.

Before they were out of sight, Tommy faced them. "Mayor Reynolds, do you need my help with anything before I head out?"

The man I assumed was the mayor said, "Tom, I think you need to get the girl out of here, and I'd like to see you in my office tomorrow morning," He turned to Kline. "What the hell? Why weren't you at your post?"

By the time I climbed into the cab of Tommy's truck, I felt overwhelmed by the strength of my visions. Since I had seen Liza, I knew for sure that my illusions of Suzy were more than intuition. But if psychics were romantic fictional characters, what was going on? Was I insane?

The ordinarily laid-back Tommy Little sulked the

entire drive to town.

"What was up with your hair?" he asked. "It was standing in the air like you were struck by lightning."

I thought it a bit rude that Tommy was insulting my windblown locks and told him so, adding that he seemed a bit testy after our adventure.

"They were up to something."

"Did Shultz leave my name out of the incident report and change the ring's location?" I asked.

"Seriously, Randa, what was that? Why were you crawling around on the ground touching things?"

"Tommy, why would Shultz do that? Doesn't Detective Miller know he's lying?"

"Those men are scary as hell, and you don't want to mess with them."

Although Tommy and I seemed to be having two different conversations, there was a silver lining to the situation. Since Tommy had witnessed me doing weird things, he was probably over his crush.

"Who was the other man with Shultz and the mayor?" I asked.

"Ian Patterson, a local businessman, and he shouldn't have been there. He doesn't have anything to do with this investigation," Tommy said.

"Who's Lowalski?" I asked.

"Lowalski? I have no idea. Why?"

"Do you know the Smith twins?"

"You mean, Pastor Smith's girls?"

"Yes." I studied Tommy's profile.

"Suzy and Liza? Liza's a super nice kid. Suzy is sweet but a bit wild. Why?"

"I think Suzy Smith is the girl I found."

Tommy glanced at me for a second before turning his

gaze back to the road. "Suzy? What makes you say that? I think she's away at college right now."

"Liza is one of my students. She says Suzy is missing." I figured I'd tell a tiny fib since I had just discovered it was one of my hidden talents. Besides, my real source wasn't one Tommy would take seriously.

"Wow. I hope not. Did her family report her missing?"

"I don't think so. Can you somehow look into it?"

"Randa, what aren't you telling me?"

"I have no idea what you're talking about?"

I bestowed the sweetest expression I could muster on my childhood friend. It was a waste of my acting skills since he wasn't looking.

Tommy Little focused on the curvy path in front of us.

Chapter 6

I forwent my un-air-conditioned sticky turret to work in the inn's comfortable grand library. Bookkeeping receipts and recipes covered Aunt Edith's desk, so I spread my project out on the oak table in the center of the room.

There was a slightly unsettling portrait of Grandma Zoey that stared at me from above the fireplace mantel. Ceiling-high bookshelves lined two of the walls. The sitting area contained a red velvet settee and an upholstered green wing-back. A ray of light from the hallway chandelier shone through the colorful leaded glass that adorned the sliding pocket door, creating a dreamy rainbow effect on my notes.

The room overflowed with character and was the perfect spot for an English professor with a flair for the romantic to pontificate. Spot sat at my feet, keeping me company. Overall, it was a quiet place to work. Russ came in once to collect some behavioral data on The Tank. And the guest, Mr. Trout-study, poked his head in to see what I was "up to" but got the hint I wasn't in the mood to talk from my monosyllabic answers.

I wasn't going out of my way to be anti-social. I was busy. I was finishing a lecture and wanted it to be perfect. I had decided to start the first day of the semester with some of my all-time favorite first lines from books. The theme of the lesson was *Firsts*. I prepared to discuss

Faulkner's *Through the fence, between the curling flower spaces, I could see them hitting,* and Márquez's *Many years later, as he faced the firing squad, Colonel Aureliano Buendía was to remember that distant afternoon when his father took him to discover ice.*

I convinced myself I was about to deliver the most astounding lecture of all time. My inspired students would spend the next four months chewing through the world's pivotal novels—or so I naively thought.

"Brilliant," I was assuring myself when Aunt Edith returned from her Town Council meeting.

Russ, his overalls covered in oil, followed her into the library.

"It was a disaster. Grainey and the pastor were at each other's throats the entire meeting, so we didn't accomplish anything." Aunt Edith plopped into the chair beside me.

Russ placed a towel on his seat and joined us at the table. "Maybe you should resign. Nobody would hold it against you. Those men are impossible, and the stress isn't worth it."

She muttered, "I can't resign."

However, the pause in her speech made me wonder if she was considering it.

"I don't want Bradley to have to face those criminals by himself." She exhaled a lengthy puff. "Are we interrupting you, honey?"

"Not at all. I just finished preparing my lecture."

I had become all ears the moment she referenced the handsome doctor, the Smith girls' father, and the notorious Greg Grainey.

The mention of criminals added an extra level of fascination.

"Is the town council made up of criminals?"

Russ grunted, Aunt Edith moaned, and Spot barked.

"So, there is some serious corruption going on. Want to talk about it?" I asked.

Aunt Edith sighed. "Patterson has decided to make a bid for Congress. He wants to be a state representative to fight the environmental regulations proposed for the coal factories. He claims his company will go out of business if he has to pay for the environmental cleanup. That is bunk! He has more money than one man can spend in five lifetimes."

"Patterson? Tell me about him. I think I ran into him yesterday when I was with Tommy."

"He owns Patterson's Energy. His company's been strippin' the land in the western part of the state for a century," Russ said.

Aunt Edith huffed out a breath. "Patterson is already trading favors. He has promised Grainey he will fight to repeal the ban on assault rifles. He has also promised that empty-headed pastor that he will support legislation that prevents evolution from being taught in public schools." Aunt Edith considered herself a staunch environmentalist and a champion for the little guy. She had no time for corrupt tycoons, hypocritical religious leaders, or irresponsible businessmen.

"Can he do that?" I asked.

"He can promise whatever he wants. He is trying to raise campaign contributions and elicit votes," Aunt Edith said.

I thought this over. "He is rich, and he still has to raise money?"

Aunt Edith rubbed her eyes. "Yes, the richest man in the county, and under the guise of campaign funding, he extorts and bribes the people around him. He plans to get himself a cushy seat and pass legislation that continues to make both him and his buddies wealthier."

"And there aren't laws against it? It seems a bit shady to me," I said.

Russ sucked at the side of his cheek. "Local politics can be corrupt as hell."

Aunt Edith nodded in agreement. "And the mayor isn't much better. He wants to funnel money from the parks and social service budgets to line the pockets of guys like Patterson and Grainey. They are supporting local businesses, my ass! The lot of them are in bed together, and they outvote me and Bradley on every issue. Tonight, the vote was four to two—again—so the upgrades to the old playground equipment aren't going to happen. Bradley tried to explain the dangers of the rusty jungle gym, but the four of them wouldn't listen." Aunt Edith's eyes were pale and weary. "We have to find a way to fight back."

Russ placed a hand sympathetically over hers. I had little understanding of local politics and attempted to process what sounded like serious ethical violations when Spot alerted us that someone was at the front door.

****

An also weary-eyed Tommy Little sat beside me on the porch swing. I perched forward so that my legs could push off the planks and gently rock us.

"I drove to the Smith place tonight. I thought I'd drop off camping literature for the youth group. The pastor wasn't there, and Mrs. Smith informed me Suzy was away at school," Tommy said.

"The pastor was at the Town Council meeting. So what did you find out?"

"Well, I passed Liza coming up the front walk, and point-blank asked her why she thought Suzy was missing. You know what she said?"

I stopped rocking us to cringe.

"She told me she never told you Suzy was missing, which I thought was odd because it meant one of you was lying."

My cheeks burned, and my heart may have missed a beat.

"Since I couldn't stand the thought that you might be the one lying to me, I convinced Liza to go into the house, and she and Mrs. Smith called Suzy's dorm room."

"And?" I asked.

"Suzy never showed up at school."

I knew it! I wasn't crazy!

Tommy was on a roll. "This morning, the mayor had my head. He is livid that you were at the crime scene. Kline received an official reprimand. Shultz has convinced Reynolds you are a troublemaker."

I sat back against the swing cushion. "Oh, Tommy, I'm sorry."

"Either tell me how you knew it was Suzy or have dinner with me, Randa Albright!" Tommy demanded. "Preferably both!"

I didn't answer him. Instead, I pulled my legs up under me and sat on my calves. I stared into the distance as I accepted my truth.

Miranda Albright, the goofy freckle-faced girl with long red ringlets, really was psychic.

Chapter 7

I celebrated my day of successful lectures with dinner at The Bear Claw Pub. The main reason for my visit was Pop's cooking. In addition to a delicious meal, I would also be able to dig up valuable intel from the all-knowing Westinghouse family. If I happened to run into Weston Westinghouse the Third, then it would be a triple bonus.

I had devoured half a cheeseburger, three mozzarella sticks, and a million fries and was playing with my food when Winona came around behind the bar. She had pulled her shoulder-length dirty blonde hair into a ponytail, and her gold hoop earrings and hazel eyes sparkled under the copper camp lanterns.

She gathered my dirty dishes. "You want anything else? My mom made a cherry pie this afternoon."

Had I known there was pie, I would have only eaten a thousand fries. "No thanks. I'm full. You mentioned there were some Satanic murders a few years ago? Tell me about them."

The enthusiastic Winona leaned across the bar, gearing up for some gossipy fun. "About three years ago, there were two cases where the cops found bodies in the woods. They were gross." She cringed, and her ponytail swung as she shook her head from side to side. "Their hearts were cut out. Then someone crucified them and put their bodies inside a spray-painted pentagram. A local reporter called them 'the cult crucifixions.'"

"*Oomph*," I muttered. "Did the cops catch the person who did it?"

"Yep! They caught the psychos who did it. It was all over the news. Didn't you hear about it down in Harrisburg?"

I hadn't lived in the capital city for quite a while. I had been away at graduate school and had heard very little news living in my I-need-to-read-ten-thousand-books-and-write-twenty-thousand-papers life of the past seven years.

"No. I didn't hear a thing," I said. "So, those murders were a Satanic ritual kind of thing?"

"Yep. The paper said they were devil worshippers."

"And they caught the guy, right?"

"Two guys and a girl," Winona said. "I think they were sacrificing virgins to keep the devil happy. You know, the devil likes things like that. He especially likes it if the girls have on white dresses, kind of like they are in a wedding gown. Then, *wonk*—someone cuts out their heart! Yuck!"

"Yeah, yuck." I shivered, then nudged Winona back on topic. "And the story made the paper?" I wondered if this was one of the articles the mutilators had referenced.

"Yep," Winona said. "Hey, if you are playing detective, can I be your assistant? I've always wanted to be a detective. My great uncle Albert said I would make a great Sherlock Holmes, and we've never had one in the family. Although Albert's sixteen-year-old hound dog once solved a crime."

I had no desire to hear about the crime-solving animal because West was coming my way. I needed my conversation with Winona to be finished so I could concentrate on the bicep-infused bartender. "Sure."

West shooed his cousin on and leaned across the bar. "Hiya, Dr. Shortcake. How's it going?"

West smiled, and I felt like we had just done something scandalous in a back alley.

"Great. You?" I blushed like a silly adolescent.

"Can't complain. Wanna beer?"

I didn't want a beer, but I did want West to hang out with me. "Sure." I tried not to get googly-eyed as he fiddled with the tap, then set a beer in front of me. I sipped and gagged.

West chuckled.

"Can we talk for a few minutes?" I asked.

"Absolutely."

West gulped water from his plastic cup, then invaded my space. He was so close I could feel his energy and smell the peppermint he sucked on.

I muttered a breathy, "Umm. Do you know who Lowalski is?"

"Lowalski?" West's gaze lifted toward the ceiling as he thought it over. "Alexander Lowalski?"

"Maybe. Who's he?"

"A bookmaker from Greenport." West flipped his mint over with his taunting tongue.

"He publishes books?" I asked, slightly confused.

West laughed so hard I thought he might bruise a rib. "God, you're adorable, Shortcake."

I pursed my lips and narrowed my eyes. I didn't want Weston Westinghouse the Third to find me adorable. Why couldn't he think of me as desirable, alluring, or gorgeous?

"A bookmaker is a bookie."

I bit my lip, rested my finger by the side of my mouth, and thought.

"A bookie takes illegal bets," West explained.

"I know what a bookie is," I snapped.

"Since this is the boonies, Lowlaski also serves double duty as a loan shark. A loan shark doesn't lend you scuba equipment or swim in the sea. He's a—"

"I know what a loan shark is, West. You're impossible!"

He gifted me with one of his butterfly-producing grins and leaned in so close we almost touched. "Why ya asking?"

"If I said Lowalski, bonds, games, and pirates to you, what would you think?"

West used his index finger to bonk my nose. "That my little shortcake was in over her head and placing bets on a baseball game with a scumball criminal."

I fought the urge to return West's touch and concentrated on my interrogation. "Do you know Lowalski?"

"I know of him. Why do you have that funny look on your face?"

I tilted my head and fluttered my eyelashes. "Can you take me to meet him?"

West's eyes popped wide, and he pushed away from the bar. "Hell no! I don't know if I'm more afraid of the Polish mob, Liam, or your aunt!"

I sighed. "Hey, Winona. I'll take a piece of that pie, now."

Chapter 8

The headline in the Thursday edition of *The Bellmount Gazette* read, *Local College Coed Gruesomely Murdered in Satanic Ritual.*

The headline in Friday's paper said *Young Man Faces Charges for Satanic Murder.* I put the newspaper down and looked around the kitchen. Aunt Edith was busy preparing French toast and bacon, and Russ had his nose in the daily funnies.

I wanted to chat, so I blurted out, "They got it wrong."

"Who got what wrong?" Aunt Edith asked.

"This investigation into Suzy Smith's murder has become a disturbing farce, void of any humor."

"It sounds like the investigation was a disaster from the get-go." Aunt Edith dunked a piece of bread in a mixing bowl.

"Shultz made a horrific mess at the crime scene, and his report doesn't mention I was there. Detective Miller seems to think it's an open and shut case. Even though Tommy, Brad, and I told him I found the ring by the road and not by the body, the official record still says it was found beside the body."

"You don't think it's open and shut?" my aunt asked.

"Not at all! It's way too staged. That kid was set up. Think about it. The ring was placed near the scene. The body was left so close to the road you could practically smell it driving past. Someone wanted it to be found. I'm surprised it took as long as it did. To top it off, it was a fake crucifixion. There was no cross, and her heart was cut out. That's overboard and crazy."

"Well, perhaps if important people want to solve the case and be done with it, there might be pressure to say the ring was closer to the body. It would make it easier to attach the murder to this boy named Skyler. Is there a reason Shultz would want to cover up that you were the one who found Suzy?" Aunt Edith asked.

Of course, there was a reason. The sheriff didn't want anyone to know he had touched, then attempted to bribe me in the middle of nowhere. Since I wasn't ready to tell my aunt those sordid details, I pushed them to the back of my mind and shrugged.

Winona peeked around the kitchen door. "Hey, are you guys talking about the cult crucifixions?"

"Winona, dear, please finish serving the guests and then clean up the sideboard." Aunt Edith walked two plates of food to the waitress.

Winona took the plates and frowned. "Okay, Edith." She lingered a second longer. Her bottom lip jutted out, and then using her hip, she slowed the door as it swung closed behind her.

Once Winona had left the room, Russ asked, "What does Tom Little think?"

"He thinks Shultz and his toadies made a mess of it, and he is livid because Detective Miller ignored his incident report. He called his supervisor with the Park Service and was told to let the Homicide Division do their job."

Aunt Edith flipped the sizzling bacon, and Russ neatly folded the section he was reading.

"Tommy thinks the police wanted it cleaned up. He feels like the mayor put pressure on them to pin it to Skyler Dubbs. They chose their guilty guy, and that's that."

Russ was nine years younger than my aunt and hadn't yet grayed, so when he shook his head, his wavy brown hair swung from side to side. "They're all a bunch of dishonest bastards. Been that way since I can remember."

"I'm sorry," Aunt Edith said. "I'm not sure there's much you can do about the investigation."

"Really? Said the lady who is taking on every plutocrat in town," I teased.

My taunt worked. She pulled her shoulders back.

"So, honey, what will we do about the troubles in Bellmount?"

I drummed my fingers on the kitchen table. "Oh, Aunt Edith, where should we start?"

Chapter 9

Weston Westinghouse the Third drove The Tank over the mountains and through the woods for twenty-five miles to Lipska's. I had discovered West's kryptonite was ugly old automobiles with V8 engines. I had offered him my car for one week in exchange for an escort to the infamous bookmaker. It appeared to be an even trade since both West and I seemed to believe we had gotten the better end of the deal.

Since Russ had adjusted the throttle, my machine no longer did its shimmy thing, although it still went roadrunner fast. Despite my protests, West had all of the windows down and had cranked the beast up to seventy-five miles an hour. His not-quite-shoulder-length hair blew every which way as he hollered out the lyrics to the country song he had pushed into The Tank's mouth. He would occasionally glance over to make sure I appreciated his performance.

I was. However, he was the worst singer I had ever heard. I was also slightly distracted, knowing my ringlets would be one large knot for the rest of my life.

Lipska's was part butcher, part deli, part office space for Alexander Lowalski. Lowalski had set up his den in the back room. An old-school chalkboard on aluminum casters sat in the corner, and numbers scrawled every which way covered it. A long receipt curled around the adding machine on his desk. A second scary-looking man, who stood by the door, silently took everything in.

"Will's nephew? What can I do for you?" Lowalski asked. He had been eating a messy sub. He wiped his greasy hand on his napkin-pants before extending it to West.

West handed him an envelope. Lowalski opened it and thumbed through the bills. Not only had I traded my car for the week, I had also put up the money for the bet and then begged his Uncle Will, who had at one time had a love for the ponies, to get us an appointment.

"Six on Thursday," Lowalski said.

"Over twenty-four for the underdogs," West responded.

Lowalski studied his board. "Since you're Will's kin, I'll give you some advice. That's a shit bet."

West cleared his throat. "The lady's call."

West had asked me for my favorite number between his bouts of caterwauling. I didn't have one, so I had randomly said twenty-four.

Lowalski chuckled. "Pretty ladies are good luck."

"I'm just learning about bookmaking, gambling, and placing bets, sir." I plopped myself into the chair across from the beefy bald man.

I must have said something wrong because Lowalski belly laughed, the man at the door bristled, and West moaned. Lowalski then extended his hand, offering West the seat beside me. West eyed the chair skeptically before sitting.

"I might even like to bet on a baseball team sometime," I added.

West rubbed his temple.

"I believe that is what you just bet on, Miss…"

"Miranda." I offered Lowalski my ungloved hand.

"Miss Miranda." He took my hand in his.

Fortunately, Lowalski found me delightful. His thoughts, not mine. Unfortunately, I knew he had broken someone's wrist earlier in the week. He hadn't even used a weapon. He had done it with the same hand that grasped mine.

"Mr. Lowalski, can I be honest?" I asked.

West placed his hands on the desk and sat forward. "Thank you for your time, Lowalski."

I supposed that since I had gone off-script, West was gearing up for our getaway.

"I'd have it no other way. And it's Alex."

"Alex, first, let me say, West didn't know I was going to ask you these things, so don't break his fingers. Second, I don't really want to place a sports bet."

Lowalski laughed, and West stood.

"Man, I'm sorry. Keep the money. We'll get out of your hair," West said.

The cool Weston Westinghouse the Third may have been the sexiest man in the solar system, and he may have liked fast vehicles and even faster women, but he was a bit of a scaredy-cat when it came to making a romantic commitment or losing a limb.

"I haven't got hair." Lowalski pointed at his shiny head. "Let her talk."

West sat down so hard it wouldn't have surprised me if the chair legs splintered. I shot him my chill-out look. "So, there are some guys who owe you money. I think it's for betting on the Pirates. I overheard them talking."

"Go on," Lowalski said.

"I assume if they owe you money, they aren't on your Nice List?"

"Now, I'm Santa Claus?" Lowalski belly laughed.

"Well, you deliver presents to some people and coal to others. Right?" I smiled.

"Right you are. Are you my little red-headed elf?"

I sat tall and pulled my shoulders back. "That's one way to look at it."

Lowalski leaned back in his chair and chuckled.

Without a second of hesitation, I made my suggestion. "I want to know who those men are, and you want your money. So, why don't we work together?"

"Man, I'm so sorry," West said.

"Young Westinghouse, don't ever try to control a pretty lady, especially a red-head." Lowlaski studied me. "So, you tell me what you know; I help you find the guys. You get your information; then they are mine?"

"Deal," I said.

I trusted this Polish mobster would do more to dole out justice than the combined efforts of the state police's Detective Miller and the slimy municipal sheriff.

"Why do you want to find these guys?" Lowalski asked.

"They wronged a friend of mine."

He thought this over as he tilted his head from side to side. Finally, he bobbed his head in the center, indicating my answer was sufficient.

"Do you know Suzy Smith?" I asked.

"Who?"

"Suzy Smith, ever hear of her?"

"Nope." He wrote down her name.

According to his thoughts, he was telling the truth.

Unfortunately, a couple of dozen stupid men with twangy accents owed him money for baseball bets. He assured me he would work with the information I had given him and be in touch. I gave him the phone number at the inn. Maybe if my "shit bet" paid off, I could buy one of those Radio World cellular phones for The Tank.

An ungloved handshake sealed my first deal with the charming hooligan.

"Miss Miranda, grab some perogies on the way out. On the house, you won't be sorry." As the door closed behind us, he bellowed, "Call me Mr. Claus."

Alex Lowalski's roaring laugh was still audible when I ordered my perogies to go. There was a silver lining to the visit. I had my suspects narrowed down to a couple of dozen gambling goons.

I thought West would be more upset with me than Tommy Little had been. He wasn't.

"Damn, Shortcake, where you been hidin' those balls?" he asked as he drove The Tank eighty miles per hour to Bellmount.

Chapter 10

Dr. Brad Gordon was a man, and I was a freckle-faced little girl, playing at being a woman. At least, that is how I felt on our date as I skipped down the inn stairway, basking in the glow that emanated from his spectacular smile.

Imagine my surprise when earlier that same morning, while I had scarfed down eggs, Aunt Edith announced, "Bradley would like to take you to dinner tonight."

A bite of omelet tumbled from my mouth, landing on the table. "What?"

"He is the nicest man I know, and he is interested in you," Aunt Edith said.

Winona called out, "Oh my God, Miranda! You are the luckiest girl in the world. Bradley looks like a movie star."

Aunt Edith placed her hand on her heart. "Oh, my. He's so handsome. And have you seen his biceps?"

I didn't know my aunt even had hormones. She and Winona giggled like school girls, and Russ rolled his eyes.

"Why does he want to go out with me?" I asked.

"He thinks you are beautiful and enchanting," Aunt Edith insisted.

The truth was, I had unruly hair and was obsessive.

I had no idea what to wear to a date that didn't involve catching wildlife. Winona and Spot sat at the window seat watching my fashion show.

"Now Brad is a doctor, so you want to look classy," Winona advised.

"I'm a doctor, too," I reminded her.

"But he's a real doctor," she informed me.

I grunted.

We finally decided on a flowing blue skirt—the same color as the wallpaper in the turret—a simple white blouse, a jean jacket, and a pair of white sandals.

Winona had dressed up her little doll and wasn't happy with the final ensemble. "Can you ditch the gloves?"

"How about these?" I slid into a white lacey pair.

Winona sighed. "For Pete's sake, Miranda, you look like that slutty pop star. I used to like her music when I was younger. I don't anymore. Well, I like some of her songs, but she went off the deep end and did a soda commercial. I still like Jesus's mother, the Virgin Mary. Now she was classy."

Winona kept on jabbering, so I gave her my nastiest of scowls. I had no idea what she was talking about, but it sounded like a major insult. Since I was the Virgin Miranda, the lace gloves were staying put.

I had hoped she would at least tell her rakish cousin that I had looked fabulous for my date.

Brad took me to an intimate Italian restaurant in the borough of Foxfield. I ordered lasagna and Italian wedding cake. He had spaghetti with meatballs and a chocolate cannoli. Winona would be disappointed to find out he ate the same food as us mere mortals.

I told him about the lunch date earlier in the week with my colleagues. I also told him about my summers in Bellmount. He even listened to me blab on about my dissertation. No one had ever done that, not even my dad. I learned he was thirty-three, had grown up in Baltimore, Maryland, had two older brothers, and had moved to Bellmount to set up his practice three years earlier.

Since we were newer residents of the mountainous Bear County, Brad and I had a lot to discuss. Bellmount was the county seat. Twenty-five miles to the west with a population of seven thousand six hundred and eighty-nine was Greenport, and twenty miles to the northeast was the four thousand seven hundred forty-eight inhabitant borough of Foxfield.

In between the triplet towns lay farmlands, trailer parks, and state forests. Harrisburg, my hometown, was a four-hour drive to the south, and Pittsburg was approximately an hour drive to the north. If one drove fifty minutes due west, they would run right into State College.

As Bellmount residents proudly confessed, they were smack dab in the middle of the boondocks.

Following dessert, Brad gave me advice. "Miranda, don't let the small-town gossip get to you. It blows over. I can tell you are the type of person who cares what others think, so whatever you do, don't fret over their opinions. If you do that in this town, you will lose your mind. If I can give you another piece of advice, buy long underwear. The winters come fast and hit hard. You'll feel like your blood has frozen in your veins for over half of the year."

We ended our perfect date on the inn's porch swing.

"I should tell you I'm recently divorced," Brad said.

That was nothing. If he had known I was a twenty-five-year-old virgin who had visions and thought she could read minds, he wouldn't have seen a little old thing like divorce as an issue.

"Do you want to talk about your wife and the divorce?" I asked.

Brad stared into my eyes. "Nah. I just wanted you to know. I like you, and I didn't want there to be any secrets between us."

He was so handsome and self-assured. I was so not his equal. I swallowed a sigh. And, no secrets? But I had so many.

"I better get going." He put his hand on the small of my back and walked me the eight feet from the porch swing to the massive front door.

We stood, facing each other, his masculine heat overpowering me. I ached for him to kiss me.

"Would you like to go see that new movie about a high school teacher at a private boys' school? I hear it's great," he said.

Brad was almost a foot taller than me. He was leaning forward so that his words caressed my cheek. I wanted him to bend lower and lean closer. I tilted my head back and peered up at him. I wanted him to lick my lips and nibble on my ear or lick my ear and nibble on my lips—either would work.

Then I wanted him to kiss me. That wasn't too much for a girl to ask.

Right?

Instead, I said in a squeaky voice, "Yes, I want to go to that movie."

Then I bolted through the door, past a wagging Spot, up three flights of stairs, and threw my aching body onto my bed.

My dating experience now included collecting turtles at the creek a decade ago, finding a corpse in the woods, and an almost kiss from a classy doctor who was even more handsome than a movie star.

I loved my new life.

Chapter 11

I was twenty minutes into overhauling my office space when I realized I had left an organizational bin in my backseat. I ran to The Tank to retrieve it and found that someone had tucked a piece of paper under the windshield wiper. I unfolded the note, and realization dawned.

I climbed into my car, wrinkled the ticket into a tight ball, threw it across my front seat, then drove three blocks, grabbed the pink wad, stomped a half block to my destination, and finally, opened the front door to the police station.

"Where's Shultz?" I called to the thin man behind the front counter.

I didn't wait for him to respond. Instead, I strode past him and barged into the office belonging to the Bellmount Municipal Sheriff. The reptile stared at me from behind a haphazard stack of files.

"What's this, Shultz?" I threw the ticket onto his desk.

Plop. My ticket landed in a plastic cup of nacho cheese. A blob of the gooey cheese had previously landed in the center of Shultz's blue shirt.

The bloated worm squinted his rat-like eyes and used his thumb and index finger to pick the paper out of his Sunday afternoon snack. "It's Sheriff Shultz to you, young lady."

"You know how the dictionary defines *sheriff*?" I asked. "I suspect you don't, so let me fill you in. 'An important official of a shire or county that is charged with judicial duties.' Let me fill you in on the definition of judicial duties—"

"Don't bother. I'm assuming you're once again going to claim you weren't breaking the law," the beast said.

"You gave me a ticket for parking in my parking spot. Campus parking isn't even under your jurisdiction, you piece of…" I trailed off because I had already called him every insult I could think of. Eventually, a new comparison hit me.

"You are maggot poo, Shultz. Worse than that. You are the maggots that live in maggot poo."

"Settle down. This ticket seems to be a mistake. See, I'm throwing it in the trash." Without even looking at it, he tossed the paper into the overflowing can beside his desk.

"What's the catch? What kind of sick, perverted proposition are you going to make this time?"

He leaned back in his chair and folded his hands behind his head."No proposition, but while you're here, maybe we should discuss a few things."

If looks could kill, Shultz would be dead. I wanted to strangle him, then shoot him eight times. Once he was good and bullet-holey, I would stab him with a knife twenty-five times. Then, I would slice his body into twelve pieces before throwing his mutilated guts into a fiery pit.

"Are you fitting in and making friends?" he asked.

"Cut the crap, Shultz. You don't give two hoots if I'm fitting in. What do you really want?"

"You know you got Tom Little into trouble with your

snooping?"

I didn't have a comeback to his statement because I still felt guilty about the issues I had caused for Tommy.

"I want to make sure you're keeping yourself out of trouble and minding your own business. I also want to make sure you're driving the speed limit. I hope you kept your end of our deal, and you haven't told your aunt about your speed warning."

"That's what this is about? You want to make sure I haven't told anyone what a perverted heel you are? FYI, we never had a deal, and I'm not telling you again; I wasn't speeding," I said, my voice sixty decibels above normal.

I stepped off my soapbox because an animal-enhanced Noah's-Arc-like commotion was coming from the lobby.

Officer Skinny peeked into the room. "Hey Sheriff, you better come out here. We got problems. Wilkes is mooning the dogs again."

"Shit," Shultz said.

I followed Shultz out of his office to quite a sight. A young police officer held a homeless-looking man in a pair of handcuffs, and three angry people stood with dogs in tow.

"Sheriff, he mooned Mr. Frenchie again," an elderly woman in a purple house dress said.

Tiny white curls topped both woman and poodle. Mr. Frenchie's human twin set him on the floor.

"Wilkes stuck his hairy ass right in Leroy's face. Look at Leroy. He's traumatized."

If Leroy was the bulldog at the end of the complaining man's leash, he looked fine to me. He poked his nose into Mr. Frenchie's butt.

"What are you going to do about it, Shultz?" a tattooed man with a humongous Great Dane asked.

"Yeah, what you gonna do about it, s-s-Shultz?" slurred the man in handcuffs.

Shultz placed his thumbs in the waistband of his pants and sighed. "Wilkes, it's Sunday afternoon. Why are you drunk already?"

"Why the hell not? Ain't got nothin' better to do." Wilkes sniffed up some snot that dripped from his nose. Discovering it was a lost cause, he used his sleeve as a tissue and smeared the mucus blob across his cheek.

"This has to stop. Wilkes is a menace. Act like a sheriff and do something. Scoobie's such a good pup, and he's distraught over this."

"I'm gonna book him this time." Shultz turned to Officer Young. "Book 'em."

"You can't book me. There ain't no law about showin' your ass to animals."

The three bumbling officers gawked at each other. Shultz lifted his palms to the ceiling. Bellmount's law enforcement agents seemed baffled about what law Wilkes had broken.

"Aren't you the new college professor?" Leroy's human asked me.

I considered lying and making a break for it. Instead, I stupidly replied, "Yes."

"Since you're a professor, what do you think? Is there a law against showing your ass to an animal? It seems to me there oughta be some law against it. Look, he traumatized Leroy."

Leroy was happily smelling Scoobie's butt.

"Yeah, what d'ya think?" Wilkes asked before losing his balance and leaning to the side. He teetered back and forth, then somehow straightened himself out.

Considering the combined IQ in the room—not including me and the dogs—might have been a negative ten, I decided to be helpful. "I would think there are laws against public indecency, public intoxication, and cruelty to animals."

"Yeah, laws again' pubic decency. You bette' lock me up and throw away the key." Wilkes waved two fingers into the air and pretended to throw something over his shoulder. The coordination it took was more than his blood alcohol of five million could handle, and he toppled onto the floor, almost taking out Mr. Frenchie.

Officer Skinny and Officer Young picked Wilkes up and brushed him off.

Shultz rested his hands on his protruding stomach and emphatically declared, "Book 'em."

"I gotta pissssss," Wilkes slurred.

"Sheriff, I'm staying here until I make sure you book him. Last time you said you would, and fifteen minutes later, his hairy ass was in Leroy's face again."

"I'm staying too," declared the other animal parents in stereo.

"I gotta piss." Wilkes crossed his right leg over his left and tilted forward at a forty-degree angle.

The room grew silent until Mr. Frenchie's human noticed me. "Are you Edith's niece?"

I once again contemplated a speedy exit but instead answered with a hesitant, "Yes."

"Isn't Edith feeding you? I'm going to have to talk with her. Some parts of you are too skinny. Not all parts, but some parts."

Mr. Frenchie's human twin stared at my breasts then poked my miniature bicep. My cheeks caught fire, and I folded my arms across my chest. Enough was enough. I needed to get back to campus.

"I gotta piss," Wilkes reminded everyone.

"Uncuff him. He can go to the bathroom. Then he's going in the holding cell for the night," Shultz said.

I pushed through the crowd to the station door, then halted at the sound of another commotion.

Wilkes was uncuffed, and his pants were around his ankles. I know I should have looked away—since there was an old man's genitalia visible—but I couldn't. I was fascinated. A yellow stream of liquid arched into the air and hit Shultz mid-shin.

"You son of a bitch!" Shultz yelled.

Officer Young and Officer Skinny stood in wide-eyed wonder as Wilkes touched his toes and mooned all of the dogs and humans behind him. Maybe Leroy was traumatized because he trotted over to Shultz, lifted his leg, and peed in the same spot as Wilkes.

Shultz let out a string of profanity. "Jesus Christ, you motherfucking cunt, you worthless piece of shit—"

I missed the rest of Wilkes's—or maybe it was Leroy's—new nickname because the door swung closed behind me. It was a tough trip to The Tank due to my chortling, snorting, and choking.

****

Fifteen minutes later, I was back on campus. However, giggling at Shultz's leg covered in multiple mammal urine specimens made my organization project difficult. I was in the middle of a side-splitting guffaw over "pubic decency" when a knock distracted me.

"Dr. Albright, I'm sorry I missed our appointment on Thursday. I needed to be with my family," Liza Smith said.

My Shultz-inspired sniggers halted at the sight of the girl. It broke my heart to see the dark circles under her red-rimmed eyes.

"Of course. Please don't worry." I extended my arm, inviting her to sit in the chair in front of my desk.

She placed her backpack on the floor and settled into the seat. "Tom Little said you were the one who found my sister's body."

I didn't have any comforting advice for the grieving girl. There was nothing anyone had ever said that dulled the pain of losing my mother. "Yes. I'm so sorry."

"Since you saw my sister and didn't know she had a twin, it must have spooked you when you first saw me, and that is why you ran off?"

I nodded in agreement. That was almost what had happened. There was no need for me to explain a body decomposing in the woods for two weeks was no longer recognizable and that I had a vision of her twin pre-decomposition.

"They have the suspect in custody."

"I read that in the newspaper."

"They arrested Skyler Dubbs."

"Do you know Skyler?" I asked.

"Yes. Skyler went to high school with us. He was a loner who kept to himself. Suzy and I were the only kids in school who were nice to him, and we didn't like the way our classmates treated him. His family was poor. They lived in a trailer outside of town. Suzy and I asked our dad to take up a church collection when Skyler's mother was diagnosed with cancer. Dad didn't think it was a good idea, but eventually, he let us." She took in a deep breath and let it out slowly. "After Skyler's mother died, he became pretty dark. He started to wear black clothes and make-up."

"How long ago was that?"

"Our senior year in high school. I wasn't as friendly with him after that, but Suzy continued to hang out with him. She would visit him every time she was home from college."

I handed Liza a tissue.

"Even though Suzy partied way too much, she was always nice to everyone, especially the kids who were different. He had a crush on her."

"I found a ring with an ankh on it by the side of the road. Does that mean anything to you?"

"The detective told my dad the ring was their most important clue. She gave it to Skyler last year on his birthday. I think that is how they figured out he was the one who murdered her."

"Do you think Skyler was capable of murder?" I asked.

"He was a bit odd, but I never thought him a murderer, and he adored Suzy. I honestly don't know. The detective seems convinced he did it."

"But what do you think, Liza? Do you think he did it?" I was looking for a compelling reason to persist with my investigation, although I would have continued no matter her answer.

Liza wiped a tear from her cheek. "I don't know what to think. My sister's gone, and even though we didn't always get along, I feel like someone cut off my right arm."

She cried, and I sat beside her, so she wasn't alone. Eventually, it occurred to me if Liza were as much like me as I thought she might be, she would be interested in my second reason for coming to campus on a Sunday—

library research. When her tears slowed, I gave it a shot.

"I'm heading to the library to learn more about the ritual killings that happened outside of Bellmount a few years back. Would you like to join me?"

"Of course," she said.

Liza and I spent the remainder of our afternoon camped out in the basement of the Lettermen Campus Library. It wasn't difficult to track down stories about the cult crucifixions. The librarian had kept the local newspaper on microfiche for three decades. A P.T. Grimwood had written the articles in 1986. He was the same reporter who had written the recent stories about Suzy and Skyler. In the original cult crucifixions, devil worshippers had cut out their victims' hearts. Their sacrifices had been crucified and left inside a red pentagram.

I concluded we had a copycat murder in which the sociopaths didn't realize they were supposed to nail a crucified body to a cross. The imbeciles had simply driven nails through her hands and feet, tacking her to the ground. It couldn't be too difficult to catch these Einsteins.

"Hey Ms. Smith, my star reporter, how would you like to take a field trip to *The Bellmount Gazette* this week to meet the masterful P.T. Grimwood?" I asked.

"Sure. We make a great team, just like Lagney and Cacey."

"Of course," I said as I planned our excursion and wondered who Lagney and Cacey might be.

Chapter 12

I was envious of Keisha Brown's pretty red car. Unlike The Tank, it fit into the parking space at Sandra's Cafe and had a CD player.

Keisha was beyond cool. Besides owning a car built in the current decade, she had silky black skin and wore stylish outfits. Dozens of long braids moved when she turned her head from side to side, and her animated speech meant her colorful hair beads continually clicked. She had a wealth of knowledge and was instrumental in setting up my personal computer.

She suggested we celebrate my new technological acquisition by skipping lunch at the overcrowded campus cafeteria. We drove to Main Street and had our midday meal at a fashionable bistro-style restaurant. I ordered the candied pecans, poached pears, and gorgonzola over greens, and the assistant to the dean ordered the House Rachel. We cleaned our plates and settled into conversation.

"Tell me about your date with that hunk of a man, Dr. Gordon," Keisha insisted.

I filled her in on almost everything. I told her about his dark hair, gorgeous smile, and tantalizing smell. I listed every detail of our Italian dinner. I topped off my story by telling her what a fabulous listener he had been.

"Did you do the humpty-hump?" she asked.

"What?"

"You know, did you knock boots?"

"I had on sandals," I said, slightly confused.

"Shit, Miranda! Do you live under a rock? Did you have sex?"

"Sex? No!" I jutted my chin back. I didn't want to tell her that he had almost kissed me, and I had run away like the absurdly shy virgin that I was.

"Did you at least kiss him? I'd kiss him. Hell, I'd—" She didn't finish her sentence because she had transitioned to a different thought. "Oh, shit. Don't look!"

"What?"

"Don't look!"

"Don't look at what? Is there a spider about to jump on my head?" I swatted around my face just in case.

"It's the Bellmount Bitches."

"The Bellmount Bitches?"

She sent a half-hearted smile and a stiff wave that could in no way be confused with a friendly greeting.

"Can I look now?" Being an odd child and an awkward coed, I had never had a girlfriend, and hanging out with the chic Keisha was exciting. I wanted to be in on whatever gossip she was alluding to.

"Okay, but be discreet."

As if staring at people in the middle of a dining establishment could ever be discreet.

I took my time turning. An impeccably dressed trio of women in their late twenties to early thirties was seated at a table along the back wall. A pretty woman with blonde hair spied me and whispered to her dark-haired companions.

"Oh," I muttered, realizing one of the brunettes was Liam's mystery girl. "Who are they?"

Keisha leaned in close. "The blonde is Holly Walton.

Her dad owns Walton Construction. The dark-haired woman in pink is Gina Schuster, of the old money Schuster family."

Liam's little playmate was the blueblood, Gina Schuster. Aunt Edith would have a cow.

"And the glamorous, exceptionally bitchy one in lavender..." She paused for a moment. "That is Jessica Grainey. Her dad is the sexy bastard who owns the gun shop."

"Ah," I said.

"Miranda..."

She paused again, and I leaned closer.

"Jessica is Bradley Gordon's ex-wife."

How had I been on almost two dates with the doctor, listened to Aunt Edith's constant complaints about the Grainey family, and not figured out the handsome Dr. Bradley Gordon had been married to the bitchy Jessica Grainey? My lunch moved from my stomach to my throat. I knew Brad wasn't hiding anything and that he had been upfront with me.

I supposed my gut-wrenching envy was because I felt so inadequate. She was tall and thin, and even her hands seemed to belong to a graceful ballerina. Each of her precisely placed silky tendrils adorned her long neck and ivory shoulders. She wore an air of confidence I couldn't have imitated, even on my best days.

My voice crackled like a croaking frog. "Why did they divorce?"

"Rumor is she was having an affair with Kyle Patterson. Sleeping with that spoiled bastard when she had a man like Dr. Gordon proves how hideous she is."

"Is Kyle related to Ian Patterson, the coal guy who is running for congress?" I asked.

"As if the country can stand any more crooked politicians?" Keisha's jaw clenched. "Kyle is his oldest son. Patterson is loaded! I guess Jessica prefers having money to having character."

Keisha's gaze focused on something above my head. I read her body language and pivoted to face our unwelcome visitor.

"Hello, Keisha," an affected voice said.

"Hi, Holly. This is Dr. Miranda Albright. She just moved to town," Keisha said.

"Hi, Dr. Albright. Is it okay if I call you Miranda?"

Holly extended her hand, and I offered mine in return. Doing nothing to hide her revulsion, she grimaced at my pink gloves.

"Miranda, I want to introduce you to the girls. Follow me."

Keisha stood to join us.

Holly dismissed Keisha with a palm and a sideway tilt of her chin. "Please excuse us for a moment."

Keisha's eyes narrowed, and her forehead creased. I supposed she thought I had about the same chances of survival as a cow in a starving village.

I gave her a tiny smile, letting her know I would be fine. I wasn't afraid of three nasty rich girls. I had dirt on the one slumming it with my handsome cousin, and I had almost kissed the cheater's ex-husband.

I followed the toady into the dragon's lair.

The thing separating a mean girl from the unconfident, slightly jealous girl next door is the former's ability to wield false politeness with the ease of a knight swinging a long sword. There was no doubt in my mind; the sharp-tongued Bellmount Bitches were truly cruel.

Keisha watched from afar with the predatory

coolness of a skulking fox as the triplets did their damage. They talked about me as if I wasn't standing a foot away.

"Wouldn't that gorgeous red hair be lovely in one of those all the rage pixie bobs?"

"Oh yes, we will have to take her to Sally's for a makeover."

"Maybe we should fix her up with Elmer McInroy. His wife of twenty years recently passed, and he requires companionship."

"Poor thing. How brave of her to show her face in town after her crazy grandmother was so scandalous."

"Let's take her to the Harvest Festival with us."

"Oh, how fun! We could introduce her to everyone."

"Yes, but we need to take her to the city and buy her something this century to wear."

Finally, Mrs. Ex-Gordon addressed me to my face. "Yes, dear, the pink gloves are a bit much."

They were lucky I didn't shove my gloves into their exposed cavernous gullets.

They twittered like hungry baby dragons, or maybe they cackled like plotting witches. Whichever it was, their laughter was truly evil.

"Someone needs to tell the Kappa Kappa Cunts they aren't in high school anymore," Keisha said on our drive back to campus.

"That was embarrassing. I felt like I was a five-year-old who just peed my pants in front of the entire school."

"Girlfriend, you gotta learn to tell people to fuck off. Who cares what they think."

I rolled my eyes but held my tongue and stifled my *whatever.*

I considered telling Liam that he needed a new sex partner since his current one was making disparaging remarks about our late grandmother. Maybe—or maybe not—Bradley Gordon would hear about his nasty ex-wife.

****

My esophagus still burned from lunch. I had finished my Monday afternoon lecture and had corrected a pile of essays on *What Makes a Novel Pivotal* when a tall man with spiky gray puffs of hair barged into my office.

"Are you Ms. Albright?"

"Yes, please come in." The invitation was moot because he was already standing in my office.

A bristly voice burst from the abrupt man. "I'm Pastor Gabriel Smith."

"Liza's father. Please have a seat." I motioned to the chair in front of my desk.

"No! This won't take long." He drew in a breath, then let loose. "Stop filling Liza's head with lies. They have caught the boy who murdered Suzy. I don't appreciate you encouraging my daughter to dig through old archives trying to invent some mystery. Leave her alone, or I will report your behavior to Dean Johnson. My family has been through enough without you inventing an additional scandal. The sheriff has informed me what a troublemaker you are."

"Shultz," I muttered. And what did he mean by "additional scandal" and reporting my behavior?

"Pastor Smith, I'm sorry you feel that way, but Liza is twenty-one years old. She isn't a child. She can think for herself."

His eyes contained hellfire, and he slammed his palms on my desk. "Stop at once, or I will withdraw her from this immoral institution. Do you understand me?" He pounded on my desk one last time. "You are as insane as your grandmother."

My poor grandmother, God rest her soul, was taking one heck of a beating. She may have been a bit eccentric, but she wasn't evil, and she certainly wasn't responsible for my fashion sense or curiosity.

Shaking—because I was afraid my soul was now damned and I might find myself unemployed—I left my office in search of Lincoln or Keisha. I hadn't even reached the hallway when I ran straight into Dean Johnson and his steaming cup of afternoon coffee.

Yes, my Monday was atrocious!

****

I stepped to the left. Then to the right. I strolled around the library, all while Grandma Zoey's emerald eyes followed me. I shivered and speculated. Grabbing the footstool from under Aunt Edith's desk, I placed it in front of the fireplace. I took off my gloves and climbed aboard.

"Please talk to me, Grandma. Help me understand. I need answers."

I ran my hands over her strawberry-colored curls and across her rosy cheeks. Grandma Zoey, with her supposed witchy ways, couldn't converse through a five-decade-old canvas.

"Do you remember the time we were playing in front of the rose trellis? You removed the thorns from a pink rose and clipped it into my butterfly barrette. I was certain I looked like a garden fairy, flitted my wings, and hopped about. You fastened a flower in your hair, and we linked hands and spun until we were dizzy. Then we lay in the grass, giggling. I remember it like it was yesterday," I told my grandma.

The *clomp* of footsteps interrupted my reverie.

I turned to see a wide-eyed, confused-looking Aunt

Edith. "Miranda, who are you talking to?"

I stepped off of the stool. "Aunt Edith, tell me about Grandma Zoey."

Aunt Edith and I parked ourselves at the oak table. She told me the story of how my grandparents had received the inn as a wedding present in 1942. Although it was now considered luxurious and nostalgic, in the forties, it had been a cheap place for traveling salesmen to stay. According to my aunt, my grandmother had been a sensitive, misunderstood woman.

Grandpa Lucas left for the European front toward the end of the Great War. Sadly, my mother never met her father, and Aunt Edith had no memory of him. When Grandpa was declared MIA and didn't return, my grandma fell into a state of melancholy. Her condition deteriorated, and a devoted caretaker, who had since passed, had kept the inn running until Aunt Edith was old enough to take over.

Eventually, Grandma Zoey had turned to magical chants and late-night dances in the garden. She had gone insane because no matter what she did, she couldn't find her husband.

"Could she read minds and see the past?" I asked.

"When I was a young woman, watching my life fall apart, afraid I was about to lose my home and my sister, I thought she was mentally ill. I sent her to doctors and psychiatrists. Nothing worked. In fact, that's how I became friends with Lincoln. He has since then retired from his practice to teach at the college, but at that time, he was a practicing psychologist. He was especially kind to her."

"I didn't know Lincoln was one of her doctors," I said.

"Yes. She adored him, but he couldn't help her. In her final months, she would take my hand in hers, and I had moments when I thought she could read my mind." Aunt Edith paused. "You know, she wore gloves for a short time too. I never understood why. She told Liam it helped dull the visions."

I clamped my lips closed and sucked up my swirl of emotions.

Aunt Edith wiped a few tears from her eyes. "Miranda, I'm plagued with guilt. I'm not sure I did right by my mother. I was embarrassed by the scandals. I never tried to understand what she went through. She was a child herself when she lost her husband and had two babies to care for."

I patted Aunt Edith's hand.

My grandmother had been kind and beautiful. Why had my family allowed her to become our shame? I knew what I was going through. How would I have fared in a less tolerant time, especially with a large inn and two young daughters? Maybe I would have danced naked in the moonlit garden and concocted silly love potions.

"Your mother told me you were sensitive, like your grandmother, but you were channeled. Your parents understood. When you were a child, they realized that you were intuitive, with heightened senses, and equipped you for the cruel world. You were loved and nurtured and ended up a successful college professor. What if I had handled your grandmother the same way?"

"You did the best you could." I wrapped an arm around my aunt's shoulder, and we spent the next half hour laughing and crying as we reminisced about past summers together.

Chapter 13

Since my car was still on loan to West for the remainder of the week, I had to borrow it back for the afternoon. Not only could I fit my six young reporters in, I still had room for all of their backpacks, a 35mm camera, and a pregnant elephant. Liza was adamant we attend our Thursday afternoon field trip to *The Bellmount Gazette*. She also insisted if the entire staff went, and if we kept the details of our trip from her zealot father, it would be "just fine."

The *Gazette* was housed in a colossal Colonial building circa 1860. It sat between the gun shop and the movie theatre. Perhaps city planners intended for Bellmountians to be able to take advantage of their unalienable American and God-given First Amendment Right to Freedom of the Press, their Second Amendment Right to buy an assault weapon, and their Twenty-eighth Amendment Right to spend a small fortune on a bucket of popcorn and a second run movie, all without having to move their car and pay extra at the parking meters.

Following our tour, I gave Michael Dunlap, our sports reporter, the keys to my car and asked him to take the rest of the class back to campus. Liza and I retraced our steps to P.T. Grimwood's office.

Grimwood required a stimulant detox of major proportions and looked as if he should be the one driving my 1970's automobile. He was only an inch taller than my five-foot-three frame and sported a black walrus mustache and frizzy sideburns. He wore yellow and orange polyester striped pants and a red shirt with a pointy collar. Old newspapers were strewn about, and his office smelled like stale cigarette smoke. He typed on a bright red manual typewriter while a personal computer sat unplugged on a bookshelf underneath a pile of papers.

"Mr. Grimwood," I said, knocking on his office door.

He continued to type. "Professor, hope your budding young writers enjoyed the tour."

"Yes. This is Liza Smith, my editor-in-chief."

He stopped typing, looked our way, and shifted his vintage horn-rimmed glasses higher on his nose. "Have a seat."

Liza and I pulled up chairs and tried to make ourselves comfortable amid the clutter.

"My future competition. Read your article "Shrinking the Fossil Fuel Footprint: Local Coal Company Battles Environmental Legislation" this past spring."

"You read my article?" Liza asked.

"Never miss an issue." He pointed at a stack of the campus newspapers sitting on the shelf beside his abandoned computer.

"Did you like my story?" Liza asked.

"You have potential, young muckraker. Share your sources with a fellow newshound?"

Liza beamed.

"Sorry about your sister," he said. "So tragic."

"That's why we're here, Mr. Grimwood," I said.

"Pat," he said.

"Pat, we were hoping you could help us with a few things. I'm the one who discovered the body."

"You discovered the body? No mention of your name

in the report. Said it was Doc Gordon."

"Shultz!" I muttered through clenched teeth.

"Quite the character," Pat said.

"Quite the character isn't how I would describe him."

Liza chimed in, "Pat, you wrote an article about Skyler, the boy in jail for killing my sister."

"Kid was arraigned last week. Won't make bail. At least a month until his preliminary trial."

"Where did you get your information?" I inquired.

"Police report."

For a man who made his living using words, Pat was a succinct speaker.

The same police report that didn't mention me. I sighed.

"Did you ever talk to Skyler?" Liza asked.

"Public defender gave me twenty minutes with him. Kid says he didn't do it. Says he follows this Goth band called Demon Succubus and dabbles with black magic but isn't a murderer. Says he loved Suzy, but she was just a friend. Claims he doesn't know how the ring got to the crime scene. Claims he was stoned out of his mind for weeks. Didn't have an alibi for the entire period in question. Not a likable human being. If you ask me, guilty as hell."

"I'm wondering if he was set up," I said.

Pat tapped at a couple of red keys before responding. "What makes you think that?"

"I think someone was restaging the murders you wrote about a few years ago and planted his ring."

He kept typing while acknowledging my comment with a nod.

"Do you think it was odd that my name wasn't on the incident report?" I asked.

"Shultz is an imbecile. Messes up everything he touches. State detective got it all straightened out. Hear Tom Little, the local park ranger got himself into trouble with the mayor. Still trying to find out what that was about."

I cleared my throat. My guilt over getting Tommy into trouble increased, serving as a reminder that I still owed him dinner.

"I assure you the incident with Tommy Little isn't a big deal," I said.

He leaned close. "What d'ya know?"

P.T. Grimwood was obviously a man who dealt in secrets and information trades.

"What do *you* know?" my feisty sidekick asked.

Pat took a sip of what appeared to be cold black coffee. "You first."

Seeing as how she didn't know anything about her current bargaining chip, Liza was behaving boldly.

I shot her a discretionary glower. "Tommy Little let me double-check the crime scene. Once I met Liza, I wanted to go back and see it through fresh eyes."

"That's all?" Pat sounded disappointed with the lack of sensationalism.

He took a cigarette from his desk drawer and a match from his clown pants pocket. Liza and I waited as he took his time lighting the cigarette and then even longer, flicking his wrist back and forth to put out the flame. Finally, after blowing a smoke cloud into the air, he divulged some information.

"Official autopsy report isn't in, but a guy at the coroner's office owed me, and I did a bit of snooping." He took a long drag and a twice as long exhale. "Suzy had a boyfriend at school?"

"Peter O'Neill," Liza said. "Her ex-boyfriend. They broke up last May."

He puffed. "Had a pretty loud break-up in front of his frat brothers."

This was news to me, but Liza seemed to know what he referenced. This time he took a long-drawn-out inhale, then a quick puff.

"The interesting part,"—*inhale puff, inhale puff*—"coroner says Suzy was two months pregnant."

"What?"

"My God!"

Puff.

Chapter 14

An exuberant wedding party occupied every nook and cranny of the inn. Aunt Edith, Russ, and Winona assisted the caterers and florists who had taken over. Liam, Spot, and I found ourselves relegated to the front porch for our Saturday morning coffee, muffins, eggs, and doggy biscuit. Liam wanted to talk about his tough week working for the accounting firm, but I had business I needed to discuss.

After twenty minutes of his *I'm-so-overworked* vent, I said, "Keisha Brown and I had lunch at the new restaurant, Sandra's Cafe.*"

"How was it?" He scratched Spot's ears.

"Great food!"

He leaned back and stretched out his long legs. "Cool. Maybe I'll try it out."

I sat forward. "I met some of the women in town. Keisha referred to them as The Bellmount Bitches."

Liam's shoulders tensed, but his face remained emotionless.

"Do you know them?" I asked.

He shrugged. "Everyone knows everyone in this town."

"I met Brad's ex-wife. She wasn't very nice to me."

"I can imagine. Jessica isn't nice to anyone."

"I met Holly Walton."

Liam rubbed his temple. "Holly has a thing for

West."

I suspected my questions gave Liam a headache. I knew his disturbing Holly pronouncement made my stomach drop to my toes. I have no idea why it upset me because every woman in town between the ages of seventeen and seventy had a thing for the alluring bartender. Still, Holly Walton moved a couple of spots higher on my ever-increasing enemy list. Liam probably reveled in relating this information since he was intent on keeping me away from West.

"I met this stunning woman named Gina Schuster. Do you know her?" I held my breath.

He took a breath, blew it over his top lip, and reached for Spot again. "Like I said, everyone knows everyone."

"Have you ever dated any of them?"

He snorted, and his scratches turned into firm pats. "Everyone has also dated everyone. One of the hazards of living in a town in the middle of nowhere."

I looked him in the eyes. "Which one of them do you think is the prettiest?"

"What the hell kind of question is that? They're all beautiful, and not one of them is nice."

Liam was sleeping with a beautiful girl he found abhorrent. Men! I supposed if he didn't like her, there was no harm in filling him in on the rest of the story.

"Gina made fun of Grandma Zoey."

His jaw tensed, and anger glimmered in his eyes. He shook it off. "A lot of people make fun of Grandma."

"But she was sweet to us. Remember when she was home from the hospital and having a good day, she used to sneak us cookies before dinner and play catch in the woods."

"Yeah," he said. "Despite everything, I think she

loved us."

I had an intense dislike of Liam's bedmate and a newfound loyalty for my misunderstood grandmother. "I don't think *your* girl should be making fun of our grandmother, do you?"

"No, she shouldn't, but she isn't my girl, Miranda. It's just, sometimes men and women, well…"

"They can't help falling into bed together, but a virgin like me wouldn't understand."

Liam frowned. "That isn't what I said or meant."

He didn't need to say it, and I was certain it was what he meant. He closed his eyes for a moment, and I crossed my arms over my chest.

After an uncomfortable silence, my body relaxed, and I changed the subject. "I have a date with Brad tonight."

"Cool," he said.

I wanted to ask Liam's advice about how I could make a man kiss me passionately, but I abstained. I knew Liam would balk at his innocent cousin having such lascivious thoughts. Besides, I needed to accept my lot. I would never kiss a man because of my touch sensitivity issues. I changed the topic again.

"I'm thinking of getting a gun." I didn't want to buy a gun, but I did want to spy on my new enemy, Jessica Grainey. While I was at it, I wanted to check out her handsome and notorious father.

"A gun? Why?"

"Protection. You know, since the body in the woods."

"If you are going to own a gun, you have to be willing to shoot it," Liam declared.

"That's ridiculous. Something good old boys say. I hope I never have to shoot it." I checked myself since I was taking *Operation Pin a Murder on the Graineys* a bit too seriously.

He laughed. "You sound like Mom."

"Because she's always right."

"Fine, but you have to learn how to use it."

Liam couldn't help himself. He was an overprotective nag.

"You have a gun, right? You can teach me." Settle down. You're not buying a gun, Miranda.

"I have a hunting rifle, and I rarely ever hunt. You need a gun safety class," he said.

"Sure," I promised, my fingers metaphorically crossed behind my back.

****

Hundreds of shotguns, muzzles high, were propped in wooden display cases. Shoppers perused the aisles, appraising pistols, revolvers, and hunting rifles as if choosing an apple or a melon from the supermarket. I wasn't sure if I was fascinated or horrified.

I followed Liam around the store as he shared his limited gun knowledge. However, I had no idea what he was saying because the slickly handsome man in the front corner of the store consumed my attention. It had been years since I had seen Greg Grainey, and the teenage Miranda hadn't understood what a playboy he was. The adult Miranda watched the tan, overly groomed man with fascination.

"What can I help you with?" a salesman asked, interrupting my gawking.

"My cousin is shopping for her first firearm," Liam said.

"What will you be using it for?" my attentive salesman inquired.

I didn't answer him immediately because I was still watching the meticulously attired store owner as he moved on to his next customer. Eventually, I exhaled. It was time to commence *Operation Pin A Murder on the Graineys.*

"I was hoping Mr. Grainey could help me," I said.

Store employees must have worked on commission because my salesman's smile turned upside down. He sought out his boss and whispered in his ear.

Greg stopped what he was doing to study me from head to toe. He lingered on my breasts, then settled on my eyes. A provocative smile that left me feeling exposed spread across his face, and my cheeks caught fire. He patted the customer he was talking to on the shoulder and traded places with the salesman I had dismissed. With his focus entirely on me, Greg sauntered our way.

"Hey, Grainey," Liam said.

Greg Grainey's gaze remained on me. "Hi, Liam."

"Do you remember my cousin, Miranda? She's looking to purchase her first firearm."

"Hi, Miranda," Greg said. "His voice slid low and became sultry. "What will you be using it for?"

"Protection."

"Ah," he said. "Everyone should have a gun, or two, or three to protect themselves. The newspapers are loaded with stories of dead people who could have saved themselves had they owned a weapon."

That propaganda was an absurd bunch of bunk. Although, in his defense, he was a slick salesman in the business of peddling weapons.

"A ravishing girl like you needs a beautiful gun. Let's head over there," Greg said.

He extended his arm to let me pass in front of him.

The heat from his stare seared a hole in my backside. He was a skillful player of the first order and, had I not been tuned in to his reprehensible nature, I may have been charmed.

Greg led us to a case and took out a pistol. "Isn't she beautiful?" He ran his hands over the gun as though he was caressing a lover.

I certainly didn't think any gun was pretty, although truthfully, I didn't look closely. It didn't matter what "she" looked like since I had no intention of purchasing a weapon.

"My lovely crimson Miranda, take off those gloves and see how she feels," Greg cajoled.

Removing my gloves was the first intelligent thing he said, so I took them off and handed them to Liam. I stood board straight with the gun hanging limply.

I supposed Greg's chuckle was at my awkwardness. He dragged us to a pretend target in the back of the store. Greg came around behind me and pressed his body into my back. He grasped my wrists and lifted them into the air toward the aiming pad.

Anyone observing would see a salesman trying to help an inexperienced shooter get the feel of a gun. I knew what the middle-aged man digging his private parts into my back while he whispered innuendos into my ear was doing.

"How does it feel?" Greg purred.

Are you kidding me? I swallowed. It was time for lie number one.

"The reason I want to protect myself is I'm the one who found—"

"Daddy?" a voice called.

I didn't finish dangling my bait because Greg surged

guilt that almost singed my wrist. He released me as though I was a hot poker. A scarlet-faced Jessica Grainey stomped toward us.

"Hi, darling," Greg said.

"Hi, Jessica," Liam said.

Jessica kissed her father on the cheek and nodded to Liam.

"I'm helping Miranda choose her first gun," declared her contrite father.

"I can see that. Daddy, this is Miranda Albright."

"Yes," he said. "Miranda and I were just reintroduced."

"Edith Marshall's niece," Jessica said.

"Yes, Liam introduced us."

"Daddy, you know—" She paused and made a small circle with her fingers before presenting her upturned hand to her father. "The one who found the body with Bradley."

Greg's jaw tensed, and his eyes flashed something I didn't recognize.

Jessica shot me a satisfied smile. I supposed she was thrilled that it had dawned on her daddy that I was her ex-husband-stealing-enemy.

"I'll wait on her, Daddy." Jessica wore a wicked smile. "She's in good hands, Liam." Her lip curled higher on one side, and her cheek quivered slightly. "Come, Miranda, let me show you some of my guns."

Linking her arm in mine, she led me away from the men. I peered over my shoulder and shot Liam my best *help-me* look. He lifted his palms to the ceiling. I finally needed his protection, and Liam was useless!

Jessica led me to a horizontal display case in the opposite corner of the vast store. My life might have been in jeopardy because she was one heck of a bitter ex, and there were a lot of weapons within reach.

"These are my second-hand guns that are for sale. Daddy got me one every Christmas and birthday. I'm quite the shot." She pointed at the case.

Neither of us blinked.

"Ten-time Bear County Female Marksmanship Champion."

I knew she was trying to unnerve me. "Congratulations," I said.

Then her sweet voice disappeared, and she growled, "My husband and Daddy? What kind of tramp are you?"

"Ex-husband," I said.

I wanted to tell her I wouldn't touch her slimy, handsome father with a ten-foot pole attached to a one-hundred-foot pole, but I didn't because of the surrounded-by-millions-of-weapons thing. I surely wasn't going to explain I couldn't be too trampy since I was a twenty-five-year-old virgin.

"Bradley is still in love with me. He is using you to make me jealous," she declared.

I searched for protection. "What's that?" I pointed at a small gun shining in her second-hand case.

"That's Princess. My first gun. I super-glued rhinestones onto her when I was about six years old."

"A six-year-old can own a gun?" I asked.

"Not most six-year-olds, but Daddy makes sure I get everything I want."

I rested a finger to my chin and thought. "Does it work?"

"Of course, she works. She's a 1969 22-caliber semi-automatic. Daddy flipped out when I decorated her, but she still fires and would be perfect for a little girl who wanted to shoot an apple off a log."

I said a prayer that the bejeweled Princess could take out both fruit and jealous ex-wives.

"Hey, Liam! I found the one I want," I yelled across the store.

Chapter 15

Brad Gordon peeked into my classroom at the same time I finished teaching my Monday morning class. Smiling absurdly, I stuttered and lost my place.

My students, realizing a visitor had caught my eye, all turned to stare at the broad-shouldered man standing in the doorway with his picnic basket.

A few of the girls muttered an "Aww," and a couple of students chuckled when, tongue-tied, I struggled to continue.

After a couple of awkward moments that seemed to last an eternity, I announced in my official end-of-class voice, "Okay, my darlings, don't forget to read pages sixty to eighty before Wednesday." I scribbled the assignment on the chalkboard and tossed my young scholars words of encouragement. "It will be awesomely joyous fun, my people, and be prepared to discuss character motivation."

Their quiet mumblings indicated they didn't wholeheartedly believe me.

As I gathered my belongings, students came forward to double-check page numbers, tell me about their weekends, ask if the man in the back of the room was my boyfriend, inquire about what was in the picnic basket— you name it, they asked it. For all their fussing, my class was in no hurry to leave. I needed a dozen barking Spots to herd them out the door.

"What a wonderful surprise," I said when I finally greeted Brad.

"Join me for lunch?" He tapped the picnic basket.

My smile was probably embarrassingly goofy. "Love to. I thought they would never leave."

Brad took hold of my gloved hand, and we made our way down the hallway and out the front door.

The sticky end of summer was gone, and the light breeze blowing over the campus quad gave the afternoon a dreamlike quality. We chose to picnic under a massive oak whose leaves were beginning their metamorphosis from green to gold. Brad set his jacket over my shoulders; then he chivalrously spread a fluffy white blanket over the ground.

"Is that from your bed?" I taunted.

He settled the basket in the middle of the cotton cloud. "Yes. I'll wash it before I put it back."

I did my best to lower myself gracefully. "It's going to be covered in grass stains."

"Better than your skirt covered in stains."

"Better than bugs crawling all over me. I hate bugs!"

It crossed my mind that, unlike West, Brad probably wouldn't throw a multi-legged critter onto my lap.

Reclining on the soft blanket that had touched Brad's skin and smelled like his cologne was a thrill. It took all of my discipline not to roll around like a contented puppy. He set out cold fried chicken, sliced strawberries, crackers, cheese, and a thermos of iced tea. Were my warm tingly feelings love?

"Brad, I had a wonderful time the other night, and this is so thoughtful. Thank you."

A few days before, Brad had taken me to dinner at the small bistro in town and then to the pub where he drank a beer and I had a cup of coffee. It had been perfect except Winona had gawked at us, West kept ruffling my hair, and Brad hadn't tried to kiss me

"I had fun too. And you deserve a relaxing lunch break. Your class is a handful. I'm impressed because you're good with them."

I fluttered my eyelashes. "I'm sure they're easier to deal with than little kids who need shots and old men who need to give up salt."

"Maybe, hungry old men can be pretty cantankerous." Brad's laugh emanated from deep within his brawny chest.

We ate and talked about literature, art, and philosophy. After our meal, he stretched out his muscular legs and leaned back on his elbows. I curled my knees under me and rearranged my skirt as the wind blew my hair every which way.

"Your hair is gorgeous," he said.

I self-consciously removed a strand from my cheek.

"So are your eyes. In this light, they are a beautiful emerald color." He paused. "You know I'd kiss you if students weren't lurking about."

Brad's eyes shimmered like sapphires. His brows were heavy and masculine, and his lashes were long and black. Bradley Gordon was prince charming incarnate. I'm sure he knew how infatuated I was from my silly grin and even sillier blush.

He tucked a flyaway ringlet behind my ear. His brief touch divulged the secret he gentlemanly tried to hide. He wanted to lay me out on his white blanket and kiss me senseless. I lifted my glove to the spot he had brushed, and he placed his hand on top of mine. I pulled back, both desiring and fearing the contact. My withdrawal didn't seem to faze him. He refocused his gaze on a group of young men tossing a Frisbee. Their joyous sounds mingled with a group of giggling girls and a chorus of chirping birds.

He checked his watch and sighed. "I have to go. I have one of those go-easy-on-your-wife's-salty-cooking appointments." He took his time repacking the basket.

"I have another class from two to three," I said. However, I wasn't thinking about my class. The images I had seen in Brad's mind consumed me. Apparently, we were both intrigued by the prospect of my moaning as he kissed my neck.

"Stay and relax," Brad said. "Keep the coat and blanket for now. It gives me a reason to visit the inn tonight."

Brad leaned forward, my insides tickled, and his lips pressed against mine. As he retreated, I placed my hand over my mouth. He smiled, stood, and strode away. Besides heating me to the core, his kiss altered me to what I meant to Dr. Bradley Gordon.

Much to Lincoln and Keisha's amusement, I pranced about like a lovesick fool for the remainder of the afternoon. I was incredibly excited for the workday to end so I could call my dad and tell him about my new boyfriend. There was the added anticipation of seeing Dr. Bradley Gordon twice in one day!

For the record, after retrieving his blanket, Brad Gordon kissed me, over and over again, as we embraced on Aunt Edith's front porch.

I was one lucky girl!

Chapter 16

I was reliving Brad's visit when Aunt Edith knocked on my bedroom door to let me know that a reporter from *The Bellmount Gazette* was on the line. I raced Spot down three flights to retrieve the olive green contraption tucked inside an oak faux hand-crank box. Out of breath, I held it to my ear and panted."Hi, Pat. It's Miranda."

"Hey, Professor. Still think that kid's innocent, because he's changing his plea to guilty. Mayor wants a story running tomorrow morning stating the killer's been caught. Advised to write law enforcement did a great job. You free? Meet me in front of the inn."

I hung up and clutched at my chest. I really needed one of those cellular phones. I shoved my feet into Aunt Edith's conveniently placed garden boots and threw Russ's oversized rain jacket over my pjs. FYI—it wasn't raining.

Before heading out the door, I called into the kitchen, "Aunt Edith, I have to run an errand with Pat Grimwood. I'll be back in a couple of hours."

I was disappointed to discover that even P.T. Grimwood, poster child circa 1971, had a newer vehicle than me. We listened to smooth jazz and talked for our twenty-five-mile drive to the Bear County Jail.

According to the journalist, we had no time to lose because it was next to impossible to get a prison interview. Skyler had requested to talk to the man who wrote the article about him. The warden had agreed and called the mayor. Since the mayor was in a hurry to have things "cleaned up," he had approved the meeting.

I hadn't been cleared for the visit, but little things like protocol didn't concern P.T. He introduced me as "Professor Albright, his colleague." I showed my driver's license and officially became P.T. Grimwood's assistant. The warden allotted us thirty minutes and an armed guard.

The reporter wore burgundy polyester bell bottoms. I was braless and decked out in pink and purple kittens. Skyler, devoid of make-up, looked quite prisoner-ish in his quilted green suicide-watch smock. What a fashion statement the three of us made.

After fifteen minutes of a useless interview, in which Skyler declared his guilt, I spoke up. "Skyler, I know you didn't do it. Why are you confessing?"

"Because I did it."

"Where did you kill her?" Pat asked.

"Man, I told you already. In the woods. You know trees, squirrels, and shit like that."

"Tell me about the pentagram," Pat said.

"I drew it. It was big, and it looked exactly like a pentagram," Skyler said.

Pat looked at me for confirmation. Since someone had spray-painted the symbol on the ground, I whispered a "No" and rolled my eyes.

"How about the crucifixion?" Pat asked.

"What about it?"

Too bad Skyler wasn't guilty because he was a belligerent jerk!

"How did you do it?" Pat asked.

"Like the Bible, asswipe. I nailed her to the cross."

"Language, mister," I blurted out. I couldn't help myself. Suzy must have been a saint to tolerate this kid. Then I looked at Pat, pursed my lips, and shook my head because there had been no cross.

Pat continued with his questions. "What did you do with her heart?"

"I um, I…" the kid sputtered.

I placed my ungloved hand on his forearm. Although he looked uncomfortable, he didn't withdraw. I divined that the heart comment had unnerved him. I took another turn questioning the young man. "What did you do with her heart?"

I thought it horrifying that the investigators hadn't found the precious organ. Those adhering to the Satanic theory believed Skyler had devoured it. It seemed more logical the wildlife had a hand in the disappearance.

Skyler closed his eyes. I saw what he saw: Suzy alive and laughing. He couldn't process that someone had ripped her heart from her body. When he opened his lids, he said, "I don't remember. I was stoned."

"How did you kill her?" Pat asked.

"First, I grabbed her." He paused. "I don't remember. I was stoned."

"Why did you kill her?"

"Because I loved her, and she didn't love me back."

"The coroner's report says she was two months pregnant," Pat said.

"Fuck," Skyler muttered. He rested his head on the table. When he lifted it, he said, "I didn't know. She never told me."

Pat sniffed. "Story's unraveling, kid."

Skyler ran a hand through his hair. "I killed her because she was pregnant to someone else, and I wanted it to be me."

"I thought you said you didn't know she was pregnant," Pat said.

"I'm always so fucked up I don't remember anything."

Pat leaned across the table and looked Skyler in the eyes. "You the kind of sick SOB that would kill a baby?"

Maybe Pat had tapped into some sort of male psychology I was unaware of because Skyler grunted then came clean.

"My attorney told me to plead guilty. She said if I go to trial and lose, I could be looking at the death penalty. If I plead guilty, they will probably charge me with voluntary manslaughter, and I'm looking at being out in ten to fifteen years. She said there is too much evidence against me, and since I was so stoned I don't remember where I was, I don't stand a chance. I don't give a fuck what happens to me. I loved her, and she's gone."

"If you loved Suzy, don't you want to find who did it?" I asked.

He rubbed his temples. "Hypothetically say, I didn't do it."

"You didn't," I reminded him.

"Okay, say I didn't. That douche bag frat guy she was dating is an ass."

"But they broke up in May," I said.

"Yeah, but he came to see her this summer."

Pat and I faced each other with wide eyes.

Skyler glared at Pat. "What are you gonna print in the paper?"

"Up to you."

"Are they gonna execute me?"

"I don't know," Pat answered.

"Then, I'm not saying another word." Skyler put his thumb and forefinger together and made a motion to indicate he was zipping his lips.

"Suit yourself." Pat packed to leave.

Praying his abrupt departure was some sort of reverse psychology, I followed his lead.

Skyler rapped his hand on the table. "Hey, wait a minute. So you know, I didn't do it. I don't remember shit, but I wouldn't have hurt her. I loved her."

On the way home, I vented in frustration. "Ten to fifteen years for voluntary manslaughter. That charge doesn't make sense. They are lying to him and forcing him to plead guilty."

Pat blew a puff of smoke out the driver's side window. "Professor, an unfortunate lesson. The system's broken. They'll punish the kid for being innocent. Important people want the fiasco cleaned up. Mark my words; after it's tidied, it'll disappear. It never happened—an unread story in a basement archive."

Chapter 17

The dinner hour had long passed when we arrived at State College. Following our fifty-minute drive, we made our way to Alpha Alpha. It was a not so balmy fifty-six degrees, and the Thursday night parties had commenced. I was overdressed for my first fraternity party. Keisha was at least colorful—which kind of fit with the beach theme. Winona had on jeans, a blue blouse, a jean jacket, and, as Keisha pointed out, "a shit-load of eyeliner."

About forty drunk twenty-year-old boys and a dozen bikini-clad, inebriated girls crowded into a basement that smelled like someone had poured week-old beer into a diaper pail. The music pumping through the dungeon-like room bounced off the walls, and the party-goers engaged in some sort of sing-off.

The girls called out, asking the boys if they would love them forever, and the boys hollered back that they would give them an answer in the morning.

An enthusiastic Winona joined the girls in their chant.

Keisha shot an eye roll in Winona's direction.

About two seconds after the song ended, an inflatable beach ball slapped Keisha in the head.

"Motherfucker!" Keisha called out, swatting it away.

What an unfortunate way to start our investigation. Nothing slapped Keisha Brown in the head without serious repercussions. Having listened to Winona sing along to a Barry Manilow cassette for the past sixty miles, Keisha's temper was already in question.

"Let's split up," Winona said.

I'm surprised she wasn't carrying a magnifying glass and wearing a tweed deerstalker cap with her *I'm a thirty-two-year-old waitress* party outfit.

"Remember, Peter O'Neill," I called.

"Got it," Winona hollered over the loud music. "Peter O'Neill."

When a beach ball hit me in the head, I handled it a lot better than Keisha. I tossed it back to a bare-chested frat brother attired in Hawaiian shorts and flip-flops. A minute later, he was at my side handing me a beer.

"Come watch." He grabbed my gloved hand and dragged me to a side room where at least thirty coeds gathered around a plastic kiddie swimming pool.

I couldn't see what was going on from my spot behind the crowd.

The revelers chanted, "Drink, Drink, Drink," a cheer would break out, and a guy, adorned in a half dozen paper leis, and standing on a chair, would call out a number. He had just called out, "Sixteen," when my new friend pushed me to the front of the gathering.

"Drink! Drink! Drink!" the crowd chanted.

A wasted kid standing in the middle of it all scooped his red cup into the pool's concoction of beer and live goldfish. He gulped, everyone cheered, and the kid on the chair called out, "Seventeen!"

I wanted to vomit, but I couldn't since there was no Dr. Brad to clean up after me. I think Number Seventeen may also have wanted to vomit. He jumped out of the pool and sprinted for the door.

"The number to beat is still thirty-one." The young

man standing on the chair yelled. "Who's next?"

I concluded that I hadn't missed much avoiding the Greek circuit during my undergrad days.

"Wanna take a turn?" my new friend, Sir Flip-flop, asked.

"No, thank you," I yelled over the din. "I don't drink alcohol or eat live pets."

Keisha made her way through the vociferous merry-makers toward me.

"I'm looking for someone. Maybe you can help me?" I said to Sir Flip-flop.

"Anything for you, babe." He winked and smiled.

The evening was going swimmingly. I was getting hit on by some nineteen-year-old kid who could have been sitting in my classroom.

Meanwhile, Keisha struggled to break through the crowd.

"I'm looking for a guy named Peter O'Neill," I said.

Sir Flip-flop didn't answer me right away because he was bopping to the old-school beachy rock clanging in the background.

Keisha finally reached my side. A gangly, pimply kid had followed her, and her ordinarily wrinkle-free brow creased in frustration.

"Pete. Yep. He's a brother. He's—" Sir Flip-flop said.

Prince Pimple stepped in front of Keisha and muffled the rest of Sir Flip-Flop's response. "How about some brown sugar, baby?"

"I will brown sugar your motherfucking ass!"

I suspect Keisha was too angry to hear her unintended innuendo.

The next sequence of events seemed to pass in slow

motion. Prince Pimple's outstretched arm reached for Keisha. Keisha balled up her fist then swung at Prince Pimple. Prince Pimple gracefully stepped to the side. My nose absorbed Keisha's punch, and I stumbled backward.

"Oh, shit," Sir Flip-flop yelled as he tried to catch me.

Splash! I took out Sir Flip-flop and ended up sitting on his lap in the kiddie pool. Coeds gasped as goldfish and beer sprayed across the room.

Winona appeared out of nowhere. "Miranda, why are you swimming in your dress? For Pete's sake, get out of there. I found Peter O'Neill."

"Fudge," I muttered.

Keisha's lip quivered. She stared at her fist; then, she swung again. This time, she smashed her mark.

"Ouch! Sexy and strong." Prince Pimple grinned as he rubbed his nose.

Keisha ignored her unlikely prince. "Shit, Miranda. I'm sorry your nose is bleeding."

A handsome boy with strawberry blond hair grabbed my forearm and pulled me from the lagoon of humiliation.

The sea of howling party-animals parted to allow my sloshing shoes and dripping dress to trudge on through. They *oohed* and *aahed* and clapped as I left a stream of yellow liquid trailing behind me.

When I reached the end of the gaping crowd, Keisha positioned herself in front of me. She unclasped the cameo pin from my neck and grabbed the beach ball from a kid standing next to her.

She stuck the sharp tip of my brooch right into that ball, gave it a good two-handed push, and a gust of air whooshed out. She handed the colorful deflating toy back to the boy. Her satisfied smile was terrifying.

Abashed and feeling as though I had no other recourse, I curtsied for the crowd, then followed Suzy Smith's ex-boyfriend up a steep stairwell.

****

The strawberry blond, Peter O'Neill, had a bedroom on the third floor of the frat house. My clothes, gloves, and undergarments were drying all about us. Peter had loaned me an XXL sweatsuit and a pair of men's size ten shower shoes.

I wrapped my ale-covered hair in a towel of questionable cleanliness. Whenever I tried to stand, the sweatpants slid down my bare hips, and I couldn't walk without tripping over the too-large toes.

Surprisingly, I didn't find Peter O'Neill to be as distasteful as I expected. He had three older women sitting in his sleeping chamber, and he was behaving quite hospitably.

"Ms. Westinghouse explained that you are private investigators," Peter said.

I shot Winona a no-you-didn't look. She flashed me a toothy grin.

"She said you have some questions about Suzy Smith. Is she okay? You know we broke up last semester. I don't think her dad let her come back to school this year. He's a total prick !"

"Suzy's dead!" Keisha was still in a foul mood and didn't feel the need to break the news gently.

"What?"

"She was murdered. A Satanic ritual. Her heart was cut out, and she was sacrificed to the devil," Winona declared.

"What?" Peter O'Neill's face paled. "I don't

119

understand. When? How?"

I held my pants in place with one hand, a tissue on my bleeding nose with the other, and opted for bare feet to make my way to the shocked boy. Since my gloves were soaked with beer and goldfish guts, I figured what the heck. I let go of my pants and hooked my lie detector up to the grieving Peter's bare forearm.

I filled him in on the tragedy.

"That weird kid from her hometown! I told her he was a psycho. That's one of the things we were arguing about. He wouldn't leave her alone. He had a thing for her, and I was afraid he might chop her into pieces," Peter said.

"Skyler Dubbs is a nutball, but it wasn't him," Keisha declared.

I gave both of my partners the evil eye. Neither of them seemed to care one iota that I was appalled by their lack of sympathy and discretion.

"Did you kill her?" Keisha put a hand on her hip. "Because the rude boys living in this house seem to have some seriously questionable judgment. Bellmount kids would never behave like this."

I needed to explain to Keisha that being a horny fraternity brother didn't necessarily make one a psychotic murderer. I was also pretty sure the students at Bellmount engaged in their share of drunken shenanigans.

"What? You think I did it? I haven't even seen her since we broke up," Peter said.

"Peter, didn't you visit her this summer?" I asked.

"I drove there to talk to her, but her dad didn't let me see her. I wanted to try to get back together, but I think there was another guy she was interested in."

"Skyler?" I asked.

"You know she was pregnant?" said Winona.

I gave my filterless backup crew a squinty-eyed glower.

"She was pregnant? Do you think it was mine?"

My previous, please-be-quiet-look, directed to the two oldest characters in the room, took on a shut-up-glare.

"The final autopsy isn't back yet, and the details haven't been released, but I think about two months."

Peter looked up to the ceiling and counted to four. "Then it couldn't be mine. I don't think it was that weird dude with all of the make-up. She was good to him, but I don't think she was sleeping with him. He might have killed her, but I'm pretty sure he didn't get her pregnant."

"Do you have any idea who the father might have been?" I asked.

"I think she had a thing for some rich dude back home."

"Rich dude?" I asked.

Winona and Keisha took turns calling out names.

"Joseph Walton—"

"James Schuster—"

"Ian Patterson—"

"Kyle Patterson—"

"Mitch Patterson—"

"Mayor Reynolds—"

"Greg Grainey—"

"Brad Gordon—"

"Lincoln Harrison—"

"Dean Johnson."

I balked at the mention of the last few unlikely men.

Winona shrugged. "Just listing guys with money."

I made a mental note to instruct my deputies in more effective questioning techniques.

"Man, I don't know. Honestly, I don't. I never asked for a name." He placed his head in his hands. "I don't know."

The handsome Peter O'Neill may have lived in a mansion-sized beer keg, but he didn't know who murdered Suzy Smith.

Chapter 18

Bradley Gordon took me to a movie on date number five point five. Since he wasn't aware that I considered our initial meeting our first date, it seemed only fair to count it as half a date. I had on my burgundy gloves, so I had to pass on the buttery popcorn. Since I wore wool, I didn't have to pass on holding his hand.

I only paid attention to the first few minutes of the movie. About ten minutes in, Brad put the popcorn bucket on the floor and grasped my hand. I was thankful he couldn't see my buffoonish grin in the dark theater. My stomach engaged in a few loop-de-loops, and butterflies fluttered in my chest. I fantasized about the sounds I might make if he kissed my ear instead of paying attention to thespian Williams and his troupe of young boys.

About thirty minutes in, Brad leaned over to whisper, "Take that off." He tapped my glove. "I'll keep your hand warm."

That was why I couldn't play with nice things like the handsome, brilliant, perfect Dr. Bradley Gordon. Before I could protest, he had removed my glove and massaged my hand.

Petrified, I recited, Eight times eight is sixty-four, eight times nine is seventy-two...

His thoughts came through loud and clear. *Rubbing it should help with the circulation and keep her warm.*

Eight times ten is eighty.

Her hand is so soft.

Eight times eleven is eighty-eight.

God, I want to kiss her hand.

Nine times one is… I—I forget!

I'm going to kiss her hand.

Then he lifted my hand to his lips, kissed it, and went back to watching the movie like he hadn't just slapped a stick of dynamite in the middle of my world. My mind-readers-end-up-in-mental-hospitals survival instincts told me to run for cover. My epicurean desires told me to kiss his hand, kiss his ear, and keep going until I had kissed every inch of him.

Since math wasn't working, I held Bradley Gordon's hand in my bare hand and recited British poetry.

Please help me, Mr. Kipling.

Unfortunately, my defense mechanism wasn't foolproof.

I wish she would rest her head on my shoulder.

I wanted to rest my head on him more than I had ever wanted anything. Since we already had skin-to-skin contact, I figured it couldn't hurt. I laid my head on Brad's shoulder, held his hand, and rehearsed my mental Rudyard. It was dreamy!

After the movie, Brad escorted me home. Our clasped hands swung between us. I gave up on my wall of defense and listened in on his thoughts. He felt my hair was beautiful, and my eyes were stunning. He wanted to kiss each of the freckles that dotted my nose. He believed I was smart and spirited and that I smelled heavenly. Why had I been so afraid?

His mind said one thing. His audible chatter said another. In between his sweet reflections, he talked about the movie and his favorite high school teacher.

Once we could see the inn, we stopped walking.

"Miranda, the Harvest Festival is in a few weeks. I was hoping you would be my date?"

Yikes! The event where his ex-wife intended to humiliate me!

I shoved the chiming warning bells into a corner of my brain. "Yes. I'd love to."

He held my chin in his hand and lifted my face to the moonlight. He bent down. I reached up, and our lips touched. He tasted like peppermint and popcorn. His tongue parted my lips and slid into my mouth. Feeling drugged, my body relaxed.

He moaned before his hand slid down my back and pulled me close. "Miranda," he whispered.

"Mmm," I uttered as my hands threaded through his hair.

Then he thought *Jessica*, and I saw a dark-haired woman in a lavender suit smirking at me.

I pulled away.

"Miranda?" He reached for me.

"Are you still in love with your ex-wife?"

His entire body stiffened. "What? No. Not even a little."

"Then why are you thinking about her?"

"What are you talking about? I haven't thought about anyone but you since I found you on the roadside."

"Then why did you call me Jessica?"

He contemplated this. "I called you Miranda. What are you talking about?"

Confused and panicky, I ran to the inn. I passed by Aunt Edith, and Spot followed me up the stairs. I didn't have the energy or desire to take a shower, so I tucked myself under my blankets and mentally replayed my disaster of a date.

Spot curled up beside me, and I scratched his ears. Then it hit me. I hadn't seen into Brad's mind. It had been my self-sabotaging thoughts tormenting me.

"Oh, no! What have I done?" I cried into my pillow.

That was the moment I knew I desperately needed help.

Chapter 19

I racked my brain, trying to figure out how to clean up my mess. I was crazy about Dr. Bradley Gordon, but even if I apologized, I was certain there was no way he would take me back. How could I explain my behavior without sounding insane? What would I do if the universe turned upside down and a man tried to kiss me again?

I had a plan. It wasn't a good one, but it was the only one I had. I waited for a stomping Dean Johnson to disappear around the corner, then headed down the hall to see my mentor.

"Hi, Lincoln. Are you busy?" I asked.

Lincoln's eyes sparkled, and a smile appeared above his beard. "Never too busy for you, Miranda. Come in. What can I do for you?"

I closed the door and sat across from him. "My aunt told me that you treated my grandmother."

He leaned back in his chair and looked at the ceiling. "Oh yes, that was a long time ago."

"Did you think she was mentally ill?"

He took off his glasses and rubbed his eyes. He was thinking or stalling, and perhaps, a little of both. Eventually, he slid his glasses into place. "Your grandmother believed she was able to read minds and predict the future. She thought she was a witch."

"Could she read minds?"

"Often, intuitive people believe they can. Intuition

has to do with skilled observation and a heightened understanding of human nature, and it doesn't mean someone has supernatural powers or is a witch," Lincoln said.

I stared into his eyes. "So you think she was mentally ill? You don't believe she could read minds?"

"I think your grandmother struggled. She often blurred the lines between reality and fantasy. Why are you asking?"

I drew in a breath and mustered courage. "What if I told you that I can read minds and sometimes see things after they've happened?"

Lincoln's shoulders tensed, and he sat forward.

When he didn't say anything, I continued. "I don't think I'm a witch, and I can't predict the future, but I can touch a person and see and hear what they're thinking. I can sometimes see an event after it happens."

Lincoln propped his chin on steepled fingers. "Your grandmother wore gloves when I first met her. Why do you wear them?"

I did my best to articulate my affliction. I explained that although my entire body seemed to be some sort of conductor, my hands were extremely sensitive, and the gloves acted as a shield that kept me from feeling the constant exhaustion associated with knowing others' thoughts. That it felt unethical to read people's minds. I told him I had no idea what caused the occasional glimpses I had into the past, and the most recent had been Suzy's murder.

He remained quiet for a minute. "Miranda, the power of the mind is a funny thing. You're a bright woman, obviously intuitive. You are living in your grandmother's house and are probably reminiscing about your childhood.

Maybe you recall some of the things she told you. Children are especially receptive to fantasy."

My courage flew out the door as my shoulders caved forward. "Thanks, Lincoln."

I sulked to the door. Then I stopped. My mentor stared at me with an odd, far-away look in his eyes. A voice in my head screamed, No! He has to help you!

I made my way back to his desk, cleared my throat, and tried again. "For years, I've told myself I'm simply sensitive, but I can see things in my mind, and..." I stuttered over my words. "I-I need help. I can't avoid all physical contact, and I'm having trouble because the line between my thoughts and the things other people think is blurring."

"You might be struggling with post-traumatic stress disorder after seeing Suzy's violent murder scene. PTSD isn't uncommon when people have experienced something they struggle to process." Lincoln paused and frowned. "I understand that your mother was murdered a few years ago."

It took me a moment to recover from Lincoln's comment. I shook the echoes of his last statement from my thoughts and continued my plea. "But this has been happening to me since I was a child, and it's getting worse. Please help me. I don't have anyone else to go to."

He studied his calendar. "Are you free next Tuesday morning? Perhaps I can help you deal with the PTSD."

I nodded. "Thank you. Thank you!"

It was a start.

Chapter 20

Weston Westinghouse the Third lived alone above the pub. To reach his studio apartment, I had to climb the steep steps that ran along the left side of the building. I knocked on his weatherbeaten screen door.

"Come in," West called.

"Hi, Randa," Tommy said before hollering a battle cry that sounded like, "Char-whaaaa!"

"Hiya, Dr. Shortcake," West said. Then he yelled, "Take that, you son-of-a-bitch!"

Neither of them took their eyes from the life-or-death video game that consumed them. I moved a crocheted afghan out of the way and made myself at home on the couch beside West.

I took in his bachelor pad. The wooden beams and frame of the building were exposed, giving the large room a rustic feel. Tommy had pushed a pile of clothes aside to sit on a threadbare yellow chair. West had his bare feet propped on an empty whiskey crate that seemed to serve as both ottoman and coffee table. The room was dark despite an out-of-place Victorian floor lamp and a lighted ceiling fan hanging from a beam. More whiskey crates had been fashioned into an entertainment center that held a TV, a VCR, a boom box, and the video game console.

A makeshift kitchen counter had been constructed in the left-hand corner of the room. Underneath the only window sat a sink full of dirty dishes, a mini-fridge, and a microwave. A pile of what appeared to be used towels obstructed the path to the bathroom. Along the back wall sat West's unmade bed, a dresser that may have been from the 1920s, and an overflowing nightstand. My traitorous body tingled at the sight of West's unmade bed.

"Woohoo! Still the king of the world," West yelled, tossing his game control and leaping to his feet to beat on his chest.

Tommy looked bummed for a moment before he shook off his defeat. "Why the long face, Randa?"

"Brad and I broke up."

"I'm sorry. Doc's loss." Tommy leaned over to pat me on the shoulder.

West grabbed a pair of rolled-up socks that sat on the all-purpose crate. "Well, good thing you have us, Shortcake. Let's head out while we still have daylight."

"Okay, but we won't tell Aunt Edith or Liam. Right?"

"Right," my childhood friends said.

****

A few hundred feet behind the pub, West constructed a target out of an upright log and empty beer cans while Tommy gave me a lesson.

"Randa?" Tommy cringed and held Princess upside down between his thumb and forefinger.

"What the hell is that? A toy? I thought you bought a .22," West called to us.

Tommy scrunched up his nose. "It has pink diamonds all over it."

"They are rhinestones, and it's what we call poetic justice," I said.

West approached us. "Explain. In words that we laymen without fancy doctorates understand."

"Meet Princess!" I took my gun from Tommy and lifted her into the air so that all three of us could admire my ridiculous excuse for an instrument of destruction. "She's Jessica Grainey's first gun, the one that she got into trouble for decorating. I thought it would be quite ironic if it were also the one that put a bullet in her icy heart."

"Oh, cool. Let's do this," West said.

Tommy laughed. "Right-handed, right?"

"Correct."

I placed my gloves on the ground beside me and spent the next forty-five minutes learning how to grip the gun, take the correct stance, and focus my eyes. Tommy was thorough in his explanations. I was impatient and wanted to blow up mean girls, sleazy cops, and righteous religious leaders.

"Come on, Little, let the girl shoot at something," West called from the rock he lounged on.

"I'm ready, Tommy."

"Okay. Remember to concentrate," Tommy said softly.

"I know; I know."

"Picture the bitch's face right in the center of the can," West yelled. "Then fire that toy gun!"

"It's a real gun, West," I hollered back.

I aimed, concentrated, squeezed the trigger, and my bullet landed somewhere that wasn't a beer can Jessica. West cheered despite my missed mark.

"Good," Tommy said. "This time, don't blink."

I aimed, concentrated on not blinking, and squeezed. I missed it again. On my seventh try, I hit my scrap aluminum enemy between her pretend blue eyes and jumped about, cheering.

"Randa," Tommy scolded. "You need to be careful. No flitting around with a weapon."

I took note that Princess danced along with me and agreed that it wasn't safe to leap about with a bullet still in the chamber.

"Sorry," I said.

West hollered, "That's my girl!"

This was when things went awry.

West strolled to the log, bent forward, and placed a new can on our makeshift stand.

I stared at his perfectly formed backside.

Tommy told me to pay attention.

I didn't mean to squeeze the trigger.

Bang!

It was a horrible trek to Tommy's truck, where he patched up the wound with a clean towel and the duct tape he kept in his first aid kit.

"Both of you stop your blubbering. The bullet barely even touched him. He's fine," Tommy insisted.

"Then why is there blood?" I asked.

West said, "Grrr."

The three of us squished into the cab of Tommy's work truck. It was excruciating to listen to West moan from his seat beside me. I begged the guys to find another doctor. I had already humiliated myself enough for a million lifetimes, and I couldn't face Brad.

"This isn't your big city, Shortcake. We've got one decent doctor in this godforsaken town," a grumpy West informed me.

No matter how many times I told Bellmountians that Harrisburg, Pennsylvania wasn't a budding metropolis, they didn't seem to get it. Since West currently had a bullet in his rear and duct tape holding his cheeks together, I figured it wasn't the best time to remind him of it.

Then the three of us argued about where to go.

"We could try the Campus Health Center. There might be someone on call tonight," I said.

Tommy said, "No, we're going to see Doc Gordon."

West said, "Grr."

"Randa, you weren't paying attention," Tommy scolded.

"It wasn't my fault. I was distracted by West," I defended myself.

"What the hell did I do?" West smiled. "Oh, I get it. You were distracted by my animal magnetism."

How West could still be conceited with a bullet in his butt defied rational explanation.

"No, West, I was distracted by your big honking head."

Yep, that was it. His absurdly large, air-filled, confident noggin, not his perfect posterior, had addled my brain.

Ten minutes later, the three of us entered Brad's examination room. Tommy set himself up so he could *ooh* and *aah* as he watched the doctor work.

I was relegated to a seat on the opposite side of the table. It wasn't that I was totally opposed to seeing West's rump, but I wasn't sure I wanted to see a bloody wound, and in any event, I wasn't given a choice since the three men in the room were opposed to me staring at West's bare bum.

Brad removed the homemade bandages. "Thank God! Little, you did a good job cleaning it."

He cleaned the wound again, poked about it, sewed a few stitches, administered antibiotics and a painkiller, checked the records for a tetanus shot, and gave West a butt pillow.

Brad assured us that he would be fine, although he would be sore for a few days and needed to take it easy. He suggested that to be on the safe side, we take West to the county hospital and have an X-ray done to ensure no shrapnel had been left in his body. It was only a precaution because Brad was ninety-nine percent sure the bullet had grazed West's glute and skidded on by.

"Hey, Doc, it stops hurting when you touch it," West said.

"Great, but I don't plan to keep my hand on your ass all night, Westinghouse," Brad informed him.

West looked crestfallen.

"You two should have taken better care of her," Brad rebuked my firearm instructors.

"Hey Doc, I'm the one with a bullet in my ass," West said.

"*You* are going to be fine," Brad told West.

From the way, he emphasized the word *you,* I suppose he thought I was the one who was too delicate to recover.

"And the bullet is in a tree somewhere, not your backside."

"Feels like it's in my ass!" West insisted.

Because I was too ashamed to tell her myself, I begged Tommy to call Aunt Edith from Brad's office phone and explain what happened.

"Hi, Edith. It's Tom Little. Yep. Fine. Wanted to let you know Randa will be late tonight…She's fine. We have to take a trip to the county hospital…No. She shot Westinghouse in the ass with her toy gun."

"It's a real gun," West and I called out.

135

****

I neatened my ringlets, applied a light layer of make-up, and threw on my Bellmount College sweatshirt. I carried a crate of cleaning supplies and a dozen of Aunt Edith's chocolate chip cookies down the hill to West's apartment.

A drowsy West stretched out on the couch, watching TV. I fixed him a snack and tackled the sink full of dishes. It was the least I could do since I had shot him, and he was convalescing.

I was scrubbing mold from West's shower when moans distracted me. I hurried to the main room. His outstretched arm reached for the television remote sitting on the whiskey crate coffee table. I retrieved the control and handed it to him.

He grinned. "Thanks, Shortcake."

"Is there anything else you need right now?" I asked.

"Man, I'm thirsty." He smacked his lips.

"Want some water?"

"There's pop in the mini-fridge."

I cringed at the Western Pennsylvanian slang. I didn't mind Pop as a name, but using it to reference a carbonated drink drove me insane. I headed to the kitchenette and fixed him a soda, then I propped him against a pillow and handed him his cup. He sipped and smiled.

"Shortcake, I'm sorry. If it isn't too much trouble, could you change the channel?"

"I handed you the remote a minute ago. Don't you have it?"

He sighed and pointed to the top of the television set.

"How did it get there?" I asked.

"I didn't want to bug you while you were getting my

drink, so I walked over to the TV by myself, but it hurt." He gave me a frowny face, and puppy dog eyes. Then he fluttered his long lashes.

I handed him the remote again. He grinned, and I returned to my chores.

I had tucked the ends of his sheet under his mattress and was about to smooth out the afghan when he called out, "Wow, I'm so cold."

I grabbed the crocheted blanket and carried it to the couch. I flipped it into the air, and it fluttered over him. As I tucked him in, he wiggled into his cocoon.

"Thanks, you're a peach."

I returned to my project and folded a pile of T-shirts.

"Man, I'm so hungry," he called.

I placed his shirts in the top dresser drawer and checked on my patient. "Do you want some more cookies?"

"Yeah, but they're gone."

"You ate them all?" I asked.

"Yep." He rubbed his belly.

"What are you hungry for?"

"There's some pizza in the fridge."

I traveled the seven feet to his makeshift open-floor kitchen. Bending low, I rooted around in the mini-fridge and found two pathetic slices under a can of unopened tuna. I placed the tuna in his tiny cupboard.

"West, how old is this pizza?" I called.

He didn't answer right away.

"What ya say, Shortcake?" he finally called back. "I'm trying to catch up on *The Leading Light*."

"Isn't that a soap opera?" I asked.

"Fuck yeah! I love me some good daytime stories."

I shook my head in disbelief, then asked again, "How

old is this pizza?"

"Two days, no three days." He counted on his fingers. "Make that nine-ish days."

"Oh, my!" I threw the foul food into the trash. "I'm heading downstairs to have Pop or Uncle Will make you something."

"No, no, you don't have—"

****

"Hey! There's the girl who shot my son!" Pop called when I entered the pub.

There was a round of applause from West's regulars. I curtsied.

Pop laughed. "What can I do ya for, kiddo?"

"I came down to get West something to eat. All he has up there is a can of tuna and nine-day-old pizza."

Pop narrowed his eyes. "Why didn't he come down himself?"

"He is watching his 'stories.'" I cringed. "And it hurts for him to move around. I came over to help out a bit, do some cleaning, keep him company, and fix him something to eat."

"I hope you're not cleaning for him," his Aunt Polly said.

"Well, I'm the one that hurt him. I feel—"

"Miranda, he's fine. He was down here playing foosball and dancing with some bimbo last night."

West's Uncle Will rolled his eyes. "He's playin' you, kiddo."

I was relieved to know that West wasn't in as bad of shape as I initially thought, so I let go of my frustration. Besides, I didn't have anything better to do since I was no longer dating Brad.

"Pop, can you pack up two burgers, mozzarella

sticks, and fries?" I asked.

****

West and I ate our dinner. He groaned about how it hurt to sit. I placated him and fluffed his pillows. Somehow, I even got suckered into hand-feeding him a couple of fries.

West made me laugh and forget my crappy week. I liked his lazy drawl and his mischievous smile and that his T-shirts were too tight for his well-formed biceps and muscular chest. I loved that he didn't take life too seriously. I enjoyed my afternoon hanging out with him so much that I decided to overlook his little trick.

After we finished eating, West had me pop a pretty steamy movie about a group of young vampires into the VCR. He stretched out on his couch but gave up the blanket so that I could stay warm as I curled into the chair. I hadn't seen many movies over the last decade, so I suspect I might have been a bit animated. West chuckled each time I squealed or covered my face in horror.

After the final credits, he sat up. "Hey, Shortcake, can you help me to my bed?"

"Sure."

I allowed him to place his arm around my shoulder and lean on me. What harm could come of it? My sweatshirt and jeans covered me, so despite his thin T-shirt, our skin wasn't touching. Besides, I figured he was tired and ready to call it a night.

"Can you help me change clothes?" he asked.

"What?"

"I've been stuck in these clothes since yesterday." He lifted his hands over his head. "Please," he pleaded.

I have no idea how I let West convince me to help him disrobe. I seemed to lose a few IQ points every time he was near. I lifted his T-shirt; he made a fake moan of pain, and then he did some absurd chest muscle pop. He observed my gaze slide over his torso. I emitted a tiny gasp, and he smirked.

"Whew, it hurts. Can you help me change my pants?" He reached for his zipper.

"You're incorrigible." I pushed into his chest and stomped across the room to the door.

"Hey, come here. I'm teasing," he called after me.

"No! I'm mad at you!" If angry, humiliated, and turned on, each had their own shade of red, then I was three shades of red.

"Hey! I need help rubbing ointment on my ass wound," he yelled as I slammed his front door.

I wanted the last word, so I opened the door, preparing to lambaste him. The idiot was laughing so hard he was doubled over.

"Weston Westinghouse the Third, you are a huge jerk. You have been since I was four when you told me a worm was Polish pasta, and then I threw up all over the yard. I have no idea why I have a crush on you!"

He stopped laughing. I slammed his door again.

"Fudge." I slapped my hand to my forehead. That wasn't what I had meant to say, and I had left Aunt Edith's cleaning supplies sitting on the counter.

West peeked out his door a moment later. "Shortcake, I'm sorry. Don't go."

"Had a crush! Had!"

It was settled. I would have to buy my aunt new supplies.

I pounded down the stairs calling over my shoulder, "And I'm never talking to you again, Weston Westinghouse!"

Chapter 21

October was in full swing, and Bellmount looked like an old-fashioned Currier and Ives print. The leaves were a colorful fall palette, and almost every residence flaunted a front porch harvest display.

If I dressed in either long colorful sweaters or tweed suits, I could make the fifteen-minute walk from the inn to the warm cup of tea waiting at the other end.

I wore my gray wool suit, white lace gloves, pearls, and was carrying a cuppa when Lincoln invited me in for our first session. Neither of us spoke for an awkward few moments. Finally, he clasped his hands together, looked up to the ceiling, and cleared his throat.

"Miranda, I've been researching something called telepathy. Do you know what it is?"

"Yes," I said.

Lincoln explained, anyway. "Scientists started researching telepathy in the nineteenth century, and probably even before that. It deals with transmitting information from one person to another without using one of the sensory channels."

I perked up because it appeared Lincoln believed me.

"I know this isn't what you want to hear, but I couldn't find a single respected scientific experiment that proves it exists. Telepathy is considered a pseudoscience because it doesn't stand up to the scientific method."

"I see." My hope deflated.

"In 1981, a researcher named Rupert Sheldrake from Cambridge proposed a theory called Morphic Resonance. This theory hypothesizes that memories are not embedded in the brain and are part of a collective consciousness, almost like a beehive. It overlaps with Carl Jung's collective unconscious, which states collective memories are shared among beings of the same species, so members can sense certain things even if that information isn't processed by one of the five senses. This has given many people who believe in telepathy hope for it to be legitimized. Still, as I'm sure you know, as fascinating as Jung's theories are, many of them are considered pseudoscience."

My gaze fell to his desk as I asked, "So you would still like to treat me for post-traumatic stress disorder?"

Lincoln nodded. "Pseudosciences provide immense inspiration for literature and movies, and they are fascinating, but they don't hold up."

I had spent most of my life feeling that same way. But my time in Bellmount had challenged everything I had known to be true, and my once impeccable common sense had leaped backward.

"I also found a study in which monkeys, wearing magnetic caps on their lower cortexes, were trained to work together and solve problems. It's fascinating and could eventually show how brains can be linked together without speech."

"That is interesting," I said.

"Fascinating, but there could have been other explanations for the monkeys' abilities to communicate. It could have been gestures, body language, or a shared goal. More research needs to be done."

"Or simply scrumptious bananas." I chuckled until I

snorted.

Lincoln was too focused to acknowledge my bad joke and humiliating chortle.

"I found a recent study that shows a connection between computer science and telepathy that is quite interesting. In 1986 scientists were able to network computers across the country. Recently, a British scientist named Tim Berners-Lee developed something called the World Wide Web, connecting information worldwide. Another researcher in Great Britain has proposed that someday we will be able to do that same thing with the brain."

"So computers can communicate with each other, like an old science fiction movie?"

"It appears so, and there is an expert in Sweden who has been working with prosthetic devices. He hooked a subject up to an electronic hand, and then using an EEG machine, was able to train the brain to move the fingers on the prosthetic. This also seems to hold some support for telepathy as a true science."

"Amazing!" I clapped and slid to the front of my seat.

"There's no evidence telepathy exists, but there are some promising studies, and once the technology is available, it could prove to be a real thing. Keep in mind, though, the technology isn't available yet." He paused. "But I have a theory I'd like to play with."

I propped my elbows on his desk. "Tell me about it."

"We know that thoughts are brain waves, and brain waves are electrical impulses, and scientists have been able to send electrical impulses through the nerves to move a prosthetic limb."

"Yes?" I leaned forward.

"Let's hypothesize that for some reason, there are

people who have an innate ability to make nerve impulses vibrate at the same frequency, almost like tapping into a telephone or the World Wide Web. They, because of some type of body chemistry, advanced neuron pathways, or genetics, become the technology."

"So a person could be like one of those mobile cellular phones?"

He nodded. "Look, Miranda, I'm not saying it will work. But since I love a good experiment, let's play with it and see where it goes."

"Really?" I sat straight and steepled my hands over my mouth in a version of a thank-you prayer.

"Yes. But I still intend to treat you for post-traumatic stress disorder as we work through my theory."

"Thank you. Thank you, Lincoln!"

"Miranda, this has to stay between us. Playing with a pseudoscience won't bode well for either of us in this academic institution."

"Of course!" I hopped to my feet and swiveled my hips in an absurd dance of joy.

Lincoln bobbled his head as he chuckled.

My life was looking up because help was on the way!

Chapter 22

Parking The Tank in front of the Madame's Brews and True Psychic Readings: Palms, Tarot, and Medium sign would have been akin to taking out a full-page advertisement in *The Bellmount Gazette* declaring that Dr. Miranda Albright was naive and gullible. Therefore, I parked two blocks away, pulled the hood of my jacket over my head—to both conceal my identity and keep out the rain—peeked around the corner, and sprinted to the entrance.

Madame's storefront promised all sorts of mystical things. Twinkling white Christmas lights surrounded the main window, a large gold palm decorated the glass, and lush purple draperies, tied back with golden fringed tassels, greeted believers.

When I pushed on the purple front door, a half dozen twinkling bells chimed. Containers of colorful herbs and teas lined the old-fashioned wooden shelves. Madame Alina, her hair wrapped in a multi-colored dikhlo headscarf and large gold hoops hanging from her ears, stood behind the counter. She wore a black shawl, a floral skirt, and brown sandals. A dozen bracelets clanked as she extended her hand in greeting.

"Hello, my dear, how can I help you?"

I took off my jacket and shook what water I could from my body. I extended my gloveless hand. Since we should have been on equal footing, there was no need to protect her privacy with my fabric mufflers. Besides, I needed to know if she was legitimate because I was desperate to find someone with whom I could commiserate. Unfortunately, Madame Alina was the only psychic listed in the Bear County Yellow Pages.

"I'm Miranda from Bellmount."

"I'm Madame Alina from the deep forests of Romania." She had an olive complexion, dark eyes, and spoke slowly, drawing out her words, making it easy to believe she was from some exotic land where vampires ran rampant.

"Romania by way of Brooklyn?" I asked.

"Vhat, my dear?"

"I thought I detected a touch of New York in your accent," I said.

"No, Romania, by way of my dear Great Great Great Great Grandmother," she lied. "Vhat are you in search of today, my dear? A love potion to capture the heart of that special man. Perhaps a tarot reading?"

"Some information."

"Please," she said, extending her hand toward a wall divider of green velvet.

On the other side of the heavy curtain was a dark room that contained a round table draped in layers of green, red, and purple velvet. A crystal ball glimmered from the center of the table. Madame took a few moments to glide around the room, sparking a flame in each of the gothic wall sconces. Once she finished creating an unearthly ambiance, she sat across from me, clasped my hands, and turned them every which way. Then she brought one of my wrists to her lips for a brief kiss.

"You are so lovely, my dear."

My eyes did an internal roll.

"Your energy is strong, and there's so much in these hands. Vhat vould you like to know?"

I withdrew them. "What do they tell you?"

"Please," she said, reaching for me. "I vill read your palm, dear."

I wasn't in the mood to be touched, so I clasped my palms in my lap.

"There's a man," she said, staring into my eyes.

I think she was waiting for a response. I clamped my lips tight.

"Someone ugly is trying to keep you from your sweetheart. Does that mean anything to you?"

It meant that most women in the world must be dealing with a Jessica Grainey. I shrugged.

"Perhaps there are two men. You must decide between light and dark. Does that mean anything to you?"

Two men? I didn't even have one man. Was she saying I needed to decide between Brad's black hair and sapphire eyes and West's sometimes sun-kissed golden hair and hazel eyes?

I had a second of panic before I remembered a couple of things. Number one, she was a fraud. Number two, I didn't have to make a choice. I was crazy about the devastatingly handsome, brilliant Brad, and I was still mad at Weston Westinghouse the Third, in his stupid tight shirts. There was nothing to decide since Brad probably thought I was insane, and West was a huge jerk. This woman, who sounded like she had stepped out of a Dracula movie, was a charlatan.

I shrugged again. She pursed her lips and drummed her bright red fingernails on the table.

"Shall we consult Anna-Marie?"

"Anna-Marie?" I asked.

She pointed one of her perfectly manicured fingers at the crystal ball.

Since I was curious, I nodded to the affirmative.

"Anna-Marie belonged to my great great grandmother. She is quite powerful, having scryed for my family in the old country for over two hundred years."

I guessed it was impressive for a fake psychic from Brooklyn, with questionable Romanian roots, who told fortunes in rural Pennsylvania, to have an ancestral hunk of quartz.

She gathered the sphere from its wooden pedestal and rolled it in her hands. Her long fingers and bright nails circled and caressed the polished glass. Finally, she focused her eyes and stared into the orb for a long time.

"The vibrations are strong for you. I see you shall have a long, happy life with two beautiful children." She looked at me for a moment before peering back into her ball. "You vill be happy, but you must choose your man carefully."

She discontinued her voodoo and set the crystal back into its holder.

"If you are interested I could prepare a special tea for you. It vill help you to—"

"Do people buy into this?"

"My dear, the crystal never lies, but you must believe for the visions—"

I waggled my finger. "You should be ashamed of yourself."

Her shoulders slumped. Her speech took on a nasally quality and tripled in speed. "Hey, what's de big idea'r? What de hell yuh want from me? I'm just tryin' tuh make an honest livin'."

There was that New Yorker I knew resided in my

fraudulent fortune teller.

"Honest?"

"I gotta'r pay de rent, yeah? I add a little excitement tuh people's lives. A little romance, a little hope. What's so bad about dat?"

She had a point.

I took two newspaper clippings from my pocket and handed them to her. I figured the adage in for a penny, in for a pound, had its merits. Since I was already there, I might as well get my forty-five dollars worth. "What do you think of these?"

"Yuh a cawp?"

"No, a college professor."

People seemed to forgive me a lot the second I said I was a professor. Of course, she's asking questions of a prisoner. Of course, she's attempting to sneak into a crime scene. Of course, she's trying to fake out a medium. Of course, she knows local animal mooning laws. Isn't that normal professor behavior?

Madame looked at the papers. "Naw. I read about it. I tell fortunes. I don't dabble in murduh if dat's what you're askin.'"

"No," I said. "I wanted to see if any of your psychic bells went off."

"Thoughtcha were a nonbelievah, yeah?"

"I hoped you could help me. I wanted to believe."

"De kid was framed," she said.

"Why do you think that?"

"Dat'll costcha anudder forty-five."

I raised an eyebrow. "Ninety dollars?"

She nodded.

I folded the articles and put them into my pocket. I needed to cut my losses. She met me at the counter, where

I handed her fifty dollars and told her to keep the change. I opened the front door, and the bells tinkled.

"She was pregnant," Madame blurted out.

The police hadn't released that detail, so how had she known? I waited for her to elaborate.

Finally, she said, "I doan get nothin' else from her."

"Thank you for your time."

"Fawh what it's wort', ya mudder says tuh let go of ya anger, and ya grandmudder' says she can't talk through an old paintin'."

I pulled my hood over my head, closed the door, and sprinted to The Tank.

I was about fifty percent certain that Madame Alina had been a disappointing fraud.

Chapter 23

Lincoln didn't look up from his notebook when I entered his office. An assortment of boxes, crayons, index cards, and books littered his ordinarily neat desk. His normally wrinkle-free shirt hadn't been ironed. The immaculate Dr. Lincoln Harrison was utterly disheveled, and he looked like the stereotypical crazy professor.

I asked him when he had last slept. He finally looked at me, dismissed my question with the wave of his hand, and explained that we would be starting with an experiment in which he would hold up an index card, and I would tell him what color dot was on it. I sat across from him and settled in.

I stared at the back of the first card. "I don't know."

He held up another.

"I don't know."

He held up a third.

"I don't know."

He wrote something in his notebook. "Miranda, would you like to try to guess the color?"

"What are my choices?" I asked.

"Think of a box of basic children's crayons, and those are your choices."

I studied the colorful crayons scattered about his desk, and he showed the back of the fourth card.

"Red," I said.

"Very good." He smiled, placed the card face up on

his desk, then recorded something in his notebook.

I contemplated the upturned red dot because it had been a lucky guess.

He picked up a card, and I guessed green.

He placed it face down.

He held up a card and stared into my eyes. I think he was trying to read my mind.

I wrinkled my nose. "Blue."

He frowned and placed the card facedown.

"Yellow."

Facedown.

"Colors can repeat," he told me.

"Okay. Good to know. Red."

Facedown.

I closed my eyes and concentrated with all my might. "Purple!"

Facedown.

He took off his glasses and rubbed his bloodshot eyes. "You have a ten percent correct response rate. Let's move on."

"Wait. Lincoln, that isn't how it works."

"How does it work?"

"Hold up a card," I said.

He lifted one high.

"Picture it in your head, and don't tell me what it is." I took off my gloves. "Picturing it?"

Wide-eyed, he nodded.

I couldn't reach him from my seat, so I stood, leaned across the desk, and placed my hand on his wrist. "Green."

He raised an eyebrow and placed the card face up. He held up another.

"Black," I declared.

He placed it face up.

"Yellow."

He turned the card over to look at the back of it, then lifted it into the light.

I laughed. "I can't see through it."

Looking thoughtful, he placed it face up and then kept going until he eventually said, "Ten out of ten. One hundred percent accuracy. Amazing." He tapped his cheek in thought. "Put on your gloves."

I did as he said.

He pointed at his wrist where my hand had been. "Now try."

"I can't do it as well wearing gloves."

"Try."

After we went through the exercise again, four of the index cards lay face up.

"Forty percent," he announced. "Why do you wear them?"

"They seem to muffle my ability to read minds. It feels slimy to lurk around in people's brains. Plus, I become exhausted if I'm constantly bombarded with other people's thoughts and feelings."

"Interesting. Very interesting." Lincoln ran his hand through his wild white hair.

He unwrapped a pack of fifty-two playing cards, and we repeated the experiment. I earned a zero percent staring at the back of the cards, a one-hundred percent touching his bare skin, and a fifty percent touching him with my gloved hand.

I remained silent while he took notes.

He set his pen down. "Miranda, this is mind-blowing. I'm not sure what it means, but it has to mean something."

"I think so, too. For years, I told myself it was intuition, but it's something else, don't you think?"

He didn't answer.

"My journalism class starts in fifteen minutes. I have to go," I told him.

Lincoln fixated on his notebook.

"Bye, Lincoln. Get some sleep. You look terrible."

He was too absorbed in his thoughts to notice my departure.

****

Knowing that my students trusted me enough to come to me for advice was a mixed blessing. Although validating my need to feel appreciated, it also meant my words were weighted, and my opinion became gospel. At the age of twenty-five, the expectation was I become one with the wisdom of the universe.

The bottom line was, I was still concentrating on making sure I showed up to work in clean underwear and praying that I had remembered to put on deodorant.

I took on responsibility for the young adults in Bellmount with gusto, while common sense for my personal life regressed at warp speed. I attributed most of my issues to the repugnant cop, who had pulled me off the smooth road leading to my new life and forced me onto an uncharted treacherous path.

Following class, Liza came to me for advice.

"Dr. Albright, I overheard my parents talking. My father told Suzy that she had to have an abortion, and if she disobeyed, she was never allowed back in the house. He threatened to cut the baby out if she refused, and he believes anyone who has an abortion is going to hell. How could he do that to her?"

There is no easy way to tell another human being that

someone they love is a monster.

"My father said that if the reporter prints that Suzy was pregnant, he will call forth a plague of locusts on the county. He says he knows the baby was Skyler's, and he wants him to burn in hell. Dr. Albright, someone strangled her, then mutilated her postmortem. I think there is more to it, but as I said, my parents received a redacted report, and my father refuses to request the complete autopsy. I don't know what he's afraid of finding out."

"Strangled?" I asked. "That's a new detail."

"I know this is stupid, considering how horrible it all is, but she had on my new bikini."

"What?" My vision of the corpse was disjointed, but I thought Suzy had been wearing underclothes and that someone had sliced the bra into pieces.

"She was wearing my pink-flowered bikini. I got upset because she was always taking my clothes without asking permission. I have no idea how I could care about something so frivolous. Maybe I'm jealous because Suzy was spoiled. She almost died when we were babies because she was born with this condition that premature twins sometimes have, called Bronchopulmonary Dysplasia. It made her susceptible to things like respiratory infections, so my mom became overprotective. Since I was physically stronger, our parents were harder on me, and Suzy got away with taking my things, partying, and staying out late." Liza wiped away a tear. "I wonder why she never confided in Mom or me that she was pregnant. Our mom would have forgiven her, and maybe if I had known, I could have helped. At least, I would have tried. I feel guilty. I don't know why, and I don't know what to do."

I dug deep and searched for the words that might bring Liza comfort. I told her that the mind does crazy things when a person you love dies. That when grieving, nothing seems to make any sense or have any rhyme or reason. To talk about her pain, let it out, forgive herself, and cry if she needed to.

Then I thought about my issues and Madame Alina's advice about letting go of my anger. Since there was a good chance she was a fraud, I decided to ignore Madame's advice. I shoved my pain under layers of skin and bone and blood. Once my little pellet of grief was pushed into its minuscule pocket, I returned to the task at hand.

But I filed that pretty bikini away in my memory. It had to be a clue.

Chapter 24

I was a master at multitasking. I could devour a spinach and tomato quiche, scratch Spot's ears, review notes for my morning lecture, and listen to Aunt Edith and Winona gossip as they prepared breakfast for the guests, all while having my morning coffee.

Russ entered the kitchen and tossed the paper onto the table in front of me. "The article's in *The Bellmount Gazette* this morning. Check out the front page."

Aunt Edith put down her spatula, and Winona turned off the stove. They gathered around me as we read P.T. Grimwood's newest article, "Recent Murder Victim Two Months Pregnant."

"He ended up writing it," Aunt Edith said.

"I don't think Pat had a choice. The problem is, everyone seems to want to cover up the facts of this case. Shultz's bumbling antics held up the investigation. The mayor and his attorney encouraged Skyler to plead guilty. The homicide detective cut corners because he's lazy, and I think he was trying to appease everyone who wanted the case closed. The official autopsy took weeks to release, and Suzy's father tried to cover up that she was pregnant. When will the lies end? Someone has to tell the truth," I said.

Aunt Edith sighed. "I know you're right, Miranda. But I can't grasp why even Detective Miller dismissed the case so easily."

"Who knows, maybe he believes he got the right guy. What I can tell you is, Skyler's still pleading guilty despite my encouraging him to tell the truth. If you meet him, you can't help but dislike him. He's deplorable; so awful, you want him to be guilty." I was rationalizing because the truth was, I agreed with Aunt Edith.

"A statement on our current judicial system that confessing to a crime you didn't commit brings you more justice than a fair trial," Aunt Edith said.

"Do you think the baby's father was a Satanist?" asked Winona.

"Winona, it isn't a cult murder for crying out loud. It's a copycat staged to look like the cult crucifixions, but the killer was too witless to get the details correct." It was the millionth time I had explained this to my addle-brained friend.

"Unless they do know what a crucifixion is, and they are trying to throw everyone off." She tapped a finger to her temple. "Or they couldn't get a cross."

I rolled my eyes. At times Winona could be almost as unbearable as her impossible cousin, with his stupid, pretty eyes.

"If you ask me, it seems like someone wanted to keep her quiet about the pregnancy," Aunt Edith said. "I think it would have to be someone who had something to lose by getting a twenty-one-year-old pastor's daughter pregnant."

"I know, which means it has to be someone rich, married, or afraid of Pastor Smith," I added.

"Unless it was the pastor himself," Winona said, "and he wanted to make it look like the devil had something to do with it."

In her enthusiasm to be helpful, Winona often threw

her theories about with the discretion of a hyperactive octopus. I glowered at her.

"Miranda, Winona could be correct. I wouldn't put it past Smith. He has a cruel streak in him, and he can't stand to look bad in front of his flock," my aunt said.

"Believe me, I have considered him. Have you ever been to his church, Aunt Edith?"

"No, but he has a huge following. A few hundred parishioners in this county make him a powerful man."

"I went once or twice," Russ said. "He was too much for me. All that hellfire and damnation stuff scared the shit out of me. If I'm goin' to hell, I don't need someone remindin' me of it on a weekly basis."

"I know someone who went to Smith's church," Winona said. Then she stared into space.

I held my breath, waiting for her to elaborate. When she didn't, I asked, "Who do you know that has been there?"

Winona brought a hand to her heart. "Well, my tooth fell out. I was only about six, seven, or maybe eight, and I had this piggy bank I loved. It was pink, and I could see straight through it and count my money. It didn't have one of those rubber stoppers. You had to smash it if you wanted your money out."

Russ studied his plate and took a bite of quiche.

"Winona, what does that have to do with Pastor Smith's church?" I asked.

"My dad was gambling so much my mom called him 'a shit for brains crapshooter.'"

"Okay," I said. "Did your dad break your piggy bank and use the money to pay his gambling bets and then have to go to church to ask for forgiveness?"

"For Pete's sake, no." Aghast, she held both hands to

her heart. "Dad would never break that piggy bank. He knew I loved it. "

I tried to shake the bewilderment from my brain. It didn't help, so I opted for honesty. "I'm confused, Winona."

"My dad gambled away all of the money, so when my tooth fell out, my mom had to break the piggy bank and steal my coins to put under my pillow. She lost all our hammers, so she broke them with her clog. I wasn't supposed to see it, but I did, and I cried."

A headache formed behind my right eye. "Well, I guess you at least got your money back when the tooth fairy came?"

"Oh no, Felix, our old three-legged tomcat ate my tooth, so I never got the money."

"A three-legged cat ate your tooth?" I asked.

"Yeah, Felix was so sick. He threw up all over the house."

I gritted my teeth. "A tiny tooth made Felix throw up?"

"No, he also ate a dead rat. The medicine was pretty expensive, so my mom had to use the tooth fairy money to pay the vet bill."

Aunt Edith wiped the crumbs from the table.

"Did your mom feel so bad about everything that went wrong that she had to go to church to pray?" I asked.

"No, Miranda. Weren't you listening? My mom says she'll never go to Smith's. She thinks he is a moralizing son of a bitch."

Russ rinsed his plate and put it in the sink.

"I'm trying to listen, Winona, but I still don't understand what your broken piggy bank, gambling father, loose tooth, and vomiting cat have to do with

Pastor Smith."

"My Aunt Ida is the one who bought me the piggy bank."

I rubbed my temple. Aunt Edith looked at the ceiling fan, and Russ stared at the refrigerator.

"So your Aunt Ida went to the church?" I asked.

"Yes, Miranda, jeez." She eyeballed me like I was the one who had spewed the absurd bunch of nonsense. "Aunt Ida agreed with Mom that Smith is a 'moralizing son-of-bitch,' so she only went once."

I considered explaining to Winona that she could have avoided the entire painful story and just told me the last line. Instead, I sighed.

"Plus, I think most people in town have gone to the church. But not Dad. He doesn't gamble anymore, and he hates Smith. And not Mom, or Uncle Pop, or West, or Willa, or me or…"

I stopped listening. My mind was whirling.

"Winona, want to go to Smith's church on Sunday?" I asked.

She bounced on her toes. "Are you kidding? Of course! Do I get to question people?"

"It's a horrible idea since that man wants my head on a platter beside John the Baptist's."

She clasped her hands together and hopped from one foot to the other.

I held a palm in the air. "Winona, we are observing. No questioning people. Got it?"

Her shoulders slumped, and her bottom lip jutted out. I had learned my lesson at the fraternity house; Winona needed to be kept occupied.

"You can take notes, though."

Her eyes brightened, and her upturned lips consumed

her face.

I was sliding my lesson plans into my backpack when I saw another interesting article. "Aunt Edith, is Ian Patterson officially announcing his bid for Congress tomorrow?"

"Yes, he's throwing his first campaign party, invitation only. He asked the town council to attend. A political move on his part, so we lead the community in backing him, but I don't think I'm going. I abhor the man. I don't know who else is going, but I know that Smith won't be there. He has already declined."

"Do you have two tickets?" I asked.

"Yes. Why?"

"I'm not goin'," Russ declared. "I don't do black-tie affairs."

"Black-tie?" I asked.

"It's at the Patterson Estate. Should be quite hoity-toity," Aunt Edith said.

"Aunt Edith, why don't you go? You can harass Patterson a bit, keep him on his toes, and I'll be your date."

She contemplated my proposal. "Harassing Patterson sounds like fun. Maybe I can annoy Grainey while I'm at it?"

"Yep! Bonus. Is it a date?" I swung my bag over my shoulder.

My aunt wore a twisted grin. "Bing. Bang. Bong. Let's torment some men!"

"Will Bradley Gordon be at the party?" Winona asked.

I scowled. "Winona, after what happened with Jessica Grainey and Kyle Patterson, why would Brad go?"

"He's on the town council." She smiled as she bobbed her head. "And to see you in your new gown."

"What are you talking about? I don't have a new gown."

Winona's head continued to bob about. "Not yet, you don't. Pick me up when you get off work. I know the perfect place to find one."

"Winona, no," I pleaded.

It was no use. Winona Westinghouse rubbed her hands together as if she was concocting a plan for world domination.

Chapter 25

Spot thought I looked like a sparkly toy. He was correct. My gown was to die for. A slit came to the middle of my left thigh and showed off my three-inch midnight blue pumps. The blue sequined fabric hugged my curves and gracefully slid off my shoulders. The matching gloves looked like something Eliza Doolittle would have worn to a ball.

I had painted my nails and lips a ruby red. I had also carefully applied make-up, added a few sprinkles of silver glitter, and pulled the left side of my hair up with a diamond clip. Hot rollers had turned my corkscrews into soft waves, and a pretty curl hung over my right shoulder. A few spritzes of Obsessive Love perfume added the finishing touch.

I needed to be fabulous if I was to get close to the untouchable Patterson men. I had to find out if one of them had been intimate with Suzy. I also needed Brad Gordon, the love of my life—if he was in attendance—to worship me from afar.

Winona wanted to see me in my slinky get-up before my night of sleuthing, so Edith and I stopped by the pub on our way out of town. My aunt waited in her normal-sized silver 1982 four-door sedan while I slid into the Westinghouse establishment.

When Pop and Uncle Will saw me, they both did a double-take and went wide-eyed.

"Holy guacamole!" Winona said. "You look unreal."

Feeling my oats, I turned around and posed.

"Dang, Miranda, I think half your body weight is in your boobs."

Leave it to Winona to humiliate me when I was feeling lovely.

Although I was still mad at West, I searched the bar for him. For some reason, I wanted him to see my glamorous gown, my fancy hair, and the extra inches I had added to my height. I was tired of him thinking I was an adorable hunk of cartoon dessert. Alas, he wasn't there. I smoothed my dress over my hips, frowned, and headed for the door.

I was about to climb into the car when West's black motorcycle pulled into the lot. He parked beside us and hung his helmet on the handle of his bike. I closed the car door and held my breath as I glided toward him.

The well-lit parking lot showcased him in a soft glow. His jeans were tucked into brown leather boots. The toes and heels were dark with wear, but the zippers along the sides were polished, and the laces in the front appeared new. The heels added to his five foot eleven inches so that even in my pumps, he towered above me. Four brass buckles shined at the waist of his matching jacket. The leather hugged his body and tapered inward to accentuate his muscular chest and lean torso.

"*Phwwwhht!* Dr. Shortcake! Where ya off to?"

If I had known how to whistle, and it wouldn't have been unseemly, I would have returned his catcall. Instead, I said, "The Patterson campaign party. Winona helped me pick out the dress and wanted to see me in it."

"Date?" he asked.

"Yes," I answered.

West sucked in his top lip.

"Aunt Edith is my date."

"Phew." He wiped the invisible sweat from his brow. "You look incredible." He followed it with a loud, "Damn." He capped off the dramatic performance with another whistle.

His gaze roamed up and down my body before settling on my lips. "I like the lipstick."

I looked at my shoes, suddenly ashamed that I had gone out of my way to seek his approval.

"I like it all." He leaned over and sniffed me. "Especially the way you smell." His voice had dropped a few octaves. It reverberated in my most intimate areas.

"I have to go," I said, desiring the safety of my aunt's automobile.

"Don't break any more hearts tonight," he called after me.

"Any more?"

"You already broke mine." He placed both of his hands on his heart and pumped his chest.

My breath caught. I opened the door and attempted to make a graceful descent into my seat. I was about to close it when West's arm intervened.

"Hi Edith," he said, leaning his head into the car.

"Hi, Weston."

"Keep an eye on this one." He pointed at me as his body invaded my space. "She has fire in her blood tonight."

"She keeps me busy. You have a good night," Aunt Edith said.

"Have fun, Shortcake. Don't do anything I wouldn't do." West gave me his I-know-I'm-so-sexy-you-had-to-parade-around-in-your-designer-gown-to-keep-up smile and closed the passenger side door.

A switch fired inside of me, and from out of nowhere, I was livid—downright, totally, outrageously furious. The fool had been taunting me and didn't think I was pretty in the least. At least I thought he had been teasing, but how could I tell when he was never serious and always cocky?

"That boy has fire in his blood, too," Aunt Edith said as we drove off, leaving Weston Westinghouse the Third smirking in The Bear Claw Pub's parking lot.

****

To get to the Patterson estate, Aunt Edith drove to the outskirts of town and up a steep and winding, tree-lined driveway. We were greeted by a gold fountain that sported water spurting from a naked cherub's arrow. Three valets sucker-punched each other until one won the battle. He said hello, winked at me, and then took Aunt Edith's keys. A seemingly seasoned butler led us into the palatial mansion.

The marble and gold front hallway was sparse except for the gilded wall sconces. A side staircase curved to the second floor, and a garish four-tiered chandelier hung from the center of the great room. Aunt Edith and I followed servers carrying trays of food up the stairs.

"Oh, my." I leaned toward Aunt Edith and whispered, "This is so…" I was at a loss for words.

"Nouveau-riche."

"I mean, wow!"

At the top of the stairwell, Aunt Edith turned toward me. "Bing. Bang. Bong!" she said.

"Make 'em sweat."

We curtsied in jest, high-fived, and parted ways, to divide and conquer. My classy aunt entered that ballroom as if she were queen of the world. I stopped short and gawked like a fool.

In the corner of the ostentatious room, a five-man ensemble played background music. Once I closed my mouth, I searched for Brad. Instead, I caught the gaze of the handsome middle-aged Greg Grainey. He stood in the corner of the room, talking to a group of women.

He placed his hand on the shoulder of the one standing next to him. She wore a glittering gold gown that would have been fabulous except for the absurd shoulder pads that overshadowed her long slender neck and made her look like she was in a million-dollar space suit. She topped off her evening attire by teasing her dark hair until it almost reached the ceiling. The resemblance was uncanny; she had to be Jessica Grainey's mother.

Greg kissed her on the cheek and sauntered my way. He tracked me with each step he took. I shivered, ashamed that I found the overly tan and well-built Greg Grainey to be alluring. To be fair, I also thought he was despicable.

"Hello, Ms. Albright," he said, extending his hand.

"Dr. Albright." I placed my gloved hand in his palm.

Correcting his greeting in any other circumstance would have been highly crass, but I knew he was searching for power in our conversation. That was the type of man he was.

"But please call me Miranda." I smiled.

He drew my name out, rolling it over his tongue. "My crimson princess, the evening was dull until you arrived. Now I have something to occupy me. You look spectacular."

He was correct about one thing. It was a dull evening for anyone who wasn't hobnobbing or sleuthing. I may have been the only person in the room under thirty-five, which meant the younger generation of Bellmount Bitches, Patterson's sons, and Bradley Gordon were not currently in attendance.

"Thank you, but your wife is quite lovely." I inclined my chin toward the shiny woman in the corner.

He studied her, and appearing disinterested, said, "Yes, Louisa is lovely."

Then his gaze traveled back to me. I found it odd that while Greg Grainey stood in the corner, undressing me with his eyes, his wife remained on the other side of the room, either oblivious or not caring.

"How do you like your new firearm?" He chuckled.

Who could blame him for being amused? A sane person should laugh when thinking about my ridiculous Princess.

"Love her!" I tossed my hair over my shoulder in a coquettish attempt to flirt with the playboyish-man who was old enough to be my father.

"Have you learned to shoot?" He moved into my personal space and peered down the front of my dress, transitioning from provocatively sexy to overly aggressive in mere moments.

Still, I continued my ruse. How wonderful it would be if his daughter got news of my flirty friendship with her father. "I shot West Westinghouse in the buttocks."

His eyes widened. "Senior or junior?"

"You haven't heard? I thought everyone knew. Junior." I smiled as I recalled West hopping around outside of Tommy's pick-up truck. "He's okay, though. He blubbered like a big baby, but I barely grazed him." Since I was once again irritated with West, I didn't mention that I had also blubbered.

Greg snorted. "I avoid gossip since I'm often the featured star. Unless it is in the newspaper, I ignore it." Then his face lit with joy. "Was Weston the Third getting a bit too friendly with the most fascinating woman in Bellmount?"

I didn't think Greg would appreciate that my beer can target had a pretend picture of his daughter with bullet holes in place of her eyes. So I left that part of the story out. "I don't know about that, but he stepped in front of my target."

"I knew we were meant to be friends." He leaned closer, and our bodies almost touched.

I took a moment to giggle at my newest fantasy. Jessica could call me mommy right before I shot her with Princess.

Once again, feeling self-conscious, I looked out over the room of about seventy guests. Many seemed to be watching Greg Grainey in the corner with the young redhead, but his wife wasn't one of them.

"Which man is Ian Patterson?" Although I had seen Ian once, I thought all of the older men in their black coats looked alike.

Greg studied my mouth. "You have a gorgeous smile. And those lips!"

Note to self: the ruby lipstick might be a keeper.

"Patterson?"

He shifted positions so that he stood beside me. "The old man over there." He pointed to a distinguished-looking man in his sixties.

"Would you introduce me?"

"But then I'd have to share you."

I fluttered my eyelashes. "But, Greg, I'm not yours to share."

He pushed out his bottom lip and crossed his arms over his chest. "Fine. Come on."

"I'd also like to meet Patterson's sons," I said as we trekked across the room.

"Obnoxious little bastards, but fine."

I would have loved to ask him if they were more obnoxious than his horrible daughter but instead concentrated on not falling off my three-inch heels and breaking my nose.

Greg interrupted Ian's group of good ol' boys.

"Excuse me, gentlemen; I would like to introduce you to Dr. Miranda Albright, our newest citizen."

I shook hands with each of the men, including Dean Johnson.

"Hello, Miranda." Johnson's gaping mouth seemed to indicate surprise at seeing me.

Even the confidence I felt in my sparkles couldn't dull my intimidation around my gruff boss. I had no idea how Keisha was so composed around him.

Greg excused himself to join his beckoning wife, who was now cornered by Aunt Edith. "I'll be right back, Crimson, don't go anywhere." He turned to Patterson. "Take good care of her while I'm gone."

"If you gentlemen will excuse me, I'd like to take some time to get to know my new constituent," Ian said.

The men said their goodbyes, leaving me alone to question my next suspect.

"Constituent?" I asked. "Isn't that a bit bold with the election still over a year away?"

"I'm a man of vision. I reach for the stars and accept nothing less."

A waitress dressed in black and white resembling a penguin waddled past, and Patterson grabbed a glass of wine from her tray. He offered one to me. I declined, afraid I might spill something on my too-expensive gown.

"So, you are the lovely Miranda Albright who has all of Bellmount abuzz," Patterson said.

"Abuzz?"

"I take it upon myself to know everything that goes on in this town. Apparently, in your short time here, you have discovered a corpse and pissed off the local sheriff, the town's religious leader, and the mayor." He took a sip. "You have enchanted our young doctor, and our smitten park ranger's job is currently in jeopardy. You also have a reporter in the palm of your hand, and he is sneaking you into prison interviews. Shall I go on?"

I was speechless.

"You shot young Westinghouse where the sun doesn't shine with some sort of controversial weapon, and you have Greg Grainey publicly drooling like a horny schoolboy. Normally Grainey has the decency to keep his little crushes private, but you are leading him around by his dick." He regarded Greg, now surrounded by his wife and the female *crème de la crème* of Bear County society.

"I'm afraid you give my influence too much credit." I tried to appear confident. The truth was I was trying to decide if I would prefer death by hungry piranhas or angry hornets.

"I'm afraid there's more. The ill-tempered Johnson can't stop gushing. Much to my chagrin, he has informed me that you are quite a promising instructor, your students adore and respect you, and the school paper is running well."

Was the statement an insult or a compliment?

"And for the grand finale, all of the single women in Bellmount—and even some of the married ones—want you tarred and feathered."

I wanted to run from the room, hop into The Tank, and return home to my father. Instead, I said, "Would you expect anything less from Edith Marshall's niece?"

Ian pointed. "Speaking of enchanted doctors…"

My gaze followed his outstretched finger. Dr. Brad Gordon had entered the room, and he stole my breath. Sharing the room with him was like being in the presence of Rhett Butler or Mr. Darcy.

Oh my God, Heathcliff's twin brother kissed me.

Brad's gaze settled on me, and he grabbed a glass of wine from a nearby tray. The bow-tied magnificent mountain of a man seemed to fill the entire room. I studied my bare thigh and tried to hide that my face was on fire.

I willed my cheeks back to their normal color and focused my attention on Patterson. "If you know everything that goes on in this town, tell me, who do you think murdered Suzy Smith? Because it wasn't Skyler Dubbs."

I was disappointed with my choice of gloves. Although they were elegant, there was no way to remove them in a public place without looking like some sort of striptease. My wardrobe snafu left me at the mercy of my unenhanced intuition.

Patterson ran his tongue over his teeth. "Young lady, you need to be careful with questions that sound a lot like accusations. You're treading on thin ice and pissing off a lot of people. I'm not fond of your aunt, but I tolerate her, which is more than I can say about how I will treat you. You may have the men of Bellmount kneeling at your feet, but I'm not one of them. I would just as soon have you return to wherever it is you came from."

Brad and Greg approached and broke into twin frowns when they reached us at the same time.

"Come on, Crimson." Greg turned to Ian. "Dr. Albright would like an introduction to your sons. I understand they are in the game room."

Patterson held his index finger up, studied it, then pointed it in my face. "My sons are off-limits to you, Ms. Albright. Heed my warning." Then he directed his attention to Brad. "If you will excuse me, Dr. Gordon." He glowered at Greg, then walked away.

Ian Patterson left me standing between two awkwardly silent men, once family, now enemies—and they had just witnessed my callous dismissal by the town's most powerful man.

I broke the silence. "Hi, Brad. It's good to see you."

"You look breathtaking," he said.

Having none of our long-lost lover's conversations, Greg grabbed me and escorted me from the room.

We found the Patterson Brothers hiding out in what looked like an All-American rec room on anabolic steroids. The masculine space contained ping pong, pool and foosball tables, a miniature basketball hoop, and a loaded entertainment center. There were shelves of equestrian trophies and ornately framed pictures of horses everywhere.

A game of pool consumed the brothers. They looked similar, except the taller one was dressed in a tuxedo, and the longer-haired one wore jeans and a sweater. Both were exceedingly handsome and appeared to be in their late twenties.

"Grainey," the one in the sweater said in passive acknowledgment of our arrival.

Greg propped himself against a brown leather chair.

"Gentleman, Miranda Albright would like to make your acquaintance."

The one in the tux concentrated on eyeing up a pool shot, so he ignored us.

The other said, "Bringing us another present?"

Greg was correct. They were beastly men. I bristled and took off my gloves in case I wanted to do a reading or punch one of them in his snotty upturned nose.

"Excuse me for interrupting your game, gentlemen. I am Dr. Albright. I'm a college professor, not a hooker or a present."

The one eyeing his shot finally looked at me. "Liam Marshall's cousin?"

"Yes." I pulled my shoulders back.

"The one dating Doc Gordon?" the brother in the sweater asked.

"Well, yes. I was dating Brad Gordon."

"I heard you shot Westinghouse in the ass with a fancy gun." Sweater boy shook my ungloved hand. "Congrats! I'm Mitch, pleased to meet you."

"Hi, Mitch," I said.

The one in the tux put down his pool stick and extended his hand. "Kyle."

So, this was the infamous Kyle Patterson, who had the affair with Jessica Grainey. He had blond hair, blue eyes, an athletic build, and reeked of money.

"Grainey, why don't you get us a bottle of Scotch from the kitchen? Charles has cut us off until we join the party. He'll give it to you, though," Kyle said.

"Don't worry, old man. She's in good hands. Hurry up," Mitch added.

As soon as Greg was out the door, Kyle turned to me. "I hate that cocksucker and his bitch of a daughter. What are you doing with him?"

One thing was for sure, in the Bellmount hierarchy, the Pattersons seemed to be at the very top, and the rest of us were so far beneath it pained them to share the air.

"Do you play, Miranda?" Mitch asked.

I shook my head.

"Here, take my shot." He rubbed chalk onto his stick and handed it to me. "You want to hit this ball into this ball and knock that ball into there."

"I might mess up your game."

"No worries," Mitch said. "We haven't bet much, only the car."

"What?" I asked.

Mitch's eyes gleamed with mirth. "I'm kidding. Kyle has already won all my cars. I just steal them back."

I set my gloves on a side table, and Mitch encouraged me to prepare for my shot. I took my time, settled in, and stuck the tip right into the green fabric that covered the table.

"Ouch," Mitch hollered. "Try again."

"Why did you want to meet us?" Kyle asked.

I held the long stick into the air and eyed it with contempt. "I might need help getting this pole correct."

"You mean cue?" Mitch laughed.

Mitch was definitely the friendlier of the two. He came around behind me and helped me steady the cue. He smelled heavenly. Undoubtedly, a man this rich could afford the most decadent spicy colognes. My backside was pressed into his body, his face was beside mine, and our gazes were lined up. His fingers gently rubbed mine as he guided my hand into position.

I procrastinated on my shot. His cheek touched mine.

"Maybe you've heard, I found Suzy Smith's body on

176

the way into town."

Mitch Patterson was unfazed by my mention of Suzy. He was much more interested in me since *she has a sweet round ass.* My pool stick made contact with a ball, and another ball headed toward a side pocket.

"Better." Mitch held onto me longer than our shot required. "The paper said they caught the guy who did it."

My hand brushed Mitch's arm one last time.

Like father, like son. Kyle Patterson was not in any way interested in me, and getting him to brush up against me would take a ton of work. If I ripped my dress, I was going to cry my eyes out.

I glided past him, feigned a trip, and fell into Kyle's arms. As he steadied me, I held onto him, acting like a simpering helpless damsel.

"Oh, thank you. Did you know Suzy Smith?" He tried to back away, but I lost my balance, falling into him again.

"These shoes and the champagne." I giggled and looked up at him through fluttering eyelashes.

Neither of us enjoyed my acting farce in the least.

He stared at me with the same haughty eyes as his father. "Yeah. Her dad is an absolute bastard. Why are you asking?" Kyle pictured Suzy, had a moment of irritation, put distance between us, and continued with his game.

I slinked to his side, caressed his arm, and set my trap. "I heard you dated her."

"You heard wrong. I'm not into college girls."

He pulled his arm out from under mine and prepared for another shot. *Click. Click. Click.* Stick and balls made contact, and he strode to the other side of the table.

He eyed me skeptically. "Why do you want to know?"

"I think I may have a bit of post-traumatic stress disorder from seeing the murder scene. I tend to obsess about it." I made up the statement, but it stuck in my mind, and while bouncing around, it took on a life of its own.

I considered falling into Kyle again, but Greg entered the room, followed by a man carrying a tray of alcohol. The uniformed man, who I assumed was the official Patterson butler, prepared four drinks, then stood and stared.

"What do you need now, Charles?" the oldest Patterson asked.

"Gentlemen, your father is about to make his speech. Master Mitchell, please make haste and put on something acceptable. I have laid your tuxedo on your bed. Your father expects you both to be in attendance."

"Shit," Mitch said. Then he added, "Thanks, Chuck, old man."

Kyle rolled his eyes.

Greg grabbed one of the glasses containing yellow liquid. "Time to go."

I put on my gloves because I looked more elegant in them, and I didn't want a single one of Greg Grainey's perverted thoughts to enter me.

Once we were outside the game room, Kyle said, "What the hell? I heard she was sweet. But she was trampy and all over us."

"Who gives a shit? Did you see those tits?" said Mitch.

Horrified, I froze in my tracks and stared into space.

"Didn't I tell you they were horrible little beasts?" Greg gulped the contents of his glass in one swig. "I hate Kyle, that home-wrecking bastard."

He used the back of his hand to wipe away the last of his Scotch, then Greg Grainey hurried me along.

A few minutes later, when he cornered me in an isolated room and pressed his lips on mine, my evening surged past hideous and became nightmarish. Greg was oblivious that my pushes, slaps, and kicks meant he needed to get away from me. I broke free and was clicking for the door when Brad Gordon entered the room.

"Brad," I cried, putting him between the red-faced gun peddler and myself.

"What's going on?" Brad asked.

"None of your god-damn business, Gordon," Greg growled.

"I'd like to go home," I said.

Brad shot Greg a look that contained shrapnel and glass. The doctor put his arm around my shoulders, escorted me out of the horrific party, and placed me in the front seat of his car. "Did that son-of-a-bitch hurt you?"

"No," I answered.

A clenched fist hung by Brad's side. "Did he touch you?"

"After his encounter with my shoe, I doubt he will ever come near me again. Would you please find Aunt Edith? I'm okay, but I want to go home."

I locked the car door, and Brad went back into the bowels of hell to find my aunt.

I hated my new dress with a passion! I kicked off my shoes and stretched and wriggled my toes as they screamed in happiness at their newfound freedom. I removed my gloves and folded them into a small square. My diamond hairpiece was giving me a headache, so I unclipped it and massaged my scalp so I could think.

My hellish evening had barely given me any information. I knew that Mitch Patterson had nothing to do with the murder. The problem was divining any information from Kyle or Ian had been impossible. I had to rely on my actual intuition, and it was telling me they were hideous men who saw people as commodities. I could see Kyle getting a girl from the wrong side of the tracks pregnant and dumping her. It wasn't too much of a stretch to believe that his father might find out and have her killed. But they were powerful and above reproach, and if I couldn't get near them, how could I possibly know for sure?

Brad returned ten minutes later. "Edith asked me to take you home. She said she was finishing an important conversation. Is that okay?"

I knew Aunt Edith would never have put an "important conversation" before me. She was probably intent on giving me time alone with Brad.

"Of course," I said.

He surveyed me, and the corners of his lips turned downward. I think he was taking in my disheveled hair and my pathetic frowny face. He ran his fingers through his hair then started the car.

We drove to the inn in silence. I stared out the window, drawing little circles on the glass with my index finger, as he concentrated on the road. It wasn't until we pulled up in front of our destination that he spoke.

"Winona Westinghouse called me this afternoon."

I cringed. "Why?"

"To tell me that you had a new gown and that I should go to the party to see it."

"Winona," I mumbled. "I'm sorry." My face felt like a flame had torched it.

"I'm not. You look beautiful." He tapped on his steering wheel. "She also informed me Jessica has been tormenting you."

I closed my eyes and sucked in a breath. "I'm a bit embarrassed at the moment, Brad."

"I suppose that somehow Jessica has led you to believe that I have feelings for her, and there is still hope for our marriage. For the record, I don't, and there is none. But now I understand your reaction on our last date."

I drew another circle with my finger before turning to him. "I behaved atrociously tonight."

"In what way?"

"I'm not sure how much you know, although it appears everyone in this town knows every move I make—every move everyone makes. I've been obsessed with Suzy Smith's murder. Tommy Little and I went back to the scene to see what we could find. As you know, there were inconsistencies in the incident reports. I also accompanied a reporter to see Skyler Dubbs in prison. The kid was framed, and he is being forced to plead guilty."

"I've heard things," Brad said.

"When I say obsessed, I mean really obsessed. I came to the party tonight determined to get information on the Pattersons because someone got Suzy pregnant, and I suspect that person had her murdered to shut her up. One of my clues led me to the Patterson men. Ian all but threatened me, and Kyle called me a tramp. Mitch commented that Greg had brought them another gift."

"He was probably referring to Grainey introducing them to my ex-wife."

"Oh," I said, feeling the fool for my *faux pas*. "The

most repulsive part was that I flirted with Greg all night. I used him to get information on the Pattersons. I played with fire, and I got burnt. I was no match for those hideous men."

"I get it. I had to rebuild my life by the time they were through with me. Now, with your aunt's help, I stand up to them every chance I get."

"I suppose you do understand." I smiled at him. "Bradley Gordon, you have a way of always coming to my rescue and making everything okay."

"Glad my misfortunes can perk you up." His warm laugh and sweet dimples almost made my awful evening fade away.

"You seem too good to be true," I said.

"I'm hardly perfect. I married into a hideous family, and I often forget to buy groceries, so I have to eat a lot of subs."

"*Pft.*" I flicked my wrist. "That's nothing."

"Would you like to hear me sing? I'm tonedeaf. Every dog in Bellmount will howl. Oh, and my feet stink when I'm nervous, and I sweat. Want to smell them?" he asked with a silly grin.

"Ew. Not today, but good to know." I pinched my nostrils. "Are you nervous right now?" I teased.

"Terribly! Apparently, I can't kiss worth a damn since the girl I'm crazy about looks like she has seen a ghost and runs away every time I try to kiss her."

His comment was unexpected, and a humbling honesty poured out of me.

"Brad, your kisses are delicious, like a wonderful drug!" I grabbed his hand. "I'm so awkward around men. I spent so much time studying that I never learned how to act around them."

"You got my attention by being yourself."

"It's more than that. When I say I'm awkward, I mean, I've never had a boyfriend or gone on a date. Tommy took me turtle hunting when I was a teenager, but that doesn't count since we've been hanging out hunting amphibians and reptiles since I was four. Brad, what I am trying to tell you is, you were my first kiss."

"Oh," he said.

"I'm a twenty-five-year-old bookworm virgin, with a thing for the most handsome, sought-after man in town. I'm complete bumbling butterfingers whenever you're near."

He rubbed two fingers along my cheek. I was overwhelmed by every emotion swirling through him and traveling into me. He was thinking about how he was falling hard for a sweet woman who had taken on an entire town and how it made him want to throw caution to the wind.

"I knew you were special the moment I saw you on the side of that road," he said.

"Me and my sexy vomit." I wrinkled my nose.

"Stop," he whispered, lifting my chin. "Kiss me, Dr. Albright. That's all you have to do. Now, just kiss me until I can't think."

"You kiss me, Dr. Gordon," I demanded, my fingers threading through his hair.

I considered how I might gracefully straddle him in my evening dress when Aunt Edith's car pulled in behind us.

"I better go." I kissed him one last time as I prepared to leave his car.

"The Harvest Festival? Will you still be my date?"

I cooed into his ear, "Only if you promise to kiss

every inch of me before the end of the festival."

Before he could respond, I jumped out of the car and headed to the inn.

"Hey, sweetheart," he called, stepping out of his car. "I promise." He placed his hand on his heart.

I smiled and waved and may have done a ridiculous hop that resembled an Irish jig in heels.

"I've been thinking if the murderer wanted to hide that Suzy was pregnant, why cut out her heart? Why not cut out her uterus?" he asked.

Hmm, good point!

Chapter 26

At least three hundred worshippers attended The First Evangelical Christian Church every Sunday to witness a fire and brimstone spectacular. Pastor Gabriel Smith's congregation was guaranteed to be treated as condemned sinners and promised the opportunity to spend eternity in the fiery pits of hell.

I'm not sure what it said about the population of Bear County that hundreds of people choose conflagration over a quiet morning drinking coffee and reading the Sunday paper in their pjs. I'm also not sure what it said about Winona Westinghouse and Keisha Brown that they chose to spend a Sunday morning with a friend who brought them nothing but trouble.

Gabriel Smith had taken over an old stone church that had been part of Bellmount's landscape since 1812. Over the years, it had also been a Lutheran and a Methodist church. Each denomination had contributed to the structure. From the front, one felt like they were about to meet God. From the back, the disjointed architecture made one feel that they were about to enter a den of iniquity.

Pastor Smith added a nasty bric-a-brac to the majestic building when he hung a neon sign that read, *Jesus Saves,* below the Gothic steeple.

The girls and I sat twelve rows from the pulpit. I attempted to look inconspicuous as we waited for the service to begin.

"Did Bradley show up last night?" Winona asked.

"Shh," I said.

"Yes or no?"

"Yes."

"How was he dressed? Did he have on a tux? Was there dancing?"

"Shh! Show some respect, you two. This is a house of worship," Keisha said, causing more of a distraction than the whispering Winona.

"You and Bradley are like Maddie and David, like Romeo and Juliet, like—"

"Maddie and David?" I asked.

"It's such a romantic show." Winona stared wistfully into the distance.

"Well, we are nothing like Romeo and Juliet. They were teenagers who drank—"

"Shh. Look!" Keisha pointed. "That's the Waltons."

Holly Walton's bleached blonde hair could be seen from Mars. She sat between her hydrogen-peroxided mother and her graying father.

"The Schusters are sitting right next to them," Winona said.

I didn't see Gina and wondered if she was with my kiss-starved cousin.

In the three minutes of quiet that ensued, I studied the parishioners in their Sunday finery. I also took in the high ceilings and beam rafters of the grand building. The juxtaposition of the arched stained-glass windows against Smith's tacky felt and plastic interior decorating touches created a slightly confusing ambiance.

The hairs on the back of my neck rose, and I pivoted to see what had caused my disquiet. Greg Grainey and his gossiping wife sat four rows behind us. He smiled. I bristled. His lips parted. I squirmed.

Then he distinctly mouthed, "You are mine."

His smile was so wicked it sent shivers from my feet to my neck. My breath caught, and I faced forward.

Keisha hit my thigh. She pointed at a little boy who scooted down the aisle behind a woman I assumed was his mother. She continued to tap on me wildly and point at the boy. A tiny gray kitten with big blue eyes peeked out of the child's pocket. I alerted Winona, who was taking notes in her spiral notebook. I gestured to the kitten, and her face lit up. The boy gently pressed his pet's ears into their hideaway. Boy, mother, and kitty sat two rows in front of us.

"Oh, that can't go well," Keisha said.

Winona drew a kitten in her notebook.

The organ music began and built in intensity. I half expected Bela Lugosi to jump from the rafters and yell *Ta-da*. Instead, Pastor Smith paraded down the aisle in a long white robe. The considerable sleeves were consumed by large black crosses. Winona sketched them.

The pastor raised his arms toward heaven. The organ music crescendoed, then abruptly stopped. The spectators sat tall and leaned forward.

"The Bible tells us to praise the Lord by lifting our hands."

Hundreds of arms lifted, and the chorus of "Praise Jesus" rang out. Winona called out a bit late since she was concentrating on taking notes. Keisha and I kept our hands on our laps.

The pastor talked and talked, and the congregation praised and amened everything.

Winona highlighted what she thought were the key

points. *If there is no hell, there is to be no heaven. The same Christ that tells us of heaven with all of its rewards tells of us hell with its fiery horrors. If we are to ignore that hell exists, we frown on the work of our holy Lord Jesus.*

Smith banged his hands on his pulpit.

"Revelations 21:8 tells us:—'but the cowardly, the unbelieving, the vile, the murderers, the sexually immoral, those who practice magical arts, the idolaters, and all liars—they will be consigned to the fiery lake of burning sulfur. This is the—"

Then a loud *Skish! Skish! Meow!* startled Smith. His eyes widened, and he froze mid-fist pump.

The kitten leaped into the air and landed on a flowered Sunday hat. The woman screamed. The kitten reclined on her head, batting at an orange silk chrysanthemum.

The boy tried to pull his pet off the screaming woman. Finally, after much commotion, the child cuddled the furball in his arms and was ushered out of the church by his red-faced mother.

The entire room hushed, and Keisha's booming laugh rang through the rafters. Smith's gaze found her. Then he spied me. His face, ignited by Satan's kindling, caught fire, and he seethed.

"Sorry, sir. Sorry, go on," Keisha said.

He continued to glower.

"I'm good, go on," she called out, stifling the last of her chortles.

I broke eye contact with the angry pastor to look down at Winona's drawing. She had sketched a big-eyed kitten attacking the woman's head. I stuck my gloved fist into my mouth and bit down. Liza Smith turned from her seat in the front row to squint at me. I bit down harder and pulled myself together for the sake of my favorite student. It wasn't her fault her father was a jerk.

Sermon time was followed by testifying time. A microphone was pulled front and center, and the pastor asked if anyone wanted to share the story of how they had "come to the Lord." About a dozen people lined up behind the microphone. I was certain this was going to be a bigger disaster than Cute-Kittygate.

The stories were lame at first. A woman found Jesus when her apple pie won first prize at the county fair. There was a mother whose son finally put away his toys. There was also a man who won twenty-five dollars on a lottery ticket. Eventually, testifier number seven, a pregnant woman in a purple striped muumuu, livened up the show.

"Well, you see, Ricky and I wanted a baby."

"Praise the Lord," echoed through the hall.

"We wanted to raise our baby with Jesus in our hearts."

"Praise the Lord!"

She hesitated, and Pastor Smith encouraged her to go on.

"Well, Ricky, my husband…" She waved, and hundreds of eyes followed her gaze to view the smiling father-to-be. "The problem was, Ricky couldn't…"

"The Lord helps all who believe," Pastor Smith told her.

"But Ricky couldn't do what men need to do to get their wives pregnant." She paused again. "He couldn't have…" She used her index finger to point into the air. "You know, an erection."

Gasps echoed throughout the room as everyone

189

stared at the beet-red Ricky.

"So, I prayed to our good Lord, Jesus Christ, for him to have an erection so I could have a baby."

"I wonder if she tried a blow job," Keisha whispered.

"Shh." Winona stopped writing and listened intently.

Pastor Smith had one hand covering his eyes. I guess he thought if he couldn't see her, that he couldn't hear her. The other was on his heart, perhaps to keep it from exploding.

"Don't worry, Pastor. We didn't fuck for fun or anything, just to bring a God-fearing baby into the world. I asked the Lord for help, and he answered." She rubbed her big round belly. "That's how I came to the Lord."

"Amen," a more subdued crowd called out.

Winona stood.

"Where are you going?" I asked.

"I'm going to testify that I found the Lord."

"You haven't found the Lord, but you have lost your mind," I said, pulling on her.

"For Pete's sake, I don't want to go to hell, Miranda," she said.

I pulled harder, and she sat with a *thunk*.

"Shh, you two," Keisha said. "I'm trying to listen. This is better than my daytime stories."

Meanwhile, a portly man in his early fifties had taken center stage.

Keisha rubbed her hands together. "Oh, this one's gonna be good. I can feel it."

"This ain't seemly, Pastor. The Devil was in me. I was drinkin' and gamblin' and fuckin' around."

"Oh, boy!" Keisha said.

"Shh," Winona whispered.

Everyone else called out, "The Lord helps all who

believe."

"The Devil made me like whores," the man confessed.

"Yeah, the Devil made him like them." Keisha rolled her eyes.

"Shh," Winona said again.

Keisha glared at her. "Shh."

"Shh," Winona said back.

They both quieted when the whore-liker continued.

"The Devil made me lay with three whores in one day." He held up three fingers then made a fist.

"Pray to Jesus," a few people cried.

"Tell those sins," Keisha yelled.

Pastor Smith paled.

"Then the next day, I itched so bad. I went to see old Doc McGee, and he says, 'Joe, you gotta give up the whores.' And I said, 'But I like whores.' And he says, 'You got bugs, Joe.' And damned if I didn't have hundreds of nasty critters in my briefs, biting me and making me itch."

Even the shushing twins remained silent.

"So I said, 'Lord, if you make the itchin' stop, I won't ever drink, or gamble, or fuck around again.' The Lord came to me that night in a dream, and he said, 'Joe, you've been saved.' I woke up the next day, and all the bugs were gone, and the itchin' stopped, and I kicked the Devil from my life. That's how I came to our Lord Jesus Christ."

"Wow," Winona said.

"It was probably the cream the doctor gave him," Keisha said.

Another person had stepped up to the microphone when the pastor said, "That's enough testifying for today."

"Darn," Winona said.

"Damn," Keisha said.

Thank God.

Pastor Smith geared up for round three.

"The Devil shows himself in many ways—adultery, drink, gambling. Sometimes he comes to us in the form of a coven of witches."

He glowered at us. Keisha eyeballed him. I shrank down in my seat until only my eyes remained above the pew. Winona perused the room, searching for who the guilty witches might be.

"These witches can take on many forms. Beware! They can be professors and waitresses and black-skinned secretaries."

"He did not just call me a secretary!" Keisha said.

Winona stopped searching for the Bellmount Coven and joined me in cowering under the pew.

"Avoid these devils, these witches. Avoid the fires of hell. Pray to Jesus for guidance."

"Amen," rang out.

He chanted his final amen. Then, seeming to enjoy the pomp and circumstance, the pastor strutted to the back of the church.

Keisha and Winona were in no hurry to leave. I, on the other hand, couldn't get away fast enough. In an attempt to avoid Greg Grainey, I fought my way through the dispersing crowd and ushered us toward the exit.

Gabriel Smith ambushed us on the front walkway. He looked murderous. "What are you doing here? I told you to stay away—"

"I think I want to come to Jesus," Winona said.

He scowled.

"Yeah, she needs her annoying, shushing, Barry-Manilow-loving-ass saved," Keisha said.

"You three witches are not welcome. Do not come back." Smoke from hell's fires seeped out of Smith's red ears.

Keisha flicked her fingers in his face. "I curse you, evil white man. You are doomed to remain in this life with your ugly clothes, bland sex, and ill humor."

****

Keisha and I sat beside Winona as she looked over her notes. Although the pages contained tons of useless information—cats, burning crosses, lines of old scripture—her chest puffed with pride.

"What's that?" I asked, looking at *G. Grainey*, a picture of an eyeball, *Miranda.*

Winona thought for a moment. "Oh yeah, I think Greg Grainey was staring at you most of the service. I know he can be a jerk, but I think he's sexy."

"Kind of creepy and kind of sexy. Like a vampire that scares the shit out of you, but you still want him to suck your blood." Keisha squirmed and licked her lips.

My stomach churned as I recalled how easily Greg had led me into a dark room and the kick to his shin that had ensued. Winona interrupted my thoughts.

"I figured it out. He did it. The pastor killed his daughter!"

"You're a moron," Keisha said. "It was that horny fraternity boy!"

I took a deep breath and considered my next move.

Chapter 27

Lincoln was as obsessed with his experiments as I was with my detective work. He drew simple pictures in an artist's sketchbook and had me imitate them without looking at them.

Then he drew intricate photos, and the results were the same. Lincoln concluded that as long as I could touch his bare skin, I could imitate, to the best of my artistic ability—which was pretty limited—whatever he had created.

He taped magnets to my cranium and tried to read my thoughts. Even with our skin touching, the experiment had abysmal results. He told me to concentrate on moving a book across the room with my mind. When that didn't work, he put a paperclip in front of me.

"Concentrate, Miranda," he would encourage.

It was no use. The paperclip stayed put. I spent absurd amounts of time attempting to move items with my thoughts, to no avail.

One day Lincoln took me to the psychology lab, where using only my mind, I tried to persuade Simon, the rat, to put a pellet in a green box. After ignoring me and running around on his wheel for ten minutes, Simon finally picked the pellet up and dropped it into the correct container. He did this three times in a row before he stuck his little rat nose into the air and continued to run on his wheel.

"Inconclusive." Lincoln buried his face in his notebook.

Lincoln insisted I learn to meditate. He studied me while I spent hours in a white-walled room. He thought that if I trained myself to relax, I could eventually learn how to build a shield to others' unwanted thoughts.

I repeatedly told him I couldn't relax in the middle of a sterile lab hooked to a biofeedback machine. Still, we were making progress. I had learned to block out forty percent of his mental messages. I was hopeful that if I continued to increase my shield-building efforts, I might someday be able to kiss a man without an ensuing disaster.

On a cold misty late afternoon in the middle of October, a mysterious-acting Lincoln handed me a rainproof windbreaker. He loaded towels and blankets into the back seat of his shiny new car.

My inquiries about what he was up to were met with, "You will see."

About twenty minutes later, we parked in a wooded clearing. He grabbed the towels, shoved them into a trash bag, slung a backpack over his shoulder, and told me to follow. I was miserable, my hands and feet were numb, and I had a moment when I wondered if I might legitimately have Raynaud's syndrome.

Lincoln counted his steps as we trudged past dozens of trees. Eventually, we arrived at the riverbed. He put down his equipment, withdrew a pair of leather gloves from his backpack, and eased into them.

He produced his notebook and thumbed through it until he found the page he wanted. He studied his notes, took in our surroundings, and, seeming satisfied, said, "Take off your socks and shoes and roll up your pant legs."

If I didn't trust Dr. Lincoln Harrison wholeheartedly, I would have thought he meant to chase me through the woods, strangle me with leather-clad hands, clean the evidence with towels, shove my corpse into a plastic bag, then throw me into the river.

"Lincoln, you are creeping me out," I told him.

"You have to trust me. This is a critical experiment."

"I do trust you, but you know, I'm not a witch. If you try to drown me, I will die."

"I would never hurt you," he said.

As unnerving as our field trip was, I took off my shoes and socks and rolled up the bottom of my black stirrup pants.

He pointed at a rock next to the river. "Sit there."

I lowered myself onto the hard, wet surface.

"Now, put your feet into the water."

"Lincoln, I will get frostbite. It's so cold. I can't."

He stuck his hand in the water and swirled it in a circle. "It isn't cold enough to give you frostbite."

I dipped my index finger in and grimaced. "It's cold enough to hurt and make me cry."

He stared into his notebook. "I have never once seen Miranda Albright cry."

That was because he wasn't there the night I made horrible accusations against Brad Gordon and ended up sobbing into my pillow.

"Use the meditation skills we've worked on," he advised.

"Of course." I rolled my eyes as I dipped my toe into the water.

The icy burn forced me to pull it out immediately.

"I can't," I told him.

"You can. Clear your mind of everything."

I took a deep breath and tried again. I dipped in one toe, breathed through the pain, my foot followed, and eventually, I had my calf submerged.

"Now your other foot," Lincoln encouraged in a gentle voice.

The wind whipped at my hooded head, the water droplets from the mist coated me, the sun was going down, and I sat on a rock in the middle of the woods, my legs submerged in icy river water.

What had happened to the Miranda Albright, who made sound choices and had lived twenty-five years without experiencing one iota of trouble? Oh, I know, she had moved to Bellmount, Pennsylvania, and was living out some sort of family curse!

"No matter what happens, keep your feet in the water. Understand?"

"Yes."

"Relax, Miranda. Relax."

I battled the elements and released the tension in my muscles. Then cleared my mind.

His voice had the same soft, mesmerizing quality he used when I practiced my meditation skills.

"Become one with the water."

I was no longer cold. I lost track of time and withdrew into myself, feeling that the wind and water were part of me.

A warm tingly sensation started at my feet and traveled up my spine as if a gentle current from the water passed through me. It wasn't unpleasant, so I let it build.

"Lincoln, something's happening."

"Relax. Let it happen."

The intensity built, my muscles contracted, and the

hair on my arms rose. "Lincoln," I called out. "It hurts."

The prickly sensation felt like fire in my veins.

"You're okay. I'm here. Relax."

A sensation akin to a fireball exploded in my chest before a large man with cruel eyes grabbed me and pushed me underwater. I fought and tried to break free, but he held me tight. The long blond hair that swirled in front of my eyes disoriented me.

Still kicking and hitting, I held my breath for as long as I could. When I finally gasped for air, I choked on a mouthful of water, and my lungs burned.

A hand held my legs down while someone said, "Miranda, you're safe. Keep your feet in the water."

I stopped fighting. I relaxed. Everything went black. I think I died.

When I came to, Lincoln was shaking me. "Miranda, Miranda, It's Lincoln. You're safe."

He lifted my feet out of the water and nudged me toward the plastic bag.

"What happened?" I asked.

He retrieved two towels from the bag, spread one onto the ground, told me to sit, and then rubbed at my feet and ankles with the other. I scratched at my itchy legs as my circulation returned.

I reached under my hood and fingered an unusually frizzy strand.

"Tell me what you experienced," Lincoln said.

Still shaking, I told him.

"Let's get you to the car and turn on the heat. Then we can talk," he said.

Lincoln didn't need to tell me twice. I practically sprinted to his automobile. As soon as the warm air blew across my feet, I rid myself of the damp rain jacket and wrapped myself in a dry blanket.

Lincoln rooted around in his backpack and handed me a thermos of hot coffee.

"Lincoln, please tell me what that was."

"I was researching local murders and found an article from 1906 in the archives. A young girl named Anna Rose Myers was drowned by her uncle in that spot. I wanted to see what would happen if I took you there."

"Why?"

"I wanted a tragic murder to test a theory, and since the uncle confessed, I knew the exact location it happened. I thought the water might aid you, acting as an additional conductor.

I played with a crimped ringlet. "It happened over eighty years ago, and I still felt like I was her. It was terrifying. My lungs hurt, and I thought I was suffocating. I felt what it was like to feel her fear and to die. And my hair? Did it stand in the air?"

"Interesting. Very interesting. Could you identify her uncle if I had a photo of him?"

"I think so. I saw the man right before he held her underwater. It was similar to when I saw Suzy Smith's body, except I didn't know what Suzy experienced when she died. I only saw afterward when they mutilated her body. I could hear the men, but I couldn't see them. I could see Suzy's corpse. What does it all mean?"

"It's very interesting," he said again.

"Lincoln, if I knew the exact location of Suzy's murder, do you think I could relive her death and see her killer?"

"That's my theory. I believe all of your abilities have something to do with energy and your innate ability to harness and conduct it. We've determined that thoughts have energy. Many parapsychologists believe that tragic emotional events can create a psychic footprint, leaving strong energy that takes years to disperse. I think you can tap into these things, and more than likely, you inherited this from your grandmother."

"Do you think I experienced the psychic footprint left by one of the men upset about what he was doing to Suzy's body? And then again from Anna Rose because she was terrified?"

"I think so," he said.

"And you believe that day to day I'm unscrambling the energy of people's thoughts?"

"That's my present theory." He put the key in the ignition.

"So I've been looking at Suzy Smith's murder all wrong. I need to change my focus from the person who killed her to the place she was murdered."

He bobbed his head. "Perhaps."

"Suzy was in a bikini, Lincoln. She may have been swimming before she was strangled."

"Perhaps," he said.

"Was my hair standing in the air?" I asked again.

"Like the Eiffel Tower."

I shivered. "What color was Anna Rose's hair?"

"Blonde, I think. The photo is black and white."

"How old was she?" I asked.

"Fifteen." He turned the key, and the engine turned over.

"Lincoln, you might be about to witness me crying." I wiped a tear from my eye as we drove toward Bellmount.

Chapter 28

I studied my reflection in the mirror. I confess I liked the way my autumn-colored sweater looked against my red hair and scrunchy brown socks. I was in the middle of a silly hand on one hip pose when there was a soft tap followed by a *woof woof* at my bedroom door.

It had taken less than an hour to teach Spot to alert me that my presence was requested on the first floor. Aunt Edith only needed to say, "Where's Miranda? Go get Miranda," and Spot would sprint up the stairs, then use his paw to knock. I handed him a doggy biscuit, and we raced down the staircase. As usual, Spot won.

"Bradley's on the phone," Aunt Edith said.

"Come on, Spot. He probably wants to talk about our Harvest Festival date today," I called over my shoulder as we dashed to the kitchen.

The only reason I beat the speedy Spot to the phone was that I was excited to hear the voice on the other end.

I hung up the receiver and frowned. "Bradley delivered a baby this morning, and there were complications. He is at the County Hospital with the Minnich family."

"That poor family. At least they're in good hands." Aunt Edith placed a comforting palm on my shoulder. "Honey, I'm sorry. I know how excited you were for your date."

"I'm okay. I know Brad needs to be with his patient."

"You can hang with Tom, West, and me," Liam offered.

My sadness lifted. "Thanks, Liam. That sounds fun."

I planned to make the most of my letdown. I was in the most charming town in the world; it was a perfect fall day, the food was rumored to be fabulous, and Liam and his gang were loads of fun. Besides, I would be hanging out with West—not that I had feelings for him anymore—but he was entertaining.

I started my whirlwind of an afternoon sitting between Tommy and West in the back of a flatbed. The two of them delighted in poking me with pieces of straw as the tractor drove around town. After a hay-throwing battle, it took me forever to untangle the thick grass from my ringlets.

Following our hayride, Aunt Edith chose Liam as the winner of our four contestant pumpkin carving contest. His prize was that Tommy, West, and I had to kiss his shiny loafers and call him "Your Highness."

Swapping spit with an entire town was even less appealing than placing my mouth on my cousin's foot, so I passed on bobbing for apples. However, I cheered for the guys with unabashed enthusiasm. West was the unmitigated champ and bragged about "The things I can do with my mouth" for hours.

We made the craft stand rounds, where I asked an adorable little girl to design my flower at the face painting booth. Good sport that he was, Tommy succumbed to having a ninja turtle painted on his forearm. It ended up looking like camouflaged roadkill and gave Liam and West ammunition in their never-ending quest to tease him. As usual, Tommy ignored them, and his face lit up when I told him I thought his turtle was cool.

One of my favorite parts of the afternoon was that many of my students wandered through the festival, calling out greetings.

While piling a plate with food, I ran into Mrs. Little, Tommy's affectionate mother. She cornered me with kisses, asking me when I was coming over for her homemade chicken pot pie. Tommy flushed. I supposed he already knew what I had divined from her sweet kisses. She hoped that her son and I would finally hit it off, marry, and give her lots of chubby babies to kiss and feed. Since I still owed Tommy a dinner, I agreed to a visit.

The four of us took our loaded plates to the riverbank. It was windy, so I had to continually remove strands of hair from my mouth before I chewed. My gaze made contact with West, and he winked. I remembered I was mad at him and looked away.

Although I spent a good deal of the day avoiding the Bellmount Bitches, the Pattersons, the uniformed Shultz, and the oddly hypnotic Greg Grainey, I enjoyed my afternoon. I was having so much fun with my childhood playmates that I almost forgot about my big girl date. Almost.

As the evening cooled off, the festivities moved into the gargantuan town hall gymnasium. My family and friends congregated at a long cafeteria-style table.

"There's a Harvest Queen?" I asked Liam.

"Yeah, usually Gina."

His face was so void of emotion that I figured he was hiding his feelings on the subject.

"You mean it isn't some little girl in a plastic tiara?"

"No, it's usually an atrocious rich girl in a diamond tiara," West added.

"Are you gonna ask Holly to dance this year, West?" Tommy asked.

"Hell no. I don't do princesses unless it's to defile them." West laughed.

"You are a pig, Mr. Westinghouse," I declared.

He used his index finger to press on his nostrils. "Oink."

Tommy groaned. Liam rolled his eyes, and I lightly punched the pig-boy in his pectorals that were awe-inspiring even in his loose-fitting flannel shirt.

"West, can't you behave for a second?" Winona asked. "Miranda, the court is made up of single women in town over the age of eighteen. Shh! Everyone needs to be quiet. They are going to announce the court soon."

"Shh, yourself," Keisha said.

"Winona, since when do you care about the Harvest Queen?" Tommy asked.

"Shh," Winona said again.

The mayor did one last sound check. "Testing one-two, testing one-two. Can everyone hear me?"

The claps and cheers indicated his microphone was working.

"I'm about to announce this year's Harvest Court."

There were a few audible moans among the cheers.

"Afterward, our queen and her court will start us off with the first dance of the evening. Be sure to stick around for the bands, and then, 'just say no,' if you have to drive. Is everyone ready?"

There were more cheers and a loud moan from Keisha. If the court consisted of cute little girls dressed as Cinderella, I would have thought it charming. No such luck. I was about to watch the Bellmount Bitches play pay-attention-to-me.

"Princesses, when your name is called, please have your escort walk you to the front." Mayor Reynolds's sweat caused his brown hair dye—or maybe it was shoe polish—to smear.

The stains started at his temple and were in a mad-dash rush to consume his forehead.

"Does someone have my box?" Like a sailor looking for land, he placed his hand above his eye and searched the room.

This appeared to be part of the show because the audience played along and laughed at his pantomime—or perhaps they were laughing at the dye that just colored his hand. Eventually, Ian Patterson strutted forward, carrying a wooden box.

"Let's hear it for Ian Patterson, one of Bellmount's leading citizens and our future state representative."

Reynolds's nose was so brown—from both dye and having it up Patterson's bum—that it needed scrubbing with bleach. It appeared the incumbent had already lost the election that hadn't even taken place. People clapped. I did not. Despite his wealth and power, I was not a fan of Patterson and the arrogant Bellmount oligarchy.

"Is everyone ready?" Reynolds asked.

Gina Schuster waved at Liam. My traitorous cousin waved back.

The mayor announced the first three princesses. The Belmount Bitches, gloating like fools, pranced to the front of the room on their fathers' arms. Keisha stuck her finger in her mouth and gagged. It took quite a bit of discipline not to encourage her with a chuckle.

"And this year, we have a new member on our court, the lovely Liza Smith."

"Yeah, Liza," I called out. "Woohoo!"

Maybe this wasn't so bad. Liza deserved a chance to be in the spotlight.

"Our final princess this evening is Miran—"

The mayor stopped to double-check what he was reading. He shook his head, looked into the box, and turned it over. The crowd sat hushed.

Dear God, no. It can't be.

"Miranda Albright," he practically growled.

"No, thank you," I called out as the people around me cheered.

"Congrats, Randa." Tommy grinned and patted me on the shoulder.

"Congrats, Shortcake," said West as he ruffled my hair.

"Woohoo!" Winona jumped up and down.

"Way to go, Dr. Albright!" some of the college students called out.

"Come on, Miranda," Liam said, reaching for my hand. "I'll go with you."

"No, I'm not going up there." I fought Liam's pull.

"There better not be any pig's blood thrown on her, or there will be some hell to pay," Keisha said.

"Miranda, you better go," Aunt Edith said. "Liam will be with you."

Liam pulled me to my feet, and I took my place beside Liza. She grabbed my gloved hand. I wanted to die, and I might have if Liza's father and the rest of the court had had any say in the matter.

"I chose a firing squad," I whispered to Liam.

He chuckled.

I was pretty sure that having a few dozen muskets firing at me would be a less bloody ordeal than the Bellmount Bitches and Pastor Smith flaying the skin from my bones.

"And this year's Bellmount Harvest Festival Queen is—" Ian handed Reynolds an envelope. "Thank you, Ian. Our queen is Liza Smith."

I exhaled in relief.

Reynolds placed a diamond tiara on Liza's head. As he slid the orange Harvest Queen sash over her, three outraged women scowled and whispered.

"Miranda," Liam said, "We have to dance."

"We have to do what?" I asked.

The music blared, and three women pushing thirty embraced their "Daddies" and danced.

Pastor Smith crossed his arms over his chest and glowered. Maybe he had a point. The entire thing did feel like the Devil's work. Instead of dancing with her pious father, Liza danced with our campus sports reporter, Michael Dunlap. Although just friends, they made an adorable couple.

Liam wrapped one hand around me and held my other.

"Liam, how did this happen?" I asked.

"Someone nominated you, and people voted for you. Probably those people." He pointed to our family and friends, who all wore giant grins.

"But half the town hates me."

"And half adores you."

"I'm so embarrassed!"

"Little cuz, you care too much what people think. You have to stop worrying about it," said my cousin with his fancy clothes and snotty girlfriend.

"*Pft*," I said. "I don't care what people think of me."

Liam's chin jutted back, and he quirked an eyebrow.

"Gina is looking at you."

"I know."

"I think she's jealous that I'm dancing with you. Kind of weird, Liam. She's jealous of your cousin."

He laughed, and his eyes took on a far-away look.

"Liam, you do like her?"

He took in a breath. "I know Gina seems hideous to you. I used to feel that way too, but she isn't all bad. She makes me feel good."

I changed the subject again. "Is someone going to throw pig's blood on me?"

"What?" he asked.

"Keisha said they better not throw blood."

He laughed so hard I thought he might choke.

"It's a reference to an old horror movie. Nobody is throwing pig's blood on anyone. We'll go to West's and watch it sometime. We need to bring you up to date on things that have happened in the last two decades."

"Good grief, this song is so long."

"First time Jessica Grainey has been single and eligible in a few years. I'm sure she and 'Daddy' want to make the dance last. I bet they paid good money for the longest song in the history of the world to be played."

"I hate Jessica."

"Doc is here." Liam inclined his chin.

Brad sought out Aunt Edith. They talked for a moment, and then he made his way to us.

"May I cut in?" he asked.

"Brad, you made it!" The heaviness of my situation faded as he took me in his arms.

"I'm sorry I missed your big moment."

"The most humiliating moment of my life. I want to die."

He smiled. "Ah, sweetheart, it's not so bad, but your

disgust makes me like you even more."

"How is it that you always know the perfect thing to say to make everything okay?" I asked.

"Because I'm awesome." His dimples deepened with his smile. "Now, want to hear me sing?"

He didn't wait for an answer. He belted out a few lines, singing something about love lifting him where he belonged.

I cringed.

"I sound just like him, don't I?" Brad's body vibrated as he laughed.

If the "him" he referenced was the man singing the song, Brad sounded nothing like him. How could a dreamy man, with an appealing deep voice, be such a terrible crooner?

"Well, you aren't quite as bad as West," I told him.

"Then Westinghouse must sound like a dying jackal."

I laughed and perused the crowd for a glimpse of West, but I couldn't find him.

"You're so awesome!" I said again.

Jessica scowled when I rested my head on Brad's chest. I couldn't reach his shoulder since he was well over six feet tall, and I was entirely too short. Since his ex-wife had shapely stilts for legs, her stupid pretty head probably hit his body at precisely the right spot.

"How is the baby you are treating?" I asked.

"Mother and child are both doing better. I needed to stay until the baby was out of danger."

The dark circles under his eyes betrayed his exhaustion.

"I know. It's okay. It makes me like you more," I said.

The song ended, and Brad held me close. "I'm not

ready to let go."

The pace of the music picked up. Liam found his way to Gina, and Aunt Edith and Russ paired off. It appeared as though Keisha and Winona were fighting over who would dance with Tommy. My friends had issues. Neither had ever paid Tommy a single bit of attention until they thought the other might be interested.

"Grainey is watching us," Brad said. "The man has no scruples."

"Jessica is watching you. Perhaps Greg is exhibiting some parental protectiveness."

"I'd have more respect for him if that were true. I'd say he is obsessed with you."

I changed the subject because Greg's obsession left me feeling like I needed a shower. "Are you still going to kiss every inch of me before the night is over?"

"Will it embarrass you if I kiss you right now?" Brad whispered in my ear.

"Please."

His lips caressed mine for about fifteen seconds before a loud commotion erupted. It ended with Jessica Grainey sitting on the floor, tears in her eyes.

"Gordon, she needs a doctor," Greg said, pushing Brad away from me.

While Brad attended to Jessica, Greg took the opportunity to whisper in my ear, "Congratulations, my crimson princess."

I ignored him.

Brad turned Jessica's ankle every which way, and with each touch, she screamed in pain. He explained that although there was no swelling, she might have sprained her ankle.

Jessica Grainey was a terrible actress. There was

nothing wrong with her. She was simply a nasty gluttonous brat demanding my boyfriend's attention. Tommy Little, the helpful guy that he was, came forward to assist.

"She's faking it," I told him.

When he attempted to lend a hand with first aid, Greg rudely dismissed him. Tommy stood beside me as the rest of the soap opera played out.

"It hurts so much, Bradley. Can't you do anything?" said Jessica, the fake crybaby.

Brad handed her a bag of ice and moved her off the dance floor, then flashed me his devastatingly gorgeous smile. Unfortunately, he never made it to my side.

"Gordon, she's in terrible pain. You need to take her to the county hospital for an X-ray," Greg demanded.

Brad sighed. "Look, I think she will be fine. Ice, rest and elevate for the next forty-eight hours. I can call in a prescription for a painkiller."

"Gordon, are you going to shirk your responsibilities to dance with a girl?" Greg pointed at me.

From his muscular thighs to his handsome jaw, Brad's body tensed. He attempted to say something, but I intervened.

I hated Jessica and Greg Grainey with every ounce of my being. I knew the purpose of their farce, and perhaps I should have called them out, but witnessing Brad's professionalism called into question, as many of his patients looked on, was more than I could handle. My heart broke as I said, "It's okay, Brad. Go ahead."

"No, Miranda, I want to dance with you."

"No, go." The Graineys would not humiliate him on my watch.

Greg leaned close and cooed in my ear, "Forget about

him. He still loves Jessica." His breath grew ragged. "Told you, you were mine, Crimson."

My heart pounded as I tried to escape the crowd. I was almost out the door when someone called, "Dr. Albright!"

I turned to face Mitch Patterson. "Please call me Miranda."

"Congrats," he said.

I moaned.

"Not into being a Harvest Princess?" he asked.

"I'd rather have fire ants crawling in my eyes, and I hate bugs. Plus, I'm a bit old to be a princess."

"Maybe you could remind the Bellmount Bitches they're on borrowed time," Mitch said.

I forced a smile. "Have a good night." I turned to leave.

"Wait! I wanted to apologize for the way my family treated you the other week. Let me make it up to you. Kyle and I are having a small get-together tomorrow around four. Would you like to come?"

"Thank you, but I highly doubt your father and brother would appreciate my being there."

"Don't mind my dad. He's a bastard to everyone who moves into town. Not a fan of change."

I didn't respond.

"Kyle isn't so bad. A bit of a snob, but his behavior had more to do with Grainey than you. You know he detests him. He had a fling with Jessica Grainey. It's a long story."

"Thank you for inviting me. I'll think about it," I said.

"Your cousin is invited."

"Liam is invited?"

"Yeah. He usually is, but since Jessica is no longer welcome, his girl doesn't like to come. So, unfortunately, Liam rarely joins us anymore."

My cousin, the scandalous Zoey Wilson's grandson, had been accepted into the upper echelons of Bellmount Society. I scanned the dance floor. Liam smiled at Gina Schuster. Yuck!

"Bring a friend. I promise you'll have a great time— food, drink, music, and swimming. Bring your suit. Although we have extra if you need one."

"Swimming?" I asked. "It's a bit cold."

"We have an indoor heated pool. Diving board. Nice this time of year."

"In a bikini?" I asked as I recovered my memory of Suzy's floral two-piece.

"Well, unless you want to borrow one or skinny dip." He laughed.

"Thanks for the invite. I would love to join you. I'll bring two friends and my suit." Before making my final break for the exit, I asked one more question. "Mitch, what would you do if you were humiliated in front of the entire town?"

He chuckled. "You mean if I had just been named a Harvest Princess?"

I nodded.

"About six stiff shots."

"Hmm," I said. "Me too."

After all, how hard could chugging six shots be?

****

Using the towel he kept tucked into the waistband of his jeans, West dried a spot at the corner of the bar. I was thrilled that he had changed back into his titillating five-dollar tee, although his flannel shirt had also been to-die-for. Who was I kidding? West would have looked sexy dressed in a bum's dirty rags.

West grinned. "Hiya, Dr. Shortcake. What you doin' here? Aren't you on a date?"

I plopped down on the barstool. "Not anymore, and I'm getting drunk."

"But you don't drink."

"Dr. Albright might not drink, but Miranda, the absurd Bellmount Harvest Princess, does."

He used his index finger to bop me on the nose. "Rough afternoon? Wanna tell old West about it?"

"I don't want to talk about it. Give me a beer," I demanded.

While standing at the tap, West gave me one of his smiles that made my body do silly things. Upon his return, I grilled him.

"Did you know about that? Did you vote for me, too? What happened to you? You disappeared."

He set the beer in front of me. "Winona nominated you."

"Winona," I said between clenched teeth.

"And, had I known how mad it would make you, I would have voted for Jessica Grainey." He chuckled. He didn't address his disappearance.

I waved a fist. "Where is that annoying cousin of yours? She will pay dearly for this one."

"She's still at the festival, along with everyone else in town, except you, me, Pop, and these few fools." He swept his arm across the almost empty bar.

"These are the smart people. This is where I'll be next year."

Leaning in close, West said, "These are the town degenerates."

Then I would be a degenerate because I would never attend anything with the word festival in it again.

"That was humiliating," I grumbled.

"You take things too seriously. Don't worry so much about what people think. Laugh it off."

I rolled my eyes. "Keep the beers coming." I attempted to chug the mug that sat in front of me. "Gross, how do people drink this stuff? It tastes like sweat socks boiled in water." I ran the back of my hand across my mouth to wipe away the wayward drips.

He chuckled, topped off my mug, and left me to pout into my foul-tasting intoxicant.

West's cocky assurance allowed him to do everything with ease, but his confidence did not in any way detract from his charisma. Although everyone ribbed him, the entire town adored the always incorrigible Weston Westinghouse's smile and easy manner. Unfortunately, staring at his biceps and forearms as he slung drinks and eavesdropping on his laugh while getting drunk for the first time was another in the long line of my ill-advised Bellmount indiscretions.

I stared him down until he walked my way.

"Another?" He picked up my mug.

I grabbed him by the collar and pulled him toward me. "If you promised to kiss every inch of me before the night was over, would you run off with stupid Jessica Grainey?"

"Doc ran off with Jessica?" he asked, his face inches from mine.

I let go of his T-shirt and flicked my wrist. "I told him to go, and I don't want to talk about it."

West leaned in and whispered, "I assure you, if I ever promise to kiss every inch of you, I won't stop until the job is done."

He was so close that if I had wanted to, I could have kissed him.

"You know why you can't kiss me, West? Give me a shot of something, and I'll tell you."

West plopped a tiny glass in front of me and filled it to the brim.

I pinched my nostrils and somehow swallowed. "Fudge." I washed it down with the slightly less offensive, dirty underclothes-flavored brew in my mug.

West refilled the shot glass, and I chugged.

"Bluck," I hollered. "Only four more to go."

"Four more?" he asked.

"Yep. I'm doing six shots to celebrate my crappy life. Give me another."

He turned the shot glass upside down. "Maybe later. Now humor me and tell me, why can't I kiss you?"

"Because I can read your mind."

He wore a smart-alec grin. "You can?"

I took off my gloves, put my hand on his cheek, and divined his thoughts. "Yep. You like me a lot. You like my lips, and right now, you want to kiss me."

He removed my hand from his face and placed it on the bar. "You're pretty drunk. I'm gonna take ya home."

"Bartender, you're the one who got me drunk, and I don't want to go home because I'm a Harvest Princess." I swirled my hand in the air like a lasso. "Get me another shot, barboy!"

"You're slurring your words, princess. Time to go." West came around from behind the bar, picked me up off the stool, and nudged me toward the door. "Hey Pop, I'll be back in a couple of minutes," he called.

I was warm, fuzzy, and loose-lipped, but the tequila

hadn't fully kicked in, so I was still coherent. Halfway across the parking lot, I turned toward him. "You know why else you can't kiss me?"

"Because you're drunk, and Liam and Edith would kill me."

"Liam says you're a scoundrel." I poked my finger into his chest.

"A scoundrel?" He smirked.

Poke, poke, poke went my finger.

He wrapped his palm around it. "Stop that." Then, he leaned in like he meant to kiss me. "Liam's correct, love."

My breath caught. "You watch too many soap operas."

He chuckled and continued to push me across the parking lot.

Once we reached the sidewalk that led up the hill to the inn, I said, "You know why else you can't kiss me?"

"I'm sure you're going to tell me."

"Because I'm crazy about Brad Gordon. I used to want you to kiss me, but now I'm mad at you, and I like Brad, but he's probably kissing Jessica."

"Okay, beautiful. This has been fun, but it's time to go home."

"You know who else wants to kiss me?"

"I'm sure you're going to tell me."

He moved me a few more steps.

"Tommy, and you. Mitch Patterson likes my body, and Greg Grainey wants to do disgusting things to me."

"I'm sure Grainey does. Now come on."

He steered me toward the inn, but I wasn't done blabbing.

"Brad Gordon promised to kiss every inch of me, but he's probably kissing Jessica." I paused to pout and then said, "I can read your mind."

"We've established that. Come on. I need to get you home."

I had lost my gloves along the way, but I didn't care. I placed my hand on his cheek. "You know what you're thinking right now, Weston Westinghouse? You want to kiss me, and then you want to fuck me." I dropped my hand and called over my shoulder, "See, told you. I can read your mind."

A couple of steps later, I plopped onto the ground. "I'm tired."

It's hard to say for sure, but as I sat on the cold ground, it may have dawned on me that I repeated shocking words when a one-hundred proof poison coursed through my veins.

"Please get up. This isn't funny anymore," West said.

"But West, you think everything's funny." I pulled on his arm. "Come sit."

"Well, this isn't funny. You're going to get us both in trouble." He lifted me and set me on my feet.

"Don't worry, because we won't get into trouble, because you won't fu—" I didn't finish the word. "You won't even kiss me because I'm a pathetic virgin. Hasn't Liam told you?"

West pulled me close. His drawl was gone, replaced by something powerful. "Such language, Shortcake."

I focused on his blurry lips.

"Liam hasn't told me a damn thing, and there's nothing pathetic about you." He ran his finger along my jaw and then wound a piece of my hair around that same finger.

I pressed my aching body into his.

"You're playing with fire tonight, my little

shortcake." His breath warmed my cheek.

"Rest assured, if I were going to kiss you or fuck you, I'd want you to remember, so I sure as hell wouldn't do it while you were drunk."

Then he tossed me over his shoulder and finished our walk up the hill, mumbling something about "a damn cold shower."

"West, put me down," I begged.

"Don't you dare throw up on me," he grunted into the night.

Eventually, I stopped fighting and relaxed into his embrace. Perhaps, I even dozed off for a moment.

West's voice brought me back to the present.

"Edith," he called into the foyer. "Hey, Edith! Special delivery."

Aunt Edith appeared out of nowhere. He plopped me down in front of her. Everything was blurry.

"I think I'm drunk, Aunt Edith. I neve' been drunk. I don' wanna be a Harvest Princess ever again."

"Okay, Miranda," she said.

"There's a murderer in this town, and nobody cares, and bein' a Harvest Princess's embarrassing!" I'm pretty sure the last sentence was slurred to the point of inaudibility. I think I followed it with, "I just wanna be a princess in my own castle." I may have pointed to the stairs, indicating my turret. I lay down on the floor and closed my eyes."I gonna sleep right here."

Everything spun.

I remember Aunt Edith asking West to help carry me to my room, and I think he said, "Only if she keeps her mouth shut."

I continued to swirl round and round on Aunt Edith's oriental rug.

"Bradley, you're back? Can you help West carry Miranda upstairs?"

It took a half-dozen strong arms to haul me up that winding staircase.

Chapter 29

The day after my drunken waggery, I slept in and missed breakfast. I only got out of bed because Spot jumped on my head and gave me a bath. He thought I smelled like chicken wings, sweat, hay, beer, and tequila. He was correct.

The glamorous kicker was that my painted rose had smeared and left what looked like a dirty bruise on my cheek. Even more fetching, my mascara coated my chin. That was probably how the handsome Dr. Bradley Gordon and the sexy Weston Westinghouse the Third had seen me right before I passed out as I begged one of them for kisses. Boy, I hoped it was Brad.

Despite the previous evening's debauchery, I dragged myself to the Patterson party and convinced the girls to join me. Although, *convinced* is incorrect verbiage to describe two women practically doing jumping jacks in their excitement over the chance to hobnob and spy.

The pool was as extravagant as the rest of the estate. Tropical plants and rock formations dotted the deck. Two Greek columns and a white marble fountain sat in the water at the low end, and a diving board marked the deep end. The fading sun meant a minimal amount of light entered through the glass ceiling. The underwater fixtures provided the rest of the illumination.

From my seat beside the fountain, I observed as almost twenty-five of the most beautiful members of Bear

County society socialized. Once I realized I wasn't gathering any valuable information, I exited the water, wrapped myself in a jumbo-sized towel, and joined my friends.

Decked out in her tropical bikini, Keisha sipped a pink umbrella drink and reclined on a chaise lounge. Winona, wearing an oversized white T-shirt, wrote ferociously in her notebook. Although one appeared to be relaxing on a sunny beach, and the other engaged in writing a novel, I knew the truth. They were using their eagle eyes to keep watch on the Patterson brothers.

"What have you guys found out?" I whispered to my partners.

Winona slid her notebook to the side so that Keisha and I could look at it.

Keisha peered at the drawing and squinted. "What the hell is that?"

"I don't understand," I said.

Winona had sketched a stick figure standing on a straight line beside something that looked like a bomb.

"Mitch Patterson likes to do cannonballs. That is all he has done for the past forty-five minutes," Winona said.

Keisha inclined her head. "Well, Kyle has spent the entire time ogling Mrs. McGinely, and the woman has to be twice his age."

The pretty woman Keisha pointed out was dressed in a red bikini, had long blonde hair, and had to be almost fifty.

"Mr. McGinely won't be happy," Winona added.

"No shit, Sherlock," Keisha said.

"What did you find out?" Winona asked. Before I could answer, she said, "For Pete's sake, Miranda, you looked a bit odd sitting in the pool with your eyes closed, pretending to be the Dali Lama."

Keisha *harrumph*ed. "I finally agree with her. You looked like a crazy woman."

The stars had aligned, and the two of them concurred. The problem was they happened to agree about how foolish I looked. I needed new friends.

"I was listening," I said, which wasn't exactly a lie. "But, all I could hear was a bunch of useless gossip."

Keisha's eyebrows rose. "Anything good?"

"No. I was trying to ignore the background chatter and only tune in to the information I need."

"You sound like you think you're a radio transmitter," Keisha said.

I bit my lip." Now I need to look for clues in other parts of the house."

"What kind of clues? Can we help?" Winona rubbed her hands together.

"No. You two need to stay here and make sure the brothers don't leave the party. I'll be back soon. Make a scene so I can slip out."

"I know, Keisha, pretend like your bikini pops open, flash some boob, and everyone will look at you," Winona suggested.

"Hell no, you flash your boobs," Keisha fired back.

"Hello! T-shirt." Winona pointed to her extra-large covering.

"You're impossible, woman." Keisha rolled her eyes, then dropped her glass onto the ceramic tile.

It shattered.

"Oops!"

"Thanks," I said.

All gazes had settled on Keisha, Winona, and Charles the Butler as they cleaned up the mess.

I stealthily made my way down the corridor that led from the pool to the main house, not passing a single person.

"Piece of cake," I whispered to the air.

I entered the first room on the ground floor hallway. It was opulently decorated and had a masculine feel; it had to be Ian Patterson's study. I sat behind a massive mahogany desk and rifled through household bills. I closed my eyes, concentrated, and attempted to become one with the room. I couldn't catch a glimpse of Suzy or feel any tragedy.

I tiptoed to the next room, which was the feminine contrast to the gentleman's study. Tall hand-painted vases overflowed with fresh-cut flowers, luxurious velvet draperies covered the ceiling-high windows, and a majestic grandfather clock kept time in the corner.

I still couldn't find Suzy's energy or detect tragedy. I was about to exit the room when heavy footsteps tromped toward me. My heartbeat quadrupled as I searched for a hiding place. I dove for a spot behind a peach couch and held my breath.

The slow, steady footfall got louder as it mingled with the metronome ticking of the grandfather clock. *Tick-tock* sang the clock. *Clip-clop* echoed the footsteps. *Lub-dup* beat my heart.

The sound of heels on the hardwood floor slowed, then changed directions as the visitor headed away from me.

I let out a breath and was about to come out of hiding when the loud *bong bong bong* of the antique timepiece startled me, and I gasped. I covered my open mouth with my hand. The *clip-clop* slowed down, then stopped. It picked up its pace, becoming a *click-click-click* as it once again moved toward me. I gritted my teeth and closed my eyes.

Heavy breathing replaced the footsteps.

Augh!

I opened my eyes and stared at a pair of shiny black shoes. I followed the length of the leg upward to a black-coated torso. My vision traveled higher until I looked into the face of my newest adversary.

"Ms. Albright, may I help you?" a high-falutin' voice asked.

I couldn't have been any more humiliated if Charles the Butler had actually dragged me by my ear out of the house to Kyle Patterson by the pool.

The butler's fingers clutched my bicep to discourage me from attempting a speedy getaway. His face was emotionless as he presented me to his lord king. "Master Kyle, Ms. Albright seems to have lost her way to the restroom and found herself in your mother's parlor."

Master Kyle's anger was smoldering but contained. I suspected he was irritated because he had been interrupted while whispering lascivious things to his paramour. It was also evident that my presence, in general, put him on edge. He already despised me. My unwelcome adventure in his home seemed to triple that aversion.

He excused himself by patting his mistress's shoulder. He called to his brother and grabbed my forearm. Keisha and Winona gaped as the three men roughly escorted me from the party.

Then the brothers argued while my wet bathing suit soaked a chair in the Patterson's game room.

"So what, man. She isn't a thief." Mitch looked at me. "You aren't a thief, are you?"

I shook my head.

"Worse, she's a troublemaker."

Kyle's eyes held so much contempt that I almost felt guilty for invading his privacy.

"You know what pisses me off? I trusted that little twin too. Despite the fact I despise immature college girls, I let her come to a party. She acted sweet and pretended to accept our hospitality, all the while she was collecting information to destroy the company and nail Dad to a cross."

The older brother could yell at me all he wanted. The longer he took, the more chlorine I would leave on his fancy chair.

Kyle glowered at me. "I loathe women like you. You act wide-eyed and innocent, and fools like my brother and Bradley Gordon fall for it. Meanwhile, you use your sexuality to manipulate and connive, all while pretending to be morally superior. You don't care that you destroy things you don't understand. Your aunt isn't much better, championing her causes, thinking the world is all black and white."

"Chill out, man. Dad brings that shit on himself. He needs to put the environmental regulations into place," Mitch said.

I wasn't fazed in the least by the colossal blowhard that was Kyle Patterson. "But you said you never dated Suzy Smith."

Kyle ran his hand through his blond locks. "Don't you ever stop? Her sister was the one that was here, the little reporter. I never dated Suzy. I didn't date either of them. I told you, I'm not into college girls."

My jaw must have hit the floor because Mitch Patterson tapped my chin from underneath.

"Yeah, he only likes women that have a jealous

husband lurking about somewhere."

"Fuck you, Mitch! I want her out of our house," Kyle said, right before he booted me from the estate.

****

Soon after my abrupt dismissal, the butler escorted Keisha and Winona to the parking lot. Winona came peacefully, but Keisha wriggled about like an angry jaguar. I filled them in as soon as we were seated in The Tank.

"Holy guacamole, Miranda. I knew it. Kyle Patterson is the murderer?" Winona cried.

"That's right. It was Kyle Patterson in the library with a revolver," Keisha declared.

"No. It was Kyle Patterson in the pool with a rope," Winona said.

"Last week, you thought it was the pastor," Keisha reminded her.

"I changed my mind. It's Patterson, isn't it, Miranda?" Winona gasped. "Do you think it was the butler?"

When I didn't answer, Keisha peered into the backseat. "You're clueless, Winona. It was that damn fraternity boy, in a frat house, with a hard-on."

I drove The Tank down the long winding driveway. "Guys, I think I might be hung over. I need to go home and sleep."

Chapter 30

I locked my office door and ate a butterscotch Kakeycake then washed it down with a chocolate bar with almonds. I laid my head on my desk and sighed loudly. I stayed like that for a very long time. I was in the middle of a full-fledged Miranda Albright pity party for one. I had so many problems.

First of all, I was learning the hard way that hangovers last more than twenty-four hours.

Problem number two was that I had stacks of papers to correct. Reading almost one hundred mediocre papers on *The Implications of the Transcendentalist Movement on American Literature* while nursing a splitting headache was abject torture.

Problem three was that all of my attempts to catch Liza Smith while she was on campus had failed, so I would risk eternal damnation and visit her at home.

My fourth problem was more of an issue for Skyler Dubbs. He was rotting in jail for a murder he hadn't committed, and not a single person cared.

My fifth problem was that Dean Johnson lurked around every corner, so avoiding him had been exhausting. The man needed an enema.

Problem number six was that Brad had not returned my calls, and my heart was breaking. I was consumed by the rumors circulating about the rekindling of the romance between the doctor and his ex, and I was convinced that my drunken exploits had turned him off. The ugly truth was I wasn't sure who I had begged for kisses while being tucked into bed by the two most desirable men in Bellmount.

Problem number seven was that I needed to humble myself and apologize to West.

My final problem, which I needed to remedy immediately, was that I needed to be kissed. My body ached so much I experienced debilitating pain.

I moaned, then gently bumped my head on my desk. Finally, resigning myself to the realization that I had experienced the climax of my private party, I sat up, corrected five papers, and did a little jig to try to send some positive energy to my despondent heart. I had a marathon evening ahead of me. It was four p.m. and time to face my troubles.

It took a lot of persuasion and a heaping dose of good luck to convince Mrs. Smith to let me talk to her daughter. "Her father will not approve" was the understatement of the century.

Then it took quite a bit of tact not to sound like I was reprimanding Liza when I said, "Why didn't you tell me you had been to the Pattersons' for a party?" and "Is there any chance that someone wanted to keep you quiet about something you found out about Patterson's company while writing your article?" And, my final nagging proclamation, "Are you sure you didn't wear your bikini to the Pattersons' pool because I think someone may have mistaken your sister for you?"

This conjecture shocked Liza. Since we thought that Shultz was more likely to accidentally kill her than protect her, we needed Tommy Little's help. I told her to pull her notes and tape recordings together, and we would meet with P.T. Grimwood and Tommy to see what they could make of them. I told her not to go anywhere by herself and to stay away from the Pattersons. Before leaving, I asked if I could have a recent photo of Suzy. I wanted to compare the twins.

I sat in The Tank and ran a finger over the picture. Suzy looked older than Liza. It was probably the heavy make-up she wore, her teased hair, and her exposed bosom. Although identical twins, Suzy looked provocative, and Liza looked like a poster child for the Milk Makes You Healthy campaign.

Pastor Smith may have controlled the moral compass of hundreds of Bellmount citizens, but his twins had minds of their own. One was an intellectual who wanted to take on the injustices of the world. The other had been a party girl who wanted to experience life. Oh, how he must pray to his vengeful Lord each night.

My next trip was to the Little home. Tom lived beside the river on the third floor of his parents' working-class duplex. Both Mr. and Mrs. Little accosted me with hugs. I sat around a king-sized dining room table surrounded by a few of Tommy's older siblings and at least a half dozen of his hyperactive nieces and nephews.

All of the Littles resembled each other. Even Mom and Dad looked like clones. The only perceptible difference was while Mrs. Little went to the beauty parlor to have her gray hair set, the rest of the female Littles had long, light brown hair, and someone took a fine-tuned buzz cutter to the male scalps a couple of times a month.

Mr. Little asked numerous questions about the murder and filled me in on the latest gossip he had gathered on his postal route. He didn't have any information to help me with my investigation, but he promised to let me know if he heard anything.

We had a not-so-light dinner of chicken pot pie, salad, homemade bread, and apple pie à la mode. After eating until I thought I might explode, Tommy walked me to my car. I filled him in on my theory about a mistaken identity murder.

"First of all, Randa, if you think Liza's in danger, you have to tell the police. Why don't you let me call Detective Miller and run it past him? Second, if Ian Patterson were behind it, he would have made sure he had the correct twin. Maybe Kyle screwed up. He has a temper, but he's pretty sharp. Mitch is a party boy, and he wouldn't hurt a flea." He shook his head. "It doesn't add up."

Tommy was correct. Maybe I still didn't have a theory or a suspect.

Then Tommy did the dumbest thing ever. I think he may have gotten confused while sitting at the table with his look-alike kin because he kissed me on the lips. It was brief and fast and not smart since I may have had a boyfriend. Besides being a stupid move, it was also a dangerous one, seeing as how I required a lot of kisses very soon.

He blushed. "Thanks. You made Mom happy, plus I like to see you."

"Thanks, Tommy. You're the best! Talk to you tomorrow." I sprinted to The Tank.

I parked my monstrosity in front of the inn and ran inside to see if Brad had called. He hadn't. I gave Spot a few belly rubs, took a look in the mirror, fluffed up my hair, reapplied my lipstick, and headed to the pub to tackle my next errand.

West was behind the bar. His face lit up when he saw

me. Then he chuckled. "Hey, Dr. Shortcake. How ya feeling? You really tied one on Saturday night."

He took entirely too much pleasure in my mortification, as he reminded me of the stupid things I had said and done.

"I came to tell you that I'm sorry. I behaved atrociously, and I'm ashamed. Please forgive me."

"No worries. You were pretty adorable. I—"

"Did I vomit all over Brad?"

West's brow furrowed, and he rubbed his chin."Did the pretty little doc vomit all over the big handsome doc? Let me think."

"West?" I stomped my foot. "Did I?"

"Not to my knowledge." He laughed.

"What did I say to you and Brad when you guys put me to bed? I can't remember."

He tapped a finger on his forehead, looked to the ceiling, and pretended as if he was trying to recall the conversation.

"Stop teasing, and tell me," I demanded.

He leaned over the bar to whisper, "You begged for kisses."

"Oh, no! I knew it. Did I ask you to kiss me, because Brad hasn't called? Stop laughing, West. This isn't funny."

West stopped laughing to clench his jaw.

"You asked the doc to kiss you, not me."

"Oh, thank God. Are you sure?"

West didn't frown often, and this particular one made me uncomfortable.

"I'm damn sure who you asked for what."

I think I may have been the only person in town who annoyed the happy-go-lucky bartender.

"What if he doesn't call me? What if the rumors about him getting back together with Jessica are true? What if he is repulsed by how hideous I am when I'm drunk?"

West held up a palm. "Slow down. Any man that would pick Jessica over you is a fool, and that lucky bastard isn't a fool. And you aren't a repulsive drunk. You talk too damn much and say stupid ass things, but you're still kind of cute." He leaned in close. "And quite kissable."

West and his perfect biceps, alluring messy hair, and the way he said kissable with puckered lips—

I cleared my throat. "So I asked Brad for kisses, and you don't think he picked Jessica over me?"

He closed his eyes as if to say, give me strength with this relentless girl, and when he opened them, said, "Give him another day. He'll call."

I took in West's long eyelashes, his soft lips, and his broad chest. "Thank you, West, and I'm sorry I got drunk and said a filthy word. And I'm sorry I annoy you. Just so you know, sometimes you annoy me, too!"

I turned my back to him, bit my lip, and strolled out of the pub. I pulled my jacket around me, trudged up the hill, climbed three flights, and showered. I put on my kitty pj's, descended the stairs, and made myself a cup of tea. I sat in the kitchen beside the olive green phone and left Grimwood a message. Then I called my dad.

"Yeah, Dad. I know. A Harvest Princess. It was ridiculous, and I was so embarrassed that I got drunk!"

My dad teased me and made me laugh until my ribs hurt and my eyes watered. Finally, Spot and I climbed to my tower, where I crawled under my covers and dreamed about sweet secrets and decadent kisses.

Chapter 31

If one were to look into the private conference room in the Lettermen Campus Library basement one fall evening, they would have seen four individuals huddled over stacks of papers and piles of cassette tapes.

We combed through Liza's notes and tapes. The article she had published about Patterson's attempts to bypass environmental regulations was well written and didn't paint Ian Patterson in a favorable light. However, it didn't include any information that wasn't public knowledge. We couldn't find proof of the scandal that I was certain existed.

"Nothing here." P.T. Grimwood took off his glasses and rubbed his eyes.

"Let's check one more time," I begged. "We're missing something."

"Randa, I agree. I don't think there's anything here," Tommy said.

"Dr. Albright, if they had mistaken Suzy for me, I think they'd have come back for me."

"I agree, Randa. It's a good theory, but I don't think it's what happened. I'm telling you Patterson wouldn't have made a mistake that big. Mitch and Kyle are spoiled rich boys, but I don't think they're murderers."

Pat took a folder from his briefcase. "Little, you see the coroner's report and official autopsy?"

"I've seen the coroner's report and the *redacted*

autopsy."

"Want to step out of the room?" Pat asked Liza.

"No. I'm fine," Liza said

"You sure?" Pat asked.

"Yes," Liza said. "If anything upsets me, I promise I'll excuse myself."

Pat called Tommy's attention to something he found in the documents as Liza and I looked on.

"What?" Liza and I asked at the same time.

"Kid, sorry. There's evidence that your sister engaged in sexual intercourse right before she died."

Liza waved a dismissive hand. "That doesn't surprise me at all."

"Tommy, what aren't you guys telling us? Was she raped?" I asked.

"No evidence of forced entry," Pat stated.

"My sister was pregnant and partied. Why would it surprise me that she had sex? I know she wasn't innocent. I think people worry that because I seem innocent and my father is a pastor, maybe I can't handle the facts, but I can!"

"You got *cojones*, kid," Pat told Liza. "Not sure I'd be so stoic if it were my sibling."

Tommy and I concurred.

"There's new science that can test DNA. Expensive, but someday every police department in the country will use it," Pat said.

"Yeah, I've read about it," Tommy said.

"Until then, gotta figure things out with our brains." Pat tapped his forehead.

He stood and faced Tommy, clutching Tommy's neck in his hands. The two of them played out a few strangling scenarios, and eventually, Liza and I joined in.

We gave our investigation everything we had, the problem being we hadn't discovered anything new almost three hours into our meeting.

"Let's sum up the facts," I said. "Suzy was about two months pregnant. She was having sex with someone and was strangled soon after. Her body was left less than twenty-five yards from the road in the state forest. She was wearing Liza's bikini. Someone cut out her heart, put her in a spray-painted pentagram, and then hammered nails into her hands and feet. This seems to be a copycat of two murders from 1986 that Pat wrote about. Finally, Skyler Dubbs was framed when a ring Suzy gave him was left like a Hansel and Gretel style clue."

"What if the kid wasn't framed? He confessed," Pat said.

"I know you're not fond of him, but he was framed," I said.

"Randa, maybe Grimwood's correct. There's nothing in these papers that indicates the Pattersons had anything to do with it. Her ex-boyfriend, Peter O'Neill, hasn't been implicated either. You don't have any other suspects."

None of us brought up the odd acting pastor in front of Liza. Maybe he was the reason Tommy and Pat seemed a bit secretive.

"Professor Albright, maybe they're right. I thought Skyler was innocent, but the state detective, the local police, the mayor—they all think that Skyler's guilty," Liza said.

"No, it wasn't him. Look, I have another lead. There are two guys I'm looking into. They owed a man in Greenport money, and they've been connected to the scene."

Tommy quirked an eyebrow. "Wanna fill us in?"

How could I "fill them in" when my lead was from sources they couldn't understand?

"As soon as I know more, I can tell you. The truth is, it's a sketchy clue."

It was a thoroughly sound clue, but I'm sure the three of them would have found a telepathic vision sketchy.

"I'll keep looking through these notes if I can keep them," Pat told Liza.

"Of course, and I'll keep looking for something on my end," Liza said.

At the end of the evening, Tommy walked me to my car so that we could talk privately.

"I'll keep working on my end, Randa. I promise. But we aren't finding anything."

"I don't trust Pastor Smith. I can't pinpoint it. But something is off. I don't like that he isn't interested in the results of the autopsy," I said.

"I agree. If you take it at face value, he is a religious man ashamed of his daughter's behavior. If you look at it less naively, he isn't acting like a grieving father."

"Is that why you and Pat seemed a bit secretive? You didn't want Liza to know that you don't think her father is being honest?"

"That, and it's sordid and a bit kinky. I remember Suzy as a little girl in pigtails. I imagine Pat remembers her as a kid too. Everyone loved the Smith girls. They were the cutest things you ever saw, always in matching dresses."

We stood in quiet reflection.

"Tommy, could I talk to you about something else?"

"Sure, you know you can talk to me about anything."

"I made such a fool of myself when I got drunk on Saturday, and Brad isn't returning my calls."

Tommy leaned on my open car door and looked thoughtful. "I don't think the rumors about him and Jessica are true. I think he's a busy guy. I think he'd be crazy to hold Saturday night against you. He'll call, and if he doesn't, well, some other man will snatch you up."

"How long do you think I should wait for him to call?"

"You mean before you go out with someone else?" he asked.

I looked at the ground before focusing back on Tommy. "I think so. Maybe? I honestly don't know what I'm thinking. How long would you wait for a girl to call you?"

"Depends on the girl, Randa." He looked above my head at something in the distance.

I tried asking my question another way. "How long should I wait for Brad to return my calls before I give up?"

He took his time responding. "If I liked a girl, I would call her as soon as I could get to a phone. But, say something went wrong, well then maybe it might take me twenty-four hours, and maybe a lot went wrong, so maybe forty-eight hours. Let's say she likes me and wants to give me the benefit of the doubt. She should give me three days. So, Randa, maybe after three days, you should let it go."

"Three days." I frowned. I was well on my way to that heartbreaking number.

"Hell, Randa. I don't know what I'm talking about. I'm probably giving you crappy advice. But I wouldn't let a girl wonder. I'd treat her like a queen."

"I know you would, Tommy. You're a sweetheart."

He rested his hand on mine. "Randa, he'll call, and if

he doesn't, I think it's time for you to give me a chance."

It was probably a low-down thing to do, but I read Tommy's mind. My dear friend thought I might be giving up on Brad and finally giving him his long-awaited shot.

The problem was, it wasn't Tommy that consumed my thoughts.

Chapter 32

I needed a lobotomy because I stood in the doorway of the pub about to add to my increasing list of poorly hatched Bellmount schemes. I took a deep breath and stared at West Westinghouse the Third until he looked my way.

He didn't call out, "Hiya, Dr. Shortcake." He didn't smile. He didn't do any of the typical West things. Instead, he froze, holding a beer in mid-air. Our connection was understood and electric. I retreated.

I waited beside the stairs that led to his apartment. I leaned against the cold brick wall and closed my eyes. When I opened them, West was watching me.

"Did you work things out with Doc?" he asked.

I shook my head.

He stepped closer, placed his hands on my waist, and pressed his forehead against mine.

"Liam will kill me," he said.

"Yes," I whispered.

"Edith won't ever forgive me."

"I know," I said.

His chest rose and fell beneath my ungloved hands. He moved his forehead back and forth just enough to tickle me with his disheveled hair. Then, he once again centered his forehead on mine.

"I want you to kiss me," I said.

He uttered a deep sounding, "Ahhhh. Where do you

want me to kiss you first?"

"Here." I pointed to my lips.

With our foreheads still pressed together, I waited. I knew how much Weston Westinghouse wanted me. I could read his mind, after all.

"West, please kiss me!" I begged.

Then I waited.

Finally, he touched my lips with his scorching finger. "Where should I kiss you after that?"

I pointed to the area that was visible above my v-neck sweater. He ran his finger along my collarbone, and my thighs tingled.

"Can you really read my mind?" he asked.

"Yes. Kiss me," I begged. "I hurt."

"What hurts?"

"My entire body. I want to be kissed so much, I hurt."

"Poor Shortcake." He brushed his mouth over mine. I whimpered.

When his lips touched the line of my sweater, I moaned. West was expertly creating a powder keg of desire that was about to take out half of Bellmount.

"Are you reading my mind right now?"

"Yes, I know you hurt too."

"I do. My body aches for you, and I'm losing my mind trying to behave."

"You behave? I thought you enjoyed defiling princesses." My voice sounded embarrassingly needy.

"But you're my innocent little Shortcake." He nuzzled his nose against mine.

"Please stop teasing, and kiss me." I lifted my lips to his.

Still taunting me, his finger moved between us in an

attempt to shield his lips.

I kissed his finger. "West, I know the things you want to do to me. Please, do them. Please!"

West lost control, and my decade-and-a-half-long dream finally came true. He grabbed my hair, his body trapped me against the building, and his lips caged mine.

He licked at my lips. I opened them, and his tongue tapped mine. We took turns—entering and retreating, entering and retreating. As inexperienced as I was, I knew what to do. His thoughts told me precisely what he wanted. My body also had its own set of demands, which included nipping and sucking on his bottom lip and running my fingers through his hair.

"If you can read my mind, say it for me," he demanded.

"I can read your mind."

"I ache from desire, too, and I want to hear you say it," he whispered as he bit my ear.

I responded with a raspy, "West, I want you to kiss me—everywhere."

Hearing me articulate my desires by using the word *everywhere* was what West longed to hear, and that was the moment he no longer saw me as a cartoon confectionary. He lost control of whatever semblance of adulation he held, and I tumbled from my virginal pedestal.

He spun me around so that I faced the wall. He used my hair as a handle and turned my head to the side to kiss me while his clothed body rubbed against my backside. His other hand roughly traveled the length of my torso, sliding under my sweater, waking up body parts that had lain dormant for twenty-five years.

With each caress, I called out his name and begged

him to continue his ministrations.

"Not here," he said.

We took the stairs as one amorphic blob of hands and lips. When we got to the landing, he kicked at his door, and when it opened, he pushed me inside. A white T-shirt, a pink sweater, and my bra were tossed somewhere in his apartment.

"Where should I kiss you next?" he asked.

"Everywhere." I shamelessly arched my breasts into the air.

I struggled to tell the difference between his vocal whispers, his filthy thoughts, and my wanton desires. His "you taste like candy," and *such sweet pink nipples* mingled with my *I need more kisses,* and our desires became inseparable.

West bestowed a crazy number of decadent kisses across my breasts. His lips circled my nipple, and he sucked until I thought I might lose my mind. Then he attended to my other breast.

"Where else do you want me to kiss you?" he asked.

Feeling self-conscious, I ran my hand over my stomach.

"Oh, yum."

He licked at me like I was a lollipop. It tickled. I giggled until it stopped being silly and turned into a scorching sensation that left me trembling.

"Where else, beautiful?"

I ran out of places to point to that didn't involve taking off my pants, and although I ached to rid myself of them, I pointed to my ear.

He laughed. "That isn't what I had in mind."

I knew what he had in mind, but he succumbed to my request, and his hand gently brushed my hair over my shoulder. In the midst of our out-of-control sexy interlude, that small gesture felt superbly romantic. I tilted my ear toward his mouth. He licked and nibbled at it. Then, in one smooth motion, he gathered my hair and moved to the other ear. He continued to nibble on me in between his whispers.

"I want to do special things for you, love. Let me kiss everything."

"Please, West!"

He led me to his unmade bed. He grasped my right hand and pressed his open lips to my wrist. He slowly pulled his lips together, and when they were almost touching, his tongue popped out and performed the tiniest of licks.

"Ahhh."

Our gazes locked as he placed a tiny kiss and a sensual lick on the tip of each finger. West worshipped a hand that spent most of its time hiding behind a layer of fabric protection. I thought my body might leave the earth and float far, far away.

Finally, he placed one of his slow open-to-closed-mouthed kisses on my palm. He finished with the most masterful of licks. I wondered if it would be a turn-on or a humiliating bumble if I orgasmed as he made love to my hand?

"Lie down," he said. He kissed me until I was lying flat, then placed two pillows under my head. "So you can watch."

He took hold of the waistband of my jeans, and I lifted my hips. My pants became part of the collateral damage scattered about his apartment. He hooked his fingers into my panties and slid them off. Before tossing them to the floor, he closed his eyes and buried his nose in them. The intimacy of the gesture made me whimper, and he smiled as if he were Lucifer himself.

He climbed on top of me. I closed my eyes and memorized the feel of every one of his kisses. He used his tongue with some and sucked with others. He kissed one spot quickly and the next so, so slowly. When he reached my belly button, he stopped. I opened my eyes as he seated himself between my thighs. The scandalous things going through his mind terrified me, and I reached for him.

"No," I said, attempting to pull him into my arms.

"I haven't kissed everything yet, and I'm starving."

I moaned.

His fingers combed through my curls. His voice was a low-grade rumble. "Love, your bush is as red and beautiful as your hair."

I whimpered. "West, I think I'm scared."

"No. You're my brave girl, and I'm going to make that horrible ache go away."

He pressed my thighs open. I tried to close them, but he didn't allow it.

"Keep them open for me," he demanded.

He blew on my curls, and my hips lifted off the bed. He blew again, and I emitted some new utterance.

"Mmm. That's a good girl." He kissed a trail that led inward on each of my thighs, and I opened wider. His fingers skillfully worked their way inside me. Then, his tongue did one long lick.

"Yum."

"Ohhh!"

"Can you still read my mind?"

"Y-yes."

"Good," he said.

His face slid between my thighs. His tongue began its exploration, and his thoughts invaded mine.

Shortcake, watch me.

At first, I obeyed.

His eyes focused on my face as his tongue continued to flutter in and out. I closed my eyes and dropped my head back, but he was having none of my indolent enjoyment.

Watch me, his mind demanded.

I opened my eyes, propped myself onto my elbows, and again tried to obey. His eyes were slits; his lips glistened; and he looked drugged.

My elbows slid out from under me, and my head hit the pillows. I didn't have the strength or energy to hold myself up while my body quaked and shivered beneath his touch.

"West, I can't. It feels too good."

His moan reverberated inside of me. His fingers searched until he found what he was looking for. He rubbed in small circles while I uttered a variety of guttural sounds. Then he planted a kiss so deep inside of me that it radiated outward and landed in my extremities. He followed it with a mental promise. *I'm going to suck on you until you come, my love.*

I said, "Oh my God," a million times as his fingers and mouth took turns massaging my special spot. My thighs quivered, and my body tensed.

Come for me, love, his mind demanded.

"Oh, God," and "Ahh," I said again.

That's it, I've got you. Come, my beautiful Shortcake.

My trembling thighs reached a fevered pitch. My body pulled itself into a tight little ball that sat beneath West's lips, and then the powder keg blew.

"Oh my God, West!" I cried out as waves of pleasure rolled over me—over and over and over—until my exhausted body relaxed.

When I opened my eyes, I didn't recognize the possessed man that hovered above me.

"Now that I have kissed every inch of you, I plan to fuck you until we both scream," he vowed.

For the record, West was justified in his bobbing for apple bravado.

****

The neon green numbers on the alarm clock read twelve forty-five a.m. when West awoke me with a kiss. The glare from his Victorian floor lamp created a halo over his not-so-angelic but glorious face. His muscular upper torso peeked out from under the covers while the rest of him remained under the blankets, keeping me warm.

I ran my finger under his jaw and was delighted to learn that our night of lovemaking was the most amazing he had ever experienced. Fortunately for him—but unfortunate for me—he had quite the carnal history.

"Hey, beautiful. I have to run downstairs. It's my turn to lock up. Uncle Will will have my head if I stick him with it. I'll be back as soon as I'm finished."

I didn't want him to go. I wanted to touch him forever, so I ran my hands over his chest. "Your T-shirts make me crazy."

"Why is that?" he asked.

"I can't concentrate because they're too tight."

He laughed. "Well, your clothes make me crazy too."

"Why is that?" I knew what he was going to say, even before it came out of his mouth.

"Because you wear too many, and they aren't tight

enough."

"I'm a professor. I spend my entire day in front of young men. I can't dress like one of your barflies."

In his unmelodious voice, he belted out something about being hot for a teacher.

"That's disgusting." I wrinkled my nose.

He ruffled my hair. "You are seriously adorable and out of it. It's lyrics from a song."

I ignored his jibe. "I have to go, too. Aunt Edith will be wondering where I am, and I have to be at the campus early tomorrow. I have a ton of papers to correct."

Moments later, neither of us had moved, and West's nose was buried in my hair.

I wrapped my palm halfway around his bicep. "Hey West, do you have a scar?"

"A scar?"

"Where I shot you?"

"No idea. You tell me. I can't see my ass." He pulled the blankets down and turned his backside to me.

I scooted down to inspect his perfectly chiseled buttocks.

"*Callipygian*," I said.

"What?" He looked over his shoulder at me.

"It's a Greek word meaning you have a beauteous backside."

"In normal people's words, you mean I have a sexy ass?"

"You have a tiny oblong scar. I'm so sorry."

He continued to study me over his shoulder. "I'm not. It's my Shortcake love tap."

I ran my finger over it, and his muscles tensed. I leaned forward and kissed our scar.

His "Oh, God" was so guttural that it sounded

painful.

He flipped over and wrapped his arms around me. "Maybe a few more minutes."

He rolled me so that I straddled him. I positioned my body upright, and his hands explored my torso. I closed my eyes and tilted my head back. My body undulated, and we both moaned. He ran his hands over my breasts, cupped them, and lifted them into the air. I opened my eyes and gasped because West's hazel eyes had become amber flames.

His hands roamed downward, tickling at my stomach, then journeying farther south. He slid two fingers inside of me and growled.

He closed his eyes for one moment, hissed, opened them, and whispered, "You're so wet."

Enraptured, I ran my fingers along the side of his face.

His palms wrapped around my waist. Then he lifted my hips and guided our union.

"Don't move," I demanded. I closed my eyes and enjoyed the way my insides tickled and sucked him in. "Oh, West. Could you feel that?"

"Uh-hum," he said. "You're so tight and warm and wet. Now ride me."

He lifted my hips and brought them down gently. My head flew back, and I cried out. He did it again. I cried out again.

"Fuck," he grunted.

He slammed my hips down hard, and we cried out together. We continued building in a harder, faster frenzy until he pulled my body to him and rolled us so that he was on top.

I wrapped my arms and legs around him and

encouraged him with pleas of, "Harder, please," and "Oh, West."

Following one particularly perfect thrust, I held him in place and called out his name as my insides spasmed around him. He held still until my body had finished using his, and then he thrust a few more times.

"I'm going to come," he whispered.

"Yes," I begged.

His jaw tensed, his head flew back, and he howled into the rafters, "Fuck, Miranda," right before pulling out of me.

After his sweaty body crashed beside mine, he used a tissue from his nightstand to pat at the creamy liquid he had deposited on my stomach. He had done that same thing hours before, and there was something about the gesture I found endearing. Perhaps it was the gentle way he groomed me after our intense love-making.

He made a show of tossing the tissues onto his messy floor, and we laughed. I tried not to intrude on his thoughts, but since I had only earned a fifty percent on my most recent filter test with Lincoln, I accidentally divined that West was happy.

"Okay," he said, "I gotta go."

"Me too."

"I'll walk you home."

"No, I'll be fine," I insisted.

He raised an eyebrow.

"West, I can see the inn from the parking lot. I'll be fine."

He rolled out of bed, and his naked body strutted around the room, picking up clothes. When he became aware of my ogling, he turned his backside to me and wiggled his bottom in the air.

I held the blanket to my chin and watched with rapt attention. He straightened and faced me.

"*Callipygian.*" He grinned. Then he tossed my clothes onto the bed and began to gather his own.

After everything we had done to each other's bodies, I have no idea why I tried to hide under the covers to dress.

"No way," he growled, pulling the covers off me. "I want to watch as you slide that sweet little pussy into your panties."

"West!" I aimed a pillow at his twisted grin.

He chuckled and zipped up his jeans.

****

West and I were no longer naked, and we were standing in the cold parking lot, taking forever to say goodbye. He had insisted he would walk me home, and I had informed him that I could walk up the hill by myself.

"I had an amazing time," he said. "It's like we can read each other's minds."

I was disappointed that he was the only one besides Lincoln that I had divulged my secret to, and he believed it was part of our flirtatious game.

"I like how you are both innocent and sensual," he said. "A crazy sexy combo."

"But I'm not innocent anymore," I reminded him.

"Being deflowered by a piggish scoundrel like me does not in any way take away from your innocence. It's part of who you are."

"It is?" I asked, confused.

"Everything about you is soft and sweet and refreshing. I could fuck you for days, and I couldn't take that away from you."

The things he had done to my body, and he still

thought of me as *refreshing*. Sigh!

"You may be saying semi-poetic things, but I know what you're thinking."

He smiled. "That tonight, you are going to visit me so that I can see what that beautiful red hair looks like spread over my thighs."

I pushed on his shoulder. "I don't know how to do that yet."

He gave me one of his crooked smirks. "Don't worry, you can read my mind, and then you will know exactly how to do it."

I bit my lip and looked up at him through fluttering eyelashes. "Then you won't think of me as innocent and refreshing? Because I would prefer you to think I'm desirable and sexy."

"Oh no, you will still be my sweet, innocent girl, only you will have my cock in your mouth." He made a funny sound in this throat that sounded like "ahem." Then he slapped me on the butt. "I gotta go. Seriously, let me walk you home."

"No, because your uncle will be angry that you didn't help lock up, and you will be dead because my aunt will strangle you when she finds us making love in her bushes."

"Making love? You're adorable. I think you mean fucking, banging, screwing, shagging, boinking—"

"West! Stop!" I half-heartedly stomped my foot. "You say those words to shock me."

He threw his head back and laughed. "Yep. Watching you blush has become my greatest pleasure in life."

I made a pouty face.

"Come here." He pulled me close. "I'm teasing. I think you are one-hundred percent absolutely desirable and sexy!" He wrapped his arms around my waist and kissed my nose. "How about tonight we make love first, then we can boink?" He winked, clicked his tongue, smiled, aimed me in the direction of the inn, and tapped me on the rear. "Now go. See you tonight?"

"Deal," I yelled over my shoulder as I took off up the hill.

"Hey, Shortcake," he called out.

I turned.

"You're skippin', like an innocent little girl."

I laughed, then yelled, "I hate you!"

"Nah," he called back. "You're crazy about me!"

"And, you're crazy about me, Weston Westinghouse the Third," I whispered into the wind.

Chapter 33

I was absurdly giddy and a little more than halfway up the hill when ominous footsteps clomped behind me. They were too fast and too unexpected to be anything but a threat to my safety. I walked faster. They walked faster. I ran. They ran. My heartbeat became an echo that mimicked my footfall.

"Help!" I screamed. "Someone help me!"

A man grabbed me from behind. Another in a black hood came around in front of me. His fist pounded my jaw, and my head snapped back. Another punch, twice as hard, landed on my nose, and blood flew into the air. I felt every sharp *bam, bam,* in my teeth and gums. I covered my face with my arms, leaving my torso exposed. Consequently, blow after blow pummeled my stomach. The man who had been holding me knocked me to the ground.

"Please stop!" I cried.

One of the men straddled me, and I swiped at his hood in an attempt to see his face. He caught my hand and pinned it to my side.

"Westinghouse's little whore. Go back to where you came from."

The reference to West alerted me that they had been waiting outside of his apartment. I tried to temper my panic and think. Figure out who they are, my common sense screamed. Unfortunately, thick layers of black clothing kept me from reading his mind.

"Get off me!" I yelled.

I freed my hand and clawed at his eye. The brief moment of contact allowed me to intrude. *She's like a feral cat, so the pastor better appreciate this.*

"Bitch!"

He slapped me across the face, then picked my head up and slammed the back of it into the sidewalk. From somewhere in the distance, a beast-like shrill rang out, mingling with my cries.

The man sitting on my chest raised his hand and was about to strike again when Spot charged toward us. My loyal companion distracted the attackers by running circles around us and howling like a grieving wolf. The upright man kicked at him.

"No!" I screamed. "Don't you dare hurt him!"

Spot backed up, growled, and then lunged. He sounded more like a snarling hound of hell than a sheepherder.

"Get off of her, or I will blow your fucking head off!"

Shik. Shik. Boom! A gunshot tore through the night, and the men scattered.

"Miranda, are you okay?"

"Russ," I called out. "I'm hurt. My teeth. I can't feel my teeth."

Russ secured his rifle on his shoulder and lifted me from the ground. Spot stared into the distance. His ears and tail remained alert, and his fangs stayed visible between his curled lips.

"Good boy!" Russ said, patting our pup on the head. "I don't know how you knew Miranda was in trouble, but you're a good, good boy."

He looped his arm around me, and my two saviors escorted me across the front yard to Aunt Edith's open arms.

Spot followed as I leaned on my aunt, and the three of us climbed the million-mile staircase to my turret. My body ached, my vision blurred, and I felt dizzy. Too afraid to see what I looked like, I avoided the mirror on the back of the bathroom door. I sat at the end of the bed while Aunt Edith laid out my bedclothes. After she finished, she took a note from the pocket of her robe and handed it to me.

I unfolded the paper. "What's this?"

"A message for you. Bradley called this evening. He got back late last night. He's been in Greenport at the hospital."

"What?" I asked as I read my aunt's neat script.

"He was with the Minnichs. Their baby passed yesterday. I have no idea why, but Bradley seems to be blaming himself."

I fought tears.

"I'll be back to check on you in about fifteen minutes." Aunt Edith closed the door behind her.

I could barely move, so I'm unsure how I managed to climb into the clawfoot tub. My blood swirled with the water and disappeared down the drain. The steam from the scalding water made it difficult to breathe. Thinking I might pass out, I got out of the tub and leaned on the sink. The room spun.

The next thing I knew, I was vomiting into the commode. I was naked and lying on the bathroom floor when Aunt Edith and Brad found me.

"Please let me brush my teeth," I begged as they tried to drag me to bed.

Aunt Edith wrapped my robe around my body and acquiesced. She stood by my side as I rinsed the wretched taste from my mouth. How unfair to have the memory of West's delicious kisses ripped from me by foul-tasting bile.

I climbed into bed, and Brad was by my side. He shined a tiny light into my eyes.

"What happened? Tell me everything."

I filled him in, minus the mention of the pastor. How could I tell him the things I had heard in my mind? How could I tell anyone other than Lincoln that I had telepathic knowledge of my attackers? Maybe I could tell West? My heart hurt. My dear wonderful West? I left a few other details of my evening out of my account to Brad, specifically those parts where I had writhed in West's bed for hours.

Brad took my blood pressure and checked my pulse. Then he gently examined my ribs and explored my face.

"Brad, it stops hurting when you touch me," I told him.

His face lit up. "Because I'm a doctor."

I tracked his finger as it traveled in the air.

"Close your eyes and touch your nose," he said.

I followed his instructions.

"Concussion?" Aunt Edith asked.

"Concussion and a fractured nose. She will need an X-ray to determine if her ribs are bruised or fractured."

"And my teeth got knocked out," I added.

"No," Brad said. "They're all there."

"No, they got knocked out."

"Let me see."

I opened my mouth, and he poked around, tapping on them.

"Nope. Your teeth are still perfect and pretty!"

"Broken nose?" I touched it, and a stabbing pain shot through my skin and smacked into my brain.

"Yes, and you'll have a black eye or two when you wake up."

"Will my nose be deformed?"

"No," he said. "Swollen for a week or two, but you will still be beautiful. Just beautiful with black eyes and a concussion. Although, if you vomit again, we should get you to the hospital right away, and you need to take it easy for about a month while your ribs heal."

Aunt Edith excused herself so that she could make a pot of two a.m. coffee.

"Edith," Brad called after her. "You have to call Shultz in the morning. You also need to let the college know she won't be in for a couple of days."

"No," I cried to both of his suggestions.

Aunt Edith agreed with Brad, then closed the door behind her.

"My God, Miranda." Dr. Gordon was gone, and Brad, the boyfriend, took over. "What were you doing wandering about in the middle of the night by yourself? Were you looking for clues and playing detective again?"

Yes. That was it. I was being a detective, not having sex with another man, while my boyfriend tried to save a baby. I was horrible, vile, and extremely dizzy.

"Brad, the baby. I'm sorry."

He kissed my wrist.

I think that "It's Thursday. I haven't heard from you since Saturday" was perhaps the most horrible self-centered thing I had ever said. Adding to my growing lack of charms was that I forwent tact when I was distraught.

An hour before, I had been experiencing the most

incredible evening of my life. Since then, my entire world had been turned upside down. My safety had been threatened, I had been seriously injured, and my heart had been ripped from my body. I had cheated on the most heroic man I had ever met with the man I couldn't resist.

"I'm sorry it took me so long to return your calls." Brad stroked my cheek. "I had an awful few days. Between the baby and Jessica, I made four trips to the hospital on Saturday. After your tangle with the bottle, I decided to let you sleep in, and then I fell asleep late afternoon and slept until the next morning. I feel terrible that I left you alone. I knew you were upset about the festival and our ruined date. I got a call Monday morning that the baby was in critical condition. I canceled my appointments and spent two days at the hospital. I sat with the baby in my arms most of that time. No matter what I did, I couldn't save her."

I was unable to divine why he felt responsible for the infant's death. But he did, and it was eating at him.

"Then I had to make up all of the appointments I canceled. Every time I tried to get to the phone to call you, something else went wrong. I knew you would understand, but I'm still sorry. The good news is the hospital is sending someone to take over Dr. McGee's practice. It took them long enough. He retired over a year ago." He rubbed his eyes. "I'm sorry, sweetheart. I've been so tired. It's like nothing I've ever experienced."

Dark circles framed his eyes. His ordinarily perfect hair looked greasy, he didn't smell like his cologne, and he wore a faded gray sweatsuit.

"I thought maybe I had scared you off with my drunken escapades," I told him.

"Nah. We've all been there. I guess you didn't want

to be a Harvest Princess, and I think you were pretty upset about not getting your kisses." He leaned over and pressed his lips to mine.

The caress should have hurt my bruised lip, but it didn't. It was sweet and gentle.

"I think any serious kisses will need to be put on hold while your body heals," he said.

"How unfair." I smiled, but putrid green guilt ate away at my insides. "I think Jessica started new rumors that you two are back together." I suppose I was trying to justify my salacious behavior.

He huffed in disgust. "You didn't believe them this time, did you?"

"Not this time," I said, even though the rumors had consumed me.

"Let me see your ribs again."

He shifted my robe, so it hid my breasts, and rearranged the blanket, so it covered me from the waist down. I closed my eyes and let his warm hands explore my injured torso. I felt drugged. Brad's hands settled on a spot, and he thought, *There it is. Please don't let them be fractured.* I had the strangest feeling that my body had healed beneath his touch.

"Hopefully, not fractured," he said, breaking the silence.

I opened my eyes and again took note of how exhausted he looked.

He rearranged my robe and blanket. He took off his shoes, lay down on the bed beside me, crossed his arms over his chest, and stared at the ceiling.

"Get some sleep, sweetheart. I think your ribs will be fine, but tomorrow morning we should get the X-rays done just in case. I know you don't want to, but you have to face Shultz. If you hurt too much, let me know, and I'll do something to help ease the pain. For now, sleep. I'll be here when you wake up."

Spot positioned himself on the window seat, and his ears jutted into the sky as he stood guard over the left end of town.

I was so tired. I closed my eyes.

Chapter 34

Dr. Lucy Biggins had taught one of my favorite undergrad classes. Biggins wasn't quite five feet tall, and I doubt she hit the ninety-pound mark on the scale. Her high-pitched voice fit her tiny stature, and she was a master at storytelling. Urban Folktales and Legends 401 was loaded with exciting tales and gruesome nightmarish gore.

For decades the miniature Lucy Biggins stood in front of her lecture hall, edifying scholars with an unrivaled flair. Her favorite telling involved an escaped convict, a dark stormy night, a lustful couple, and a bloody hook.

"What do we learn from this urban story repeated around campfires for the last three decades?" Biggins had asked us.

That lecture was running through my head as I sat beside Brad on the way home from the hospital. Apparently, I needed a refresher course from Dr. Biggins because I had forgotten that girls who didn't behave ended up on the wrong side of a tale. Instead of a hook chopping off my head for my wanton ways, Pastor Smith's goons had beaten me to a pulp, and it would be at least a month before I could engage in licentious activities again.

My index finger traced circles on the passenger side window of Brad's car as I desperately sought an answer to my man dilemma. *You must decide between the light and the dark,* Madame Alina had said. Maybe the fraud had known what she was talking about.

After my return from the hospital, Aunt Edith and Russ sat with me while I met with Shultz in the library. His rodent-like eyes almost disappeared into his spider-veined cheeks, and his nonexistent chin seemed symbolic of his missing morals. The crooked cop was quite full of himself.

"Your niece finds trouble everywhere she goes, Edith. You need to put a leash on her."

Aunt Edith remained the calm before the storm and offered Shultz another cookie. Russ blew like an unplugged grenade. He leaped out of his seat.

"You useless son-of-a-bitch, are you gonna look for the men who did this, or am I gonna need to skin your fat ass?"

Shultz quaked for a moment. "It would have helped if you called it in last night. Can you give me a description, young lady?"

"No, I can't. It was dark, and the men had on hoods." I put my hands on my hips and deepened my voice. "Did you fill out the paperwork for me to carry my firearm yet?"

"Shultz, fill it out, sooner than later." Russ looked like someone had just peed in his toolbox.

Shultz never did answer my question. I found the entire conversation to be a fascinating exchange. Not only was he intimidated by Aunt Edith, the sheriff was also afraid of Russ.

Oh, the onion peel layers of drama that could be pulled back in one small town of eight thousand inhabitants.

Tommy Little took his lunch break to bring me a present.

"Hey, Randa." He presented me with a shoebox. "I didn't have time to go to the store."

I knew Tommy well enough to ask, "Is it something that will bite?"

"I hope not."

Since he was smiling, I peeked into the box. It contained an adorable turtle that fit into the palm of my hand. It had striking yellow and orange markings. Tommy blushed.

"To keep you company while you rest. It's an Eastern Box Turtle. He was sick when I found him, and I nursed him back to health. He's been a bit pampered, so I've been afraid to release him into the wild. You could help me take care of him."

"I don't have to chop up bugs for him, do I?"

"Just a few earthworms and snails," he teased.

"Oh, Tommy, you know I hate bugs."

"Then we can get him pellets at the pet store." He grinned and produced a box of food from his jacket.

I playfully slapped at his shoulder. "Tommy, you're almost as bad as West these days."

"Don't say that. Nobody's as bad as West." Tommy laughed.

Something pinged at my heart. "What's his name?"

"I never named him. I thought I would release him as soon as he was well."

"Do you remember when we were little, and I named every turtle we found Princess Pickles?"

"This Princess Pickles has a penis," Tommy informed me.

Despite his additional body parts, Princess Pickles it

was. Spot and I had a new friend.

"Did you call Detective Miller?" I asked.

"Yep. Miller said the case is closed, but I plan to call him back to let him know what happened to you last night."

This time Tommy exhibited discretion and kissed me on the forehead.

"Bye, Randa, take care of yourself, and enjoy Princess Pickles with a Penis."

Lincoln and Keisha visited when they got off work. Keisha placed a vase of aromatic red roses and purple asters on my nightstand. She sat on the edge of my bed, filling me in on my missed day of campus gossip, the most crucial tidbit being that crazy Professor Michaelson had a new wart on his big toe.

"Keisha, I hate to ask, but could you see if Aunt Edith will fix me a glass of iced tea. I'm so thirsty."

It wasn't exactly a lie because I did want a drink.

"Of course, darling," she said.

Keisha was always making me cups of tea and fixing my computer, but she had never called me "darling." How pathetic had I become? I took advantage of her absence and peppered Lincoln with questions.

"I don't know who the men were. I couldn't see their faces, but I knew the pastor was behind them. The problem is, I know because of my abilities, not because of any hard facts. What do I do?" and "Lincoln, I'm pretty sure I can communicate with Spot. I think he heard me calling for help, but I wasn't touching him at the time. Why do you think that is?"

Lincoln responded with his "Interesting. Very interesting," at the same time that Keisha entered carrying a tray of pastries and drinks.

"What's interesting?" she asked.

"Nothing. I asked Lincoln to bring me the stack of papers I left on my desk."

Keisha eyed us with what I'm sure was skepticism.

"I'll stop by the office this weekend and get them for you."

Brad and Liam came for dinner. Aunt Edith had prepared a pot roast with big potatoes and little carrots. I wasn't hungry. I was more interested in the conversation.

Liam filled us in on his rough work week. "I know I shouldn't say anything, Mom, but I may need to leave the firm. I'm not liking some of the things I'm seeing. I tried to talk to Lancaster. He doesn't want to hear anything about anybody."

"What's going on?" Aunt Edith asked, piling more meat and vegetables onto his plate.

Aunt Edith was a genius. I was learning her secret— food equals men divulging information. I filed it away for later.

"This goes nowhere," Liam said, looking around the table.

Four individuals were all ears.

"Patterson is raising huge amounts of money all over the state and filtering some of it through his personal account."

Aunt Edith put her fork down. "Bradley and I knew it."

Liam relinquished another secret. "Smith's church made one hell of a big donation."

"Patterson is promising to meet with lobbyists and discuss legislation that prohibits evolution from being taught in public schools," Brad said.

Liam nodded and clenched his jaw. "These donations

are shocking. Pretty much all of the old coal and lumber families in the county are also donating, and this money isn't showing up in Patterson's campaign fund. Some of the families...well, it's eating at me."

The Schuster family had to be one of those shocking donation-bribes. I had a feeling Gina Schuster was challenging everything Liam had grown up believing to be true.

"Oh, and get this, Grainey made a big contribution. The lucky son-of-a-bitch's profits are way up. It seems like every fool in western Pennsylvania went out and bought an extra few guns after Suzy Smith's murder," Liam said.

"The same thing happened a few years ago," Russ said. "That reporter published those stories about the cult crucifixions, and gun sales skyrocketed."

"I'm going to carry Princess with me everywhere from now on," I declared, pushing my dinner around my plate.

"Just don't carry concealed until you have your permit," Liam said. "And whatever you do, don't take a loaded weapon onto the campus."

I made a face at my meat before stabbing it a few times with the sharp prongs of my fork.

"Grainey is afraid the Roberti-Roos Assault Weapons Control Act will make its way from California to Pennsylvania. He's fighting it with everything he has. Patterson has promised to block it." Brad paused. "Liam, have you considered opening a firm, maybe running a business with some ethics in this town?"

"I don't know. I think I'd have to leave Bellmount to do it. Lancaster already takes care of almost every business in town."

"I think you would have two clients off the bat." Brad pointed at himself, then Aunt Edith.

The conversation halted. I assumed everyone at the table was considering Liam going into business for himself.

The silence broke when Spot barked, the doorbell rang, and Russ excused himself. Russ and Spot returned moments later, followed by West.

West took in my bruised face and muttered, "Ew."

"I know it isn't pretty, but I will live." I laughed.

West frowned. He greeted each of the people at the table, hesitating at Brad. "Doc," he said.

"Westinghouse," Brad said.

They appeared to be eyeing each other with something akin to irritated apprehension. West's gaze traveled from Brad to me. My heart ached with feelings I didn't fully understand. Guilt? Regret? Embarrassment? Sorrow? Lust? Loss? Some sort of combination?

"Pull up a chair, and I'll grab you a plate, Weston," Aunt Edith said.

"I can't stay because we're busy tonight. Winona told me what happened." West sat but waved off Aunt Edith's offer of a plate. "Tell me everything."

"Miranda decided to follow some lead in her mystery and ran into some thugs in the middle of the night," Liam said. "She has sleuthed herself right into a fractured nose, a concussion, bruised ribs, and a beautiful shiner."

"Yes, but some creep is walking around with a slapped face and a ton of scratches. I gave it to him good." I pretended to box. It was an absurd gesture, but I was dying a million deaths.

There was a wistfulness in West's gaze and a softness in his voice when he said, "I bet you did, Shortcake."

Brad cleared his throat and placed his hand over mine.

West stood. "I have to go. Miranda, please take care of yourself."

West had only called me by my name twice. Once as he orgasmed on top of me, and in that awkward moment in front of my family and Brad Gordon.

"West, did you get that information I asked you about?"

He furrowed his brow.

"You know, that information about Suzy's murder?" I bobbed my head around and pressed into the table to lift my bruised body out of the chair. "Please excuse me. I'll be back in a minute." I followed West toward the exit. "He was checking out a lead for me," I said over my shoulder.

"Westinghouse, don't you dare encourage this shit right now," Liam said.

"Weston, she needs to rest," Aunt Edith called after us.

"Fuck!" West said once we reached the porch. "I should've walked you home. I'm a piece of shit."

"West! Stop it. You aren't."

"I'm not? Then why are my best friend and your aunt losing their minds because I'm standing on your front porch? And why is Doc sitting beside you, taking care of you, while I pour beers for the town drunks?"

"West, you're the one I want to be with. I'm going to tell Brad about us. I'm just waiting for the right moment."

"Don't bother," he said.

I reached for him, and he took a step back.

"Shit, Miranda!"

"I'm Shortcake, or Dr. Shortcake, or love, or

269

beautiful. I'm not Miranda to you. Please smile, or laugh, or tease me."

He looked like he might reach for me but stopped himself. "Lowalski called."

"He did?"

"He thinks he knows who your guys are."

"Why didn't he call me?" I asked.

West shrugged. "I guess even a criminal realizes you need a babysitter."

Since it was partially West's fault that I was no longer demure, I decided to practice my rude gesture repertoire out on him. His statement earned him a raspberry and a middle finger. My first crude hand signal was immensely satisfying. Since West was intent on proving to me how frustrated he was, he tried not to smile at my uncouth reaction.

It took him forever to straighten the line of his lips. "Lowalski says he should have something by next week and wanted to know if we could stop by his place." Then he lost control, his mouth cracked, and he grinned.

My West was back.

"We have to wait until next week?" I sighed. "Fine, I should be feeling better in a few days. I get off work at four."

"No. You're done. It's too dangerous."

My West had disappeared.

"Who are you to tell me what I can and can't do? Don't try to lock me away because you think I'm too delicate. Don't you dare treat me like the rest of them in there." I pointed in the direction of the family dining table. "I couldn't take it from you. Don't shut me out of your life, and don't you dare try to pretend like there isn't something between us."

West's nostrils flared. It wasn't a look that suited his happy-go-lucky personality. "I'll go and check it out. I'll take Little with me. But this," he pointed back and forth between us. "There's no *us*. It was one night. I'm a pig, remember? You're better off with Doc."

"Don't say that, and I'm going with you to talk to Lowalski."

Aunt Edith leaned out the door. "Miranda, your dinner's getting cold."

"Shit!" West muttered as he retreated down the front stairs.

Even though my bruised ribs left me unable to take a step without pain, I would have chased after him if Aunt Edith hadn't been staring at me like I had snakes for hair.

A dizzy spell forced me to sit. My mind, body, and soul hurt so much I didn't know where the pain from one picked up and the other left off. I rested my face in my palms.

To top off my mess of a life, I had broken the invincible Weston Westinghouse the Third.

Chapter 35

If I had a nickel for every time someone informed me that winter came early in Bellmount, I could have afforded one of the new Radio World Cellular Phones I desired.

"Hey, little cuz, let's have breakfast on the porch this morning. It might be the last Saturday we can sit outside until the spring thaw. Winters come early and hit hard in Bellmount," Liam informed me.

I wore my gloves, sweater, and jacket, then wrapped myself in an afghan so that Liam and I could sit on the front porch. We ate Belgian pecan waffles and drank steaming cups of coffee.

Liam placed his plate on the patio table and studied my face. "You look like you went twelve rounds and lost every one of them."

I held my warm cup to my cheek. "Is the bruising getting worse?"

"Yep."

He continued to stare at my Quasimodo-ish face and furrowed his brow.

"Hey Miranda, is there something going on between you and Westinghouse? Brad's a hell of a good guy. I don't want to see you throw it away. Westinghouse has a different girl every other week."

"Nothing's going on between West and me."

A horrible ache landed in the pit of my stomach as I

recalled West's rejection.

"I'm crazy about Brad." I changed the subject. "So, let's talk about you and Gina."

Liam took a sip of coffee.

A boy riding a bike pulled into the driveway. He dismounted and trotted over to us, carrying a package.

"This is for a lady named Miranda," our young visitor said.

"I'm Miranda. Come on up."

The boy climbed the steps and handed me a box wrapped in pink paper and topped with a silver bow. "Some man asked me to give this to you."

"Who was the man?" Liam asked.

The boy shrugged. "I don't know. I didn't ask. He gave me ten dollars and asked me to deliver it to Miranda at The Bellmount Inn." He descended the porch, mounted his bike, and rode off.

"That's weird," Liam said. "You better let me open it."

"No way. It's mine." I knocked Liam's hand away. We continued to slap-fight until we were laughing.

Liam chuckled. "Knowing you, it's some thug's thumb."

"You're just jealous because you wish a mobster would send you a body part," I taunted.

I wasn't sure if I hoped it was a bracelet from Brad or a silly lets-be-best-friends-again bubble gum ring from West. In case it was the latter, I hid my package under my afghan so that Liam couldn't see it. I took off my gloves and scraped at the scotch tape.

I screamed, grabbing at my heart. "It's a… it's a…"

Liam jumped to my side.

"A bloody ear!"

"What the hell?" Liam's voice rose to operatic octaves.

I laughed so hard, I snorted, and my eyes watered.

"Damn you," he said when he realized I was teasing.

"You need to stop worrying about me. I haven't even opened it."

"Let me see." Liam attempted to peek under my blanket.

"Go sit down." I pointed to his chair.

Liam pouted but obeyed. I lifted the lid off the box and stared at my present. My surprise was an inexplicably beautiful rose gold necklace. A pink diamond shined from the center of a gun-shaped charm.

Liam came around to my side to stare at it. "Who's it from? Did you look at the card?"

A white note adorned with an embossed red rose sat between the necklace and a layer of cotton. I didn't plan to read it in front of Liam.

"It's from Lincoln. He said it reminded him of me."

The truth was, I knew who had sent it, and it wasn't Brad, West, or Lincoln. I put the lid back on the box.

"That Lincoln's a damn nice guy," Liam said.

I filled my lungs with cold air. "When do you think we'll have our first snow?"

****

I found my perplexing present fascinating and disturbing. I held the chain under my blue tiffany lamp, and the diamond sparkled and shined as I turned it every which way. Spot startled me when he tapped to let me know my Saturday evening dates had arrived. I ran my gloved finger over the embossed card that read, *Get well soon, my crimson princess. Yours, Greg.*

I placed the note on top of the necklace and shoved

the box into my dresser drawer. I opened my castle door, scratched my pup's ears, and gave him a doggy biscuit. Winona, Keisha, and a stack of ungraded essays greeted me at the bottom of the stairs.

"That is so cool," Keisha said. "He runs right up there to get you."

"Yep," Winona said, her shoulders pulled back and her chin held high. "Spot's super smart."

I suspected Winona was attempting to assume a position of superiority in our friendship since the inn was her second home.

"More than we can say about you," Keisha said, taking back her status.

I rubbed my temple. It was going to be a long night.

Aunt Edith had loaned us the library for the evening and prepared a snack tray of cheese, crackers, veggies, and dip. Winona had baked brownies with walnuts, and Pop and Uncle Will had sent a bottle of wine.

I took a sip of my water, Keisha stood below the fireplace mantel studying Grandma Zoey's portrait, and Winona asked, "Why was West just here?"

"West, here?" A surge of tingles shot through me.

"We just passed him. He was standing in your front yard, so I thought maybe he was visiting." Winona shrugged. "I guess not."

"Maybe he was with Russ, asking questions about cars or motorcycles." I didn't know why West had been to the inn because it hadn't been to see me.

"Maybe," Winona said.

Keisha pointed to the portrait. "Is this your Grandma Wilson that Lincoln treated?"

"Yes. Isn't she beautiful?"

"That is a grandma with some serious *juju*. I know

'cause my Nana Brown has *juju* too."

"Your grandma?" I asked. "In what way?"

Keisha never had a chance to answer because Winona blurted out, "Have you guys ever watched goats play? They're so cute. They jump on each other's backs."

I will give her this; Winona looked happy as she hopped about pretending to be a baby goat. Keisha's eyes narrowed, and she scratched her nose.

"Winona, what do baby goats have to do with what we are talking about?" I tried to think in Winona-speak. "Oh, I get it. Your grandma had goats?"

"No. Grandma Westinghouse hated goats and never let them in the house. I don't have any idea why because they're so cute."

"Maybe because they shit on the floor," Keisha said.

Winona was all seriousness when she said, "No, they mostly go to the bathroom outdoors, but Great-Aunt Gerty's goats used a kitty litter box when they went in the house."

This time Keisha used her middle finger to rub at her nose. "There is no way in hell you can teach a goat to shit in a kitty litter box."

"Yes, siree, Bob," Winona said. "You can teach goats lots of tricks."

I took a sip of water, and against my better judgment, asked, "What kind of tricks?"

"Even though Pluto had an eye patch, he could count to four. He used his hoof." Winona tapped her foot as she counted, "One, two, three, four."

"Who exactly was Pluto?" I asked.

"He was my Great-Aunt Gerty's one-eyed goat."

"He only had one eye?" I asked.

I was pretty sure Keisha's eye daggers might slice me

in two.

"Yes, he was jumping around on King's back. King was getting old, and he didn't like it when the babies jumped on him."

"So, did King the old goat scratch out Pluto, the baby goat's eye?" I asked.

Winona brought her hand to her mouth and gasped. "No. King wasn't mean, just old. Pluto jumped on him and leaped right into a briar, and the briar scratched his eye out. Grandma Westinghouse hated goats, but she liked to sew, so she made him an eye-patch." Winona formed buck-teeth, made mini animal claws, and spoke in a baby voice. "He looked so cute, like a little goat pirate."

"Shiver me mother fucking timbers and make the dingbat shut up," Keisha said.

"Keisha, don't be mean. Their entire house burnt down," Winona said.

Keisha had an arm on the fireplace mantel and had propped herself below Grandma Zoey's portrait. She gulped her wine and poured herself another drink.

Winona's story wasn't helping my concussion, but I was in too deep.

"Whose house burned down?"

"My Great-Aunt Gerty and Uncle Saul Shapiro's. One night Grandma and Grandpa Westinghouse were visiting them, and my grandma left Pluto in the house. She said since Aunt Gerty was always letting filthy animals in, she didn't think she would care. Aunt Gerty told her to stop calling Uncle Sal names. Then Grandpa Westinghouse snuck Pluto a cookie. Pluto got excited and jumped around, and knocked the Hanukkah menorah over. The latkes went up in flames, and then the curtains, and pretty soon, the entire house was burning. Everyone got out okay, even Pluto. But Great-Aunt Gerty never forgave Grandma Westinghouse. She said Grandma was a nasty Catholic who never got over people marrying outside the faith—and that's why she tried to burn her house down during a sacred holiday."

Both Keisha and Grandma Zoey's stares had glazed over.

Winona and I both jumped when out of nowhere, Keisha hollered, "What the hell? Not Jewish, you twit. *Juju*, as in magical ability."

Winona's cheeks flushed. "I was just saying." Her voice was soft as she confessed, "I like goats and Grandma Westinghouse and cookies."

Keisha had reached the end of her rope and issued her final threat to Winona. "Don't make me walk over there and slap you, woman."

I took pity on my inept storytelling friend. "Did you bring your notebook, Winona?"

"Yep." She retrieved it from her backpack.

"You have one too?" I asked Keisha.

"Damn straight, girlfriend." Keisha reached for her oversized purse.

I wasn't about to let little things like bruised ribs, a broken nose, overprotective relatives, and a guilty conscience get in the way of freeing the despicable Skyler Dubbs and bringing Suzy's killer to justice. Since I was cursed with Grandma Zoey's affliction, I would put it to good use. Perhaps, it would have been easier to set up shop with Madame Alina or go to Vegas and become an expert at cards.

Being telepathic had to make one good at gambling. Right? But that wasn't my calling. My mission was to find a ruthless killer.

"They have me locked in this house, and Brad is only letting me climb the stairs twice a day. I need you guys to handle some things."

The girls sat forward.

"I don't think Suzy was murdered at the Patterson pool, but it was probably somewhere people swim. I need you two to make a list of all of the pools within a sixty-mile radius. Include both indoor and outdoor, and any other places people might go. Maybe lakes?" I said.

"Aye aye, captain." Winona saluted me.

"We need to contact each of those places to see if Suzy visited and if someone was with her. See if you can narrow the search down, and once I can sneak past my guards, I'll go with you to check it out."

"It's a plan," Keisha said. "But the outdoor pools will be closed for the winter, so we might have problems getting the information we need. The good news is there are only two lakes in Bear County."

"There are a ton of swimming holes along the river, though. How will we check them all?" Winona asked.

"There is also a chance she may have been sunbathing," Keisha added.

"I know. Do the best you can," I said. "We need to move this along. We might be running out of time."

Neither of them commented on my plea for urgency. Keisha sat in quiet reflection, and Winona flipped through her notebook.

"Miranda, I've been thinking, what if it was Shultz? He's a pervert and likes younger women. What if he purposely messed up the investigation to cover up his crime?" Winona asked.

As I have previously indicated, I had concluded that Shultz had thrown a wrench into the investigation for three reasons. First of all, he was a klutzy cretin. Second, he was trying to keep Mayor Reynolds happy, and the mayor wanted the crime solved and closed so that nothing reflected poorly on his perfect little town. Third, and the most disturbing realization to me, was that he had tried to erase me from the scene because he was terrified someone would discover he had stopped a woman on her way into town and behaved like an atrocious debauchee.

"Hey, Winona, you're a moron. She would never have slept with that piece of shit cop, meaning it wasn't his baby, meaning it wasn't him. It was those damn frat boys. I could see it in their lecherous little eyes."

The Albright Detective Agency was working like clockwork.

Kind of.

Chapter 36

Dr. Bradley Gordon smelled like intoxicating musk when he picked me up in his fancy 1986 black convertible. I wore my red lipstick, a short floral skirt, an emerald blouse, and since I wouldn't have to walk far, my three-inch brown leather mules.

Brad dressed in a purple polo shirt that brought out his blue eyes and complemented his ebony hair. My gloves sat in my backpack, alongside Princess. I didn't anticipate needing either.

Brad's Main Street office was on the first floor of an ivy-colored Arts and Craft Style Bungalow. A line of white paned shaker windows made up the front of the building. Built-in light fixtures, affixed to the pine beams, lined the ceiling. A red brick fireplace with its massive oak mantel dominated his waiting room, and medical textbooks were crammed into the built-in shelving units.

Brad and I climbed the cherry staircase to the second floor.

He opened the door and ushered me inside. "Jessica got our house and the furniture in the divorce. I got my office and the clothes on my back."

I think he felt ashamed of his small apartment. He needn't have been. It was way nicer than West's pigsty and had real furniture.

"Have a seat." Brad pointed to a plush brown couch. "I'll finish dinner. Wait until you see what I prepared."

He smiled.

A butterfly, or ten, slapped at my chest.

I was excited for my big girl date, although I hoped he didn't plan on serving me something exotic, like escargot, caviar, or calamari. I craved a cheeseburger or a piece of pizza.

A table and two chairs sat between the living room and galley kitchen. Brad lit the candle on the dining table and the one on the coffee table in front of me. From my seat, I could talk to him as he prepared our dinner.

"How did you feel today?" Brad asked.

"I spent all day correcting essays. They were rough. I'm still a little dizzy, and I have headaches on and off, but my ribs feel better, and I think I'm ready to go back to work tomorrow."

He faced me. "I don't think that's a good idea. Why don't you rest a couple more days, and I'll give you a doctor's note."

I thought it over but didn't respond because I wanted to return to campus.

His back was to me, and his head was in his refrigerator when he asked, "How's the Smith investigation going?"

"So-so. I've been locked in my high tower. Right now, I have to rely on Winona and Keisha to look into things."

He chuckled. "You three are like Chuck's Angels?"

I was thrilled to finally understand a pop culture reference from the last two decades.

"Sure, if there's an angel with a bad attitude and another that is twenty-four cents short of a quarter." I beamed at Brad's laughter.

"Dinner's ready."

I took my seat at the table, and he dramatically called out, "Ta-da!" as he placed half a homemade turkey sub and a handful of potato chips in front of me.

"Sorry," he said. "I was going to cook for you, but I figured you'd experienced enough trauma over the past couple of months. I didn't want to add to it by forcing you to taste my cooking. It's even worse than my singing."

"That bad?" I taunted.

"Pretty much. Wine?"

"Water. I'm never drinking alcohol again."

He filled my glass with tap water and poured himself some wine.

"I'm sorry," he said again. "I know it isn't as fancy as your aunt's cooking."

"Are you kidding? I'm relieved. I was afraid you might make me something gourmet like raw oysters." I took a big bite and spoke with my mouth full. "I wub subs."

His eyes sparkled. "I think you might have me on a pedestal."

"Because you're perfect, and everyone says you look like a charming prince."

"A charming prince?" he asked.

"Yes."

"Who says I look like a prince?"

"Winona, Aunt Edith, Keisha, the girls in my class, every woman in town."

His chest puffed with pride. However, my loose tongue had me feeling the fool.

After we finished eating, Brad took a package of pink and white coconut cream cookies from his cupboard. He gathered the treat and his glass of wine. I grabbed my water, and we headed to the couch.

He disappeared for a minute and came back carrying a book and the same fluffy blanket we had used on our picnic date.

"A snowball picnic?" I asked.

"Better. I have a surprise for you."

He sat beside me and tapped his lap. I laid my head on his thighs, and he pulled the blanket over me.

"A restful evening with a book. Perfect for healing brains and ribs, and no laughing at my British accent," he said.

I stared up at him as he read. "There was no possibility of taking a walk that day. We had been wandering, indeed, in the leafless shrubbery—"

I popped up. "*Jane Eyre*? You remembered. Pink and white snowball cookies and *Jane Eyre*."

He cleared his throat. "Do you mind, I'm reading," he teased.

I lay down, closed my eyes, and listened to his deep baritone imitate a British accent. I was warm and cozy. His skin wasn't touching mine, so I couldn't divine his thoughts, but a woman doesn't need to be telepathic to know what a man reading her classic literature in a fake accent while feeding her nostalgic cookies is thinking.

After thirty minutes, he stopped reading to take a sip of wine. I used the break to push the blanket to the side and help myself to dessert.

"Yum." I bit into my cookie. I made a show of licking it and uttered scrumptious food sounds that I supposed were not all that different from succulent sex sounds.

Brad's eyes widened, and his lips parted as he watched me.

"Take a bite." I put my cookie to his mouth.

His tongue popped out, and he licked at it. Then he took a tiny nibble. I wasn't trying to be sensual when I licked where his tongue had been. I simply wanted to see if I could taste him on my cookie. He groaned. I popped the remainder of the sweet into my mouth, chewed, and swallowed.

Brad Gordon looked like a naked harem had just danced for him.

"Want another cookie?" I reached for the package.

He tossed Jane onto the table. "About those kisses, I owe you." His voice was so deep, I shivered.

"I thought you said I couldn't have kisses for an entire month."

"These are prescription kisses."

Brad's arm wrapped around my torso, and he gently pulled my body to his. His other hand cradled my face, and his lips, so soft and gentle brushed mine. I relaxed into his arms. He stopped kissing me to look into my eyes. He ran his finger over the bridge of my nose.

"Does it hurt?" he asked.

"No," I said. "You're so gentle."

"I'll be so gentle. So, so, gentle. If anything hurts, tell me." His voice became quieter as he spoke, demonstrating just how careful he would be.

He ran his finger under my eye, where my bruising looked ungodly.

"It doesn't hurt. Your hands are like medicine," I whispered.

"Good," he said, untucking my blouse from my skirt. "Lean back."

I pressed my torso against the couch, closed my eyes, and listened in on his thoughts. He wasn't making a pass. He was trying to take away my pain.

Gentle. Gentle. Don't hurt her.

His fingers danced over my bruised ribs.

"Let me see if they're healing," he said.

I let him lift my blouse to peer under it.

"Ew." He shook his head.

"Brad, don't be angry. Just touch me, so I don't hurt," I begged.

I closed my eyes, and his fingers dragged over my ribs, just barely, but enough. It felt as if a pain reliever pumped through my body. "Your hands are magic."

I opened my eyes and studied his visage because his thoughts had changed. He no longer wanted to treat my injury. He wanted to rid me of my shirt and bra. Dr. Brad—and boyfriend Brad—argued with each other. The doctor won. He would wait until my body healed. I inwardly smiled at my gentlemanly boyfriend's lustful thoughts.

"Brad, kiss me," I demanded.

His lips crushed mine.

"Sorry," he said, as he contained his passion and once again became gentle.

I tapped his lips with my tongue, and he allowed me to enter. I withdrew and bit his bottom lip. He bit mine. I kissed softly. He kissed softly. I kissed harder. He kissed harder. I smiled. He smiled.

"Brad, I like your dimples and your kisses."

"I'm glad," he whispered.

My hands traveled under his shirt, and I lifted it over his head. My chivalrous doctor had some pretty impure thoughts. They weren't quite as naughty as West's desires, but they possessed their own bawdy charm.

"Your chest is so muscular." I scratched my nails through his coarse dark curls.

"Chopping wood."

The raw sound of his voice made me tingle.

"Really?"

"I like to chop wood," he said.

Yes, he did like chopping wood, and he thought about it for one-sixtieth of a minute before he returned to thinking about my body. His kisses traveled from my lips to my neck and settled on my ear.

My week's entertainment led me to realize that I loved to have my ear attended to. I now knew that my favorite thing in life was to have a man lean close and softly intimate at seductive, racy things. I also discovered that I didn't appreciate it when those quiet utterances included telling me that my luscious messages were about to stop.

"Miranda," Brad whispered. "We have to stop. I'm…" *I'm so turned on, I ache.*

I ignored his plea and continued running my hands over his chest.

"Please stop," he said. "I want you, sweetheart, and I'll hurt you."

"Hurt me?"

"You're injured, and so tiny, and I'm so big, and I'm not sure how much longer I can be gentle." *And you may be a bit drugged right now.*

It was a strange thing for him to think because I hadn't had anything to drink. Although truth be told, his touches left me with a warm fuzzy buzz, and I no longer felt injured. Besides, I liked how big he was, and I didn't care if he stopped being gentle, so I continued exploring his muscles with my hands and mouth until his mind said terrifying things. *Damn, she's so sexy! Pull yourself together, man. She's still a virgin. She's so sweet! She wants you, too! Not tonight, you'll hurt her! I think I could love her forever! I think she is the one!*

I pulled away. I had been ignoring my problem for days, and now here it was, slapping at me. My poisonous putrid guilt lodged itself between Brad and me. He still thought I was a virgin, and if I was *the one*, he had to know the truth.

"Brad, we have to talk."

He dressed as I confessed.

"You're my superhero. You have made every awful thing that has happened to me since I came to town better."

"I'm glad," he said.

"But you were supposed to take me on a perfect date and kiss me all over."

"Go on, Miranda." His jaw tensed.

"And, there were so many rumors about you and Jessica. I tried not to believe them, but after a while, they got in my head. Then you saw me drunk, and I behaved atrociously. I assumed I had upset you. I kept calling and leaving messages."

"I know, I received the messages." He clenched his hands into fists.

"I even drove here to your office—twice."

"I didn't know that," he said.

I looked at my hand, then grabbed his.

He knew what I was about to say, and he thought he might even know who my partner in crime was.

"Tell me." He held his breath.

"I'm so sorry. I thought you had broken up with me. I was sad and lonely. Now I know you were trying to save a life, but then all I knew was I couldn't find you."

I paused for a moment to let him talk. He didn't.

"Please forgive me. I was with West." I didn't need to finish because he had figured it out even before I spoke the words.

He didn't say anything, but he thought a million painful things. *I thought she was different. I thought she was better than all the other women. I thought she was the one. Damn, I can't breathe.*

"Please say something, Brad."

He let go of my hand and blew out the candle in front of us. "I guess I better take you home."

Chapter 37

Even though I longed to be released from my tower, my return to campus after my extended weekend was bittersweet. I was apprehensive because I was defying my doctor's orders in returning so soon after sustaining my injuries. I also knew that asking Brad to forgive me for my fling with West was a tall order.

The bottom line was, I didn't understand my feelings for West. I thought about him all of the time but had to face reality. West had a collection of beautiful women. A nerdy bookworm who barely knew how to kiss could never satisfy a man like him. Of course, I also thought about Brad. He was too good to be true and had adored me. I had carelessly blown up whatever future we had because of my ever-increasing inadequate willpower and my growing impatience.

Adding to my misgivings, I had dizzy spells, my ribs ached, and I continued to struggle with headaches. There was also the issue of my hideous appearance.

I stood in front of the classroom, writing notes on the chalkboard, when someone called out, "Hey, Dr. Albright. You look like you ran headfirst into a wall."

I didn't have to see him to know my heckler was John Gibbons.

"Don't take this personally, but you used to be hot, now you look, well, not hot."

I ignored the comment.

"Is it gonna heal up, and are you gonna be pretty again? I don't think I can concentrate and learn if you are going to look like that all semester," Mr. Gibbons added.

If the throbbing in my head hadn't felt like someone was trying to suck my brain out through my nostrils, I might have taken the comment personally.

"You're an idiot, John. You hurt her feelings," chided Missy Henderson.

"Rest assured, my doctor has said when the bruising and swelling go away, I will look like my old self." I'm not sure if this reassurance was for the benefit of my class or myself.

"I heard a rumor that your boyfriend beat you up," Gibbons said.

I bristled. I hadn't had a boyfriend for almost fourteen hours, and Brad was the most gentle man in the world.

"Not the handsome doctor with the picnic basket?" Shelly Byers gasped as she held her hand to her heart.

I didn't have time to respond before the next rumor rang out.

"I heard you and the bartender at the pub tied one after the harvest festival, and you fell in the middle of the street," Myles Allen said.

"You heard wrong!" Unfortunately, after accessing the accusation, I realized that the rumor had elements of truth to it.

"I heard you are trying to figure out who killed Liza's sister, and since her dad is an ass, he keeps beating the shit out of you," chimed in Dante Santiago.

Yikes! That was true, but how could my students know? It had to have been a lucky guess. I rubbed at my temple, trying to decide if bashing my head into the chalkboard might alleviate the growing headache.

"I heard you looked at Ms. Brown the wrong way, and she popped you," said Mason Bitz.

I attempted a chuckle at the hysterical comment but ended up with my forehead in my hands.

"Listen up, people." I cringed at the sound of my voice as my class waited in anxious anticipation. "This may be the most important lesson you will learn from me all semester. If you value your life, don't ever slap Ms. Brown in the face with a beach ball, don't ever hit on her, and don't ask her to deliver an unedited paper to me."

"Albright, you hit on Ms. Brown? So cool!" John Gibbons was intrigued, as were about fifteen other nineteen-year-old boys.

"The point, John." I swung my finger into the air, pointing to something above his head, indicating my etude had whizzed past his tiny brain.

My students laughed.

"People, about these papers!" I took the corrected stack from my backpack.

****

I returned to my office to find Simon the rat's cage on my desk. "What are you doing here, little fellow?" I asked.

I looked at him. He looked at me. I wrinkled my nose. He wrinkled his nose. I bent down to peer into his house and sent him a message. He sent a message back.

"I will not put the pellet in the box myself!" I picked up the cage and marched to Lincoln's office.

"What's this?" I held up the despicable beast in his blue plastic lair.

"A present and our new experiment."

"I don't want any more presents; my head hurts, and

Simon and I don't like each other. Right, Simon?"

Simon stuck his nose into the air, grabbed his carrot, and turned his back to me. I stuck my tongue out at his backside.

Lincoln laughed. "I think the two of you are getting along splendidly. I want you to practice your telepathic communication skills with him."

"Do I have to feed him and brush him too?" I asked, my temper on edge.

Simon stood, turned in a circle, and presented his hindquarters—again. The indolent jerk was taunting me.

"Come in and close the door," Lincoln said.

I secured our privacy, set Simon's cage on Lincoln's desk, and sat.

"I find it fascinating that you can communicate with your dog when you aren't physically touching him, so I want to see how things go with the rat. For now, just get to know him. Take him home, introduce him to your turtle and dog."

"Seriously?"

"Yes, bring him with you for our Thursday sessions, and we'll take it from there."

"Fine." I turned Simon's crate so that he had to face me, then glared at him.

"Miranda, the question about your attackers, I don't think you need to tell the police you gleaned the details telepathically. Just say you heard them. Nobody needs to know the specifics. Chances are these men will have been so hyped up on adrenaline their thoughts and vocalizations will be confused in their memories."

I bestowed menacing grimaces on my rodent. "Don't worry about that. I think I know how I'm going to deal with Smith's toadies."

"What are you up to?" Lincoln tapped his pen on his desk as he stared into my eyes.

I think he was trying to read my mind.

"Right now, I'm teaching this creature who the boss is." I lifted the lid to Simon's house, confiscated his carrot stick, and carried my bratty rat to my office.

****

Later that evening, I peeked around the back of the pub, looking for West's motorcycle. I was relieved to see it parked in its spot. I fluffed my hair, mustered my courage, and headed into the Westinghouse establishment.

I had grown accustomed to the way West called out, "Hiya, Dr. Shortcake," when he greeted me. I was addicted to the contagious warm feeling that washed over me when he smiled. I was unprepared for the cold man who didn't say "hi" or clean a spot for me when I sat at the bar. I surely didn't expect him to ignore me and wait on another customer.

"West?" I implored.

His chin tilted down and to the side. "What do you want?"

"Can we talk?"

He slammed a beer down in front of the customer beside me and threw a plate into the dishpan. "I'm busy right now."

Unfortunately, I had a knack for putting the carefree Westinghouse in a foul mood.

"Please, West. Can you spare a few minutes?"

He tucked the tip of his towel into the waistband of his jeans and followed me into the parking lot. It was so cold that the condensation from my breath hovered in the air. "Why are you mad at me?"

"I'm not mad. I'm trying to convince you to move on."

"Move on? Why?" I asked.

"I have a date tonight," he said.

An invisible punch jabbed at my chest. "I told Brad about us."

"Why? I told you not to do that." He shook his head and sputtered, "*Pft!*"

I wondered what his vocalization meant but didn't ask. "I had to tell him the truth. I can't lie to him."

West continued to shake his head. "What did he say?"

"Nothing. Nothing at all. I think I hurt him. He thought I was different and that I was the one."

Instead of looking at me as I spoke, West scanned the parking lot. "Okay then, I need to get back to work."

I wanted to reach for him but was unsure he would allow it. To steady myself, I dug my fingers into my palms as I clenched my fists. "Why were you at the inn the other night?"

He bit his lip and huffed. "Miranda, what do you want from me?"

"I want you to stop calling me Miranda. I want you to tease me and make me laugh."

He waved his hands in the air. "Okay, Dr. Shortcake, why did the chicken cross the road?"

His outburst left me horrified and wondering if he was the womanizing jerk everyone accused him of being. I wanted him to understand my current torment, so I willed him to look into my eyes. Eventually, he did.

"Now, I have to escort you home." He kicked at the pavement. "Thanks a lot. I'm going to be late for my date."

A date? No, please don't go! Stay with me. "You don't have to take me home."

"Yes, I do. Now walk." He turned his palm toward the ground, and his index and middle finger stepped through air. Then he inclined his head toward the inn.

His footsteps clomped behind me as I began my climb. Eventually, I turned. "What are you doing?"

"Making sure you get home safe."

"I'm fine. It's still light out."

He grunted.

"You can walk beside me," I said.

"No, I can't." He waved a hand toward the inn.

I sighed, then continued.

His footfall heavy, he followed a few feet behind. I faced him again, but before I could say anything, he said, "Walk!"

No matter what happened, I would not let him see me cry. Unfortunately, I was unable to conceal the effort I put into composing myself. Ashamed, I turned my back to him and took three more steps.

Before I could take step number four, he whistled and called out, "Wowwee, Dr. Shortcake! Look at that adorable little ass!"

I pivoted to face him. "West, you can't see my behind. I have on a long sweater."

"Oh no, I can see it just fine. It's etched in the West-vault." He pointed to his forehead and smiled. Then, his voice became firm. "Now, move it !"

I continued up the hill, and I'm ashamed to confess, swung my hips—just a little.

"Look at that *callipygian*," he yelled.

I traveled backward as I called, "It's an adjective. You used it as a noun."

He scrunched up his nose and formed his fingers into claws. He scooted low and took on the stance of a beast stalking its prey. "*Callipygian*-ing, that *callipygian*, *callipygian*. There—noun, verb, and adjective. Happy, Dr. Beautiful?"

He straightened, and his face lit up with so much mirth that I thought I might explode from giddiness.

"You're almost home, love. Turn around and keep that ass swinging."

Once I reached the porch, I positioned myself in what I hoped was an attractive pose and gawked. West stayed ten feet away. His hair blew about in the wind, and he shoved his hands into the front pockets of his Levis. From the way he shifted his weight back and forth, it was apparent that his meager T-shirt was too flimsy to ward off the chill. I tried to decide which I liked more, his perfectly fitting jeans or his tight-fitting shirt.

"Do you really have a date tonight?" I asked.

He took a hand out of his pocket to tap on his forehead. "Let me check Old West's chick calendar. Nope! I have lots of dates tonight." He held a finger in the air each time he called out a name. "Holly, Jessica, Gina, Monica, Erica, Rita, Sandra, Mary, oh and Jessica again." Then he burst into song. "One, two, three-four-five. Everybody's in the car, come on, let's drive, 'cause West has nine dates tonight."

Even though I knew he was teasing, I stared at him with puppy dog eyes.

He slid his hand back into his pocket. "It's a song, Shortcake. A song."

I tried to laugh, but it came out as some sort of garbled grunt.

"By the way, Little's going to ride with us to see

Lowalski. You're paying for the gas, and we're taking your car."

"Really?" I called out, clapping.

"Really, and you aren't going to read anybody's mind, especially mine. And you will lay your pretty self down in the back seat and rest while I drive. And you will do what Little and I say. No negotiating on any of it."

"Deal!" I'd decide later on if some of the terms needed negotiating.

He turned to trek down the hill.

"Hey, West!" I yelled.

He faced me. "What?"

"You believe me? That I can read minds?" I hoped no one heard me ask the silly question.

"Yeah, I believe you."

"Hey, West?"

"What, Shortcake?"

"Thank you!" I said it so quietly that even the wind struggled to hear me. Then I bellowed across the distance that separated us, "Thank you for everything."

Chapter 38

Brad shined a medical penlight into my eyes as Grandma Zoey watched from her perch above the mantel. He was worried because my concussion testing wasn't showing the improvements he expected. He firmly declared I was pushing myself too hard and needed to take a few days off work.

A shoulder-slumped Aunt Edith carried a tray of refreshments into the library. I think the realization that she wasn't going to marry me off to her handsome friend-crush had finally dawned on her.

Brad and I received a lecture with our tea and cookies.

"Remember, relationships are hard and require give and take... The keys to success are compromise and forgiveness... The work you put in will make it all worthwhile..."

Clearly, Aunt Edith didn't know what a cheating strumpet her niece was. She left us alone, sliding the pocket door shut, locking us away until we talked it out.

Once Aunt Edith was gone, Brad placed his hand on my forehead. "Close your eyes for a minute. I'm concerned about the concussion, and I need to examine you."

His warm fingers brushed over me as he thought, *I need to get the swelling down.* His hand settled on the right side of my hairline, then slowly traveled in a semicircle until it cradled the base of my neck.

I was so tired I dozed off for a moment.

Brad tapped on my shoulder, waking me from my mini nap. "Last night, I had quite the humbling experience."

"What happened?" I asked, shaking off the fog.

Brad cleared his throat and said the most shocking thing ever. "I got boyfriend advice from Westinghouse."

"What?"

"He showed up at my office and defended your honor."

All possible responses seemed both shallow and incriminating.

"The bottom line is, he made me see the error of my ways."

"You didn't make the mistakes, Brad. I did."

He grabbed my gloved hand. "I was wrong to allow Jessica to torment and humiliate you. I shouldn't have left with her when I knew she was faking the ankle injury. I needed to take care of my patients, but it was inexcusable to go for five days without returning your calls. It was selfish to allow you to worry and expect you to suck it up."

"Brad, stop! I was the selfish one. If I'm going to date a doctor, I need to understand how important your work is. You were exhausted. I could see it in your face."

"Hear me out. According to Westinghouse, if I'm going to make a relationship work, I have to do a better job of communicating with my partner."

Good grief. What is the world coming to? West, the Love Doctor?

"The truth is I felt run down and wasn't thinking, and I took you for granted. Don't think I'm saying you can run around kissing Westinghouse, or any other man for that matter, because if you're my girl, I only want you kissing me."

I tried to tell Brad that I had done more than kiss West.

"Please let me finish. Westinghouse reminded me of how sweet and innocent you are, and he explained that he didn't do anything to change that."

West had played a game of semantics, but I let Brad continue.

"Then he made me punch him."

"He made you punch him?"

"Sweetheart, Westinghouse told me how crazy you are about me and that all you did was talk about kissing me for weeks. He said he deserved to be punched for taking advantage of the situation. He promised never to touch or kiss you again, and then he made me punch him."

I tried to call forth an image of my sweet doctor punching the bartender. I couldn't because it was absurd. To be clear, I disapproved of West's promise because I had total say over who did or didn't kiss me.

"You didn't punch him, did you?"

"I didn't want to, but he kept poking at me until I finally did. Then I had to administer first aid."

My eyebrows hit the ceiling as my chin made contact with the floor.

"The point is, I want to be exclusive. I'm not sure that I've ever told you that is how I feel, so I'm telling you now. No Jessica demanding my attention. No Westinghouse flirting with you. Communication and honesty."

"I did more than kiss West," I blurted out. "I made

love to him."

An all-consuming frown settled on Brad's handsome face. "I see."

"When you didn't call me back, I thought you were breaking up with me. I'm so sorry. West and I are just friends." I held my breath and waited.

"Westinghouse insisted you are just friends and that he is seeing other girls. Although he led me to believe that nothing sexual happened."

My heart hurt at the thought of West dismissing our connection, although hadn't I just done the same thing?

I had been foolish to think there was something between us. No girl in her right mind would think that a night with Weston Westinghouse the Third meant a romantic relationship.

"Do you have feelings for him?" he asked.

"No," I said, knowing that was the way it had to be. I studied our hands. "But, I have an important trip coming up with Tommy and West."

"I know. Westinghouse told me. I was upset at first, but he pointed out that if he and Little didn't take you, then you would go with Winona and Keisha, and that would get all three of you killed. I have resigned myself to accept that there is nothing any of us will do to stop you from your investigation, and I think it would be wrong for me to be the one to try. So go, and if you decide you still want to be my girl, please don't touch or kiss Westinghouse again."

"I don't plan to be with him ever again," I promised. "I want to be your girlfriend. But how can you forgive me so easily when I behaved so atrociously?"

He placed a single intoxicating kiss on my lips. "The past is the past. Let's start over."

Chapter 39

Tommy and West argued about who got to drive The Tank to Lipska's. Heads or Tails and Rock Paper Scissors both failed to crown a victor. After much ado, I told them it was my car and my choice. Tommy would take us there, and West would bring us home. We would eat perogies for dinner and have ice cream for dessert.

Tommy harassed West about his black eye. West informed us that "jealous boyfriends are a bitch, but the sweet piece of ass he got in the deal was worth it." If West was trying to make me hate him, it was working—kind of. Maybe.

Order had been restored to my life. Brad had forgiven me and didn't seem upset about my venture. Additionally, I was quite cozy in the back seat since it was almost as big as my bed, and I had my pillow and an afghan.

The best part of it all being, West once again relentlessly teased me. I smiled and hugged my arms to my chest.

Tommy took a moment of the long ride to check on our baby. "How's Princess Pickles with a Penis?"

West chuckled at the name.

"Great, he eats a lot for a little guy. He and Spot get along well. Neither of them can stand the rat. Simon is so full of himself."

"Reading minds again, Shortcake?"

"Only things that have a brain, West. For instance, I

303

don't have any idea what you are thinking right now," I said.

"Ouch!" West said.

"What is up with the two of you?" Tommy asked. "Something seems off."

"Nothing," we said not so convincingly.

"West, how was your date with Holly?" Tommy asked.

I sat up. "You had a date with Holly?"

"None of your business, Shortcake. Lay your pretty self down and rest. We don't want to get into trouble with your boyfriend and aunt! The date sucked. I can't stand Holly. Snotty bitch!"

Tommy added his two cents. "She's gorgeous, but I figure not worth the trouble."

"Not even close. She keeps calling, but I'm not interested."

I lay down. The silence only lasted a few seconds.

"Little, when you gonna get up the balls to ask out my cousin?" West asked.

I sat up. "Tommy, are you going to ask out Winona?"

"I don't know, and it's none of your business, Randa. Now rest! We aren't going to tell you again."

I plopped onto my back.

"Hey, Randa, I haven't made up my mind, so you can't say a word. I might ask Keisha out instead."

"What?" I sat up, and it took all of my discipline not to jump into the front seat. "You can't, Tommy. They will scratch each other's eyes out!"

"And who knows, Randa, there's another girl I like. I'm still hoping she decides to give me a chance."

The energy in the front seat grew heavy. I was certain that some momentous look of acknowledgment that had to do with me just transpired between my childhood friends.

"Little, pick one, and make a move!"

For being the hands-down winner of Bellmount's most notorious relationship avoider, West was chock full of advice—it was probably too many daytime television dramas.

"And make sure the one you pick is my cousin, so she stops snoopin' in my life."

West leaned over the seat to stare at my reclined body. "Shortcake, keep the lips zipped, and stop being a pain in the arse, or we cut you off. No more bodyguards for your visits to your mobster friends."

"You know, forcing me to rest in this back seat is ridiculous," I said.

He winked at me. I glared at him.

He faced front. "We need some music."

One of them popped a cassette into The Tank's mouth.

West bellowed something about standing in a doorway and hearing a mission bell. Tommy screeched something about lighting a candle and finding the way. Then they sang a duet about some hotel in California. West honked out how lovely it was.

"Blah, blah, blah," echoed Tommy.

I placed my hands over my ears and moaned. There had to be something in Bellmount's water. Tommy was even more tone-deaf than Brad and West.

The discordant duo belted out lyrics for a millennium. Finally, we pulled up in front of the deli. Before entering, I told the guys I needed to run back to the car because I had a "girl issue." In reality, I hid the cassette in my backpack beside Princess.

As soon as Alexander Lowalski saw me, he wrapped me in a warm embrace. Although half of the residents of Bellmount hated me, I had endeared myself to the neighboring town's version of The Godfather. Go figure!

Unfortunately, he didn't provide me with as much information as I had hoped. He knew who had set up Suzy's horrific murder scene and mutilated her, but he wouldn't give me names. He claimed he couldn't "get blood from a stone." West explained this meant he couldn't collect his money if the guys were dead or in jail.

The story went something like this: Goon one and goon two had gotten a call from an anonymous man to pick up the corpse by the dock at Pickett's Dam.

Tommy explained that Pickett's Dam was a resort area on the outskirts of Bellmount where there were a lot of hunting camps, a picnic area, canoe rentals, and "the best damn fishing in western Pennsylvania."

The story got even crazier. The men were told there would be an envelope containing a newspaper article and a ring attached to the body. They were to imitate the crime scene described in the paper. Dispose of the heart and the newspaper elsewhere, plant the ring by the body, then leave the bikini-clad corpse in the forest where it would be found.

The henchmen had been paid a small fortune to do the deed. And yes, they made a habit of doing "some pretty disturbing shit for money," but neither had ever committed murder.

"Who in Bellmount owns a camp in Pickett's Dam?" I asked the four men.

"Who doesn't would be an easier question to answer," Tommy said.

"Every man in the county pretty much owns or co-owns a camp," said West.

"Do you, West?" I asked.

"Nope."

"Do you, Tommy?"

"No."

"Do you, Alex?"

"No, I loathe the woods."

"Do you, big scary man in the corner?"

He scowled and shook his head.

Apparently, I was misinformed because none of my present company could take me to their camp at Pickett's Dam.

"Miss Miranda, it's quite clear, someone strangled the pastor's pregnant daughter, framed a kid from the wrong side of the tracks that nobody gives a shit about, and then hired two low-life scum to make some sort of dramatic statement."

"You've been studying the murder, Alex."

"You asked for my help, didn't you? Now let's address the elephant in the room. This had better not be the result of a lover's quarrel?"

He looked back and forth between West's black eye and my bruise-covered face.

"We aren't lovers." West was an expert at playing with semantics. "I ran into the fist of a jealous boyfriend."

"And you, Miss Miranda?"

"I ran into a couple of thugs who would like me to leave Bellmount and return home to my father."

"Connected to Suzy Smith's murder?" Lowalski asked.

"Indirectly," I said.

"Get me names. I'll take care of them." Lowalski's eyes contained a far-away look, and the edges of his mouth turned up in a disturbing grimace.

I approached the hulking man that leaned against the wall watching our every move. He snarled and crossed his tree-trunk-sized arms across his chest.

I had to look into the sky to meet his gaze. "We haven't been formally introduced. I'm Miranda."

"Wochowska," he said.

"Hi, Mr. Wochowska."

"Just Wochowska."

His deep garbled voice sounded a lot like the one my imagination assigned to Dr. Jekyll's alter ego, the evil Mr. Hyde.

I removed my glove and ran my finger over the vicious bulldog inked into the skin of his bulky forearm. He giggled. His dog held a bloody knife in its sharp teeth and wore a spiked red collar. Beneath the fierce animal, a fancy script spelled out, *Celer silens mortalis.*

"Swift. Silent. Deadly," I said as my finger traced the lettering.

He giggled again.

I couldn't decide if the ticklish mobster Marine's missing front tooth was terrifying or adorable.

"Wochowska, how much would it cost me to commission your services for an afternoon?" I asked.

Chapter 40

"…So then Lenny looked out into the distance, 'And I get to tend the rabbits, George, and we gonna live on the fat of the land. Let's do it now. Let's get that place now.'"

"'Sure, Lenny, right now, I gotta, We gotta,' and then…bam!"

Wochowska jumped.

"And that is the condensed version of Steinbeck's classic story," I concluded.

"Damn, Dr. Miranda. George shot Lenny in the back of the head?" asked Wochowska.

"Yes, it was the ultimate act of friendship and love."

"Damn. I don't know, seems sad to me. The saddest damn story I ever heard."

Even though my personal goon could crack a human skull with his thumb, he was a bit of a fluffy bunny. West and Tommy didn't see it, but what did that matter? I hadn't invited them to be part of the mission.

"Tragic and beautiful," I muttered wistfully.

I wiped the fog from the passenger side window of Wochowska's 1980 two-toned monstrosity. It was the only vehicle I had seen that rivaled The Tank in its lack of aesthetic appeal. In the misty afternoon, it was hard to make out much more than the red electric glow of a Jesus Saves sign.

I pressed my face to the window, hoping it might help me to see better. It took my eyes a moment to focus and see that the Sunday throng had dispersed.

I tapped Wochowska on the shoulder. "I think everyone is gone now. Ready?"

"Ready, Dr. Miranda," he said.

Wochowska and I exited his car and made our way through the damp gray fog to Smith's House of Shame and Guilt.

With its empty pews and absence of organ music, The Fifth Evangelical Church of Christ was extraordinarily foreboding. Wearing his long white robe, Pastor Smith was the only person in the pulpit, although an angry redhead and a Himalayan-sized ex-marine were headed his way. His lips twisted into an annoyed sneer as we approached.

The pastor's voice echoed in the lofty atrium. "I have told you, you are not welcome here, Ms. Albright!"

"Dr. Albright, to you," Wochowska reminded him. "You wanna tell me I'm not welcome here, too?"

"Who are you?" Smith asked.

"Dr. Miranda's friend."

The events of the last few weeks had me a bit on edge, so I wasn't feeling very sweet or patient. "Listen up, Pastor. I know you are the one who had me beat up. Your toadies messed me up good. I didn't go to the police for Liza's sake."

The truth was going to the police was pointless since Shultz was a useless pile of maggot excrement.

Wochowska stepped closer to Smith. The pastor backed up. Wochowska stepped forward again, and I went with them. We performed our odd little dance until the three of us reached the back wall of the church.

I took off my glove and placed my hand on the simpering excuse of a father's cheek. "Tell me, why don't you want to know who killed Suzy?"

"They got the man who killed Suzy. I've talked to the police and mayor, and they have locked up the man who impregnated and defiled her. You are filling Liza's head with tales."

The clueless man wanted to believe the things he was saying. There were tears in his eyes, and I felt a tiny bit sorry for him.

"Why did you have me roughed up?" I asked.

"I can't lose another child, and if I pull Liza from college, it will break her heart, and I will lose her too. I want you to leave her alone. You are evil, a witch, like your grandmother."

Taking offense to this statement, Wochowska grabbed the pastor by the neck and lifted him a few inches off the ground. A gasping red-faced Smith hung suspended in the air beneath a tacky felt Come to Jesus banner. His eyes bulged until I feared the beady balls might pop out of their sockets.

"This is the deal. Are you listening?" I asked.

Smith attempted to nod, although he struggled since his neck was being squeezed in a fleshy vise.

"It's okay, Wochowska." I indicated he could set the pastor back onto his feet.

"You will stay away from me unless I come to you. If you ever have anyone threaten me again, you will answer to my friend here." I pointed to my hired gun. "And know this, he will be a cuddly teddy bear next to my aunt and Russ."

Wochowska snarled and showed some teeth. He looked like his bulldog, minus the blood-stained incisors.

"Skyler Dubbs did not kill Suzy. They got the wrong man. You can't hide behind your absurd doctrine, proclaiming truths out of falsehoods. It won't bring justice to your daughter. Do you understand what I'm saying?" I asked.

I suspected the pastor quivered in both terror and anger.

Wochowska lifted Smith off the ground again and grinned. The loveable lug seemed to enjoy himself.

"So tell me, Pastor, who else in this town may have snuck off with your daughter? Someone important? Someone with money? Someone married? Someone you're afraid of?"

"I don't know," he said.

The weak-willed man did know. He was in denial and had shoved the name into his subconscious.

"Got it. Let's go, Wochowska," I said.

Wochowska dropped Smith, then popped him hard. Blood splatter landed on my cheek. I took the edge of Smith's robe and cleaned my face. The crimson liquid stained his white sleeve. Before I left the church, I took one last glimpse at our Lord and Savior's pathetic conduit. Pastor Smith sat against the wall. He used his wrist to wipe away the blood that trickled from his nose. A Jesus hanging from a plastic cross looked down at him.

"Pastor Smith," I called. "I hope Jesus forgives you." Then I closed the blood-red church door.

Once we stood in front of the building, I handed Wochowska an envelope containing the money I owed him.

"Dr. Miranda, I've been thinking, maybe instead of paying me, you could, well, I don't know how to read, and I'd like to read that *Of Mice and Men* story."

How exciting! A new student! "I'd love to teach you." I reached into the clouds and ruffled the ex-marine's hair before we made a break for our getaway vehicle.

****

The girls had gotten "bupkis," according to Winona, and less than "one of Simon's turds," according to Keisha. Winona said that Suzy had not checked into the Bear County Recreation Center or the college pool. Keisha had compiled a list of all outdoor pools and couldn't connect Suzy to any of them. I had switched gears, and instead of working on my location theory, I was back to finding a suspect. Once again, we were strategizing at the Bellmount Inn Library.

"Tell me about Greg Grainey," I said.

"What do you want to know?" Winona asked.

"Everything."

"He makes my belly tickle," the grinning Winona said.

"What does that mean?"

"Means he makes her panties wet," Keisha clarified.

"Good grief!" I rolled my eyes.

"He's kind of swoon-worthy." Winona rested two fingers to her forehead and tilted her head back dramatically.

"Swoon-worthy?"

Brad Gordon was swoon-worthy. He was a gentleman; he saved lives; his muscles had muscles; and a woman could lose herself in his long dark lashes and bright blue eyes. West Westinghouse the Third was swoon-worthy. He had hair you wanted to run your fingers through, pectorals that threatened to shred his T-shirts, and a good-old-boy drawl that whispered secrets a woman felt deep inside her most intimate parts.

Although Liam was my cousin, he was swoon-worthy. He was tall and lean, wore tailored suits, and had hair the color of a copper penny in the sun. Even Tommy Little had enchanting charms. Tom was sweet and genuine. He would give you the shirt off his back, and he saw beauty in the most insignificant of details.

But Greg Grainey? What was it? He was handsome, he caused the hair on my neck to stand, and he made me want to run for cover. Was a fight or flight response linked to a man's swoon-worthiness?

"Miranda, haven't you ever wanted a man to tie your wrists to the headboard and hold you captive? 'Cause Greg's a tie'r'upper," Winona said.

"Do you want that?" I asked.

"No, but if I did, I'd want him to do it."

"Miranda, say you wanted to have a man bite your neck until you bleed and then lick the blood while he made love to you? Grainey would be the guy." Judging from her numerous references to bloodsuckers, Keisha clearly had some sort of vampire fetish.

"Gross! Would you do that?" I asked her.

"No, but I like to think about it," Keisha admitted.

"Or say you wanted to make out in the park, while half a dozen people watched. One name, Greg!" Winona grinned.

"In other words, he's a sick pervert! And Bellmount is full of sick, perverted women?" I asked.

"He's kinky, Miranda. And no woman with half a brain would play with his fire for real. But it doesn't hurt to fantasize a little; it's healthy, and if you ever did accidentally dabble a tiny bit, Grainey would be the guy. The best part is, he would keep your little indiscretion to himself," Keisha said.

"Accidentally?" I shook my head and grunted. "He's

not discriminate at all when it comes to me. He pretty much flaunts his desire in front of his wife, Brad, everyone. It isn't helping my status in this town. It's humiliating."

"But is it sexy?" Winona still had her silly smiling nod thing going.

Keisha cut her gaze to Winona and made a whirligig motion with her index finger before turning to me. "Miranda, you're the new girl in town—the fiery redhead that has upset the status quo. Grainey could rub you in every other man's face. You're what a small town like this calls fresh meat!"

I shuddered. Fresh meat was the word Liam had used to describe me.

"It's not like there's much to do in this town, and the bachelor pool is limited. I guess sometimes things need spiced up. You don't understand because you happen to have the hottest man in the county in your bed."

I didn't have the energy to address the inaccuracies in that statement. Telling them that I wasn't sleeping with my fabulous boyfriend because I was wanton and hadn't kept my panties on when I was left alone with the bartender was too humiliating to repeat.

"What about Greg's wife?" I asked.

"Bitchy! Gossipy! Cold marriage. Sometimes I kind of feel sorry for him," Keisha said.

"What if I was a twenty-one-year-old girl that liked to party hardcore, and I wanted to upset my strict daddy? Would Greg be my man?" I asked.

"Oh, Miranda! Miranda!" Keisha said as my meaning hit her.

Winona must have been fantasizing about a vampire tying her up and biting her while the entire town watched her fornicate because she seemed oblivious to our newest revelation.

"Hey? Wanna hear something super kink?"

Keisha and I were all eyebrows and ears.

"Once, I went skinny dipping in Grainey's hot tub. Nothing happened. I didn't let it. But he invited me, and I went."

"W.T.F., girl?" Keisha looked like someone had hit her in the face with a beach ball.

"I told you nothing happened?" Winona said.

"Who cares? You dolt. A hot tub! A bikini!" said Keisha.

I leaped to Winona's side. "The hot tub, Winona, where was it?"

"A bikini? But we skinny-dipped." Then her eyes widened as realization dawned. "Oh, crap! His camp. Pickett's Dam."

"Address, Winona? Address?" I implored.

"I don't know. Greg drove me. It was in the woods. We passed the lake and a lot of camps."

"Could you find it again?" I asked.

"I was only there once. He drove. It was dark. I was drinking wine." She frantically waved her hands. "No. I don't think so."

"I have to ask Brad where it is. He has to take me."

"Miranda, don't go by yourself. Grainey will get you naked in his hot tub and do things to you, and you won't be able to stop yourself or him. He has this tongue—" Winona said.

Keisha interrupted before we could hear any more of the scandalous details. "Hey dingbat, you said nothing happened."

Winona closed her eyes, squished up her face, and

looked guilty.

"Miranda, the fucker might strangle you, fuck you, and then chop you into pieces. And that ain't fun kink, girlfriend, that's serial murder kind of shit."

I shivered. "I'm going to see Brad."

After this proclamation, a case of monkey brain hit me. Brad will never take me. I'll ask Tommy. No, I almost ruined Tommy's life. West is my man, but I'm not allowed to play with West without a chaperone. Liam? Liam is way too overprotective. Augh! I have to convince Brad.

"Are you sure neither of you knows where the camp is?" I asked.

"Don't you dare go to his camp alone," Keisha said.

Winona wrapped her arms around herself and rolled her large body into a tiny ball.

"I'm going to see Brad," I declared more emphatically this time. Before running off, I had one more question. "Would either of you let Tommy tie you to a headboard?"

"Tom Little?" Keisha asked.

"Tom?" Winona smiled.

At the same time, they both said, "Sure, Tom's adorable."

Interesting.

Chapter 41

Greg Grainey's dark hair was slicked into place, and he had fastened a gold chain around his neck. For the record, I didn't find either of these things to be swoon-worthy. I waved and smiled. His gaze caressed my curves, his lips parted, and his breath ambled.

He slid toward me with the confidence of a sure-footed feline about to corner its prey. A low-grade hum sparked in my belly and traveled along the sides of my body. It gathered steam and rose even higher, becoming a prickle at the back of my neck. Were there women who found this sensation to be a turn-on because I was pretty sure it was fear?

I peered up at him and performed my recently mastered eyelash flutter that worked like a charm on Brad, West, and Tommy. Greg hissed. As I suspected, it also worked on Greg Grainey. Although, to be fair, everything worked on Greg Grainey.

I tilted my head and ran a finger over my gun charm. "I haven't properly thanked you."

He motioned for me to follow. I secured my backpack on my shoulder, and he led me through the store, into his office. The trek past rows and rows of weapons afforded me time to think. Was there something about Greg that would make him appealing to a misguided coed? An aging waitress or a bored housewife finding him enticing was one thing, but a beautiful twenty-one-year-old girl, with college boys eating out of her hand, was quite another.

Greg left a heady smell of citrus and musk in his wake. His shoulders were broad, his hips were narrow, and it appeared he spent quite a bit of time in the gym. Although he was much older, his clothes were youthful and stylish, and he could easily pass for a young forty.

If I wanted to attend a bacchanalian party where masked revelers danced naked and then writhed together in the moonlight, would I want Greg to be my date? That would be a hard no. I had no desire to dance naked in the moonlight, and if I did, there was only one man who could convince me to frolic.

I tried another fantasy. What would it be like to kiss a man who was so disturbingly sexual? Would it feel different than Brad's drug-like romantic caresses and West's toe-curling sensual explorations?

Maybe I was a tiny bit curious. Would Greg's kisses contain a dark intoxicating pleasure that ripped me from reality and spun me into an alternate sphere where my mind left my body?

Perhaps, but the entire thing was preposterous. Grainey was a predator and probably a cold-blooded murderer! But, if I was Suzy, might I decide to play with a handsome older man who smelled tantalizing and sent me an occasional present? And who wouldn't want to torment Pastor Smith? It was immensely rewarding to watch him cower after his arrogant moralizing.

Greg cornered me in his office. He ran his finger over the necklace and then along my collarbone. I shivered. I suspect he interpreted this to mean I was putty in his hands. It was more that I had seen into his soul, and he was Kinky, Kinky, Kinky, with triple capital Ks. Of

course, I had a few capital letters of my own. I was
S.O.R.—Stubborn, Obsessed, and Relentless.

He firmly planted himself in my personal space. "I
knew you would come."

I searched for an emergency exit but stood my
ground.

"I heard about your attack and have been crazed with
worry."

He was a murder suspect and was livid about my
attack? Go figure.

In case Greg got any funny ideas, I wanted him to
know not to mess with me. "Don't worry. I can take care
of myself."

He ran his finger over the now yellowish bruise under
my eye. Once again, I quivered.

"Mmm," he said. "Let's get out of here. The manager
will lock up the store tonight."

"Greg, you know I can't. I have a boyfriend."

He grasped my waist and pulled me to him. "Just a
*boy*friend. I'm sure I don't need to remind you that I am a
man."

I finally understood his appeal to Suzy. Greg Grainey
epitomized the promise of being a man. A man that made
you feel like a woman and fueled your most inappropriate
desires. He was a gun-toting, money-spending, sex-
starved, All-American man, and some women couldn't
resist that.

I was not one of those women.

I had to duck and weave to keep his lips from
touching mine. "Greg, the thing is, I'm injured, and
everything hurts. I have to be careful."

There was no way that I was telling Greg that my
headaches and dizzy spells had miraculously stopped and

that my ribs no longer ached. I still looked bruised enough to garner a few sympathy votes.

His bottom lip jutted out. "How disappointing."

"I know. The only physical activities I'm permitted to do are swimming and splashing around in the water." Oh, that's a good one, I congratulated myself.

A bleached-white toothy grin replaced his pout. "This is your lucky day. I have a hot tub?"

Bingo! I was a genius.

"You do? Where?" I asked.

"At my camp."

He was a piece of cake. "Where's your camp?"

"Pickett's Dam."

"I've been there with Liam." Oh, how I could lie for the sake of sleuthing. "Which one is your camp?"

Greg had mastered speaking with a predatory purr, and his "I'll show you" terrified me.

I concentrated on slowing my breathing. "What's your address? Maybe I could bring a couple of my friends and meet you there later."

Greg pushed me out the back door of his store, saying, "Let's go now, my crimson princess. I can worship you as you splash in my hot tub."

I was not a genius. I was a stupid, foolish woman. Why hadn't I been more patient and waited for Brad to get off work? Why hadn't I at least tried to ask Liam or Tommy for help? Why couldn't I exhibit more self-control so that I could have requested West come with me? Why hadn't I brought Keisha and Winona to the gun store?

Why had I changed from an honor student ruled by common sense into an undisciplined, impatient risk-taker who attracted trouble like a little boy attracted dirt?

Perhaps I needed a prescription for the behavioral stimulant that doctors prescribed, like candy.

Winona had warned me, and still, I had let him take control of the situation. The last time I had played this game with Greg, I had lost. This time I was in so far over my head, I had no idea how I would untangle myself from the mess.

****

Miranda, the first snowfall of the season makes surfaces slick. You're going to have to be extra cautious when driving over the mountains. You don't get snow like this down there in the big city, said Aunt Edith, Liam, Keisha, Brad, Tommy, and other Bellmount inhabitants.

Apparently, nobody had taken the time to remind Greg Grainey of this hazard because his bright red sports car took those dark snowy curves at eighty miles per hour. I was thankful he drove a stick shift; it kept his hands from wandering over me as we drove away from Bellmount toward his secluded camp.

The excessive energy bouncing off of Greg, and slapping at me, made me dizzy. He smiled. I couldn't smile back because icy surfaces, mutilated corpses, lecherous men, and isolated cabins consumed my thoughts.

"You're so beautiful. You take my breath away," he said.

I responded to this provocative declaration with the unsexy plea of, "Greg, could you please drive slower?"

"Of course, your wish is my command," he said.

The speedometer dropped to seventy-five.

"More," I begged.

"*More*. The word I hear you say over and over again in my fantasies."

I tried again. "Slower, please."

He made some sort of guttural sound as if I were touching his private parts.

"Augh. Greg, please drive slower."

He chuckled, and our speed dropped to fifty-five.

"I was thinking closer to twenty-five miles per hour."

He laughed again. It dropped to forty.

I gave up.

"Greg, tell me about your wife."

"My wife?" We took a sharp curve, and his hand pulled on the gear shift.

"I want to get to know you," I said.

"There are plenty of ways to get to know me that don't involve talking about my wife."

"Humor me," I said.

"She's beautiful."

"Tell me more."

He sighed. "I think Louise loved me once, but after she had Jessica…" He shook his head. "She hasn't loved me for a very long time."

"Is that why you sleep with other women?"

He took his gaze off the treacherous lane to look at me.

"Eyes. Road," I reminded him. "It wouldn't be any of my business, but you have been relentless in your pursuit of me, and I'm sitting in the front seat of your car. Given the circumstances, I think I have the right to know."

He *harrumph*ed. "No other woman has asked me these things. I like women. I like the way they smell, and the feel of their skin, the way they taste, and the way they cry out my name when they orgasm." He peeked out the corner of his eye.

I assumed he was checking out my reaction to his

dirty talk. I pointed to the windshield.

He refocused his attention on driving. "I don't remember anymore if my desire for other women caused her to fall out of love with me, or if I desire other women because she fell out of love with me."

"How many women have there been?" I needed to understand his motivation for possibly ending a girl's life.

"A lot. Too many to keep count."

"The town is only so big," I said.

"The county is much larger, and there is a new crop of college girls each fall."

Now we were getting somewhere.

"Do you take all of your women to your camp?"

"So many questions, my little professor. Liaisons can happen anywhere and everywhere. As far as the camp, sometimes I take my buddies, sometimes Jessica, sometimes a special girl. I used to take my son-in-law. Can we cease with the inquisition now?"

"I guess professors are annoyingly inquisitive." And so are psychics who know that the wrong man has been accused of a crime.

"What attracts you to the woman you date?"

"Date?" He chuckled. "Most of the time, it's just a fling, but not you. You're different."

"Why am I different?"

"I picture how you would look with your gorgeous red hair cascading over those amazing naked breasts, and how you would blush, and look at me with those innocent green eyes, and how I would cherish that forever."

I took a moment to think about his statement. "Are you attracted to me because you want to take away my innocence?"

"Maybe," he said. "Maybe it's that you play hard to

get, and I enjoy the chase."

His voice had become raspy, and the crotch of his pants may have been becoming tight because he looked uncomfortable.

"I can't be innocent forever. Once you caught me, the chase would be over, and the fun would be gone."

"No. You will always be fun, and I couldn't take your innocence away from you, even if I fucked you for a million years."

That statement scared me to death. It was the same thing West had said to me. West wasn't like Grainey, was he? Maybe I was afraid he was. Perhaps it was why I held the bartender at bay and hid behind the gentlemanly doctor.

On second thought, that wasn't true! West was nothing like Grainey. He didn't murder coeds or have a wife he cheated on. West looked out for me. When he wasn't acting impossible, he made me laugh. Besides, West was my childhood friend, and I was pretty sure I had a special place in his non-committing heart.

"What would you do with a fling?" I asked.

"So many wonderful things…" His voice trailed off. "What do you want me to do with you, my crimson princess?"

I hadn't been talking about myself. I had been referencing Suzy. I wanted to go home.

"Greg, I'm trying to be your friend. I have a boyfriend. I just want to get to know you."

"I love all women. I like them old, young, big, small, blonde, brunette, white-skinned, brown-skinned, black-skinned. But my favorites are redheads with innocent eyes and bodies built for sex that I can hunt down, and when I finally catch them, listen to them scream my name in ecstasy."

My stomach did some sort of floppy thing that felt like lust for a second and then like I wanted to regurgitate.

"I'm done talking for now because there's nothing else you need to know." He pushed a CD into the player. "How about some music?"

Greg's velvety voice melded with the voice from the speakers as he sang about running with the night.

"Greg, you can sing?"

It was clear that he hadn't had the same choral director as Brad, West, and Tommy.

"Of course, I can sing." He grinned. "And I can do a lot of other wonderful things you might enjoy."

"Greg, I'm sorry. I'm not feeling well. Could you take me home? Please!" I begged.

We pulled up in front of his cabin. "Maybe you're motion-sick. We're here. A little fresh air and you will be feeling better in no time."

Fresh air wasn't the solution to my woes.

****

I triple-checked to make sure Princess was both loaded and wrapped in a towel. I set my backpack on the floor beside me and plopped myself onto a plush couch. Although frigid from being uninhabited, the camp was lovely. It was all pine boards and rich shades of red, green, and brown. I shivered even though I was under a warm wool blanket. While Greg piled wood into the stone fireplace, I tried to send Suzy a mental message.

Suzy, I'm Miranda. Please talk to me. Tell me what happened to you.

Although she didn't answer, an unsettling tug similar to the one I sensed at the Smith crime scene overtook me.

"Wake up, sleepyhead. The heat is on, the fire is

going, and the hot tub is warming up. You should be toasty soon," Greg said.

I opened my eyes to a glass of wine dangling in the air in front of me. I was a non-drinker, with one night of tippling in my history. Since then, I had sworn off all forms of liquor and returned to tee-totaling.

At that moment, I found myself chugging the poison, proffered by a probable butcher. Since my circulation was taking its good old time returning, the liquid helped warm my insides.

"Where's the hot tub?" I asked.

Greg pointed to a glass-paned door that was underneath a wooden loft. There was a large bed high in the rafters. Goosebumps traveled from my feet to the roots of my hair. *Suzy, if I have to go up there to find you, I don't think I can do it.*

"You seem a million miles away, Crimson."

"I told you. I'm not feeling well. You should take me home."

He took a deep breath, closed his eyes, then chugged.

"See, I'm a huge disappointment. Not sexy at all. So, time to go. I'll just look at the hot tub, and we can be on our way."

"We drove all this way. It would be a shame not to take a quick dip. How about twenty minutes? It will help you feel better." He ran a finger over my facial bruises, then looked at his shiny gold watch. "It's a quarter after eight. We'll be on our way home by nine."

I don't know why I bothered to explain, "I don't have my bathing suit with me," when I knew what his response would be. There was no way!

He chuckled. "You don't need a bathing suit in my hot tub."

"I'm not getting naked and splashing in your hot tub. I want to go home. Now, Greg! I'm not joking. I don't feel well."

He disappeared for a moment and returned with a skimpy purple polka dot bikini swinging from his outstretched fingers. I made my way to the bathroom, locking the door behind me. I squeezed into the bikini and then stared at myself in the mirror. I wasn't blinking. My eyes had frozen in a terrified maniacal expression, and my face was an odd motley colored purple, black, and yellow mass of bruising.

There was nothing seductive about me unless a man found my D cup size spilling out over a small B cup appealing. The stupid suit had to belong to a tall thin woman with the body of a ballerina.

"Stupid Jessica Grainey," I said, trying to tuck my breasts into the miniature bra.

It was pointless. They popped back out.

"Fudge!" I whispered to my image in the mirror, "What are you going to do if he murders you? No Brad, no Bellmount, no saying goodbye to Spot or Dad, and no West. Help me, Suzy. Where are you?"

I settled my rapid breathing and wrapped a towel around me. Then I left the safety of the bathroom and tip-toed past a fire-attending Greg.

"Twenty minutes," I called over my shoulder as I tried to conceal my torso under the tiny towel.

The hot tub was inside a windowed patio. Two glass walls provided a sublime snow-globe kind of view of the fluffy powder coating the tree branches.

Greg joined me. His eyes went wide as I discarded the towel and slid into the steaming water.

"Damn," he said, gawking at my breasts, bursting out

of his atrocious daughter's bikini.

Augh! I sunk into the water.

I closed my eyes and leaned back because Greg wasn't going to kill me. That wasn't his energy. My life wasn't in danger because I wasn't carrying his baby. He wanted to do lewd things to me, but murder wasn't one of them.

The water was heavenly, and I felt like I was in a peaceful dream. I listened to the mesmerizing sound of the water jets, and all my tension washed away. Why had I been so scared? It was wonderful, and Greg was almost behaving like a gentleman—almost!

A heavy splash interrupted my reverie. I kept my eyes closed.

"You better have on your swim trunks!"

He withdrew from the water and left the room. The moment of peace and the absence of anxiety caused by his advances allowed me to focus. *Where are you, Suzy?* I was about to accept that I had hit upon a bum theory when an extra charge mixed with the bubbling water.

Hold steady, hold steady, you've got it, don't let go, I told myself. The electric current grabbed at me, and the hair on my arms rose. I thought the hair on my head might also be standing in the air. I tried to ignore the sensation I was being boiled alive. An image faded in and out, reformed, and then hit so hard, it knocked the wind out of me.

I was staring at Suzy. I knew it wasn't Liza because this girl was in no way innocent, and she was smack dab in the middle of the throes of passion.

The image was clear and horrible. I was licking at Suzy's lips.

"Yes, Greg, please," she said as I kissed her.

I think I was sliding a body part inside of her as her head tilted back.

Greg's guttural voice came from my body. "Tap if you get scared, love."

"Yes," she said as I—or was it Greg—slid into her again.

To be clear, I did not find ghost sex underwater to be to my liking.

Large hands stroked Suzy's collarbone before they slid a thick black cord around her neck. Why isn't she terrified? Why is her head tilted back in ecstasy? I felt myself slide inside her again and again and watched her face redden. I experienced a sensation that might have been pleasure, although it filled me with dread. I didn't know how to separate myself from Greg's energy.

Minutes seemed to pass, and I didn't know if the "*Let go! Let go! She's dying!*" was in my mind or if I was screaming it out loud. Instead of releasing the cord, the hands pulled it tighter. It was as if I was in a horrible nightmare I couldn't wake from. No matter how hard my mind worked, I couldn't control the scene or make the cord release.

Suzy's face distorted, and her body slumped forward. I panicked, but Greg was oblivious and caught up in a frenzy that brewed, then exploded like some sort of destructive firework.

It felt as if I was the one who pulled Suzy's limp body from the hot tub, while Greg's voice called out, "Suzy! Suzy! Wake up! God damn it. Wake up!"

"Miranda, Miranda!" Greg shook me. "Are you okay?"

I wish I had said, *Please take me home. I don't feel well* because I think he might have consented if those had been the first words out of my mouth. "Why didn't you give her CPR?"

"What are you talking about? Give who CPR?" His facial muscles became taut.

"I'm not feeling well. Will you take me home?"

High-pitched words poured forth, fast and clipped, replacing Greg's smooth voice. "Miranda, what the hell is going on, and who were you talking to?"

I stepped out of the hot tub and moved deliberately so as not to spook him. His face was the same color as his red swim trunks, and the energy bouncing off of him terrified me.

I backed up toward the main room. "I don't feel well."

I had to work at moving purposefully because my body was telling me to run. If I thought he looked predatory before, I had no idea. He had become an I'm-going-to-pounce-on-you-and-rip-out-your-throat kind of blood-thirsty.

"Miranda, answer me! What the fuck just happened? Your hair?" He raised his hands over his head and waved his fingers.

"You're scaring me, Greg." I backed up a few more steps.

"Good! Tell me what the hell you are talking about, and what I just saw you doing, and why your hair was standing in the air like you were struck by lightning?"

I wasn't sure what I was doing or why my hair was "standing in the air," although I did have a few theories. I might have been making love to a ghost, strangling an already dead girl, and screaming Suzy's name. I knew I hadn't found Suzy's psychic footprint. She had died in the throes of pleasure, one minute in ecstasy, three minutes later dead. She had never felt terror, so she hadn't left anything behind.

What I had experienced was Greg's panicked energy trapped in that whirlpool. It was the same thing I had tapped into when I experienced the horror the thugs had felt when mutilating Suzy's body.

"Miranda, are you like your grandmother?" Greg asked.

The jig was up for both of us. There were no longer any secrets. Had he believed in Grandma Zoey's abilities while the rest of the town thought she was insane? I needed to get closer to my backpack.

"Greg, I know you didn't mean to do it. I know it was an accident. Was it your baby?" What a stupid question. What in God's name was wrong with me?

"I didn't know she was pregnant until the newspaper article came out," Greg said.

His admission explained a lot.

"Did you love her?" I took another step.

"No," he answered as he took two steps.

"Did you want the baby?"

"I didn't know there was a baby, and I don't know for sure if it was mine, but if it were, I would have taken care of both of them." He stepped closer.

"How did you get Skyler's ring?"

"The kid is a burn-out. A waste. No idea why she looked out for him. All I had to do was feed him a little pill and confiscate the ring."

"Why was the ring left along the side of the road and not by the body?" I asked.

"Because I hired simpletons. They fucked up everything. I suspect they dropped it in the wrong place—unless an animal moved it."

I snorted. Had a chipmunk moved the heart and ring, causing a firestorm of controversy?

"Did her father know?" I asked.

"I don't know if he knew about the baby, but he suspected the fling. I think she wanted him to know about it. Lucky for me, he would prefer to believe it was that asshole kid rather than me—for the sake of the town's conservative agenda—not due to any feelings of loyalty toward me." Greg's laugh sent chills up my spine. "Smith is the worst kind of son-of-a-bitch."

"Worse than you?" I asked.

Perhaps the type of man he was had just dawned on him because the color drained from Greg's face.

"Yes. Everyone knows what I am. I don't hide it. The pastor hides behind his Bible."

He took another step. I took three.

"Why mutilate her when it was an accident?" Me and my relentless questions.

Two more steps, and I could reach my backpack. I would be okay. I needed to get to Princess, demand his car keys at gunpoint, then drive myself home. A stick shift couldn't be too hard to figure out. I looked wistfully at my concealed firearm. Greg's gaze followed mine, and his understanding dawned. We lunged for my bag at the same time. I landed on the floor, and he was on top of me in an instant.

"I don't want to hurt you, but I will," he said.

As we wrestled, his thoughts invaded mine.

"You opportunistic bastard," I cried out. "You mutilated her to sell guns. You left her alone on the side of the road to be eaten by maggots." I punched him as he held me down.

"She was already dead, and I didn't mean to do it,"

he said as if that made it okay. "And I dressed her first," was his pathetic afterthought.

I supposed that was what he told himself so he could look in the mirror each day. How ironic that the small gesture of affection he had shown for her, in the end, was the one that had led me to him.

"I hate you!" I screamed.

I wanted to hit him in his hideous private parts, but he straddled me and pinned my arms by my side. I fought like a wild beast and somehow freed my hand. I swiped, and my fingernails made contact with his eye.

"Shit!" he yelled.

He covered his eye, and I reached for my backpack. He jumped off of me, grabbed my bag, and threw it across the room.

I took off, crawling after it. I had just reached it when he called for me.

"*Phwwwwwht*," he whistled. "Look here, my crimson princess."

I cringed at the sound of a click and the discovery that Greg pointed a gun at me. "Augh!"

What a gross misjudgment on my part. Of course, a man like Greg Grainey would have a gun hidden away in every nook and cranny of his dwelling.

"Move away from your bag." He shifted the gun slightly to herd me in the direction he wanted me to travel.

"Please, don't hurt me. I'm sure we can work this out."

"Damn it. I don't want to hurt you. I like you. Patterson, Shultz, Smith, Reynolds, Jessica, they all warned me you were trouble. 'Leading me around by my dick,' they said. Shit!"

A pounding at the door startled us both.

"Grainey!" Brad called. "Grainey, let me in!"

"Fuck!" Greg let out a slow exhale and shook his head from side to side.

"He has a gun," I yelled, hoping Brad could hear me through the door.

"Fuck," Grainey said again.

The lock turned, and the front door opened. Greg pointed his gun toward our visitor, and I took advantage of the distraction to retrieve Princess. Brad lifted his hands into the air to show he was unarmed, and a key dangled from his right hand. He cautiously moved into the bowels of the camp.

"Damn. I forgot to change the locks when you abandoned my daughter." Greg's laugh was twisted and disturbed. "I don't want to kill you, Gordon, but I will. I'll put a bullet in you; then I'll fucking blow our girl's head off."

"If you shoot him, I will shoot you, Greg. I swear, I will." My hand was shaking so much I wasn't sure if I could pull the trigger or hit a target that wasn't West's behind, but I would sure as heck try.

Brad held his hands in the air as he tried to maneuver himself into a strategic position between us. "Let's all calm down. Nobody's going to shoot anyone. Someone explain to me what's going on?"

"He killed Suzy, Brad. He was having sex with her and was playing some sort of strangling game. He accidentally killed her, but instead of calling for help, he had her mutilated to scare people into buying guns."

"Damn!" Brad stomped a foot then composed himself. "Suzy was born with a weak heart and lungs. Didn't you know, Grainey? She shouldn't have been playing around with those things."

From the horrified look on Greg's face, it was apparent that this was the first time he had heard about Suzy's condition. Although, the revelation did nothing to dissuade his threatening stance.

"Miranda's a crazy one, Gordon. Everyone else in town knew, but we both fell for her." He sighted Brad over the barrel of his weapon.

"Okay, Dad. Let's put the gun down. We'll take Miranda somewhere and get her help," Brad said.

Shocked, I cut my gaze to Brad, wondering how he could believe such things. It took me a moment to realize he was placating Greg. He knew I was telling the truth and that our lives were in danger.

My hand shook. Greg's didn't. He appeared calm and steady, and his disturbing laugh had returned.

"Dad. I've missed that, Son." He paused. "Now stand the fuck still, Gordon."

Brad stopped moving.

"Gordon, you know how she knew it was me? You might want to hear this if she hasn't filled you in?"

"Shut up, Greg," I yelled.

"She's psychic, just like that crazy grandmother of hers. That's why she wears those damn gloves."

The three of us jumped when Liam and Tommy barged through the open door.

"Fuck," Greg said.

The end of the gun traveled a slow path from Brad to me.

Brad cried out, "God, no!"

Greg said, "Take care of Jessica, while I'm locked up, Son." Then his index finger clicked on the safety.

Brad lunged for Greg screaming, "No!"

Bang! A horrifying sound echoed off the beams and stone. The blood, and things I can't begin to explain, exploded and hung in mid-air before splattering on Brad and an exquisite stone mountain fireplace.

Liam dropped to the ground, pulled my face to his chest, and held me tight.

West strolled into the massacre holding Brad's cellular phone high. He stopped short and gawked. "Jesus Christ!"

Liam emptied the cartridge of the bejeweled gun and deposited the bullets into his pocket. He wrapped Princess in the blue towel and tucked her into my backpack.

West ran both hands through his hair. "Fuck!"

Tommy hovered above the blood and gore. "Doc, he's gone. Come on." He reached an arm for Brad.

Brad swatted him away as he attempted to resuscitate a corpse with half a face.

I stood and forced my shaky legs to carry me to Brad. I sucked back tears and screams. "Brad."

He continued to administer pointless first aid.

"Brad," I said again. "It was an accident."

Liam wrapped an arm around my shoulder and nudged me away from the scene as Tommy and West pulled Brad to his feet.

It was then that the horrifying energy loop took hold. I experienced Greg's death over and over again until West's embrace pulled me outside into the fresh air.

****

Blinking lights from the police cars, the coroner's van, and an ambulance bounced off the snow and lit up the night at Pickett's Dam. Attempts to change back into my clothes had not gone well since the camp contained a whirlwind of violence that made me dizzy and nauseous. I didn't experience the horrifying energy loop in the front yard, so that is where I stood. The ice fell, coating the wool blanket I had wrapped around my bikini-clad body. I trembled and shivered as an exhausted, red-eyed Brad Gordon cradled me in his arms.

Brad had washed the gunk from his hands and face. He had discarded his shirt and hadn't zippered the too-small jacket he had borrowed from Tommy. I didn't mind. It was comforting to feel his warm chest against me.

"Miranda, I begged you not to do this on your own. Why didn't you wait? I told you I would help you as soon as I got time off work. I'm supposed to save lives. I watched him die. I couldn't do anything to help." Brad's voice was harsh, but his caresses were soft.

I was privy to the horrible images in Brad's mind. We both observed his hands in the muck that had once been Greg's handsome face. He had wanted to stop the bleeding and make the pieces form into a whole.

I reached inside and pulled my filter into place. I held onto it for as long as I could. I was exhausted when I let go. Brad's thoughts crashed into me like a river pulverizing a dam. He held me tight. I rested my cheek on his chest and finally understood my doctor.

"Brad, you can heal with your touch? That's why West recovered from his gunshot wound quickly, and why I healed from my injuries at record speed?"

"Yes, sweetheart."

"But you couldn't save the Minnichs' baby?"

"No, sweetheart. I wasn't strong enough. I really tried."

"I know you did." I pulled back from his embrace just far enough to look into his eyes. "You couldn't save

Greg, either?"

"No." He sighed. "No, I couldn't."

"When you give people your energy, does it make you tired?"

"Very."

I swallowed. My boyfriend carried his burden like a tormented saint.

"I'm sorry I didn't wait, but I knew it wasn't Skyler, and nobody believed me."

"I believed you."

I ran a finger along his cheek. "I'm sorry," I said again.

"Miranda, the thing he said about you being psychic, about your grandmother?"

As soon as "Greg made that up" left my lips, I regretted my response. Brad believed me and sealed my untruthful confession with a kiss to the forehead.

How could I betray Brad's trust? He had confided in me, and I had bold-faced lied to him. I had trusted Lincoln with my secret out of necessity. But why had I gotten drunk and entrusted West, and why was I afraid to tell Brad, the man I thought I might love? Brad had bared his soul to me, and I had looked him in the eyes and fibbed.

The truth was, I had known there was something different about Brad the first day we met, and he had placed his hands on the scorching hood of The Tank like it was a room-temperature wooden table. So, why was I afraid to tell him about my abilities?

Detective Miller approached. "Dr. Gordon, we're ready for your statement."

Before Brad walked away, I came clean. "Brad, I don't know why I lied. It's true. I can read minds," I whispered.

His beautiful blue eyes appeared gray in the odd lighting. "Miranda, I don't understand? Why would you feel the need to hide your gift from me?"

I finally understood that my reluctance and doubt were wrapped in layers of self-loathing and shame. "It's not a gift, Brad. It's a horrible curse. I hate being like this."

It felt as if he were staring into my soul. "It is an incredible gift when you learn to use it correctly. I'm sorry, but you were wrong to try to do this by yourself."

Brad turned his back to me and walked away.

"I'm sorry, Brad, but I couldn't wait any longer. Waiting is why they never caught the person who murdered my mother," I whispered to his receding back.

The only person who heard me was a wizen-faced detective.

"Dr. Albright," Miller said, interrupting my despair. "As soon as I'm done with Dr. Gordon, I'll be ready for your statement."

"Oh, so now you want to talk to me, Detective Miller. I think you are way too late!" I grumbled as I watched Brad walk out of my life and back into that camp.

****

West and I sat in the front seat of Tommy's warm work truck. I was still wrapped in the blanket, and my bathing suit bottom had finally begun to dry. The windshield wipers obliterated the icy flakes before the heat could melt them. Headlights from the numerous vehicles lit the front yard of the camp.

A car parked in front of us. In the red glow of taillights, Mayor Reynolds stepped from the driver's side, and Louise Grainey climbed from the passenger side. She stood tall, her shoulders pulled back, as Shultz approached her.

The back door opened, and Jessica Grainey tumbled out. She walked to her mother's side and stood for a moment before she took off in a run. Brad intervened. He caught her and wrapped his arms around her. She hit him, and he held her tighter.

The metronome wiper kept ticking, flakes kept hitting the windshield, and Brad Gordon held his ex-wife in his arms to keep her from seeing her father.

West's voice broke into my nightmare. "You were wrong to come here on your own."

I stopped tracing circles on the window to wipe a tear from my eye.

West's voice was gentle. "But Shortcake, I think you're brave as hell."

It wasn't possible to wipe away the downpour of tears that followed. West grasped an end of the wool blanket and wrapped it around his hand.

He placed that hand over mine. "In fact, Dr. Miranda Albright, I think you are the bravest woman I've ever met."

Chapter 42

The entire town turned out for Greg Grainey's funeral, minus one unpopular redhead and one grieving family. I had been officially uninvited with an un-invitation sent by Jessica Grainey's attorney.

I hoped the Smith family was hauled up at home, holding each other close. Spot, Princess Pickles, Simon, and I sat on our throne in the high tower and watched as the town crowded into Konicki's Funeral Home.

I wasn't at all startled when Spot barked and ran to greet our guest. I gazed out my bay window as my visitor approached from behind.

"I'm glad you're here. We need to discuss your boundaries."

"Happy to see me, my crimson princess?"

"Boundaries, Greg! You can't keep popping in when I'm in the shower. It's rude, not to mention it's perverted!"

My visitor laughed.

"Greg, clothes, you need to put on clothes." I closed my eyes.

He chuckled. "You can look now. I'm dressed."

"You better be." I opened my eyes. "Why aren't you at your funeral?"

"Apparently, if they falsely accuse you of offing yourself, not only do they not admit you into heaven, they also don't let you attend your funeral service."

"Actually, I don't think they let you into heaven if you're a murderer," I reminded him.

"Let's be fair. We both know Suzy's death was an accident and that you and Gordon shot me."

I sighed. "For the millionth time, you shot yourself with your own gun. Although, everyone in town hates me and blames me for it."

"Fuck them all. You worry too much about what people think."

I pulled my shoulders back. "You are wrong. I don't care what people think of me."

Greg quirked an eyebrow. "You know, I was pissed, but I never would have pulled that trigger?"

"Don't you have anyone else to haunt?" I asked.

"No. You're it right now. Everyone else is at my funeral. And although I can haunt whoever I want, I can only talk to three people in this god-forsaken county. FYI, Gordon is a huge ass bore. All he does is mope around about you and pretend like I don't exist."

He gave me one of his sleazy grins.

"For the record, Alina is way more hospitable during my late-night visits than you."

"Ew," I said. "Too much information. And you better not be making Brad think he is seeing things."

"Me, do something that sinister?" Greg placed his hands on his heart.

The only possible way I could respond to his comment was with a grunt.

"Greg, are you getting younger?"

"You noticed. What do you think?" He spun his ghostly form around and posed.

"I think if you keep going, you are going to end up a zygote in your momma's womb."

He laughed. I don't think Greg saw the irony. He had spent his life so consumed with youth, beauty, and material possessions, that he had accidentally murdered a woman half his age. He had died trying to cover up the consequences of his shallow materialism and vanity. The cruel twist was that he would spend eternity as a handsome non-aging dead man.

"By the way, I saved your obituary." I pointed to the newspaper on the table.

Greg slid to my round table and picked up the paper. "I was an upstanding businessman who championed the Second Amendment Right. A loving father and husband, and a devoted member of the town council." His lips tilted downward. "It doesn't mention I was sexy."

I couldn't help but smile at my self-absorbed ghost.

"There's another article on the front page."

He flipped the newspaper over and read the headline out loud. "Romance Between Businessman and College Coed Ends in Tragedy." He read the article silently, then snorted. "That ass of a kid was acquitted."

"He was innocent, Greg."

"Yeah, but he's still a little fuckhead."

I poked my finger into his intangible shoulder. "Greg, you were a frustrating human, and you are an even more impossible ghost."

Unfazed by my comment, he grinned. "Hey, I have a surprise for you."

I grimaced and looked out the window. "I'm not interested. Keep it in your pants."

He chuckled. "You will like this one. I hid Shultz's keys this morning. I hid 'em good. The crazy-fuck was still looking for 'em last time I checked."

I took my chances and peered at him with one eye.

Luckily he was fully clothed.

"Really?"

"Really." He puffed up his ghost chest.

Then we both laughed.

"Hey Greg, if you promise to behave yourself and keep your clothes on, you can sit with me."

"I promise. For today anyway, since it's my funeral and all."

Greg Grainey's ghost sat in my blue turret and watched his grieving friends and family disperse from the funeral parlor.

I still had so many questions. "I don't understand. Why did everyone cover for you? Why was Suzy's murder brushed over?"

"You have a lot to learn about small-town living, darling. Nobody knew it was me. Rumors are one thing. Everyone loves a rumor. Dark secrets are another. If one secret unravels, the entire fabric of the town rips wide open, and important people go down."

I frowned as I contemplated this. "Greg, I think we should take this time to review the boundaries?"

"Go ahead, Crimson, but it will be a huge waste of your time," my ghost informed me.

****

Winona teared up as she told me what a beautiful service it was. Keisha said Winona had cried like a heartbroken lover as West cradled her in his arms. Aunt Edith told me that Jessica and Louise Grainey had held their heads high and presented themselves with admirable dignity.

Brad Gordon had stoically stood by Jessica's side in front of the town. Aunt Edith was the only one who had seen that, following the service, he had walked away, leaving his ex-wife staring after him.

Over time, my bruises healed, but my heart shattered into a million pieces because Brad Gordon did not return my calls.

Gordon is no fun. You need a real man, my ghost told me.

Miranda, you have to give him time. He adores you, but he watched a man he once loved die, and he blames himself. Be there for him when he has healed, Aunt Edith advised.

Miranda, how are things going with Simon? Are you communicating better? Concentrate on that for now, Lincoln said.

Randa, sometimes, men need space. He'll come back around, and if he doesn't, you know how I feel, Tommy said.

Miranda, you need some serious girl time right now. I got ya, sister, Keisha promised.

Little cuz, I love you like a baby sister, but you worry us all. Thank God Winona had the sense to call me, or Grainey would have killed you. You used to have common sense, but you have become reckless, and Doc probably can't deal with it right now, Liam lovingly nagged me.

Miranda! Everyone is talking about how Greg and Suzy were like Romeo and Juliet. You and Brad are like Romeo and Juliet, too, exclaimed Winona.

You have a special gift, Miranda. Learn to use it wisely, I told myself every time I looked in the mirror.

Meanwhile, day in and day out, the snow kept falling.

Chapter 43

Early November passed, and I was too cold to care that half of the inhabitants of Bellmount considered me to be *scandalous*. Fortunately, the only people who mattered happened to adore me. Besides, life wasn't all bad because receiving a noogie from a man who has given you three orgasms in one night—is in its way—a special sort of love tap.

"Cowabunga!" West called as he jumped on me and rubbed his knuckle into the top of my head.

I sniggered as Tommy and Liam pulled him off of me.

"Time out, Westinghouse." Liam pointed to the chair. "Sit down and eat." He handed West a paper plate piled with pepperoni pizza.

I stifled my giggles as I demurely sat in the center of the couch with my hands folded. Liam and Tommy, beers in hand, sat down on either side of me. West plopped himself into his chair and pouted. Like a bratty child, I stuck my tongue out at him. He hid his mouth behind his hand and directed lewd gestures toward me.

I confess I had a fondness for West's inventive tongue.

Liam caught sight of West in the middle of a particularly suggestive curl and asked, "What's going on between you two?"

West *harrumph*ed. "Nothing. Nothing at all." He

347

took a sip of water.

"Is it time for the movie?" I asked.

"Movie time is a go." West placed his snacks on his whiskey crate and retrieved the VHS tape. "Moviegoers, prepare for a night of classic horror this evening."

I sat sandwiched between Liam and Tommy as horrified and delighted, I watched the saga of a reluctant high school psychic, covered in animal blood, play out.

West leaned back in his threadbare yellow chair, occasionally peeking at me. Eventually, our gazes met. His eyes twinkled, and he grinned. I bit my lip.

That was the moment I knew.

Weston Westinghouse the Third was my soulmate.

A word about the author...

Nicki Pascarella lives in Pennsylvania with her husband, daughter, and hyperactive Shetland Sheepdogs. When she isn't writing fiction, you will find her reading, belly dancing, or running 5ks with her furry partner.

https://www.nickipascarella.com

If you enjoyed this story, leaving a review at your favorite book retailer or reader website would be much appreciated. Thank you!